GEARS OF WAR®
JACINTO'S REMNANT

GEARS OF WAR®

JACINTO'S REMNANT

KAREN TRAVISS

BALLANTINE BOOKS

NEW YORK

For Alasdair Hogg,
emergency planning chief without equal,
who would have had Jacinto sorted
and squared away in no time.

ACKNOWLEDGMENTS

Grateful thanks go to: Mike Capps, Rod Fergusson, Cliff Bleszinski, and everyone at Epic for creating a thing of perfect beauty; editor Tricia Narwani (Del Rey) for providing top cover; super-fixer Sue Moe (Del Rey) for manning the guns; Penny Arcade—Mike "Gabe" Krahulik and Jerry "Tycho" Holkins—for talking me into all this; and Jim Gilmer, for logistics support, above and beyond.

GEARS OF WAR®
JACINTO'S REMNANT

CONFIDENTIAL

FROM: HOFFMAN, COLONEL VICTOR S., 26 RTI
TO: SURVIVING REPRESENTATIVES OF THE COALITION OF
ORDERED GOVERNMENTS

RE: DECISION TO DESTROY JACINTO, 2ND DAY OF FROST, 14 A.E.

I write this in full knowledge that this record may not survive, but if it does, then I wish our command decisions to be understood by any future generations.

At 1410 today, after the Locust began to mine tunnels beneath Jacinto to sink it, Chairman Richard Prescott authorized a preemptive plan to sink the city ourselves. This was designed not only to flood the Locust tunnels, but also to trap and destroy the Locust army that had infiltrated the center of Jacinto itself. A mass evacuation of citizens via land, air, and sea routes began an hour ago.

We believe there was no alternative. The Landown assault, in which we engaged the enemy within their own tunnels, resulted in major losses and failed to stop the Locust advance. Members of Delta Squad, under the command of Sergeant M. Fenix, E.S., located the Locust queen, and were made aware that the enemy also planned to create a sinkhole to destroy Jacinto. With insufficient forces to prevent this, we took the view that sinking and flooding the city ourselves, to trap the enemy and drown them within their tunnels, was our only option, and justified the destruction of our last stronghold.

We were unaware until Delta Squad penetrated the enemy command center that the Locust Horde is engaged on a second front underground with another faction of their species, which they call the Lambent and regard as a plague. The Locust plan to flood Jacinto themselves would have inundated their own positions, and seems to be as much aimed at destroying the Lambent as wiping out humankind. We do not yet fully understand the nature of that conflict, and may never do so.

We have been left with no option but to try to inflict maximum casualties on Locust forces so that a remnant of humanity can be saved to reconstruct our world. We have some certainty that they will never recover from this blow. Not only do they appear to think flooding will be effective in defeating the Lambent, but records have been found to indicate that the late Professor Adam Fenix believed that flooding would destroy the Locust threat itself.

At this stage, we do not know the extent of our own losses; evacuation under these circumstances will inevitably result in high civilian casualties. But the alternative is the extinction of the human race.

Chairman Richard Prescott and I are no strangers to this magnitude of decision. Fourteen years ago, we took the decision to deploy the Hammer of Dawn. I cannot speak for his private views, but as a soldier, I am fully aware of the deaths I have on my conscience, and I grieve for every man, woman, and child who has paid the price for my actions. If there had been any alternative, I would have fought to the end to take it. Sometimes you can save what you love most only by destroying it.

Again, we ask: please forgive us. It was the only way.

—**Victor Hoffman, E.S.,**
Colonel, Chief of Defense Staff
of the Coalition of Ordered Governments

PROLOGUE

We're fucked now. That's for sure.

Just take a look down there. Boats, bodies, sea rushing in. Jacinto's history, baby.

I mean, this is *sick*. I'm standing here looking out the Raven's door while it's circling around like I'm on some weird sightseeing trip. That's the Octus Tower going under—what's left of it. All that water, but the place is still burning, stinking of smoke and fuel. Shit, it's sinking. It's just *sinking*. The whole goddamn city is *gone*.

And we sunk it. Fifteen years fighting to save it, and we have to trash it ourselves in the end. But at least the grubs are drowning with it. They're history, too. That's *justice*.

Shit . . . I hate flying. I'm going to puke. But I can't look away from the water.

I can just about hear Lieutenant Stroud over the noise of the chopper. "Hey, Cole?"

Look at all the bodies in the water—humans, not grubs. Rescue boats didn't get to everybody, then. How many folks in Jacinto? A few million. Even if we had a proper navy, we can't ship out everyone. Glad I wasn't the one deciding who got to live and who didn't. Must be shitty for those navy guys. And look at that—

a goddamn *yacht* heading out. Who the hell's kept a big-ass yacht going since E-Day? Well, you better pick up some citizens on the way out, rich boy.

"Cole . . ." Anya Stroud's been sitting behind me with a comms set on her lap. She has to yell to make herself heard. We got pretty well all that's left of Command on board—Chairman Prescott, Colonel Hoffman, and Anya. She can't raise anyone on the radio, and she's sweating over it. So am I. "Cole, you think they made it?"

"Say again?"

"Marcus. Dom. Baird."

"Ma'am, they ain't the dying kind." Sometimes I believe that. I want to believe it now, and so does Anya. And I want to believe Bernie made it—damn, Boomer Lady *hates* water. She'll be real pissed off now. "They're on another bird. Count on it."

Anya nods like she heard me okay. Yeah, it's all bullshit. I've lost so many buddies that I can't sleep some nights for seeing their faces. But I've got to *believe*. If I stop believing, it'll start catching. Soon everyone else stops believing, too. Team morale. That's what counts, same in war as in thrashball.

"They'll make it, Lieutenant," Colonel Hoffman yells. He looks like he's searching for someone, leaning from the safety rail, watching the city go down the crapper. "They'll make it."

Prescott's sitting in one of the transverse bulkhead seats, head bent like he's praying—too late for that, man. He looks like he hasn't got a clue how to get us out of this shit, and Hoffman's looking at him like he *knows* he don't know.

Anya's still going on about Marcus. I don't catch everything she says. Ravens are real noisy bastards. "I didn't even . . . chance . . . talk about . . . with Sergeant Fenix," she says, all formal, like I haven't guessed about him and her. "Not . . . properly."

I can fill in the gaps. Hell, what does it matter now if you *say* it? Most of the world's dead. Whoever's left is hurting and mourning. And you and Marcus been edging around each other for sixteen, seventeen years. Is that what sane folks do?

"Okay, make a list of all the things you gonna tell him, ma'am," I shout. "'Cause you gonna forget again."

"Say again?"

"*Make a list.*"

She forces a smile and nods.

I can't stand staring at the shit below me anymore. So I look up instead. The sky's full of smoke and King Ravens, every last airframe we can get off the ground, heading for nowhere, just like the boats and whatever got out of Jacinto by road. Funny, it almost looks like we still got an air force when you cram all them Ravens into the same patch of sky.

But this is *all we got left.* The whole fucking Coalition.

The pilot's in a hurry. We're cutting through the other Ravens, and I'm looking into every open bay that we pass, searching. And you know what? I swear this believing shit *works.* Most Gears got the sense to wear a helmet, except crazies like Delta and me, of course—and man, can you see Baird's blond hair a long way off. There he is. He's seen us. We draw level.

Yeah, there they are, standing in the crew bay opposite now— Baird, Dom, Marcus. Baird's got a dumb-ass smirk on his face, closest he's ever come to looking pleased to see me, so I tap my chest plate in respect, 'cause he can't hear me. Marcus and Dom, though—they nod back at me, but they ain't smiling. They look like shit.

But they're alive. And that's all that matters, right?

"Ma'am, port side. Look."

Anya's going to shake the guts out of that comms set if someone don't answer soon. "What?"

"Just look."

She gets up and stands next to me, and suddenly she looks like she don't know what to do next. But she does a little wave at Marcus, like she's embarrassed, and hangs on, staring across at him until the chopper banks away. And he stares back until he's just a distant blur.

"Okay," she says to herself, sort of smiling without looking happy. I can lip-read it this time. "See you in Port Farrall." Then she sits down and begins cycling through the comms frequencies again. We'll be at the RV point in maybe thirty minutes.

Hoffman's still looking down at Prescott like he's a big steaming pile of something real nasty. You never know what goes on between those two, but it ain't brotherly love, that's for sure. Hoffman looks like he's still mad as hell about not being told shit. I catch a few words.

"Any *other* classified information . . . share . . . sir?" Hoffman's got his fuck-you voice on. I can tell from his face even if I can't hear it all. "Because right now . . . any . . . surprises."

Prescott pokes around inside his jacket—still wearing all his medals, however the hell he earned 'em—and takes out a small notepad or something. " . . . going to take days to process the refugees," he shouts back.

Hoffman's got his jaw clamped tight shut now. He's pissed off, all right. Just as I think he's going to dropkick Prescott out the Raven to see if the asshole flies or floats, Anya jumps up.

"Sir, sir—comms are back online again." She's got one hand pressed to her ear. Something clicks and my earpiece is working again. No more yelling. "The emergency relay on *Sovereign* is operational. Very limited range. Hundred klicks, max."

"Good enough," says Hoffman. "Everyone knows the RV procedure if they lose contact again."

I just got to listen in to the voice traffic now. I need to know who's out there, who else made it. I want to hear Bernie cussing out someone. She's been missing since the Landown assault.

What the hell. Let's see where Baird's bird is.

"Hey, Delta. You receivin'?"

"Yeah, Cole Train," says Marcus's voice.

I just want to know they're all okay. "So, still no sign of Dom's lady? False lead?"

I don't get a response. Maybe I've lost the damn signal again. But then I realize I can hear Marcus breathing like he can't get the next word out.

"I found her . . . yeah. I found her."

But that's Dom talking now. It's *Dom*. He's been looking for

Maria for ten years, going crazy, but he don't sound happy he found her. I'm waiting. I don't know what the hell to ask next, because I can guess what's coming, but I can't stop now.

"Dom, she okay? What happened?"

Yeah, I bet I know what's coming next. Aww, shit . . .

"She's dead," Dom says, all quiet and steady and *normal*. "I did it. I helped her go. She's okay now."

No. That *ain't* what I was expecting.

I think I heard wrong. I know I didn't. There's a million things in my head right then, and none of 'em look good. What the hell do I say to Dom now?

You think it's finally over, that the pain's all stopped, and then you find that the hurt's just moved on somewhere new.

Aww, *shit*.

CHAPTER 1

If you want to flood the city, we can handle it. The evacuation's already under way by road, we've got ships on standby, and this is a population that's used to emergency drills. They move when we say move. But that's the easy part. It's winter, and somehow we've got to carry enough equipment and supplies to create a giant refugee camp from scratch in the middle of nowhere, then sustain it for maybe a year. We're going to lose a lot of people, whatever happens. So let's start by accepting that.

(ROYSTON SHARLE, HEAD OF EMERGENCY MANAGEMENT, JACINTO.)

JACINTO, ONE HOUR INTO THE FLOOD.

Dying really did bring its own moments of clarity, just like they said.

Bernie Mataki didn't see her life flash before her. Instead, she found herself weirdly detached, reflecting on the shitty irony of sailing halfway around the world only to drown in Jacinto.

Water. I bloody hate it. No bastard should have to drown in the middle of a city.

She could see a patch of whirling sea ten meters away, like a sink emptying down a plughole. Debris rushed toward it. Chunks of wood, vegetation, plastic, and even a dead dog—a little brown terrier thing with a red collar—raced past her on the surface to vanish into the maelstrom. A chunk of metal pipe bobbed along in its wake, clanging against her shoulder-plate and nearly taking her eye out before it spun away with the rest of the flotsam.

I'm next. Sink. Get it over with. Nowhere to swim to. Drown here now or there later . . . no, screw that, I'm a survival specialist, aren't I? Get a grip. Do something. I'm not dead yet.

"Sorrens? *Sorrens?*" All she could see was columns of black smoke and the occasional flash of sunlight on a distant rotor blade. The last Ravens were heading away from the stricken city. Saltwater slopped into her mouth. "Sorrens, you still there?"

There was no answer. He was the last man left of her squad; they'd fought their way to the surface, radios dead, staying a few desperate meters ahead of the flood. But the Ravens had already gone, and the sea engulfed the city. It pissed her off that Sorrens had survived the battle but that she'd lost him because the frigging COG itself pulled the plug. That felt worse than losing him to the grubs somehow.

But they thought we were dead. We can't have been the only ones who missed the RV point. How many got out alive?

Jacinto, which had always seemed so ancient and eternal, was vanishing a landmark at a time. The sea didn't give a shit about humanity's little nest-building efforts. Buildings were subsiding into the caverns beneath the city, creating whirlpools that dragged in everything on the surface. She'd be next. Her hands were aching with cold as she struggled to hang on to a roof gutter that was now at sea level. The roof itself was gone, and only the end gable jutted at a sharp angle above the water. She looked for some refuge, but there were no surfaces she could balance on, just a finial, a twin-headed heraldic eagle that loomed over her and offered nothing to settle on.

Two minutes, they said. Two minutes in icy water before hypothermia killed you. She'd been here longer than that, she was sure. And then there was the fuel floating everywhere. That wasn't going to do her a lot of good, either.

Can't let go. Bloody radio . . .

Bernie steadied herself, timing the moment to take one hand off the gutter and try her radio again. The current tugged impatiently. Once she lost her grip on her last fragile link to solid ground, the weight of her armor would drag her under. It was the modern stuff, heavier, a two-handed job to remove, not designed for long immersion. She needed both hands free to jettison any plates, and once she let go she was dead. She couldn't tread water: too exhausted, too heavy, too far from dry land.

All she could hear was the roar and crash of the sea filling the sunken city, creaks of buckling metal that sounded like screams, and a fading *chakka-chakka-chakka* as the last Ravens shrank to dots on the amber horizon. There was a stench of unidentifiable chemicals and sulfur, as if some kind of gas was pooling on the surface.

Shit, don't let that catch fire. I can't handle burning to death in water as well. That's one fucking irony too many.

She had to get on with it.

One . . . two . . . three.

Bernie took one hand off the gutter and waved her arm. But it was a waste of time, and she knew it; the choppers were too far away. Even the ships and small vessels were out of range. She was just one more tiny speck in a chaotic soup of debris. But now that her hand was free and she hadn't been snatched from her refuge by the force of the water, she risked turning around, trying to scan the choppy surface for signs of other survivors.

There were bodies. She could see how fast the current was running by the speed at which they shot past her.

Did they get left behind? Or did they decide to die here rather than keep running?

People did the damnedest things in disasters. Wanting to stay put was common. Bernie always prided herself on getting the hell out.

She pressed her finger hard against her earpiece, rocking it slightly to make sure the switch made contact. There was an encouraging hiss of static. It was still working despite being soaked.

"Sierra One to Control, this is Mataki . . ." *Time.* She just didn't have time. Even if anyone heard her, could they loop back and find her before she went under? There were no bloody miracles on the way, that she knew. If she was going to survive, she'd have to perform her own. "Sierra One to Control, this is Mataki, are you receiving?"

There was just the empty random hiss of background interference. Maybe they could hear her, though. Maybe they couldn't respond. She needed to give them a location, just in case, and tried to work out where she was in this suddenly unfamiliar landscape, but it was hard to orient herself when only her head was above water. She racked her brain for where she'd seen the eagle finial before, trying to visualize Jacinto as it had been only hours ago.

"Sierra One, this is Sergeant Bernadette Mataki . . . I need extraction urgently, repeat, urgent extraction . . . my position is . . . wait one . . ." *Shit. Where the hell am I? What's that dome over there?* Suddenly it came to her. "Allfathers Library, south side of the roof. I'm facing the Ginnet Mausoleum. Request immediate extraction, over."

This was the point where it suddenly got harder and demanded decisions. How long did she wait before she decided they were never coming?

Bernie found herself scanning the horizon to the east, looking to see if any of the small islands around the harbor had survived the seismic activity. If she could shed at least some of her plates—maybe grab the next chunk of debris that passed as a flotation device—then she might make it to dry ground. She could see only the outer harbor wall now, a stump of granite that had once held a lighthouse. It was a very long swim, even under the best circumstances.

"Control, I'll hang on as long as I can," she said at last. "Request immediate extraction, repeat, immediate extraction."

Bernie decided that if anyone had heard, then she'd given them long enough to triangulate on her signal. She shut down the radio to conserve power. All she could do now was stay put and try to avoid being hit by the flood of rushing debris.

How long before it gets dark?

She had two or three hours' light left. Maybe getting up on that gable end was feasible after all—if it didn't crash down on her or sink with everything else. If she moved around to the other side, a little further along the gutter, the sloping gable would be facing away from her. She could edge her way up it.

For a moment, she felt inexplicably pleased with herself, and realized that it was because of the water—her worst nightmare, the thing she dreaded, and yet she was in control. It hadn't beaten her. If she could deal with this, anything was possible.

"Screw you," she said aloud to nobody in particular, and felt carefully beneath the water for her belt. If she took it slowly, she could find a length of line even with fingers so cold they felt like they were being crushed between rollers.

Don't drop it. No, don't open the pouch, lift it so the stuff doesn't float out.

Bernie shook out the line and almost lost it. Now the challenge was to form a loop to anchor it to something solid. Tying a bowline one-handed when someone threw you a line was a basic survival skill, but with nothing to secure it to, she had to slide the line under her other hand, the one gripping the gutter. It seemed to take ages. Eventually, gathering the line with slow care, she managed to form a noose, and clamped the end between her teeth to avoid losing the thing if she dropped it.

Pirate time. Shit, I must look like a complete dickhead.

Then she made her way hand over hand along the gutter until she was looking at the inside of the gable end. It took every scrap of strength she had left, but she dragged herself over the gutter, taking her weight on her chest, then swung one leg as if mounting a horse. The sea had now overtopped the wall. She straddled the brickwork for a moment, struggling to balance properly because her thigh-plate had caught on something she couldn't see, and slowly lifted the line in both hands to try to lasso the finial.

Shit.

She missed twice. She missed a third time. Either the polymer rope was too light or she didn't have the strength now to heave it.

Again . . .

As long as she was trying, she was alive. And the effort was warming her up.

And again . . .

The loop of rope caught around the neck of the eagle with a wet slap, and she pulled the line tight. It held. The gable leaned at around fifty degrees; all she had to do was walk up that slope, even crawl, and the rope wouldn't have to take her whole weight.

It was weird how the brain compensated, she thought. Something that was plainly as dangerous as staying put had now become a sensible option. She found out just how dangerous when she tried to work out how to stand up.

The wall, of course, wasn't level. It was at the same canted angle as the gable, because the whole building had tilted. It was just the fact that it was broken—split vertically—that gave her hands and backside the illusion of being level. When she pulled one leg out of the water and jammed the heel of her boot into a gap in the brickwork, she found herself slipping toward the gable. Standing up took a massive effort that was more like an explosive squat. Her face smacked into the bricks, and she found herself spread-eagled on the inner surface of the gable, one boot on the wall and the other dangling in the sea that had filled the building.

But she had the rope in one fist, and she was mostly out of the water. It left her feeling heavy and oddly warm. Now all she had to do was climb.

Easy. Really, it is.

Bernie had to believe that. And she had to think no further than the next step. That was how you kept going, one hurdle at a time, then the next, and the next, until the huge task had been chipped away.

Now she was halfway up the slope. When she got close to the top, she'd work out how to secure herself with the rope, free both hands so she could assess any injuries, check that her Lancer still worked, and see what kit she still had in her belt pouches.

And time to call in again. Shit, they can't have lost all comms, can they?

She lay flat and listened for a moment. The city still groaned

and screamed as the weight of water crushed it. But that was a little further away; closer to her, she could hear rhythmic slaps on
the water, as if someone was swimming.

I'm not alone. God, I'm not alone. It's Sorrens. He made it.

Bernie took a few breaths and gathered her strength to sit up as
best she could and take a look. Before she did, she tried calling
Control again.

"Control, this is Mataki, requesting immediate extraction. My
position is the Allfathers Library roof." She could still hear the
splashing. It was getting closer. "Control, come in . . ."

The splashing stopped.

Bernie raised her head and looked down at the sea. Now that
she was facing away from Jacinto's death throes, the seascape simply looked stormy, the drifting smoke more like dark clouds than
the end of urban society. She couldn't see anyone in the water—
nobody alive, anyway.

"Sorrens?"

She couldn't ignore what she'd heard. She tugged on the line
to make sure it was secure, then tied the other end around her
waist like a safety line. She was losing body heat, she reminded
herself, and there was a cold night ahead, so any survivors would
stand a better chance if they huddled together.

Braking her slide with her heels, she edged down to the top of
the wall again, wondering how she'd haul him inboard. The sea
looked almost solid, like churning, oily lumps rather than water.
She strained to see a head bobbing between waves. Nothing.

Then the water erupted.

A body burst through the surface like a porpoise breaching.
She sucked in a breath, jerking back, because it wasn't Sorrens,
and it took her a second in her exhausted state to register that fact.

She was face-to-face with a Locust drone, a big gray bastard of
a grub. It could swim. It should have been dead. It wasn't. It
scrambled for the wall, *her* wall, *her* safe haven.

"*Shit,*" she said, and reached for the knife in her boot.

———————

The comms link crackled in Dominic Santiago's earpiece. "KR-Two-Three-Nine to Control. Are you receiving that signal?"

Oh shit oh shit oh shit, did I do it? Oh God, I did it, I killed her. I killed her.

Dom could hear the chatter between the two Raven pilots, but it was just noise, words, sounds without meaning. His body was carrying on without him; he felt like he was coming around from an anesthetic. Whatever instinct had held him together during the mission was now wearing off, leaving behind it a paralyzing horror that drove out everything else except the sheer choking pain from that last look into her eyes.

I killed Maria. I killed my own fucking wife. It couldn't have been her, could it? Did I really do it? Oh God oh God oh God, *how am I going to breathe again—*

"Roger that, Two-Three-Nine. It's Mataki. We lost the signal, but she's somewhere on the Allfathers' roof."

"We're low on fuel."

"Okay, we're just calculating which KR can get back to her—"

Marcus's voice cut in. "Control, I'm up for it. If Sorotki thinks he can make it."

"And if not?" Sorotki said.

"Then drop me off and I'll frigging *swim* back for her." It wasn't a growl. Marcus just sounded exhausted. "Baird, you got any objections?"

Baird must have shaken his head, because Dom didn't hear a reply. The guy always came back with some smart-ass retort about Mataki. But not this time.

"Just so you understand," Sorotki said, "we don't have the fuel for anything fancy. We just winch her clear and go, okay? We'll be flying back on vapor as it is. Hey, Mitchell, quit the sightseeing and get your ass back here. Crunch me some numbers."

"On my way." The co-pilot abandoned the aerial recon and

stowed the camera. "Mataki punched out Baird. We've *got* to rescue her, so she can do it again."

Marcus put his hand on Dom's shoulder. "Hey . . . you with us?"

"Yeah. Yeah, let's do it." The words were out of Dom's mouth before he could think. Shit, he *couldn't* think. There was a loop playing in his brain now, over and over, disjointed but agonizingly vivid, and it wouldn't stop even when he shut his eyes.

It was just the beginning. It wasn't going to go away. He wanted to die; nothing mattered now, not even breathing. But when he turned his head and met Marcus's eyes, he was jerked back into a world where people depended on him, where friends put themselves on the line *for him*. That included Bernie. There was no giving up now.

The co-pilot returned to the cockpit and Sorotki banked the Raven in a loop to retrace their course back to Jacinto. Dom stayed at the door, staring down onto the ocean as the chopper skimmed over an extraordinary fleet of vessels that ranged from hovercraft and rust-streaked beam trawlers to tankers. A group of carriers—*Raven's Nest* class—led a flotilla of shabby warships. One was just a matte black lump right on the waterline, then the helicopter tilted, and Dom picked out a solid sail and the bulbous outline of a sonar dome on the bow.

"Shit, look at that," Baird said. Dom felt something clack against his back plate, and realized Baird had clipped a safety line to his belt. That wasn't like him at all. "We still got a *submarine*. Hey, I just *got* to play with that. Torps away, flood Q, all that shit."

Dom felt Baird was humoring him, like he was a kid who'd just woken screaming from a nightmare and needed distracting. Baird had heard what he'd told Cole. He hadn't realized Dom had found Maria, let alone that he'd taken his sidearm and—

Dom could still see it, over and over, whether he wanted to or not. But he couldn't say it even in the privacy of his own mind. He stared at the carrier beneath, trying to shut out everything else.

"That's *Sovereign*." Dom could see the pennant code under

the bridge wing, peeling and faded. He couldn't remember the other carrier's name. "They were overdue for the scrapyard even before E-Day."

It was the sheer volume of small civilian craft that surprised Dom—tiny clinker-built dinghies, rigid inflatables, grimy white motor cruisers with wheelhouses covered in nets and wicker fenders. He'd never known this navy-in-waiting existed; all these shabby hulls must have been carefully laid up on blocks in garages or derelict buildings for years, waiting for the worst to happen. People still ventured out to fish in the estuary after E-Day to supplement their meager diet. And everyone knew there were distant islands out there—for those willing to risk the journey, anyway.

Like Bernie. Island-hopping from the other side of Sera. *Crazy woman.* Dom had experienced the sheer terror of the sea in his commando days, and the idea of spending months afloat in a boat that size almost made him shit himself.

"Pretty impressive that they can hold a convoy formation," Baird said. "We haven't had a fighting navy since E-Day, let alone exercising with civilian vessels."

"Discipline, man." Dom tried to imagine how many people could cram into a carrier. "We got an orderly, well-drilled bunch of—"

She's gone.

And I killed her.

Dom ground to a halt midsentence. For a few moments he'd thought about something other than Maria, but now it had all come crashing back again. His free hand shook. He grabbed the adjacent rail just to keep it steady. All he wanted was oblivion—fuck it, just five minutes of *nothing* in his head so he could pull himself together. The images superimposed on everything he looked at. He found himself screwing his eyes shut and turning his face away from the open door. It was like that night on board *Pomeroy,* when he'd lost his brother at Aspho Fields, lost half his buddies, and heard his daughter had been born—a terrible chaos of agony and joy, unbearable, so disabling that he didn't know how to get through the next hour. All the time he was fighting to stay alive, he could cope. Once the pressure was off, the tidal wave flooded back.

The Locust were finally gone. The world could start over. But Maria was gone, too, more gone than she'd been for the ten years she was missing, and he was the one who'd killed her.

Maybe I could have saved her. Why didn't I get to her sooner? Why did I pull the trigger?

He knew why. He knew she was past saving. He also knew that wouldn't stop him tearing himself apart thinking about all the things he could have done differently.

His torment must have showed on his face. Baird nudged him with his elbow but didn't say anything. Baird wasn't good at reassurance. He didn't have Marcus's unerring ability to say the right thing when it really mattered, but at least he wasn't carrying on as if nothing had happened, like he usually did.

"Ten minutes." Sorotki's voice interrupted their short-range comms. "Lots of smoke drifting down there. I hope we can spot her. Fenix, you're winchman. If Mataki's not in any shape to help herself, you'll have to go down yourself and put the sling on her."

Marcus checked the clips, tugging the sling and cable hard and scrutinizing them. "Under the arms?"

"Yeah. Cable to the front, slip the sling over her shoulders and under the armpits, then get her to keep her arms down at her sides or hands clasped in front and *relax*. Grab her when she's level with the deck, and pull her inboard. Simple."

Marcus nodded to himself and sat with the harness on his lap, head bent as if he was meditating over it. Baird didn't seem to know what to do with himself. There was no small talk to pass the time, not now.

"Two hundred meters, port side," Sorotki said. "I have a visual on the building."

Dom moved across the bay deck to the other door and stared out. Jacinto looked just like someone had thrown a pile of broken dollhouses into a bucket of water. The scale was somehow distorted; the landmarks were all in the wrong place, or at least it seemed that way because some of the ornate towers and domes were missing. Even when the Raven dropped to twenty meters above the sea, the city didn't look life-sized any longer.

"Oh, shit," said Sorotki.

Marcus leaned out of the door, hanging on by one hand. Dom was blinded by the mass of rolling smoke. But the pilot could detect something they couldn't. Baird put his goggles on and peered out as well.

"What's up?" he asked. "Can't you see her?"

"I see her, all right. Which of you is the best shot?"

It was the worst thing Sorotki could have said. Dom felt his guts knot. His mind raced ahead to fill in the gaps. No, Sorotki didn't mean *that* at all.

"*She* is," Marcus said calmly, still gripping the sling. "She's a sniper. What's the problem?"

"She's got company, and not the let's-keep-our-spirits-up kind . . ."

The wind parted the smoke for a moment, and Dom caught a glimpse of someone else's hell for a change. A Gear—it could have been anyone in that armor—clung to a jutting section of brickwork while a grub tried to climb aboard too.

"Time to break up the party," Marcus said. "Sorotki, get me in close as you can."

ALLFATHERS LIBRARY.

Bernie heard the sound of a Raven getting closer but didn't dare take her eyes off the grub to look up.

The thing was struggling, trying to heave itself out of the water. That didn't mean it wasn't going to kill her. Locust were tougher than humans, harder to kill, and all that nearly drowning had done to this one was exhaust it. It looked right at her—vile pale gray eyes with pinprick pupils—as if it was surprised that a human had survived.

And she was stuck.

She was now lying flat on her back on the sloping wall, trapped and hanging from the length of line. Her Lancer, slung on her back, was jammed underneath her. All she had to rely on was her knife and a very bad attitude toward anything that wasn't a Gear. The grub gripped the brickwork with one huge clawed hand, then tried to lunge upward. She kicked out at it.

"Fuck off," she yelled, trying to work out the best place to strike. The nearest target would be its head or hand, not exactly effective places to stab an assailant. She needed to slice into a major artery or somewhere blindingly painful. Stabbing was a slow kill, or a distraction to slow someone down while you tried something else, but that was all she had. "This is *my* frigging wall. Just piss off and *die.*"

The chopper was definitely very close. The noise was deafening, and she could feel the downdraft. She still couldn't take her eyes off the grub. If the pilot hadn't seen her by now, he never would. The grub looked up, though, and she could almost see its thoughts; it was too exhausted to swim away, its enemy was hovering above, and all it could do was revert to instinct and grab for safety, however short-lived that was.

And it did.

It must have found purchase on the submerged brick, because it sprang up from the water with a massive bark of effort, crashing down on top of her. It landed with its head level with her waist. Its claws hooked on her belt, and it began hauling itself upward.

Its breath stank.

This was just a frozen second, but the smell and the sheer weight of the frigging thing on top of her triggered a memory in Bernie that she still tried hard to bury: helpless, pinned down, unable to fight back. She wanted to kill. It was all she could see, think, feel, taste. *Kill it.* She rammed the knife into the first place she could reach—its shoulder—but it was like trying to stab concrete.

It bellowed. Had she even scratched the thing? It still clung to her, crushing the breath out of her. She drew back her cold-numbed arm to stab blindly again, and again, and again, until the blade didn't pull clear and she didn't know if she'd finally pierced its thick hide or snagged the knife in something. She struggled to pull it out. All she was aware of was a fierce downward wind sand-blasting grit onto her face, a wall of screaming noise that made her head hurt, and a frenzied rage that closed her throat as tight as a stranglehold.

Yes, there was a Raven right above. She thought she caught a glimpse of someone aiming a rifle at her. But the grub was still clinging to her, one hand on her belt and the other hooked into her chest-plate; it *had* to die. She pulled the knife back one more time, looked down into the grub's nightmarish face—mouth open, venting meaningless noises and terrible, rotting smells— and rammed the slim blade as hard as she could into its ear canal.

Now . . . *that* worked.

The grub screamed, a long gurgling noise, and hung from her belt by one fist as it flailed helplessly at the knife. It was going to drag her down with it. And she wanted her knife back. A fight was never cold logic, and all kinds of insane shit went through her mind at times like this, but right now her knife mattered more than anything, and she yanked it clear. Then she dug the point hard into the back of the grub's massive hand and ground the point around like a screwdriver.

The grub was still screaming. Her belt broke. The creature thrashed for a second as it fell back into the water below, and then it was gone.

Now she could look up. The downdraft from the Raven almost blinded her. The chopper backed off a little, and she could see someone with a black do-rag squatting on the open deck, gestur-ing with a bright orange rescue sling.

Marcus.

Bernie couldn't hear him above the noise, but she knew what to do. She just didn't know if she had the strength to do it. The line hit her in the face, not that she could feel much now, and she grabbed it one-handed. But that was as far as she got. She couldn't get the loop under her arms because her back-plate and rifle kept snagging it, and she didn't have the energy or strength to struggle with it. The harness slid out of her grip and

vanished back into the Raven. Shit, were they giving up, or trying again?

It was Delta. They wouldn't leave her here.

She shut her eyes for a moment to get her second wind. Then
something heavy crashed down next to her. If that grub had come
back, she was going to have to bite out the bastard's windpipe this
time—but when she looked, Marcus was standing on the steep
slope of the gable, hanging on to the winch cable.

"Brace your feet against my boot," he yelled over the noise. "Sit
up. Come on. *Up.*"

She reached above her head and cut the line that now tethered
her to the sinking building. Whether she sat up on her own or
Marcus hauled her, she wasn't sure, but the sling was around her
and she crunched hard against Marcus as the cable went taut
again and her boots left the brickwork.

"Shit, am I glad to see you." She was so cold that she had trouble making her mouth work. "I owe you one."

"No, you don't."

Dom and Baird reached to pull them inboard when they were
level with the deck. It was an undignified scramble and she ended
up in a tangled heap with Marcus while Baird disconnected the
slings. She was still slumped on the deck as the Raven swung
around and headed north again. Dom closed the doors on both
sides of the Raven's bay. The noise level dropped instantly.

"It's damn cold," he said. "You need to get your body temperature up again."

"Thanks, Dom." She propped herself up but could only reach
his leg, so she patted that. He nodded, then slipped through into
the gunner's compartment as if he wanted to leave them to it.
"And you, Blondie. Thank you. No sign of Niall Sorrens? He was
right behind me."

Baird helped her to the aft bulkhead seat and draped a blanket
around her. That was so unlike him that she really wasn't sure
what to say. She wondered if she was in worse shape than she
thought.

"Nobody else, Granny," he said. Well, at least a bit of the normal *me, me, me* Baird was functioning. "Creative knife work, by the way. Very entertaining."

"I'd do it to every last frigging one of them," she said, carefully reburying all the memories that the fight had dredged up. She was shaking uncontrollably—from cold, fatigue, ebbing adrenaline—and she didn't want to look weak in front of Baird. "But we finally finished the bastards, didn't we? Except the stragglers. Just send them my way. I've got scores to settle."

"Yeah, Granny," said Baird, still unnaturally civil. The jibe didn't even feel offensive anymore. "Next grub we find is all yours."

She craned her neck to see what Dom was doing. Through the narrow hatch, she could see him manning the gun position, staring out into the growing dusk. He looked *wrong* somehow; so did Marcus. Even Baird didn't have his usual perma-sneer in place. Bad news was imminent. She could feel it. And there was someone missing, someone she expected to see with Delta Squad.

"Cole?" Her gut somersaulted. Cole was a force of nature, an endearing blend of raucous humor and solid wisdom, and she had a soft spot for him. He was *not* replaceable. "*Where's Cole? No, not Cole, I couldn't*—"

"Don't worry, he got out on Hoffman's flight," Baird said. "With Anya."

No jokes, no sarcasm, even from Blondie. Shit. What's coming?

Bernie was running out of names to play guess-who-didn't-make-it. Marcus braced one hand on the bulkhead above her, leaning over with a look in his eyes that said he was working up to telling her something that even he couldn't quite handle. And that was starting to scare her. She'd known him—and Dom—when they were young Gears in the Royal Tyran Infantry, before anyone had ever heard of the Locust. Even in a world where everyone had suffered and grieved, though, Marcus looked especially ravaged by loss, and it wasn't just those facial scars.

"Just tell me," she said.

"Tai's gone." His voice was almost a whisper. Tai Kaliso was a South Islander, like her, another comrade they'd both fought with at Aspho Fields. "Did you ever meet Benjamin Carmine? He's gone, too."

Marcus paused. It was clear he hadn't finished. He'd always been self-contained, but she could see accumulated years of anguish in his eyes. This was the Marcus she'd glimpsed a long time ago, distraught at the death of his buddy Carlos, Dom's brother.

"Marcus," she said, "just *tell* me, sweetheart." She could call him that. She was twenty-odd years older, so she could play the veteran sergeant with him. "Whatever it is."

"It's Dom," he said at last. She couldn't hear him now. She had to read his lips. "He found Maria. He had to . . . stop her suffering. Shit, Bernie, he had to *shoot* her. She was just this skeleton, this brain-damaged *skeleton*. I told him it was okay."

Bernie had steeled herself not to react. But it was so far from what she was expecting to hear that she actually felt her mouth open in shock. Her immediate instinct was to go to Dom as if he was still that teenage kid she first knew, give him a hug, tell him he'd get through it, that everyone would help him. But it was complete bollocks.

She knew, because she'd been seconds from putting Carlos Santiago out of his misery at Aspho Fields. And she knew that if she'd pulled the trigger, then she would have found that bloody hard to get out of her head every night, every time she tried to fall asleep, every unguarded moment.

She didn't ask for details. There'd be a proper time for that. She caught Baird's eye as he watched her and Marcus, but he looked away fast.

"Does everyone else know?" she asked.

"No." Marcus straightened up. His eyes looked distinctly glassy. "And I want to make it as easy as I can for him."

"Want me to warn people off?" Every Gear who knew Dom would ask him if he'd found his wife yet. Every Stranded, too, if they'd survived. The man had spent ten years shoving a photograph of Maria in front of everyone he met, asking if they'd seen her. "It'll save a lot of painful questions."

"Sounds like a plan."

"No detail. Just that he found a body, so they'll shut up about it."

"Thanks, Bernie." Marcus patted her shoulder, distracted. "He'll know we've got his back."

Bernie rested her head in her hands and let the airframe's vibration lull her into something approaching sleep. *Shit, what a letdown.* She'd always thought that defeating the Locust would be a cause for celebration, but if there was one thing she'd learned about wars, it was that their endings were just temporary lulls. Rebuilding human society was going to be hard, slow, and generations long; the entire human species—the tiny remnant that remained—was bereaved. And it no longer had an external threat to hold it together. It didn't have something to live for yet, just the shared instinct that said *stay alive.*

Survival's an ugly thing. Seen it. Done it.

Bernie found it was a lot easier to forget her own traumatic memories when she thought of Dom.

Poor little bastard. What a shitty way to begin the first peace we've ever known.

She looked up and started to rise from her seat, planning to make her way to the gun bay and just sit with Dom to let him know everyone was there for him. But when she glanced through the opening Marcus was already there, just standing over him with one hand on his shoulder, staring out into the dusk.

If anything was going to rebuild humanity, it was comradeship. Gears had that in shitloads. Bernie knew exactly what kind of society she wanted to see emerge from the ruins.

CHAPTER 2

The first thing you do is split the team into two shifts—because this is going to go on for a lot longer than you think, and by the time you realize you're too tired to think straight, you won't have anyone ready to take over.

(STAFF SERGEANT LENNARD PARRY, COG LOGISTICS CORPS, BRIEFING CIVILIANS CO-OPTED FOR EMERGENCY CONSTRUCTION DUTIES.)

PORT FARRALL EVACUATION ASSEMBLY AREA, NORTH TYRAN COAST, THREE HOURS AFTER FIRST FLOODING.

Anya Stroud couldn't tell if she was looking at fifty thousand people or half a million.

She stood on the Armadillo's open ramp with her jacket wrapped tightly around her, hands thrust in pockets, watching a slow-flowing river of refugees streaming past, many clinging to junkers that didn't look capable of carrying so many people. The icy sleet had now turned to snow. It was the worst possible time to evacuate.

And it was the first time in fifteen years that Anya had absolutely nothing to do for the time being, except worry—about Marcus, about whatever the hell Dom had meant about Maria, about the next twenty-six hours, about whatever *tomorrow* meant now. Their Raven had landed safely, she knew that much. She didn't dare hog overloaded comms channels for personal chit-chat. Behind her in the rear of the APC, Lieutenant Mathieson was manning comms, keeping a tally of Gears and tasking them as they reported in. He was diverting some to security duty, others to rest periods. It was a well-rehearsed plan.

How many civilians did we lose? How many Gears? How long is it going to take to check everyone on the list?

"Anya, you should get some sleep." Mathieson turned in his seat. He'd lost both legs in combat and hadn't taken enforced desk duties well. "You're back on watch in seven hours."

"I'm okay," she said. "If I sleep now, I'll feel like hell when I wake up."

"Suit yourself."

Mathieson turned back to the comms console again. Anya went on scanning the scene around her. To her right, she could see the abandoned city of Port Farrall through the line of parked trucks and Centaur tanks. The nearest buildings were backlit by APC lights as Gears moved in to secure the area before the EM teams and sappers moved in. Nobody was under any illusion that the Locust threat was entirely over. There'd be pockets of strag-glers. And they'd be just as dangerous. When she turned to face the rear of the Armadillo, the upperworks of CNV *Sovereign* were visible, picked out by navigation lights as the warship sat along-side in Merrenat Naval Base.

We all know the drill. We've had evacuation plans in place for years. But even so . . . how are we going to pull this off? How do we get an abandoned city habitable in days?

No, not days. *Hours.* The temperature was plummeting. No-body had the luxury of time.

"Anya?" Hoffman strode up to the APC, boots crunching on the frozen slush, and indicated somewhere back down the line of parked vehicles with his thumb. "The CIC truck's operational now—heating and coffee, people. Get down there. No point freez-ing your asses off. Stroud, you're rostered off. Get some sleep."

"I told her, sir—" said Mathieson.

"I'm fine," she said.

"Maintaining rest breaks is part of your duties, Stroud. Got to keep you operational."

That was Hoffmanese for "I worry about you." She found it rather endearing. "Understood, sir. But I can't sleep now. Don't they need people to . . . well, at least hand out hot drinks or something?"

"I said *rest*. What's the key thing in any planned emergency?"

"Know your task and carry it out, sir."

"Right. Let the designated teams worry about everything else until they ask for assistance. You'll be busy tasking Gears sooner than you think. Public order, security details . . . yes, it's a different kind of soldiering now."

Hoffman paused and looked past her at something in the crowd of refugees. A Gear—forties, with a wild beard and a straw hat that marked him out as press-ganged from the Stranded—was working his way back through the tide of bodies, calling out a name: "Maralin? *Maralin!* Sweetie, you okay? Where's Teresa?"

A teenage girl struggled through the press of bodies and flung her arms around his neck. People parted to avoid them, and Anya watched a tearful reunion. Then another girl, just like her—no, *exactly* like her, a twin—appeared in the crowd and elbowed her way through, yelling, "Daddy! *Daddy!*"

"Well, *someone's* happy," Hoffman muttered. "Grindlift driver. Glad he found his kids."

Anya had a hard time distinguishing Stranded from citizens now. Many refugees were so ragged and scruffy that they could have been either. And while that Gear had found his family, others were still searching the human chaos for faces they recognized. A man stood to one side of the stream of people, calling out: "Anyone seen my son? Tylor Morley. Fourteen, brown hair, skinny. Anyone?"

He repeated it over and over, like someone standing on a street corner selling newspapers. Anya knew there'd be many more desperate searches like that in the days to come. The satisfaction at evacuating most of Jacinto was now giving way to the guilt and dismay of realizing how many had been lost.

"That's the hard stuff," Hoffman said. "I'm thankful that the emergency guys can handle all that. Fighting grubs was the easy bit." He paused. "When Santiago reports in, ask him to see me."

"Will do, sir."

Hoffman looked as if he was going to say something else, but he just turned around and walked back toward the EM truck. Anya wiped her face with the back of her hand. Her skin was starting to sting with the steady barrage of snow.

"Better get moving," she said. She shut the hatches and started the engine. "I want to check out the medical tent. I'll drop you off at CIC."

"What's all that about Dom?" Mathieson asked.

Anya went into protective mode. Dom had defended her from intrusive interest when her mother was killed, and now it was her turn to watch his back.

"I didn't think you knew him," she said.

"Everyone knows Dom. Won the Embry Star at Aspho. Screwed his career defending Fenix at the court-martial. Hoffman's favorite. Spends all his free time looking for his missus."

"Yes, that's Dom." Anya steered the 'Dill out of the line, keeping to the vehicle lane marked in the grass by reflective cones. She kept a wary eye out for stray pedestrians. "Like you said, Hoffman's favorite."

It was as good an explanation as any. She'd get to Dom before the gossip started. So far, the only people who knew weren't the gossiping kind: Delta Squad, Hoffman, and herself. It was nobody else's business.

When she reached the CIC truck, she jumped out of the 'Dill's cab to find herself ankle deep in slush and regretting not changing into combat boots and fatigues. Mathieson swung himself out on prosthetic legs that were the best that the COG could manage to make, and that wasn't very good at all. Anya made a note to sweet-talk Baird into seeing what modifications might be possible. Baird wasn't exactly the most bighearted Gear, but he couldn't resist a mechanical challenge.

And humanity was now facing a future with even less technol-

ogy at its disposal. Although that was obvious, and everyone knew
that abandoning Jacinto meant leaving behind almost all the trap-
pings of modern society, the full realization hadn't hit Anya until
then.

*No workshops. No bakeries. No computer network. No drugs
manufacturing. We didn't have much in Jacinto, but now we've
even lost most of that.*

The CIC truck's interior looked like any small office, minus
windows. It smelled of damp wool, fuel, coffee, and sweat, packed
with weary and stressed people trying to grab a hot drink to keep
them going while they worked out humanity's chances of survival
on the back of a used and reused notepad.

This was an old emergency management command vehicle
from the pre-Locust days, a mobile base for the response team,
designed to go wherever a civil disaster occurred. Anya almost
didn't recognize Prescott when she walked in; he was sitting on
one of the desks, in a thick pullover and ordinary pants like the
rest of the civilian team—no smart tunic, no medals, no gold
braid. It might have been common sense—civilian rig *was*
warmer than his uniform—but it looked like a subtle message
that he was in it with the common people, suffering what they
suffered. Design or accident, it certainly seemed to have had the
right effect. The EM team looked energized. Even Dr. Hayman
looked more relaxed. After what they'd all been through, that was
some impressive inspiration in action.

No, you're not just any old bureaucrat, are you, sir?

"Okay." Prescott was partway through some agenda item. "So
we'll leave people on board ships for the time being, except for
those in open vessels who need immediate shelter. Can the larger
vessels take any of them?"

"Stuffed to the gunwales already, sir." Royston Sharle had
drawn the shortest straw of all as the EM chief. He'd served in the
COG navy, and it showed to Anya in all the *right* ways. "Disease
is going to be an issue if we push that. You know—confined
spaces, overloaded waste discharge. We've rigged tents with
heaters for the time being, and for tonight, we just have to get as

many under cover as we can. Those in vehicles—they're better off staying put until we can move into the buildings. Latrines and water in place, and soup wagons will be operational within the hour."

"Good job, Sharle." Prescott rubbed his forehead, looking down at a sheaf of notes in his hand. If it was an act, it was beautifully performed. "Thank you. Fuel?"

"*Sovereign* sent a marine recon team into Merrenat and there's still imulsion in at least half the tanks that Stranded couldn't get at. And there's no telling what else is still stored in that complex—it was built to withstand a full Indie attack in the last war."

Anya listened, the landscape of crisis shifting before her eyes. From a single city under siege, held together by necessity, defined by a physical defensive line, humankind was now in free fall. The biggest threat was itself. The word *secure* brought that home to her. Citizens had probably stolen, feuded, and connived throughout the war, but the Locust threat was right on their doorstep—easy to focus upon, familiar, oddly unifying. Now the Locust were gone. Simply staying alive was suddenly even harder. Anya could sense a communal fear of the truly unknown.

Prescott glanced up at her and looked relieved; he even managed a quick smile. Maybe that was his political psyops at work again. The sobering thing was that she felt herself respond to it like everyone else did. She was willing to work until she dropped.

"How many people did we lose?" Prescott asked quietly. "Do we have any idea yet?"

There was a brief silence. Hayman looked at Sharle for a moment.

"I can only tell you how many haven't made it out of the treatment station alive so far," she said. Hayman had to be at least seventy years old; she was in the vulnerable elderly category herself, even if her don't-mess-with-me attitude disguised that. "And that includes trauma and those who've died of heart attacks in transit. But if you're asking for an estimate overall—we're thinking in terms of thirty percent losses."

But we said we'd evacuated most of the city. I said it. Anya tried to come to terms with what *most* meant. *Is that the best we could do?*

Yes, 70 percent was a good majority, achieved under attack and with the city literally vanishing under them. It still didn't make 30 percent acceptable. And it didn't include any Stranded, because the COG had no real idea of how many people lived in wretched shantytowns outside the protection of Jacinto. There could have been more than a million dead now. A drop in the ocean after so many over the years, but—

No, Anya couldn't take it in. She just let it register on her brain as a statistic, allowing the shock do what it was designed to do—to numb the pain temporarily so that you could concentrate on surviving. Prescott chewed over the news for a few moments, then slipped off the table to stand upright, fully in command. It was perfect use of body language; he probably did it automatically, a habit learned at his father's knee. This was simply how statesmen behaved.

"I'm not going to give you a stirring speech," he said. "We face facts. Our society's changed out of all recognition in three hours. We're more at risk now than we were under Locust attack. We've lost even the most basic comforts we had in Jacinto. People *will* die of cold and hunger. People *will* become angry and scared very, very fast, and that's the point at which we face collapse. It's going to get a lot worse before it gets better. And it's going to put enormous pressure not only on you, but on our Gears—we're taking them out of a terrible war and plunging them straight into policing their own people, keeping order, because order *will* break down if we don't impose it. Some Gears will find it impossible, and so might some of us. But the only other choice is to degenerate into savagery, and then the Locust will have won because we handed them the victory."

Prescott stopped and looked around at the assembled team. Anya had been so transfixed by the pep talk that she hadn't noticed Hoffman behind her. She had no idea where he'd been, but he was here now, coffee in one hand, freshly shaven, smelling of soap. That was his substitute for sleep—coffee and a shower. Where he'd found running water and privacy, she had absolutely no idea, but Hoffman would have rubbed himself down with snow if he had to.

"Well said, sir," Hoffman said quietly, and sounded as if he meant it. "We now have security patrols on task."

So that was where he'd been. Anya had expected to be central to that tasking, but things *were* changing. The meeting broke up, and Hoffman beckoned her into another compartment of the vehicle.

"I can't find Santiago," he said. "Now, what the hell went on with his wife? I *heard* that transmission."

Anya shook her head, trying not to think the worst. "I only know as much as you do, sir."

"Permission to go find out some *more*, seeing as you're not going to sleep." Hoffman folded his cap and tucked it in his belt. "I've got to do my quality time with the chairman. And please give Sergeant Mataki my compliments if you see her."

"Understood, sir."

It was all code. If Hoffman had ever been the type to openly admit he was worried sick about individuals, it was long buried. No commander had that luxury. Anya felt she had moral permission to use the radio now and leaned over Mathieson at the comms desk.

"Okay, where's Sergeant Fenix?"

Mathieson consulted his roster. "Delta's on stand-easy and they're all logged off the radio net. Try looking in marshaling zone G. Tents should be up by now."

If Dom was losing it, Marcus would be with him. All she had to do was find Marcus. She drove the 'Dill slowly along the marked lanes, slowing to a crawl every time she saw a group of Gears. It took a long time, and then the APC's headlights picked out a familiar figure—Augustus Cole. Apart from his sheer size, no other Gear was crazy enough to go around with bare arms in this weather. Baird and Mataki stood there with him, looking as if they were arguing, completely oblivious of the snow.

Anya stopped and rolled back the Armadillo's hatch. "Hi, guys. Where's Dom? I'm on a mission from Hoffman."

"Marcus went lookin' for him, ma'am," Cole said. "Some seri-

ous shit's goin' down. What happened? I heard him, *you* heard
him—"

Baird cut in. "I don't believe it. The man was totally *normal*
when we met up. Not a word about it. When you blow your wife's
brains out, you don't just shrug and carry on, do you?"

"Blondie, you're all fucking heart," Bernie said sourly. "Sorry,
ma'am. Look, I say we shut up and leave this to Marcus for now.
We don't know what went on yet. We tell anyone who asks about
Maria that Dom's got proof she's dead, and not to ask him about
it. Okay?"

"Good idea," Anya said.

Baird seemed genuinely shaken by it. "I mean, I saw what the
grubs did to our guys down there, and shooting her had to be
the—"

"Shut up before I *shut* you up." Bernie prodded him hard in
the chest. "Dom's in shock. We do what we have to, to get him
through it, okay? And from *you*, that means no crass advice. Keep
it zipped."

Anya was satisfied that Bernie had the situation—and Baird's
mouth—under control. She'd try raising Marcus again.

"Hoffman thought you'd been killed, Bernie," she said. "He
wants to know you're okay."

Bernie's face was cut and bruised. She glanced away as if she
was embarrassed at Hoffman's concern. "Not in quite those
words, I'll bet."

"I'll tell him you're happy he's okay, too."

"Yes, ma'am," Bernie said.

In this game, a girl had to be multilingual. Anya could speak
Hoffmanese, and she understood Bernie-speak pretty well too.
She turned the APC around at the end of the lane and resumed
her search.

SOUTHERN PERIMETER, ASSEMBLY AREA.

There was just enough light from his armor's power status indicators for Dom to see the detail on the photograph.

He squatted in the lee of a boulder, bent over so that his body shielded the picture from the falling snow, and went through the sequence that was now pure reflex after so many years. He studied Maria's face—her cheek pressed to his as they posed for the camera—and recalled where they'd been when the picture was taken, then turned the print over to read what she'd written on the back. He'd done the same thing a dozen times a day for ten years. The photo was cracked and creased; Maria's handwriting was gradually fading, the lines more smeared each time he took it from the pocket under his armor.

So you always have me with you. I love you, Dominic. Always, Maria.

That was the Maria he had to remember: beautiful, enjoying life, not the scarred and tortured shell in the Locust detention cell. Dom tried to fix it in his memory. That was how he'd been trained. When a commando was in the worst shit imaginable, he had to be able to think his way out of it—to concentrate on survival, tell himself a whole new story, believe the best, and ignore the nagging voice that told him he'd never get out of this shit-hole alive.

Dom tried. But all he could see was her sightless eyes flickering back and forth as he tried to get her to recognize him, and a face that was only scarred and ulcerated skin stretched over a skull.

Why can't I see the rest?

The last thing he could visualize was placing the muzzle of his sidearm to her temple as he held her. He shut his eyes at that point. He remembered lowering her carefully to the floor and taking off the necklace she still wore, the one he'd bought her when Benedicto was born, but the rest was a blank, and somehow he couldn't see any blood in his mind's eye.

Was it her?

You know damn well it was.

Why didn't I take her out of there and get her to a doctor? Wouldn't any man do that without thinking?

Why didn't I find her sooner, try harder, go looking down there earlier?

I had ten fucking years and I let her down.

Dom knew the answers and that he could have done no more. But there was knowing and there was believing, and believing wasn't much influenced by facts.

He fumbled under his chest-plate for the sheaf of photographs he kept in his shirt pocket. It was the size of a slim pack of playing cards, carefully sealed in a plastic bag, and he could visualize each of the photos at will. His life was preserved in those fragile sheets of glossy card: his brother, Carlos; his parents; his son and daughter; Malcolm Benjafield and Georg Timiou from his commando unit. There was only one person in those pictures who was still alive now, and that was Marcus.

Dom put Maria's photo back in the pack and resealed it. He wouldn't need to show it to anyone else again. He'd found her.

What am I going to feel like tomorrow, or the day after, or the day after that?

He got to his feet and walked on, staring out into the snow, cradling his Lancer. Despite the noise from the camp—'Dill and Centaur motors, generators, the murmur of thousands of voices, occasional shouts and instructions—it was quieter here than anywhere he'd been in years. He could hear boots crunching in the snow, gradually getting closer. He didn't need to turn and look.

"Dom."

Marcus just appeared beside him, matching his pace as if they'd planned this patrol. He didn't ask if Dom was all right; he knew he wasn't. And he didn't ask if Dom wanted to let it all out or talk it through, or why he'd gone off without telling anyone. It didn't need saying or asking. It was simply *understood*. The two of them knew each other too well to do anything else.

"Nothing moving out there," Dom said.

"Hoffman's set up patrols in the camp in case the civilians get out of hand."

"Yeah, it's a whole new pile of shit now."

"You said it."

"Everyone thinks I'm a bastard, don't they?"

"The whole camp? I didn't ask them all. But if you mean the squad—no. They don't."

"They know what I did."

Dom was ready to freeze to death out here rather than go back and look Baird, Cole, or Bernie in the eye—or anyone else, come to that. It was like he'd sobered up after a crazy night and had to admit he'd been an asshole. He felt he had things buttoned down all the time he was in the Locust tunnels, but now he was safe—whatever that meant now—things were starting to come apart again. He didn't know what the next minute would bring for him.

Denial, anger, bargaining, depression, acceptance. Dom could repeat it like a litany. The well-meaning woman who'd counseled Maria after the kids died had listed it for Dom like a transport timetable, all the stations where you would stop on your way to the terminal marked Normal Life Again. But she'd never warned him that he'd feel all of it at once, or in random order, or that he'd never reach normal.

"Dom, say the word, and I'll tell them what happened. You don't have to." Marcus stopped to sight up on something. The snow was easing off; the cloud cover was thinning out. "They'll understand."

"How can *they* understand if I can't?"

"We've all lost family. Nobody's judging you."

"I should have saved her."

Marcus just shook his head. They were now a couple of kilometers south of the camp, in ankle-deep snow pitted with criss-crossing animal tracks. Dom had been certain that he'd react like Tai and blow his own head off rather than live with the horror that was trapped in his mind, but it didn't feel that way at all. He could have done it ten times over by now. He hadn't.

Part of him had started grieving for Maria the day she really fell apart—when Benedicto and Sylvia had been killed. Whatever was happening in his head now wasn't nice, clean, noble, *predictable* grief. It was full of other shit and debris, like the snow around here. It wasn't as white as it seemed.

"You did save her," Marcus said at last. "Remember Tai.

Toughest guy we knew, and he *wanted* to die. That was after *hours* of what the grubs did to him, not weeks or years. If anything like that happened to me, I'd want you to cap me right away, because I'd sure as shit do it for you."

Dom didn't know if Marcus could do it, because he hadn't slotted Carlos when he'd begged him to. Marcus had still tried to save him. But that didn't matter now.

"We better report in," Dom said.

"Yeah."

"You spoken to Anya yet?"

"No."

"You thought she hadn't made it. Don't kid me that you don't need her."

Marcus made the usual noncommittal rumbling sound at the back of his throat. "Yeah."

They turned back to camp, following a wide arc. Dom tried to imagine how he'd have felt if Anya had been the one to die and it had been Maria on that Raven. He was damned sure he'd have rushed to Maria's side and never let her out of his sight again. But Marcus had been raised in a big cold house full of silence, where emotions were kept on a leash, so he probably didn't even know where to start.

The temperature was falling fast now. The snow was turning rock hard, and the sounds it made had changed slightly. Dom strained to listen.

"Shit." Marcus held up his hand to halt him. They covered each other's backs automatically. "Hear that?"

Dom had to hold his breath to hear it. Whatever it was sounded a long way off, like something moving erratically through the belt of forest to their south, breaking branches as it went. It could have been an animal. There were enough varieties of hoof and paw prints on the ground to fill a zoo. But some sounds were deeply embedded in memory, and Dom wanted it to be just his tormented mind misreading everything and trying to fit it to familiar patterns.

"Corpser?" Dom said.

Corpsers were too big to manage a stealthy approach, and they had too many legs—great for excavating the grubs' tunnels and ferrying drones around, but piss-poor at surprise attacks on open ground. Something was crashing in this direction at high speed.

"I hope his mother knows he's out late." Marcus pressed his radio earpiece. "Fenix to Control, enemy contact, two klicks southwest of camp, possible Corpser approaching. We're engaging."

"Roger that, Fenix," Mathieson said. "You're not rostered on patrol. Are you alone?"

"Santiago's here. Consider it voluntary overtime. We love our work."

"I'm tasking fire support and a KR to get some light on those grubs. Don't hog all the fun, Fenix."

Stragglers were inevitable. And this time, they were almost welcome. Dom had unfinished business that drowning the grub bastards hadn't resolved. Yes, it was a Corpser. He could see its lights in the darkness now, wobbling as it worked its way through the trees.

"So, we wait here, or we go get it?"

Marcus started walking. "Manners are the bedrock of civilization. Let's meet the asshole halfway."

Dom was up for that. A switch flipped somewhere inside, and he wanted destruction, vengeance, some vent for the pressure building within. He was jogging some way ahead of Marcus when he heard the Raven approaching. It swooped low overhead and the brilliant blue-white searchlights lit the field up like moonlight. Dom saw movement behind the Corpser. Shit, it was a mixed bag of Locust—a dozen drones, a couple of Boomers, and a Bloodmount.

Marcus sighed. "Ahh, shit . . ."

"You think they're a recon party?"

"I think that's a bunch of grub refugees doing what we're doing and getting the hell out. Higher ground, old e-holes—they've kept ahead of the flood."

Well, they weren't coming to kiss and make up, that was for sure. Dom could already hear the noise of 'Dills behind, racing to the contact point. He dropped behind the nearest cover with Marcus, took aim, and waited. On open ground the motley band looked grotesque rather than terrifying, but if they got into the camp—no solid buildings for protection, masses of civilians who were already scared shitless—the panicked stampede alone would cost lives, let alone any damage the grubs might inflict.

Maybe the grubs didn't realize they were on an intercept course for a human camp. They looked in complete disarray. The Bloodmount was going nuts, thrashing its head from side to side even with its rider hanging on to it for grim death. If the rider was thrown, the thing would revert to blind instinct and sniff out the nearest human flesh.

Maybe the grubs would veer away when they realized how outnumbered they were.

No. Bring it on. Come to me. Come and die.

As far as Dom was concerned, one grub was too many. Prescott was right: it was a genocidal war. The Locust started it. But now humans had to finish it, and grub stragglers weren't just a hazard, they were potential breeding stock. They all had to die.

This is why I'm still alive. This is what I'm meant to do. I get it now.

Dom could now see headlights playing on the hummocks in the snow from behind him as the APCs raced to their position. There was no way the grubs could miss that, not in complete darkness on open land. Dom bet on them feeling just like he did then—that they wanted to make someone pay for what had happened to their buddies and their shitty little bit of Sera, and they didn't much care if they died doing it.

"Want to take a bet on how many Locust were down there?" Marcus said.

"No idea. Thousands. Hundreds of thousands. Millions."

"I think we've got about fifty or sixty heading this way."

"Maybe some of the Lambent made it out, too, and that's who they're running from."

"Like we're the softer option?"

Dom centered his sights on a Boomer. "They got that wrong, then," he said, and opened fire.

ARMADILLO PERSONNEL CARRIER PA-776,
RESPONDING.

"Cole, let me in." Anya Stroud hammered her fist on the 'Dill's hull as it revved up. *"Cole!"*

Anya was only a little slip of a thing by Cole's scale of reckoning, but she was close to putting a dent in the metal. Bernie leaned across the crew cab and went to hit the hatch control.

Baird snapped his goggles into place with a loud *thwack* of the strap. "It's ladies' night, Cole."

"Anya ain't *frontline.*" Cole would have driven off, but he couldn't see exactly where Anya was standing and he was afraid of flattening her. "She's gonna have to sit this one out."

"Bollocks, her mother was my CO, and she's coming with us," Bernie said. She hit the switch. "Mount up, ma'am."

Cole wasn't sure that answer made sense. But he didn't have time to argue, and Bernie had her killing face on. She was still mad as hell about her squad—or something. There was plenty to be mad about. Anya scrambled into the cab.

"Okay, ma'am, just be careful, that's all." Cole understood that rush of blood that made a Gear want to get stuck into a bunch of grubs. It was only natural, but not in a skirt and high heels. That was asking for trouble. He sent the 'Dill racing down the perimeter lane. "If I bring you back with holes in you, Hoffman's gonna yell bad words at me."

Baird rummaged in a locker. Cole caught a glimpse of a Lancer being handed over as he focused on the driver's periscope.

"Okay, ma'am," Baird said. "Tell me which end makes the big noise."

"I still have to requalify with this weapon every year, Baird." Anya checked the safety and the ammo clip, then powered up.

The short burst of chainsaw noise in the confined space made Cole wince. "Think of this as saving me from skills fade."

"We only got a few grubs, and there's a whole army of Gears headin' their way, so form a line," Cole said.

"Just in case, then."

Maybe she felt she still had something to prove, what with having a kick-ass mother like Helena Stroud and everything. Shit, that was some serious lady to live up to. Bernie had told Cole some hairy stories about the major, and he believed every word. He glanced at Anya for a moment to check whether her expression said *scared shitless* or *red mist*, but it looked more like she was trying to recite some drill under her breath. She had a point, though—frontline meant squat now. Nobody was going to get the luxury of sitting at a fancy desk all day, even if the COG still had any of those. Which it didn't.

"Whoa, they started without us," Baird said, finger pressed to one ear as he listened to the comms chatter. There was a weird mood going around, that crazy state between finding everything funny and wanting to cry for days. People did dumb shit when they felt like that, but it was sinking in that the grubs were busted and humans were back on top again, even if that was top of a pile of nothing. You had to make allowances. "Hey, Cole, see all the muzzle flash? It's a mixed grill. A little of everything on the Locust menu."

"Shit, it'll all be over by the time we dismount." Bernie didn't sound like she was joking. "But they won't be the last."

"I promised I'd save a live one for you, Granny."

"That's my boy. I'll remember you in my will."

"Not fair," Cole said. "You promised to leave the kitty-fur boots to *me*, Boomer Lady."

"You get the country estate. You're my favorite." Bernie's voice wasn't right. Her mind was on something else. "Is it true what they did to Tai?"

Cole didn't want to think about it yet. It wasn't the right time to lose it. *Maybe later.* "Depends what you heard. But he's out of it now, so—"

"I told her," Baird said.

Everyone stopped yapping. Anya laid the Lancer on her lap. Baird hadn't told Anya, and now Cole could tell she was imagining the worst. Maybe she couldn't imagine anything that bad.

No, she was a CIC dispatcher. The bots' cameras had shown her the war in close-up for years. It'd take a lot to shock her, but then maybe Tai was one mutilated body too many.

"Now, where am I gonna park?" The 'Dill bounced over the rough ground. This was close enough. Cole brought it to a halt next to three other APCs—none of which had their full armor plating—to provide extra cover. "End of the line, ladies. Check you got all your luggage with you."

Another squad was already laying down fire to the right, and when Cole followed their aim, he could see that the Corpser had broken away and was trying to circle around the defenses. *Shit, get a Centaur down here and pop this bitch with a few shells.* They were now in a meadow due south of the camp, running parallel with the road to Jacinto. More refugees were still streaming in. And they'd heard that the grubs were back in town, judging by the screaming.

Shit, the last thing anyone needed now was some kind of stampede and civilians rushing every damn where. They had nowhere to hide. But there was no point telling them to leave the cleanup to the Gears and carry on into the camp like nothing was happening. They knew the grubs were around, and grubs meant ending up dead.

"Ma'am, get up in the 'Dill's hatch and give us fire cover." Bernie gestured to Anya. "Because you're not fully mobile in what you're wearing. We'll put that right later. Okay?"

"Who's herding the civilians?" Cole asked. "Someone ought to be keeping a line between them and the grubs in case they bolt the wrong way."

Anya vanished and the top hatch flew open. She had a vantage point now, and she could see stuff Cole couldn't. She rested her Lancer on the hatch coaming while she activated her radio. "We need some crowd control down here, Mathieson."

"Tell him to put some armor between us and the refugees," Baird said. "We're overmanned down here. Just keep the civvies out of our way and stop 'em going shitless."

"Control's blind, man." Cole felt sorry for Mathieson, trying to task units without any visual on the battlefield. "Shit, the things I'm missin' about Jacinto already . . ."

Bernie pointed toward the road. "Ma'am, if you want to head off any civvies, move the 'Dill—we'll be fine."

"Roger that, Sergeant."

Bernie smiled to herself and jogged away in the direction of the firefight. Baird shoved Cole in the back. "Hey, come on, Cole. We got to keep an eye on Granny. She's the one who knows how to cook all that wildlife shit, remember? That's *important* now. *Skills,* man."

Every Gear seemed to be converging on that bunch of Locust like they'd never seen one before. It was now total overkill; relief, probably, everyone finally seeing the last of the grubs and wanting to get a whole lot of shit out of their systems. The biggest danger now was probably getting in some other Gear's arc of fire. APCs screamed out of the assembly area and headed for the road, tail-lights bouncing in a staggered line. Cole could hear a Raven heading his way.

But he had some shit to get out of his system, too.

He focused on a wounded Boomer trying to reload—baby, you had to be *faster* than that with Cole Train around—and ran at it, firing short bursts. Marcus was down there somewhere to the right, yelling at someone else.

"Stop pissing ammo!" Marcus didn't yell much, but when he did, you could hear him the other side of Jacinto. "Shit, *save your fucking ammo!*" There was a roar of chainsaw, then a loud grunt. "We can't *replace* this shit yet."

"Yeah, that's right, baby!" The Boomer looked up just as Cole put a burst into its legs to distract it. He sprinted inside its reach before it could aim its Boomshot and put two rounds through its eye socket—a handy ready-made hole in the skull, a whole lot easier than trying to get through that thick hide. "I'm on an economy drive. Baird, where you got to? Talk to me—whoo, we got *light*!"

The Raven was now overhead, sweeping the snow with search-lights, and Cole got an instant snapshot of the battle as far as the visible horizon. Dark gray mounds lay scattered: dead grubs. Baird and Bernie were running to intercept one moving toward the road. Cole could see it staggering, leaving a trail of blood on the snow. A massive explosion followed almost immediately by a second—a kind of *boom-boom* like a heartbeat—left him blinded for a few moments.

"Corpser down," said a deadpan voice on the comms channel. A Centaur rumbled into the circling pools of brilliant white light as if it was taking a bow at an ice show. The tank was in its element, with plenty of space to do its thing. "KR-Three-Five, you see the Bloodmount? They're just nasty. We want it."

"KR-Three-Five to all squads, we have visual on the Blood-mount and rider. C-Twenty-Eight will engage. Stand clear."

The Centaur fired another volley of shells just as the Blood-mount came racing toward the camp. Man, they were big ugly bastards even by grub standards. They ate humans if they got a chance. The rider must have known he was going to get his ass fried, and his pony's, too, but he kept on coming like he had a chance of trampling the place.

They hate us that much?

Hell, that's what I'd do . . .

"Fire."

The Centaur trembled on its massive tires from the recoil. The Bloodmount was an instant ball of flame, and its rider was hurled so high into the air that a couple of Gears had time to start a run for his landing spot. The meadow was suddenly still except for the Raven tracking back and forth in a search pattern as it scanned the battlefield. It didn't look like any grub had made it out.

The show distracted Cole for a moment, and he lost sight of Baird and Bernie when the searchlights moved. Then a 'Dill's headlamps picked out the two of them. The grub they'd been chasing was down. And Bernie was on its back, like she'd tackled it. She probably had. Baird waved at him.

"Cole!" he yelled. "I promised Granny, okay?"

"What the hell you doin', man?" Cole jogged across the snow. Another 'Dill rolled in, lights angled down, like it was illuminating the area for them. "Give her a hand. She's gonna get hurt. You out of ammo or something?"

The grub was badly wounded, all blood and frayed flesh, but that didn't mean it still wasn't dangerous. Cole didn't want to see Bernie survive the war—hell, *two* wars and whatever shit she did in between—just to end up creamed because she couldn't resist settling one last score with grubkind. But she had the thing in a headlock, pinned it to the ground.

That was a sight to behold in itself. She was no kid, and she still wasn't carrying enough weight to brawl like that, but she didn't seem to care. She drew her knife and shoved the tip under its jawline. Shit, why didn't Baird shoot the thing?

Baird looked at Cole and shrugged. "We got a live one. Hey, ladies first . . ."

"Damon baby, just kill it so we can go. I ain't had my dinner yet."

"Why? We never took one alive before. It's *interesting.*"

Cole suddenly realized what Bernie was up to. Her teeth were clenched, and she didn't look like the Bernie he knew. And it wasn't just the sharp angles that the headlights threw up on her face.

"You know what I'm going to do with *this*, tosser?" Her face was right in the grub's, close enough to get it bitten off if the thing had the strength left to go for her. "I'm going to do to you what you did to my mate Tai. Yeah. You like that idea? And I'm old, so I'm going to be a bit slow about it. Understand?"

The grub struggled weakly. Baird moved around and put one boot on its back to pin it down. Cole thought it was to stop the thing from throwing Bernie off if it got its second wind, but some of the Gears who were watching took it as an invitation to join in.

Cole didn't mind chainsawing any number of grubs, but this wasn't right. Bernie—and she was a *kind* woman, she really was—

had kicked up a notch into something he hadn't seen before. Andresen's squad cheered. Nobody seemed to have any doubts; they all knew now what grubs did to human prisoners. And that was without the grievance about a few billion dead since E-Day.

"Bernie, just shoot the thing." Cole debated whether to end the show himself. Baird wasn't exactly helping calm things down. "Damon, that ain't nice. Don't get Boomer Lady all fired up when she's had a shitty day."

Baird shouldered his Lancer. "Why haven't we taken any of these things prisoner before? Maybe this is a chance to learn something." He lifted his boot and moved around to the grub's head, kneeling down to look it in the eye. It just kept bellowing. It might have been crying for its mother or cursing them all to hell. Nobody knew; Baird was just about the only guy who stood a chance of working it out. He was smart when it came to grubs. "Hey, asshole—look at me. I know you get a kick out of this shit, but why pick on us? Your war was with your own buddies. Not our problem. And, seeing as we're chatting, where the hell did you all come from?"

The Locust just went on bellowing, and Bernie dragged the tip of her blade down its neck, looking like she was putting all her weight into it. Grubs had thick hides; she wasn't joking when she said that slicing it up would take some time. Cole was starting to feel really uncomfortable now, wondering if he'd have sawed up so many grubs if he'd had the chance to take his time over it. Something told him he wouldn't have, but that didn't help him work out why one felt okay and the other didn't. It didn't make the grub any happier, either way.

I never lost any sleep over 'em. Just over my folks. And my buddies. This ain't the time to start judgin' Bernie, maybe.

"I've got plenty of time, grub," Bernie said. "Blondie, you think you'd understand an answer if it gave you one?"

Baird was still on his knees, peering at the grub like it was the underside of a truck. "Dunno. Try it and see."

The group of spectators parted. Marcus wandered across, Dom behind him, and stood looking down at Bernie and Baird.

"Just shoot it," he said.

Bernie still had a murderous grip on the grub, but she twisted around to look at Marcus. "Give me a reason."

Marcus shrugged. "You'll be bitching that your back's giving you hell tomorrow."

Bernie looked at him for a few moments, seemed to catch her breath, then eased off a fraction. She reached for her sidearm.

"Good point," she said, and put the muzzle to the back of its head. "Okay, Blondie—clear."

Crack.

If Marcus had just walked away like he'd put her in her place, it would have been awkward, seeing as she was the veteran sergeant. But he just held out his hand to help her to her feet. She took it. Everyone else thinned out. Getting a few hours' sleep suddenly seemed a lot more interesting than messing up a grub or two.

"Terrific," Baird said. "Now I'll never know. Next time we find one—"

"I don't give a shit what any grub's got to say." Marcus gave Bernie a shove toward the 'Dill. Cole reminded himself that they had history, *regimental* history. "Control? We're done here. Returning to base."

They piled into the 'Dill and headed back. Anya took the wheel. Cole sat back and tried to read what was going on—and there was a lot a guy could read in a bunch of tired, shattered people.

Bernie linked her arm through Dom's, not a word said, and Dom let her, then shut his eyes. It was a real nice motherly thing to do. Anya took a quick look at Marcus a couple of times, and he looked back in a way that wasn't exactly a smile but wiped a few lines off his face for a moment. Baird sat dismantling a Lancer chain, not making eye contact, probably because he didn't know how to tell everyone how glad he was that they were all alive and could actually think about a *real* future, not just the bullshit one that Prescott always used to talk about to make people forget they probably wouldn't see tomorrow.

Yeah, nobody had to say a word. Everyone understood.

"I'd like to think that wasn't me back there," Bernie said quietly. "But it was, and that's the thing that's going to be the thin end of the wedge if we let it."

Dom didn't open his eyes. "You'd have stopped yourself. I'm not sure if I would have."

Nobody needed to add that they wouldn't have blamed him. Cole hoped he knew that.

CHAPTER 3

We can't stop them. We don't know where they come from. We don't know what they want. They don't even seem to want territory. All they do is kill. We can't even begin to negotiate with them, or work out their objectives, because we just don't know the first damn thing about them. That's not an enemy, Mr. Chairman. That's a monster.
(GENERAL BARDRY SALAMAN, CHIEF OF THE COG DEFENSE STAFF.)

Father was dead, but even if he'd still been alive, he would have had no advice or answers to give his son now.

Richard Prescott wasn't fighting his father's war anyway. It wasn't about energy supplies or land. Nobody on Sera had ever fought this kind of enemy before; there were no rules or precedents, and a year and a month after the Locust Horde had erupted from the ground, Sera—human Sera—was close to collapse.

I've been in office two months. I wouldn't even be here if Dalyell hadn't dropped dead. What do I know?

I know that we're all going to die if I don't pull this out of the fire now.

"Sir?" The office door opened slowly. "Sir, I've got Premier Deschenko on the line now. I'm sorry about the delay."

The delay had been ten hours; Prescott had been trying to get hold of the man since last night. Jillian, his secretary, hadn't left the office in days, but then few of his staff went home regularly each night now, and it wasn't just a primal human need to huddle together with familiar faces. It was desperation. Somehow, there was a feeling that the answer might be around the next corner if they just kept on trying, or spent one more hour looking for a break.

"Good," Prescott said. "Put him through."

He pressed the phone to his ear and shut his eyes. It was easier to concentrate that way. He needed to hear every nuance in Deschenko's voice, because he was going to ask the impossible, and he had to know if he was actually going to get it.

"Yori? How are you?"

"I've just had to order the retreat from Ostri." Deschenko sounded hoarse and exhausted. "I mean *the whole country.* I've lost nearly twenty brigades since E-Day, and now I need the few troops I have left to defend Pelles."

Prescott hadn't expected good news anyway. But that wasn't what he was seeking. "You know what I'm going to ask."

"Richard, I can't send troops to Tyrus or anywhere else. I have millions of refugees pouring over the border, and the best I can do is try to hold the north."

"You still have chemical weapons."

Deschenko fell silent. The Coalition of Ordered Governments was a strange beast to control. Prescott was its chairman, and its heart was—and always had been—in Ephyra, in Tyrus, but the operational reality was very different. It was a global alliance. Heads of COG states had to *want* to cooperate, or at least fear the wrath of the others if they tried to break ranks. Unilateral enforcement—the kind that didn't require extreme measures, at least—wasn't in Prescott's gift.

And he was on his own now. He knew it.

Where was the coalition? Every state had been hit hard by Lo-

cust attacks, and each was fighting its own war for the privilege of
being the last to fold and die.

You've all given up. You cowards. You parochial little cowards.

"Yes, I have weapons," Deschenko said. "But they're my last resort, to defend Pelles. And they'll kill us along with the grubs.
They're for the endgame, Richard."

Oh yes. They are.

Apart from the names of cities and precise numbers of dead,
this was a script that Prescott had almost learned by heart over the
past few weeks, because every COG leader so far had taken the
same position. They couldn't think beyond their own boundaries.
Nobody was ready to sacrifice the defense of their own citizens to
support a combined strike.

They've given up. They're just letting these bastards pick us off.

This wasn't about Pelles, or Ostri, or Tyrus, or any other member state. This was about Sera, the entire world. This was about
the survival of humankind.

"I realize I'm asking a great deal," Prescott said carefully. "And
I know I'm seen as the boy who's just taken over the family firm
and has to learn how things are really done around here. But I
don't have time, and neither does Sera."

"Spell it out, Richard."

"I'm asking you what I've asked every member state. Agree to
this—a joint and coordinated assault on the main Locust infesta-
tions. Break their back."

"Many of those locations happen to be in Tyrus . . ."

"There are no national boundaries now, Yori. The Locust
don't give a damn about our petty administrative detail. We're all
the same to them. Are you with me?"

Deschenko sounded as if he was swallowing repeatedly. He
might have been grabbing a coffee, or just agonizing over a
choice between disaster and apocalypse. But Prescott knew the
answer would be the same either way. He just needed to know
he'd done all he could to carry the argument.

"No, Richard," Deschenko said at last. "I'm afraid I'm not."

It was such a polite way to usher in mass destruction.

"Thank you, Yori. I understand your position." Prescott paused, almost automatically wishing the man well, or luck, or some other banal blessing that would never come to pass. But it felt like a lie. He hadn't yet learned to lie that easily. "Goodbye."

Prescott stood staring out the window for a few minutes, aware of the TV screens on the walls on both sides of him, sound muted, spewing news bulletins that never seemed to change, but focused instead on the physical world he could see with his own eyes. Helicopters tracked across the sky. It was a beautiful sunny day, at odds with the ugly work that had to be done. If he switched off those TV sets, he could almost believe that life was going on as normal. He didn't. He walked to the other window, the one that overlooked the rest of Ephyra, and stared at a view that stretched for twenty miles. Palls of smoke were visible, and old skyline landmarks had vanished. The Locust were almost at the gates.

One more try?

They've all turned me down, except the South Islands, and they've got nothing to contribute except Gears. This is going to take more than manpower.

"Jillian?" He held his finger on the intercom. "Get me the Attorney General, please. Not on the phone — ask him to come here as soon as he can."

"Yes, sir. You know his brother's still missing, don't you?"

Everyone was grieving. "I do."

Prescott sat down to wait, and turned up the sound on the monitors to watch the latest headlines. It astonished him that camera crews were still willing to go out and film the destruction. But what else could they do? In crisis, humans reverted to doing what they knew, part reflex, part comfort.

He was doing the same. He sat wondering why the final refusal from Deschenko — the confirmation that he had no control, that he'd failed to convince the rest of the COG that drastic action was all that was left — hadn't crushed him. He felt *cleansed* by it. A burden had lifted.

God help me, do I actually want to do this?

No, he wasn't a monster. He was sure of that. He knew what

monsters looked like now. They were gray, and they came in many hideous forms, and they delighted in the suffering of humans.

And they *had* to die, or all of humanity would be wiped out.

What have we done?

We should never have let it get this far. It has to stop, right now. Any way we can.

He pressed the intercom again. "Jillian, it's time you went home."

"I'm fine, sir."

"Do you have family anywhere else? Outside Jacinto, I mean."

"Only my sister, sir. She's in Tollen."

"You might want to ask her to come and stay with you. Ephyra's going to be the only part of Tyrus that's safe from Locust. In fact, make it soon. The grubs are getting closer every day."

Jillian paused, and that wasn't like her. Prescott hoped she understood the urgency of moving her sister, and from that pause, he knew she understood at least a little of what he had in mind.

"Thank you, sir," she said at last. "But I'll wait here until the AG's shown up. Is there anything else I can do in the meantime?"

Prescott wanted to sleep now. He decided he could manage a half-hour nap before anyone answered his summons.

"Yes," he said. If it had to be done, it could be rolled up in one meeting. "I need to see General Salaman, too. And the Director of Special Forces—Hoffman. That rough little colonel with all the medals."

"Yes, sir."

Prescott had his quorum now. "And Adam Fenix. Get Professor Fenix. The meeting's going to get technical."

THE SANTIAGO HOUSEHOLD, EPHYRA.

"Maria? Maria, honey, are you there?"

Of course she was there. She hardly ever left the house now.

Dom stood in the hallway and waited for a response. He knew

where she'd be, and he could simply have walked upstairs and opened that bedroom door, but it was just too hard to see her sitting there staring at the cot. She wanted that quiet time, too. In the last year, they'd reached an understanding about no-go areas in this house as complex as any minefield in the war.

He'd rented this house for them to be happy in it, for the kids to have a big backyard to play in, but it didn't work out that way.

"Maria, I brought Marcus back." Dom waited, listening for movement, giving her time to get herself together. "I'm going to cook dinner. You come down when you're ready, baby."

Marcus was still standing on the doorstep, staring up at the birds. He always waited to be invited over the threshold now, as if he felt he was intruding, and that upset Dom; Marcus was family, and Dom's house was his, anytime. With Bennie and Sylvia gone, Dom took nobody for granted now. He tugged at Marcus's sleeve.

"Hey, come on. Kitchen duties."

"You sure I'm not making this worse?"

"No. She likes to see you. You know that."

They peeled vegetables and jointed the chicken in silence, while sounds of movement from upstairs indicated that Maria had left Sylvia's room and gone into the bathroom. Dom knew her ritual: she'd close the door, and then spend fifteen minutes, almost to the second, putting a soaked ice-cold washcloth on her eyes to reduce the swelling.

But he'd still know she'd been crying for hours. No amount of sympathy or tablets could change the fact that their kids were dead—and their parents, and cousins, and half their friends. The fact that the Santiagos were like millions of other utterly broken and bereaved people across Tyrus—across the whole world—didn't ease the pain one bit.

It just meant that the neighbors didn't ask dumb-ass questions, or make stupid but well-meaning comments about time being such a great fucking healer, because they were mostly bereaved, too.

Bullshit. I haven't even healed about Carlos, and that was three years ago.

Well, if they weren't bereaved yet, they had family serving as Gears. It was only a matter of time.

"What do I do with these?" Marcus held up the wine. He was raiding his father's priceless cellar a few bottles at a time, but he wasn't much of a drinker, and he certainly wasn't a chef. "Which one's for the chicken?"

"The white one. Red makes everything a funny color."

Marcus studied both labels, then uncorked the bottle of white. "I'm impressed."

"Why?"

"You, learning to cook like this."

"Well . . . you know." Maria had problems getting her act together around the house some days, and Dom began doing stuff to stop her from feeling bad about it. Then it seemed to cheer her up a little to have dinner cooked for her. As long as he was cooking, he knew she was eating properly, even if it was only when he was home on leave. "I don't know what else to do for her."

"Look, I'm passing this on because I promised I would," Marcus said. "Dad says Maria can stay at the estate anytime. He's worried about her being here alone. He'll hire someone to keep her company. And he's got access to all the top doctors." Marcus stopped dead. The quiet embarrassment on his face said that he knew his father meant well, but that Dom's answer would be no. "Sorry, Dom. You know my father. He thinks science can fix anything."

Dom looked away and found the pan of rice suddenly of great interest. Gestures like that choked him up instantly. The Fenix family estate was a huge empty mausoleum of a place, intimidating and magnificent, and Adam Fenix was a bit too much like his home, a man with no idea how to be anything other than distant and focused on his work. But there was a kind father in there trying to get out, desperate to do the right thing; he just didn't seem sure how regular people showed that they cared.

"That's really, *really* generous, Marcus." Dom felt his voice cracking. "Your dad's a good man. Tell him thanks, but Maria needs to be *here*. You know. The bedrooms are . . ."

He didn't finish the sentence. The word was *shrines.* Dom understood that completely, but it still freaked him out. He'd done it himself. He didn't want to touch his father's workshop; he could still see them all in it, tinkering with some engine—Carlos, Marcus, Dad, Mom wandering in with sandwiches. But he walked away from it, because that was how you made yourself accept that they were never coming back.

Maria walked into the kitchen and gave Marcus a big deliberate smile, but her eyes were dead. As always, though, she looked beautiful—perfectly groomed, hair immaculate, full makeup. That gave Dom hope that she'd mend, because she hadn't let herself go. Shit, it was just over a year; how could anyone finish grieving in that time? He was expecting too much. But he just wanted to see her pain stop.

And then I'll have nothing left to do but look at my own.

"Have you seen your dad?"

Maria's voice sounded hoarse and thick. She had a habit of plunging straight into topics now, as if she'd been having a conversation in her head that had just leaked out. Marcus accepted a peck on the cheek from her, blinking as if he'd noticed.

"I haven't seen him since I got back," he said. "He's pretty busy."

"You've got to spend time with him." Maria took firm hold of Marcus's hand. "Promise me."

"I'll see him." Marcus nodded, looking embarrassed. "I promise."

"Come on, sit down, both of you," Dom said, shepherding them toward the living room. It had to be her medication. She seemed much more spacey today. "Let's have a drink while the dinner's cooking."

It was good wine. Dom didn't know much about vintages, but the Fenix family was rich, *seriously* rich, and this stuff was twenty-six years old—older than him. Whatever it was, it had cost a fortune; the chicken was swimming in something that had probably cost a week's wages. But with rationing, money was ceasing to mean much. The chicken was a rare treat, not because he couldn't afford it on a Gear's pay—shit, they were getting paid on time, even now—but because the Locust had trashed farms and food factories, disrupted freight traffic, all the little invisible things that put food on the table of a big capital city.

"Animals," Dom said, holding the glass up to the light while he racked his brains for another neutral topic of conversation. The wine looked more brick-red than ruby. Marcus always said that showed it had bottle age. "Animals are smarter than us. We get a power outage or some factory gets blown up, and we fall apart. We need so much *stuff*. Animals—they just get up in the morning, find food, and carry on. No piped water supply—we drown in our own sewage, but animals just stay *clean*. If they've got white fur, it *stays* white. Imagine the state we'd be in if *we* had white fur."

Marcus looked as if he was going to say something, but just did a slow blink and nodded. He'd stopped himself at the last moment. Whatever it was he'd been planning to say, it probably had the word *death* or *kill* in it, and he never used either in front of Maria. It was one of those little silent clues that told Dom what really went on in Marcus's head.

"That's what shaving's for," Marcus said at last.

"You okay, honey?" Dom topped up Maria's glass. She was looking distinctly distant now. "You didn't get much sleep last night."

"I remembered to take my pills." The doctor had prescribed antidepressants. "I've got to go out later. Just a nap, and then I'll go out. I go out every day when you're not here. I have to."

Dom didn't have a clue what she was talking about, and hoped it was the medication talking. He wasn't sure if she felt hemmed in by this house and its memories and needed a break from the four walls, or if she just went for a walk to stretch her legs.

"Yeah, you're too sleepy to go out now." He stroked her hair. "Maybe the doc needs to look at your dose again."

"Have a nap if you feel like it," Marcus said. "You don't have to entertain me. We'll wake you up when dinner's ready."

Maria leaned back in the chair and fell asleep in minutes. Dom crept over to her to check, listening to her breathing; yes, she was definitely out of it.

Marcus got up slowly and gestured to the kitchen.

"It's just a year," Dom said, closing the door behind him. "I'm pushing her too fast."

"Anything I can do. Just say."

"Yeah."

"And stop blaming yourself."

"She's the one with the blame problem. She's still saying that if she hadn't sent the kids to her folks' for the day, they'd be alive now. She thinks she let the grubs get them."

"Shit, Dom . . ." It wasn't as if Marcus hadn't heard it before. But it always seemed to upset him to be reminded of it, and he looked as if he was about to offer some insight. "Ah, forget it. Explaining to someone why they're not to blame doesn't actually help. They have to work it out for themselves."

Dom assumed it was all about Marcus's mother. When she went missing, he was sure that Marcus felt responsible, in that weird way that anxious kids often did.

"I need you to see something," Dom said. "I feel bad showing you, but I have to show someone." He beckoned Marcus to follow him, and led him upstairs to the bedrooms. "I don't even know why I'm doing this, but . . . maybe it'll make more sense to you next time I come out with some crazy shit or other."

Dom opened the door of Sylvia's room. Marcus just peered inside, going no further than the doorway.

So it hits him that way, too.

Nothing had been changed since the day that Sylvia—two years old, born the night Dom had taken part in the raid on Aspho Point—had been collected by her grandparents for a day out. Her stuffed toys were still on the windowsill, minus the green striped caterpillar she insisted on taking everywhere.

All her bedding, the clothes in the drawers, even the clothes in the laundry basket hadn't been moved. Maria just cleaned around it all.

Marcus drew a deep breath and stepped back. He might have said *shit* to himself. Dom wanted him to understand what haunted him when he tried to sleep. If Marcus couldn't make sense of it, then nobody could. Dom shut the door and then opened Benedicto's room.

Marcus leaned against the door frame as if he expected the paint to be wet, and just scanned the room again, halted at that invisible barrier. It was hard not to follow his eyes; they were almost unnaturally pale blue, so they always drew Dom's focus. Marcus started blinking a lot. Even if he'd been the chatty kind, he probably wouldn't have had much to say about this. He drew back after a minute or so and wandered across to the window on the landing.

If he was anything like Dom, then it would have been the tiny pair of thrashball boots on the bed that finished him off.

"Yeah, I just can't go in there," Dom said. "Not even Bennie's room. Maria spends hours in one room or the other. Now, is it me who's nuts for not being able to go in, or her for not being able to get rid of it all?"

Life had to go on, war or no war, and Maria's folks wanted as much time with the kids as possible. Bennie—four, Dom's heart and soul—had been really excited about seeing their new apartment. They had a cat, a stray that had shown up out of nowhere, and Bennie wanted to play with it.

"Nobody's nuts," Marcus said. "Everyone finds their own way of coping."

"I shouldn't lay all this shit on you."

"It's okay."

Marcus could usually make Dom feel that things really were okay, but some situations were beyond that. They went back to the kitchen, listened to the radio news channel in silence, and then served dinner, all three of them somehow managing to keep up the illusion of enjoying the event. Maria seemed a little brighter.

No, it wasn't an illusion. It was an affirmation. Dom had to see it that way. He believed that if he tried hard enough, if the state put enough effort into it, then the war would end and life could begin to get back to normal, even if it took five years—ten, maybe. But it would come.

He just didn't know what it was going to take to turn the tide.

Marcus kept taking a discreet look at his watch, probably trying to work out the best time to call his father. He might even have been working up to it. He never seemed to find it easy to talk to him.

Maria picked up the phone from the sideboard and set it down in front of Marcus. "Nobody's too busy to want to hear from their own son." Then she started clearing the table.

It was the first time she'd said anything like that in a normal tone—even the word *son*—since E-Day. Dom followed her into the kitchen while Marcus called his dad.

"You okay, baby?"

"He's got to talk to his dad. They shouldn't be apart this much."

So that was starting to get to her: separation, not letting kids get too far from you. "We'll get through this, I promise."

"You never give in. That's what I love about you. You never quit."

Dom seized the briefest change of mood and clarity. This was how recovery started, the doctor said. "I'd never give up on you." He took her hand out of the dishes and wiped away the soapsuds. "I need to get you another ring, don't I?"

Maria's hands had swollen so much when she was pregnant that she'd had to have her wedding band cut off. She hadn't worn a ring since. It made Dom feel uneasy, because a guy's wife *had* to have a nice ring, a symbol that someone loved her more than anything.

She touched the pendant he'd given her. "I've got this, Dom. I'll wear it until the day I die."

"Yeah, but—"

"What have *you* got? You don't have a ring." It was true; rings snagged inside his gloves, and they were a real hazard when handling cables and machinery. "You've got to have something. I've never given you something to keep with you. We've got to have something so that we're *together*."

She wiped her hands and started looking through the kitchen drawers where most of the household paperwork ended up. Eventually she pulled out a photograph and grabbed a pen.

"Here." She wrote something on the back of the photo and handed it to him. "Remember this?"

It was a picture that Carlos had taken of them in a bar off Embry Square, just before Dom began commando training. Dom turned over the photo to read what she'd written.

"So you'll always have me with you," she said. "Don't let me go. Keep it in your pocket. Please."

"You know I will."

When he put his arms around her these days, he felt as if she was clinging to him for safety. There was nothing harder than picking up his holdall and leaving her behind. He was determined to cherish every minute of the leave he had left, even if it meant stopping her from sitting in those dead, frozen bedrooms.

"He's busy."

Marcus's voice made Dom jump. "Your dad . . ."

"He got a call to see the man." Marcus shrugged. He'd put his I-don't-really-care face on. "His secretary at the uni said she didn't know when he'd be back. Can't say no to Prescott."

"Sorry, Marcus."

"Hey, got to go. I'll pick you up when it's time to ship out, Dom. Take care of yourself, Maria."

And Marcus was gone, just like that: no hugs, no gradually edging toward the door, just a clear signal that he was going, and he never looked back. He wasn't keen on goodbyes.

Was anybody these days? Goodbyes had a habit of being permanent. The worst thing, Dom decided, was that he could remember none of his.

CHAIRMAN'S OFFICE, HOUSE OF THE SOVEREIGNS.

All politicians were assholes, but at least Prescott cut the crap and said what was on his mind.

Hoffman could find something in that to admire. How long would it last, though? The idealistic and the outspoken all got ground flat in the end—not that some of them had far to go.

Adam Fenix was supposed to be here.

And Prescott wants me here because . . .

The last time Hoffman had been summoned to this level of meeting with Fenix present, he'd been tasked with sabotaging a weapon of mass destruction. The damn grubs must have come up with a new toy. It wasn't as if they needed it. Maybe they were just getting bored with having to gut every human by hand, and they wanted the planet to themselves sooner rather than later.

"Attorney General," Prescott said, "what are my options under the Fortification Act?"

The AG, Milon Audley, was past retirement age and looked like he'd seen it all before. "You may use it to declare martial law in part or all of the COG territories. Normally, the vote is carried even if—"

"No voting." Prescott faced them across a table, not lounging behind his desk or staring out the window as if they were incidental to his plans. "I have the authority to declare martial law without consulting the assembly, haven't I?"

Hoffman had the kind of peripheral vision honed by years of trying to keep an eye on superior officers about to drop him in the shit. Salaman didn't seem to be bothered. Martial law was just turning up the volume on what was happening now, after all. Prescott obviously wanted to keep his fledgling administration looking clean, doing everything by the book. Maybe he wanted to go down in history as the last and only moral leader.

"You *do*," Audley said, "but it's ill-advised, because you won't be able to enforce it outside Tyran borders without effectively declaring war on every other COG state. You don't want to do that, do you, sir?"

"All I want to know is whether it's legal. Whether it's constitutional."

Audley was on the spot, and it was clear that even his lawyer's shark brain couldn't work out Prescott's angle. Hoffman knew that look: the quick lick of the lips, a flicker of the eyes, the moment any adviser dreaded, when a yes or no to an apparently straight question would become something with a frightening life of its own, something that would come back to bite you hard on the ass. Hoffman had been there.

"It's legal, Chairman, but it's not a good move," Audley said at last. Bets were hedged. Asses were covered. "I'd advise discussion with the Secretary for Interstate Relations."

"I've passed that stage, Milon. I just needed to know that I wouldn't be acting illegally. I do have a pragmatic reason."

"Not a constitutional one, then . . ."

"I'm going to restore the Fortification Act and declare martial law throughout the COG." Prescott looked away toward the door as it opened and Adam Fenix walked in. "Good evening, Professor. Take a seat."

"Apologies, Chairman. Roadblocks."

"Just so that we're all up to speed . . . the Attorney General has advised me that I'm within my rights to use the Fortification Act to declare martial law."

Hoffman had decided some years ago that whatever was admirable in Adam Fenix's son had come from the maternal side of the gene pool. Fenix put a folder of papers on the desk in front of him but didn't open it, almost as if he wasn't sure he was in the right meeting and might have to up sticks and go find the right room.

"Would you like to give me some *context*, Chairman?" he said.

Prescott meshed his fingers and leaned his elbows on the table. "I want you all to understand that what I'm about to say is born of last resort. General, in layman's terms, as of today, how do you evaluate our chances against the Locust?"

Salaman perked up a little. "Depends who you mean by *us*, sir."

"I think I mean Tyrus. I've seen enough in the last few weeks to know that some states are closer to collapse than others, whatever they say."

"We'll still be overrun in a month, then," Salaman said. "Militarily—we're hemorrhaging. The infrastructure is collapsing globally. Civilian casualties—if they're not slaughtered by the grubs, then they're dying of disease, and refugee movement is spreading more cross-border infection. You can't dump millions of corpses on the system and maintain disease control. We're *finished*, sir. I'm sorry. The grubs are in pretty well every city on the planet."

Fenix looked at Hoffman. Maybe he thought they had some kind of rapport and that Hoffman would have a different opinion. He didn't.

"Remember that we no longer have any emergency command bunkers outside Ephyra, either," Hoffman said. "We don't even have the option of saving the chosen few and the art treasures and sitting it out, as we had in the last war."

"All destroyed?" Prescott didn't look disappointed for some reason. "Even Cherrit?"

"That's the problem with underground facilities and a burrowing enemy, sir. I hope they appreciate fine art and canned beans."

Prescott took a breath. He looked too young. He was in his late thirties, and there were a few gray hairs in his beard, but he was remarkably unlined. A few more months in office would put that straight.

But we don't have months. It's weeks.

"Gentlemen, I'm going to deploy the Hammer of Dawn," Prescott said.

It wasn't the first time that Hoffman had been caught totally off guard by a COG chairman, nor the first when the realization hit him that Adam Fenix was here to do the dirty science work.

And me. Now I know why I'm here, too.

"Sir, that's just not possible." Fenix seemed to think that Prescott was just kiting an idea. Hoffman could see he wasn't. The man had a stillness about him—no fidgeting, no sweating, not a hint of uncertainty—that said he'd made his decision. "It's not a tactical weapon. It's strategic. You can't deploy it in urban areas, and that's the kind of war we're fighting."

"Losing," Prescott said quietly. "Right now, we're *losing* the war. And that will *not* happen on my watch. This is where it ends."

Hoffman glanced at Salaman, and they both knew this was

now about *how* it would be carried out, not *if.* Audley simply bowed his head and said nothing.

Fenix was still staring at Prescott, demanding an answer with raised eyebrows. Hoffman wondered if he ever yelled or lost his temper.

"You *do* know how the Hammer works, Chairman?" Fenix said.

"Not the physics, but I do grasp the fact that the satellite platforms cover the entire planet, which is what I require."

"What are you going to target? Is that what you need me for, to advise on blast coverage?"

Salaman cut in. "Grubs don't take over cities, sir. They *clear* them. They'll only be in areas where there are humans to kill and resources to plunder. They strip a city and move on."

"I *know* that, General," Prescott said. "I know that very well. They're using our own equipment and supplies against us. They adapt our own technology to kill us. *We're feeding their war effort.* So we stop them. We destroy everything in their path. And a lot of grubs will die, too—not all, but this is about asset denial."

I know where this is going now. God help us.

Hoffman found himself wanting to call Margaret, not to warn her but just to hear her voice, and he hadn't felt that way about her for years. It was as close as he'd come in his adult life to panic. Fear—he'd lived with it for so long that he wasn't sure if he could perform well without it. But this was *different.* There was no border across which life would go on after surrender or a victory.

"Okay, sir," Salaman said. "Have you thought about what we'll have left to fight the grubs who survive?"

"The only major center of population that they don't appear to be able to penetrate far is Ephyra—Jacinto in particular," Prescott said. He stood up and unfurled the global map on his wall. "Largest unbroken area of granite on Sera. And that's where we'll regroup. I want the entire Hammer network deployed. Salaman, I need a priority list, because we're going to have to do this in stages—am I right, Professor?" Prescott turned around, one finger still on the black type that said EPHYRA. "We feed in the coordinates for the first batch of targets, activate the lasers, then feed in the next batch, move the orbital platforms, and so on. We don't have enough orbital devices to sweep Sera in one simultaneous attack, do we?"

Shit.

Shit, this is planet *denial, not asset denial.*

"What the hell do you propose to do with the people in those cities, Chairman?" Fenix sat back in his chair as if he'd been winded. "This is going to incinerate millions of our own people. Do you understand me? This is wholesale slaughter."

I don't want to hear this.

I know what the options are going to be.

And I helped the COG grab the Hammer technology.

Prescott waited a few beats, looking at Fenix as if he was the difficult kid in the class who just didn't get the math and needed a bit of prompting. For a moment, Audley looked as if he was going to intervene, but he just shifted position and looked as if he'd given up. He wouldn't be alone. Everyone else except Prescott had.

"I'm ordering an evacuation to Ephyra," Prescott said. "We'll give refuge to anyone who can make their way here. Three days after the announcement we deploy the Hammer."

"We—can't—move—millions—of—people—in—three—days." Fenix slammed his fist on the table to emphasize every word. Fenix, Mr. Stiff Upper Lip, the man who never reacted, had finally lost it. Hoffman didn't want to watch this disintegration; there was no satisfaction in it. It just confirmed that he was right to feel that he should be shitting himself right now. "They'll die. They'll all *die.*"

Prescott looked to Salaman and nodded for a response.

"Once we announce the recall, we have to assume the grubs will know," Salaman said. "And when people start moving in numbers, they'll just home in on them. So it has to be fast—or it has to be covert."

"What, we don't tell people we're going to fry the goddamn *planet*?" Hoffman said. "So we just sparc Tyrus? And who gets told it's time to run?"

"There's a balance to be struck between giving people adequate time to evacuate without giving the enemy time to react," Prescott said. "I have to tell the people what the stakes are, but we want to catch the Locust on the wrong foot, too. That's always an ethical dilemma in war. How many of our own people did we allow to die in the Pendulum Wars because alerting them to attacks would reveal too much about our latest intelligence?"

Fenix spread his hands. "*Ethical?* Good God, this is about a weapon of mass destruction, not a single conventional attack."

"Don't start on the old ethics shit again, Fenix," Hoffman snapped. "*You* made the Hammer technology operational, so don't tell me we can't use it when we need it most. My men died to get it for you. It's *your* fucking bomb. What did you think we'd use it for, a toaster? And just how bad did you think things would have to get before we'd need to use it?"

"It was intended as a deterrent."

"Oh, I'm sorry. You didn't realize it was loaded. It was just there to scare burglars."

"This is precisely the kind of extreme scenario we envisaged using the Hammer for," Prescott said, ignoring the spat. "If you can think of a more extreme one, Professor, do say."

"This means destroying most of our civilization to save a fraction of it—if we save any of it at all." Fenix started fiddling with his pen, turning it over between his fingers like he was tightening a bolt. "And what will we be left with? That level of destruction has two phases—what it kills immediately, and what it kills for months or years afterward by debris thrown into the atmosphere, by chemicals released by combustion into water tables and—"

"Professor, *do you have an alternative?* That's not rhetorical. You've been a Gear. Do you disagree with the military assessment?"

"Not substantially."

"Then is there *anything* we can do differently, other than wait to be picked off? If you have anything at all to suggest, *any* avenue we haven't explored, then I urge you to say so now."

The argument took Hoffman back three years, to when he'd clashed with Fenix over who needed to die to seize the Hammer technology from the Union of Independent Republics. Fenix couldn't stomach the need to kill enemy weapons scientists. He was great at saying what was wrong, what was immoral, but he was shit at making the hard call between ugly and uglier. And those were usually the only choices in war.

Prescott was still waiting.

Fenix looked as if he was going to say something, then shook his head. It took a few more moments for him to answer. Prescott didn't hurry him.

"I can't think of anything else that will stop them in the time we have," Fenix said eventually. "The incursions have gone too far. If we'd had more time . . . there could have been other ways we might have stopped them."

"Let me be clear. There might be alternatives? Can you develop those in the *weeks* we have left?"

"No." Fenix looked defocused again for a moment, anguished, probably crunching numbers in his head and unable to make them add up. "No. We've run out of time. It's all too late."

Prescott's gaze flickered for a moment. "Thank you, Professor."

"But we can't accommodate everyone who wants to evacuate, even if they can reach Ephyra in time. The city can't absorb the global population. Not even with millions already dead."

"I know," Prescott said. "It's brutal. I accept that it's the illusion of compassion. But either we save who we can, what we can, and preserve humankind, or we do the equitable thing and let everyone share extinction. It's my call. We're taking back Sera, starting now."

"Kill it to save it." Fenix shook his head. "And what the hell do you think our *society* will become?"

"A human society that's fit to survive," said Prescott. He walked over to the inlaid desk that had been used by every COG chairman for nearly eighty years and laid some sheets of paper on it as if he was going to make notes. "I'm taking full personal responsibility. You don't need to. You're only following orders. Milon, you don't have to take any further part in this. Thank you for your counsel."

The Attorney General rose slowly, as if his back hurt him, and walked to the door. He looked even older than he had when he'd come in. "I'll prepare the legal instrument, sir. After all, what you're doing is . . . *constitutional*, and I have no grounds to refuse."

"This remains strictly confidential, Milon. Within this room."

"I took that as a given, sir."

The door closed behind Audley, and there was a moment's silence punctuated by the distant *whoomp-whoomp* of artillery fire. Hoffman rarely noticed it. It was a permanent background noise now.

"I'm not just following orders, Chairman," said Salaman. "Either I'm with you or I have to quit this post. What about you, Victor?"

"There's nothing else I can offer, General."

Hoffman tried to freeze the moment to examine why he was agreeing to it—not that opposing it would make any difference. It was lawful, and he had agreed to involvement. Was he being selfish? *Ephyra first—we're all right, screw the rest of you.* Maybe he was just resigned to the inevitable. "Maybe we should have thought about concentrating on asset denial earlier, before the grubs got a foothold, and when we had more time to evacuate people."

Hindsight was a wonderful thing. Fenix stared at him as if he was a pile of shit.

"We'd still have been killing people," Fenix said quietly. He placed his briefcase on the table and unlocked it, rummaging around inside. "Our *own* people. And the numbers don't change that."

"Keys, gentlemen," said Prescott. He opened a desk drawer and took out a small socket-shaped metal cap. "General?"

Salaman reached inside the collar of his shirt and eased out his COG-tag. His Hammer command key was on the same chain.

It was all very low-tech and banal, this global destruction business. Hoffman fished his key out of his pants pocket, unclipped the chain, and held it up. His front door keys were next to it.

"I never knew," Fenix said, staring at Hoffman's hand.

Hoffman hadn't realized that Fenix didn't know who held the third command key to activate the weapon. "It goes with the DSF job. Don't take it personally."

"Professor, do you understand now why I wanted to be reassured this was legal?" Prescott was still very calm, all business, not bad at all for a brand-new chairman whose first big headline was going to be WORLD ENDS TODAY. "I wouldn't ask you to be complicit in an unlawful act. I now need your best estimate of how hard we can strike and how far. General Salaman will keep you apprised of Locust movement so that we make every Hammer strike count. Within the next three weeks, I want a window of three to four days when we have the Hammer ready to deploy, and when I can announce the recall to Ephyra. Of course, if you object, I'll have to co-opt one of your staff."

"The Hammer is my responsibility," Fenix said. "I wouldn't pass the buck to anyone else."

Prescott sat down at his desk and began writing. "Thank you, gentlemen. I'll inform the Cabinet of my decision a short time before I make the public announcement to invoke martial law and declare Ephyra a sanctuary zone. How short depends on how we assess the risk of information leaking and starting a panic. The evacuation period starts from then. I favor three days, unless anyone has a compelling practical argument otherwise. But this has to be fast."

Three, five, ten—it didn't make much difference. There wasn't enough room for the whole world.

"Three it is, sir," said Salaman.

"A *panic*," Fenix repeated quietly. "What do you think we already have?"

"I don't know quite how you work, Professor." Prescott just kept going. "Can you keep this under wraps at your end, or will you have staff who need to be briefed?"

Fenix's shoulders sagged. "I can do it on my own. Like I said— this is my responsibility."

Fenix grabbed his briefcase and walked out. Hoffman headed

for the side exit with Salaman, and found that his hands were
shaking.

"Shit," Salaman said. "I'm going to grab a drink."

"I miss my NCO days," said Hoffman. "See you in the morning."

Hoffman walked back to the apartment, rehearsing how and
when he would tell Margaret that he'd just put his name to the
destruction of almost every city on Sera, and most of its citizens.

Yes, he missed being a sergeant.

CHAPTER 4

We only achieve unity through order.
(NASSAR EMBRY, ALLFATHER PRIME, FOUNDER OF THE COALITION
OF ORDERED GOVERNMENTS.)

PORT FARRALL, TYRUS, ONE WEEK AFTER THE
FLOODING OF JACINTO, 14 A.E.

"Your vehicle camo sucks," Baird said, puffing clouds into the freezing air. "Saw you coming *way* off."

Bernie brought the battered 'Dill to a halt at the outer checkpoint. "Aren't you going to ask me how I got them on the roof?" She jumped out to admire the haul of deer carcasses strapped to the hatch surfaces and panniers of the APC. "Four. That's a *lot* of meat, Blondie. And leather. If you're a good boy, I'll teach you how to dress it."

"You're loving this, aren't you?"

"You want to live on dry rations and a roast rat for special occasions? Come on, mount up."

Bernie drove into the reclaimed city with mixed feelings. Her whole reason for struggling across Sera to reach Jacinto was to get rid of the grubs, to get her world back before she was too old or too dead to do it. Now that the grubs were mostly gone, she wasn't sure what would fill that space.

For the meantime, being uniquely useful would do. She could survive off the land in any terrain, any climate, and teach others to do the same. That knowledge was now vital in the literal sense of the word. It was central to staying alive.

But one week after the destruction of Jacinto, the reality of what they'd left behind—squalid as it was—was really starting to bite hard.

"How many dead today?" she asked.

"You got some recipes?"

"Don't even joke about that, Blondie."

"Forty-three," Baird said. "Hypothermia. Elderly. Make sure you wear your cat-fur booties, Granny."

Dr. Hayman posted the list at CIC daily. The winter was bitter and the accommodations grim, despite the engineers doing their best to bring the most habitable part of Port Farrall back to life. It was all about timing. A different season and this would have been a little easier. They could have grown crops. But at this time of year, all they had was the emergency rations shipped out with the convoy and whatever they could forage.

As Bernie drove slowly through the streets, she spotted four civilians carrying a plastic sheet between them like a battlefield litter. Another dead body? No, whatever was in it was throwing reflections onto the walls. When the 'Dill passed, she could see it was bulging with fish, so brilliantly silver that they sparkled in the sun.

"The boom-and-bust cycle of nature," she said.

"You Islanders talk some mystic shit."

"Not mystic, Blondie. Humans die off, so other animal populations boom. Especially marine life."

"Handy."

"In a pie. Lovely." At least there'd be a reliable source of fat and protein around, even if the diet got monotonous. "You know, I'd rather be on the ships. Got to be warmer and more comfortable."

"Put me down for that yacht Cole spotted."

Gears patrolled the streets. Civilians were combing the place looking for missing friends and relatives. They'd reached the stage where the shock of displacement was beginning to wear off and they were working out just how wrecked their lives were. People with nothing to do but wait for food and watch others die were a recipe for unrest.

Even Jacinto's citizens had limits to their stoicism. "Do we even have a head count yet?"

Baird shrugged. "No, stragglers are still arriving. Cole says some civvies have left to see if the local Stranded settlements will take them in."

"Ungrateful tossers. Anyway, shouldn't we be assimilating the Stranded if this is all that's left of us?"

"Stranded aren't *us*, Granny."

They were the savages beyond the wire, and it had nothing to do with hygiene. "Hang on, what about the Operation Lifeboat guys?"

"Come on. You don't like Stranded either." Baird paused a beat. "You're lost, aren't you?"

"I know where I am, dickhead."

Everything bounced off Baird. He took it in the same way that he dished it out. "I meant that now the fighting's stopped, you don't know what to do except harass the local wildlife."

"Haven't noticed you happily taking up knitting, either."

"I haven't gone this long without a firefight in fifteen years. I don't know what comes next."

When Baird wasn't being mouthy or smug, he could say things that brought her up short. Life *had* changed out of all recognition again, just as it did on E-Day, but the COG had been at war—one way or another—for the best part of ninety years. Peace was unknown territory.

Bernie inhaled discreetly. Baird smelled faintly of phenol. "You going on a date? Where'd you get the disinfectant?"

"Dr. Hayman's having the whole place sprayed. Infection control."

Gears had banged out of Jacinto in just the armor and kit they stood up in, no personal effects, or even a change of pants for some. "I'll go scavenging later."

"You mean robbing civvies."

"I mean seeking redistribution of assets for the good of the wider community."

"Yeah. Right."

Civvies had been given enough warning of the evacuation to take grab bags. They'd been drilled to keep a bag of essentials by the door, ready to run, because they'd been used to moving from one part of Ephyra to another each time the grubs infiltrated. So now civvies had *stuff*, and Gears mostly didn't. It was something of a role reversal.

"I meant bartering a few steaks for clothing, razors, whatever," Bernie said.

"Prescott says we'll get the basics we need."

"Yeah, but he can't pull supplies out of his arse, and that means taking stuff off civvies. They used to resent us for getting bigger food rations. We don't need all that aggro fermenting again now. Hearts-and-minds works wonders, Blondie."

As the 'Dill wound its way through the streets, Gears stood out like a separate species even in borrowed overalls — tall, muscular, well fed. The civvies were stick-thin. Anyone between the two extremes was probably in a noncombat role, like the sappers and drivers, fed a little less generously than the frontline.

We're getting just like the frigging grubs. Splitting into different types.

"You're going to butcher all this shit in the open, right?" Baird said. "Entrails. Gross."

"See it as sausages. Nothing gets wasted."

Hoffman had set up the new HQ and barracks in an abandoned boarding school, confined to the ground floor until the engineers could carry out repairs to the upper floors. Bernie drove the 'Dill into what had once been the staff car park and jumped out to unload with Baird. Gears wandered out to watch as she managed to drape the smallest animal across her shoulders and tottered toward the entrance with it. She could hear Cole's bellowing laugh even before he burst through the main doors.

"Shit, baby, you *never* gonna get that through the cat flap." He held out his arms. "Let the Cole Train take your burden."

"You think it's too dressy as a collar? Maybe if I took off the hooves."

Cole lifted the carcass as if it was weightless. "I'm glad you're givin' up eating kitties, Boomer Lady. They got *worms*."

Dom stood outside the entrance, leaning on a shovel where he'd been clearing snow. The poor little bastard was trying hard to look as if nothing in particular had happened to him. Bernie was still trying to gauge the right time to get him to talk, but Dom would probably pick his own moment. He certainly had over Carlos's death.

"I'll give you a hand, Cole," Dom said. "I've never had venison. What's it like?"

Baird lowered another carcass from the 'Dill's roof, letting Dom take up the slack. "You'll hate it. I'll have your share. Hey, I want the antlers for the mess wall."

They were all trying hard—even Baird. Delta had closed ranks around Dom, looking out for him and making sure he wasn't left on his own. Bernie didn't think that a man who could live with losing his kids and parents was a suicide risk now, but then he hadn't had to blow their brains out himself, so maybe caution was a good idea. She left them to unload and headed for CIC—an old laundry—to clear things with Hoffman, finding herself stepping over Gears dismantling their armor plates down to the components to scrub them. Some were boiling shirts and pants in an open vat of soapy water, standing around in an assortment of borrowed work clothes.

Combat was a smelly business. This was the first real break they'd had to get the stench of grubs, blood, and sweat out of their kit. The scent of damp decay—wood, brick, mold—still lingered under the assault of newer, cleaner odors.

And shit, it was *cold* in here.

Hoffman was leaning over a paper chart with Anya and the EM chief when Bernie walked in. They seemed to be checking routes between the docks and the inhabited part of the city. Nobody had debarked from the larger vessels in the evacuation fleet yet. Bernie wasn't the only one who thought they were a better place to be.

"Mataki," Hoffman said, glancing up for a moment, "I want you to set up daily bushcraft classes for the civvies. Is there anything practical they can do in the field?"

"Berries and traps, sir. I don't recommend the river. Civvies and thin ice don't mix."

"And see Parry about supply recon teams. One of his men says there's a lot of recoverables on the south side of the city—machinery, raw materials."

"And the Stranded didn't sniff it out?"

"*Another* secure COG facility that we kept to ourselves."

Ouch. Hoffman was still livid that Prescott had hung on to classified information right up to the final battle. Maybe he'd beaten the rest of it out of him. *Good for you, Vic.* Anya, now wearing sensible working rig and flat boots, gave her a quick flash of the eyebrows. Fights had been had, evidently.

"Will do, sir. Permission to barter some venison with the civvies?"

He leaned over the chart again, both hands flat on the table. "Go ahead. I'll file it under public relations."

"I found some cattle tracks, too—farm livestock got loose and bred, probably. Might be well worth a foray for steak and milk in the weeks to come. Oh, and signs of feral dog packs. If they come near the camp, it's shoot on sight."

Hoffman managed a smile. "You're a damn useful woman, Mataki. See what you can do about the feral cats, too."

Great. I'm catering and pest control. Still, nobody needs a sniper for much else now.

He didn't ask if she'd save some venison for him. He probably knew she would.

When she walked back outside, the carcasses had a small audience, so it seemed a good time for a spot of skills transfer. They were mostly city boys who'd known nothing except hunting Locust. They probably hadn't seen a deer this close, if at all.

"Right, you lot, gather around for training, or sod off and do something useful." She pulled out her knife. "And someone fetch me a hacksaw."

She put on her instructor's voice and began indicating with the tip of her knife what needed cutting first and why. Anya wandered into her field of view and stood watching with her arms folded; without makeup, she looked so much like her mother that it was upsetting. Bernie almost lost her thread. She paused for a second to get back on track.

All these years, and it still isn't over.

"Sorry, where did I get to?" Bernie said, not caring if she sounded like she'd plunged into senility.

"The balls, Granny," Baird called.

"Oh, right." *Smart-arse.* "Yes, testicles." She couldn't resist it. She sliced carefully, then lobbed them at Baird. "You'll be wanting a pair."

Everyone needed to have a laugh when they had to watch guts being removed. Inevitably, though, someone would throw up. Gears who had managed to chainsaw their way through any number of grubs would lose their lunch soon, she knew it. Sometimes it almost tipped her stomach over the edge, too.

"You don't need to throw any of this away—well, not much." The carcass still felt comfortingly warm, but her hands would stink for a week no matter how many times she scrubbed them. "Lungs, heart . . . chop those up, and you can make a nourishing filling for—"

Her voice was drowned out by the rumble of a vehicle coming through the entrance gates. A huge grindlift rig squeezed between the pillars. Dom turned around, stared, and then jogged over to it as if he'd never seen one before. It was only when the driver scrambled down from the cab and the backslapping started that she realized this was a reunion, and decided to call it a day on the lesson. She dropped the offal back in the deer's body cavity for safekeeping and wiped her hands as best she could on its coat.

"Bernie, this is Dizzy Wallin," Dom said. "He saved my ass, and Marcus's. He took on that grub bastard Skorge so we could get clear in the grindlift."

Bernie could smell stale alcohol. The man stuck out his hand and she shook it. "He's buildin' me up, Sergeant—Tai was the one who stopped that weird streak o' piss, not me. He saved *my* ass. Where is he? I got some extra-smooth moonshine I want to share with him."

Tai Kaliso's name stopped the conversation dead. Dizzy looked into Dom's face, read what was there, and screwed his eyes shut for a moment.

"Shit," he said.

"Sorry, Dizzy. He didn't make it."

"What happened? Last I saw, he was givin' that grub bastard hell with a chainsaw and yellin' at me to get away."

Dom caught Bernie's eye, and she wondered if he was hesitating to spell out what had happened to Tai because of her or for Dizzy's sake. Maybe he'd just had enough of reliving nightmares.

"The grubs took him," he said. "He was . . . ah, shit, they just carved him up, man. They really made a mess of him."

Dom looked down at the ground for a few moments. Dizzy looked at Bernie and she just shook her head. The detail could wait, if it had to be told at all. A movement caught her eye, and she looked up at the cab of the rig to see two teenage girls staring down at them.

"My girls," Dizzy said. "I'm gonna be able to look after them now, like I oughta." He gripped Dom's shoulder. "Let's all meet up later and sample that moonshine. For Tai."

"We'll do that," Bernie said. "Nice to meet you, Dizzy."

She walked away to get on with butchering the deer, but she'd only gone a few steps when the alarm sounded. Cole jogged past her to the gate with his hand pressed to his earpiece, followed by Baird.

"Grubs?" she asked. "I'm in the right mood for them."

"Civvies shapin' up for a riot," Cole said. "Hey, Marcus? You down there already?"

One of the Ravens was now airborne, circling over the area, so whatever had triggered the incident, CIC was making a show of cracking down on it. Bernie collected her rifle and put in her earpiece. Human civilization was a fragile thing.

She knew that all too well, not only because she'd seen what replaced it in far too many places, but also because she straddled that line between reason and savagery herself. Her own grasp on civilization was as fragile as anyone's.

Yeah, making that grub suffer would have been a dangerous release for her anger. She'd find another way to do right by Tai.

FOOD DISTRIBUTION CENTER, PORT FARRALL.

So much for cold weather keeping trouble at home.

Dom could now see the crowd. He was about a hundred meters away when the scuffle spilled over into something uglier, but Marcus was already there.

A guy went down hard on the concrete; the screaming mob closed like a sea. Marcus waded into the center of about eighty men and women, Lancer held close to his body, and just shouldered his way through.

Dom felt his guts knot and started sprinting. Armor or not, Marcus was taking a big risk. Without a helmet, he'd get a serious kicking if he went down, and that was the kind of dumb thing that killed you when a shitload of grubs couldn't.

Marcus vanished in the press of bodies for a moment. When Dom caught sight of him again, he was standing his ground and letting blows bounce off his plates. Then a space began opening around him.

"Hey, *enough!*" His yell was loud enough to cut right through the screaming. "I said *enough*—back off!"

The scuffle stopped, but the crowd was still yelling and cursing. Dom and whoever was behind him—he didn't even look— slowed and spread out, rifles aimed.

The target of the mob's anger lay on the ground, huddled in a ball, and Marcus stood over him like a dog guarding a bone. Dom almost expected to see him bare his teeth and snarl. And it wasn't the men in the crowd who were gesticulating and swearing now; it was the women.

It wasn't easy to get heavy with a bunch of women.

Shit, we're not trained for this.

Dom remembered the food riots in Ephyra not long after the Hammer was fired, and he would rather have faced down grubs bare-handed than have to charge civvies again. He never felt right going after them. He didn't know if he had what it took to shoot if he had to.

Marcus just stood there, immovable, and signaled to the approaching Gears to hold it without even looking in their direction. Dom braked. Cole caught up with him, and now it was a matter of seeing what happened next.

"I want you to step back, folks," Marcus said firmly. "Now. Move it. I'm dealing. Okay?"

The shouting died down, and there was suddenly a little more space around Marcus.

"That's it." He held out his left arm and made a calm-down gesture. But he still had his Lancer in his right hand, muzzle lowered, finger inside the trigger guard. "That's better. Just go home. Okay?"

He was doing his it'll-be-all-right voice. He could usually pitch it perfectly, quiet enough not to make anyone feel threatened but firm enough for them to know he meant business.

A woman started up again. "That *animal* shouldn't be here." She had that same well-bred tone as poor old Major Stroud. Her clothes were threadbare, but Dom could see they'd once cost a lot of money. "They're parasites. We're struggling to stay alive, and he just walks in to steal our food."

"That's my problem, ma'am. Not yours." Marcus switched instantly to a voice Dom hadn't heard in years—the wealthy, educated Marcus, one posh person talking to another in some sort of code they both understood. "Just go home." He turned slowly, spotted Dom, and gestured discreetly. *Stay back.* "I'm not moving until this area is cleared."

The woman must have been used to getting her own way. "We're supposed to be under martial law. Unless he's punished, they'll all be in swarming in here before long. We'll be overrun by Stranded."

Marcus just looked at her for a few beats in absolute silence. Dom could hardly hear him now. "Martial law? Yes. I can arrest you all, or shoot you for unlawful assembly. But you'd rather walk away now and let me deal with him. Wouldn't you?"

The King Raven was holding position at about two hundred meters, not directly overhead, but close enough for Dom to feel some downdraft. It was there to keep an eye on crowd movement. That was another police job that Gears weren't trained for. It would either reinforce Marcus's point or make things worse; in this mood, a mob needed only one trigger to kick the whole thing off again.

"Okay." Marcus squatted slowly and grabbed the man by his collar, hauling him upright. "We're done here."

The guy looked like he'd had the shit kicked out of him, face covered in blood, clothes ripped. For a moment, Dom thought the whole crowd—silent now—was on that knife-edge of either breaking up or pitching in again, and Dom's only focus was on getting Marcus out of there if it blew up. Marcus was effectively surrounded. He had to walk through a few men to get the guy out. And that was the likely flash point.

Dom got ready to fire a burst over their heads. Then Marcus took a couple of steps, setting his shoulders in that don't-fuck-with-me way, and the men in his path just stepped aside. People usually did.

Dom took the cue to move in behind him with the others, forming an extended line to walk slowly toward the crowd until the civilians all decided to move away at the same time like a shoal of fish. It might have been the sobering effect of seeing Cole ambling toward them, too.

"We don't take much pushin' to go over the edge as a species, do we?" Cole said. He waited with Dom until the street emptied. "Shit, we all *behaved* ourselves when the grubs were around."

"We're too used to having an enemy." Dom looked up to watch the Raven bank away. "Come on, let's see what the bum has to say for himself."

Marcus took the Stranded guy around the nearest corner and

checked him over, while Dom and Cole watched. The man was scared shitless. He seemed to be expecting another good kicking.

"And *I'm* supposed to be the frigging animal?" Blood trickled from his scalp and nostrils in bright, shiny trails, and he kept wiping his split lip with the back of his hand. Despite the crap he was giving Marcus, he was still shaking. "Shit, you COG fascists never change."

Marcus ignored him, tilting the guy's head with both hands to look at his scalp. "The doc should check you out. Skull fractures. Delayed onset of symptoms."

"What you gonna do with me?"

"Kick your ass out of here, if you don't want the doc."

"Why'd you save me, then? Why didn't you let 'em kill me?"

Marcus leaned over him. "Because if I let them do it once, they'll do it again. And again. And then we've got *anarchy*. It's not for your sake. It's for ours."

"Gee, thanks, asshole."

"You're welcome. Come in, or stay outside. But inside—it's our rules."

The bum didn't respond. Cole gestured to him to get up. "Come on, fella, let me escort you out the restaurant. You ain't wearin' a tie. We're kinda formal."

Cole strolled off with the bum, heading for the checkpoint, but Dom saw him reach into his belt and hand the guy a small ration pack. They disappeared around the corner.

"One week," Dom said. "Shit."

"Yeah. Better work out a way to stop them from getting in and upsetting the more sensitive citizens. Not exactly a secured perimeter."

"That was pretty impressive crowd handling, by the way."

"Yeah. I'm great with housewives." Marcus shrugged and walked out into the main street again, looking uncomfortable. "Anyway, I didn't like the odds. Let's dump this on Hoffman and get the food supplies sorted."

Without any discussion or briefing, every Gear who'd responded to the call was now patrolling a little differently. Dom could see the sudden change. They weren't keeping an eye on buildings or potential emergence holes any longer. They were watching the civilians around them. It was weird how something could shift the balance so fast. Grubs were easy to see, obviously a threat, but any one of the folks in Port Farrall could suddenly become the disgruntled hothead with a grudge now. At least they weren't armed, for the most part.

This is what gets to me. I need a clear line between who's on my side and who isn't.

Unity through order. Shit, I used to think that was just a slogan.

Boots thudded behind him at a jog, and Cole caught up with him. "Dom, baby, how you doin'?"

I don't know how I'm doing. I'm existing. That's about it. "So, how far did you have to drop-kick him?"

"Aww, I just advised him to stay out the way of crazy women. Shit, maybe we're gonna *need* Stranded now."

"Yeah, well, they know the membership rules. It's up to them."

They're no use to us. How many times did I walk through their stinking slums looking for Maria? Ten years, all their networks and bush telegraph and shit, and they didn't know she was out there? Then some bastard finally thinks he recognizes her when it's too damn late? Fuck them.

Dom knew—in a weird, distant way—that he'd split off the functioning parts of himself to get through the day. There was the terrified Dom who had nightmares, and struggled to face each morning when he woke. Then there was the Dom who kept his body moving and going through the motions of being a Gear. There was also the Dom who endlessly replayed those last few minutes with Maria, torturing himself with what he might have done differently, and—half ashamed, half enraged—even blaming others.

But I did it. It's all down to me.

"Dom, we been talking to Parry." Cole jogged his elbow to get his attention. "His guys and the civvy builders are gettin' some of the small rooms habitable. You want a cabin to yourself?"

"We've all got to put up with some discomfort." Sleeping quarters were no more than rows of camp beds and bare mattresses in derelict classrooms. "Why would I want my own room?"

"So you got some privacy, man. You know?"

"No . . ." *Yes.* Dom knew what he meant.

"You wake up. Every time you wake up, you go, *Oh God,* and . . ."

Dom's face burned. "Shit, I'm waking up the whole barracks when I have nightmares. Is that it? I've got to move out?"

"No, man. It ain't that at all. *Everyone's* got their nightmares. Nobody's sore at you. Just offerin'. You want it, I'll make it happen."

In some ways, Dom would have found it easier if everyone had told him to snap out of it. Nobody did. They just got kinder and tried harder. There was nothing they could do, though.

"Thanks, Cole Train."

Shit, I'm going to lose it . . .

Dom blinked and tried to clear his eyes. Bernie was a little way ahead of him, a bloody handprint on the backside of her pants. When they walked through the school entrance, she made for her precious deer carcasses and seemed to be searching for something.

"Bastards," she snarled. "Where's my frigging liver gone?"

Dom joined her, because it was something to do, anything to distract him. The deer's innards were scattered. Small blood-tinted paw prints led into a culvert.

"Cats," Dom said.

"That's it. Time I got some fur gloves." She checked her Lancer's ammo clip, then her watch. "They need putting down. Vermin. I've got a couple of hours. Coming?"

Being Bernie, she just wanted to be kind. Dom wasn't stupid; he knew the whole squad—his *social* squad, nothing defined by call signs—kept a constant watch on him.

Putting down. Euthanizing. Whatever fancy name you want. Oh God, Maria . . .

It tipped him over the edge.

"Just stop being *nice* to me, all right?" The shout was out of his mouth before he could think. Everything in his peripheral vision vanished. It was just rage and shame and pain erupting, uncontrolled. "Just *frigging stop it*, all of you. I couldn't save my own fucking wife. I couldn't find her in time. I couldn't save her. I had to shoot my own fucking wife because *I couldn't save her.* Okay? Are we done now? Are we done with crazy Dom? Fuck you all."

Then he burst out sobbing. The next second—he could have punched someone out. He didn't know what the next breath would bring. He heard Cole like he was miles away, telling someone to beat it, that there was nothing to see here, and Bernie just grabbed him as if he was going under for the third time. He sobbed on her shoulder. It didn't matter what anyone thought, because his life wasn't worth shit now.

"Come on, sweetheart, it's okay . . . okay . . ." Bernie must have beckoned someone, because he felt her shoulders move. "Take it easy. It's okay."

Someone took his elbow. "Dom, it's freezing. Get inside."

Marcus had promised Carlos that he'd always look after Dom. And he *was* always there; he'd just show up, like he showed up now.

Dom wasn't sure how long he sat in the janitor's room with his head in his hands. He could hear sawing and conversation outside as Bernie cut up the carcasses. Later, he heard single shots from a distance, shattering the still air.

"Waste of ammo," Marcus muttered.

But that was all he said. He simply sat there and waited until Dom decided he could stand up again and face the rest of the day.

Despite his expectations, he did.

CIC CONTROL ROOM, 2200 HOURS.

It was way past dinnertime. Hoffman's energy was flagging. He wanted to take a leak, and he wanted the steak that Bernie had surely put aside for him very badly indeed, but he also wanted commitments from the Chairman before he rostered off, or at least some acknowledgment that plans might have to . . . *adapt.*

"Look, I *agree* with you, Victor," Prescott said. "We *haven't* trained Gears for civil policing. But if it worked for fifteen years in Jacinto, we can still make it work now."

"That was when we had grubs knocking on the door, sir." Hoffman's biggest fear had been that he would screw up the defense of Jacinto and humankind would be wiped out because he wasn't up to the job. He'd dodged the bullet on that, and now another fear had taken its place: that he didn't have the peacetime skills that this beleaguered society needed to pull itself together again. "The grubs have gone, so the lid's finally off—plus we really *are* in deeper shit than we were a week ago."

"I'm going to visit the local Stranded and offer them amnesty. Usual terms."

You're not listening to me. "And if they tell you to ram it?"

"Then, because of the acute supply shortages, I authorize Gears to shoot Stranded as looters if they're found inside the perimeter."

"You tell them that."

"I will. And I expect your men to follow that order."

"What makes you think they won't?"

"It's very hard to shoot civilians, Victor. Any Gear will open fire if he feels his life's threatened, but it's another thing entirely to pull the trigger when the target is making off with a loaf of bread."

Hoffman tried not to lean back in the rickety chair. Once his shoulders touched the backrest, he knew he'd slump, and then he'd find it hard to stay awake. The Stranded were just a fraction of the problem, one of a list of potential flash points. Most of the trouble, he suspected, would come from a simple question asked over and over by the people in this makeshift city: why did food, medicine, or any other resource go to another person and not to them? They were already griping about how much easier folks had it on the ships, and that they didn't have enough ashore.

"The only thing we have on our side at the moment is a windfall of fuel," Hoffman said. "And that was luck. Nobody expected Merrenat to have imulsion left where the Stranded couldn't get at it. But we don't have the hardware yet to make decent use of it. Heating systems. Buildings with roofs and doors and windows.

Plumbing. People can only take so much, Chairman. We took them out of their last familiar haven, squalid as it was, and dumped them in a freezing hole."

"That's Sharle's problem to address. And he *is* dealing with it."

"But he's using my engineers. And the security situation is my problem, too. So I can't ignore the root causes."

"What are you asking, Victor?"

"When will we decide that Port Farrall isn't viable? Because this was a last-minute panic choice. It's too far north, given the infrastructure we don't have."

"We don't have that option. This was a last resort, after all. Every city we considered as an evacuation center is going to be like this, or worse."

"But we've got another three or four months of this weather, plus serious shortages. Ask Hayman how many will be left alive then. We've already got rustlung and some kind of dysentery."

Out of uniform, Prescott sometimes looked like an art teacher on a day off. It was the pullover and the beard. Without that tunic and medals, he looked pretty ordinary—until he moved or opened his mouth, and then everything about him exuded a certainty that he was in charge, and that it was the natural order of things. Hoffman couldn't imagine him having a single moment of self-doubt. From the time he took over the COG and deployed the Hammer, the man knew exactly what he wanted done.

"We're ultimately talking about restocking Sera with humans, Victor. If we lose vulnerable people, the older ones, we can still . . . oh, I hate to use the word *breed*, but that's the reality."

"Hayman says you can keep humankind going just fine on a gene pool of two thousand people, but do we want to run on empty if we have a choice? Otherwise we might as well be the Stranded."

"To make it worth leaving here," Prescott said, "it would have to be more than hardship. I would need to be convinced that staying here would endanger the majority of survivors."

"I'll monitor that situation. Sharle or no Sharle."

"Where else would we go? Where *is* the proverbial *better hole?*"

"Islands," Hoffman said. "There have to be plenty out there that never had a visit from the Locust. Somewhere warmer."

"Would any of them be large enough, though?"

"We lost a lot of people on evacuation. I think it's going to reach fifty percent losses."

Prescott just looked past him in slight defocus, stroking his beard.

"Let's consider it," he said eventually. "Talk to Sharle. And it's going to put the naval contingent on a different footing."

"Meaning?"

"We've let the navy decline."

"It was always peripheral, even in the Pendulum Wars." *And they didn't like that much.* Hoffman had probably spent more time with amphibious ops than any other COG commander. "You only have to look in the dockyard now to see that."

"Well, if we ever decide to reestablish the COG offshore, then we need more than a trawler navy, and not just for transport. When you're ready, let's assess their officers. I admit I've neglected the service badly." Someone knocked at the door, and Prescott looked around. "Any other business before I turn in?"

"Any other classified information you haven't shared with me, sir?"

Prescott gave him that look—the I-hate-apologizing-to-the-hired-help look. "I'm sorry about that, Victor. Yes, I've told you about every facility in COG territory now. The trouble with politics is that *not* volunteering information becomes a default in the best of us. It's a mechanism we learn to stop ourselves from blurting out things at inopportune moments."

That's not an answer. But you've told me what I need to know anyway. Asshole.

"Thank you, sir," Hoffman said. "Sleep well." He raised his voice. "Come in."

Prescott reached the door just as Bernie Mataki walked in. She held something balanced on a large sheet of metal, covered in a piece of camo fabric, and managed to salute the Chairman without dropping it.

Hoffman waited for Prescott's footsteps to fade. The man had a lair overlooking the sports field, with one of his priceless rugs on the floor, and for a man born to rule he seemed oddly happy with that.

"Asshole," Hoffman said. It felt better to say it out loud.

"That's no way to talk to room service, Colonel."

He smiled. "One day you're going to have to peel me off his throat."

"Well, better keep your strength up, then, sir." She laid the metal sheet on his desk and whipped off the cover like a waitress to reveal a mess tin cradling a lump of brown meat and a few pale root vegetables that could have been anything. She'd even found some decent cutlery. "It's as tough as old boots, but we didn't have time to hang it. Cole hammered it with a mallet for a while, though."

"Steak?"

"Venison steak. You could have had liver pâté, too, but some bastard cat got it. But I got the cat, so we're even."

Bernie could always make him smile. He looked down at the tabby-fur boot liners that had instantly cemented her reputation with Delta Squad. Anyone who could skin and eat cats earned a certain cautious respect.

"You're *primal*, Sergeant Mataki."

"Go on. Eat."

"Don't go. I need company."

Hoffman hadn't had a steak in nine, ten years—maybe longer. He certainly couldn't remember having game at all. He chewed, eyes closed, overwhelmed by the intensity of the flavor, and suddenly found tears running down his face.

She sounded as if she'd sighed. "Are *you* okay?"

Maybe it was just fatigue, or the lid finally coming off after years of keeping it clipped down, or just vague memories of a vanished world that had restaurants. Either way, he was embarrassed.

"Yes," he said, wiping his face with his palm. "Hell . . . I don't know. Things you forgot existed."

"A few nights' sleep would do you the world of good, sir."

"It's Vic. Remember? Let's pretend it's still the NCOs' mess and all this tinsel on my collar never happened." He opened the bag he kept under the desk—everything he owned—and took out the flask of brandy he'd been keeping for something special. He'd always imagined it would be one last toast to absent friends before he took a final stand, or used that one last round any sensible man saved for himself. "Here, rinse that cup out. Drink with me, will you?"

Bernie considered him with her head cocked to one side, then chuckled. "Yeah, Vic, I will."

She took a metal object from her belt pouch that he first thought was a pocket watch, but she gave it a shake in her hand and it extended into a small cup. She placed it on the desk.

Hoffman examined it, fascinated. It was made of concentric tapering steel rings. "That's very clever."

"Collapsible. I travel light."

"We're the last of our kind, Bernie." He poured a generous and gentlemanly measure for her. "To the Twenty-Sixth Royal Tyran Infantry."

"Two-Six RTI," she said. "The Unvanquished."

"We beat the goddamn grubs, anyway."

"And we're not the last. There's Fenix and Santiago."

"I meant *our* generation."

"Then we're definitely the last." She stared into the cup, then raised it again. "Absent friends."

There were so many of those now. Hoffman used to be able to recite names, but the best he could do now was remember individuals sporadically. "I heard about Tai Kaliso."

"Ah, the Baird Broadcasting Service."

"And Santiago."

"All of it?"

"Maybe not. I haven't caught up with him yet. I keep meaning to."

"It's grim. He found his wife in some grub cell. Marcus said she was blind, couldn't speak, couldn't recognize Dom, looked like a corpse. He didn't know what the hell to do. She was too far gone."

Bernie took a pull at the cup, then put her forefinger to her temple, thumb extended, and squeezed an imaginary trigger. Hoffman was about to take another mouthful of steak. He couldn't.

"Oh God . . ."

"Bloody hard. Doesn't matter if it's the kindest option or not. Been there. Or been close, anyway."

Hoffman thought of Margaret more these days. It wasn't that he missed her, not like Dom Santiago would mourn his wife; he just felt worse about her each year. It wasn't even a tragic love story, just a mediocre, mutual toleration like so many marriages. But even if he hadn't pulled any trigger, he'd certainly killed Margaret.

"I'll talk to him," Hoffman said, and started eating again. "I'm still his CO. Hell, I remember the night his daughter was born."

"Aspho won't go away, will it?"

"Do you want it to?"

"Not really."

So it was Bernie and Vic again for a while, just an hour or so, and one of the few times in his life when he regretted the path he'd taken, not as a soldier but as a man.

"Is it ever too late in life to put things right?" he said.

"If I thought it was, I wouldn't be here."

Bernie probably meant that insane journey across Sera to rejoin the COG ranks after so many years. But maybe she didn't.

He'd find out.

CHAPTER 5

The Coalition of Ordered Governments still exists, the rule of law still exists, and our social covenants still exist. We may no longer be in a state of war, but we still have a battle ahead to survive and rebuild, and in these difficult days there will be no tolerance of lawlessness and antisocial behavior. Unity defeated the Locust. But disunity will be the certain end of us all.

(CHAIRMAN RICHARD PRESCOTT, TO THE REMNANT OF JACINTO'S POPULATION, PORT FARRALL.)

CNV *SOVEREIGN*, MERRENAT NAVAL BASE, TEN DAYS AFTER THE EVACUATION OF JACINTO, 14 A.E.

"Would you mind stepping in the footbath, sir?"

There was a large metal tray full of purple liquid at the foot of the ship's brow. A commander—Alisder Fyne, Anya's list said, the most senior serving officer left in the COG navy—stood sentry at the top, making it clear that not even the chief of defense staff and the chief medical officer would get on board unless they followed procedure.

"What a good boy," said Dr. Hayman. "Up you go, Colonel."

Anya watched Hoffman carefully. A lesser man would have snarled, but the colonel just paused as if someone had reminded him he'd forgotten his keys. He paddled his boots in the disinfectant, shook off the surplus, and strode up the brow. Dr. Hayman followed.

"Opposed boarding," Marcus muttered. "Send in the shock troops first."

"I'm sure Fyne will see sense . . ."

Marcus was so close behind Anya that she could smell carbolic soap. Everyone was scrubbing themselves raw these days. It wasn't just infection control. There was some psychological tic sweeping the ranks, like a need to wash off the past.

At the top of the brow, there was a bucket of soapy, strongly scented water.

"Hands," said Fyne. "Please."

"I'm glad to see you're taking hygiene seriously." Hoffman washed like a surgeon. "Dr. Hayman's going to give you a great report."

"We're a confined space." Fyne, definitely wary, beckoned them to follow. "I've got more than eight thousand people on board. We don't need any more problems."

Once they were off the weather deck, the air inside the ship was blissfully warm. Anya inhaled a heady cocktail of oil, cooking, and bodies—not unpleasant, just a silent reminder that the carrier was crammed to the deckheads.

Fyne stood back to usher them into a compartment with CAG BRIEFING T-6 stenciled on the bulkhead next to the door. As Anya stepped over the coaming, she caught Fyne looking past her at Marcus with a wary look on his face. Maybe he thought he was the security detail; it was clear that the community of ships here was starting to see Port Farrall as Anarchy HQ as well as a source of contagion.

"Marcus Fenix?" he said.

"Correct . . . sir."

Marcus had subtly different ways of saying *sir* according to whether he had any regard for the officer concerned or not. Anya thought for a moment that Fyne knew him from a previous operation or had known his family.

Then it struck her that some only knew Marcus as the Sergeant

Fenix who'd been jailed for abandoning his post. The court-martial of an Embry Star hero tended to stick in people's minds.

Anya felt herself brace instinctively, ready to defend him against whatever sneer or comment followed, but Fyne said nothing more, and they sat down at the table. Flight suits hung against the bulkheads; not enough locker room, then. All the King Raven pilots were now based in *Sovereign*. It had taken just days for the beginning of a divide to emerge between the refugee existence ashore and the relatively comfortable world afloat. The navy had declined to send more medic-trained personnel ashore to support Hayman's struggling unit. And it claimed it couldn't accommodate anyone else.

"Commander." Hoffman rested his elbows on the table. "I'd like to do this by negotiation. But I often have to do things I don't like. Dr. Hayman's team is going under, and I'd *really* like you to release some of your corpsmen."

Fyne nodded at Hoffman, then aimed his reply at the doctor. "When you evacuated Jacinto Medical Center, ma'am, we made *Unity* the infirmary ship. We've got a lot of critically injured Gears and civilians who need acute care. I know what my job is, what my orders are—to preserve this crew, this ship, and this fleet. I'm not going to second-guess JMC's chief of medicine about who we can afford to let die."

This was the game. Hoffman would growl, Hayman would indulge in some shroud waving, and then Anya would suggest a compromise position.

And if that didn't work, Marcus had orders to remove Fyne from the ship. He hadn't been happy with that.

Yes, it's not going to inspire anyone to pull together. Authority's fine, but when you impose it in a situation like this . . .

"I'm losing a long list of civvies every day, sonny," Hayman said. Fyne must have been in his forties. "You can't do much about hypothermia, and we don't have that many surgical cases because they've conveniently *died*, the poor bastards, but you sure as hell can help with the medical ones. Respiratory cases, mainly."

"Rustlung and viruses. I'm aware of the disease issue."

"By the way, footbaths are terrific for controlling livestock diseases, but not the ones we're likely to develop. Five points for trying, though."

Anya felt sorry for Fyne. Hayman could emasculate any man with a razor-edged word. It was diplomacy time.

"How about pooling our resources?" Anya said. "Trade you a few surgical staff for nursing assistance. Or we can look at making *Unity* into the central COG medical facility and move all our cases on board."

Anya learned the lines Hayman fed her. It was a threat. Hoffman could have forced anything on Fyne, of course, or shot him for failing to jump when he said so, but there was a time to crack down and a time for restraint. It always surprised her that Hoffman—gruff to the core, not even a veneer—could navigate that psychological maze.

"Look," Fyne said. "Let's start as we mean to go on. I'm a supply officer. I can't fight a war, although I'd die trying. For the last fifteen years, we've kept a skeleton fleet operational. Maintained ships. Ferried supplies. Managed stockpiles. The COG gave up pretending to have a navy on E-Day, but the navy kept going. Now, I'm not claiming we've been through the hell that land forces have, but we were tasked to keep a core navy afloat, just in case, and that's what we've done. You can understand my reluctance to compromise the people we've rescued."

Anya felt bad for Fyne. Yes, she'd have done the same. Hayman went to answer, but Hoffman cut in.

"You did good, son," he said. "Here's the problem I've got, though—we're less than a month out of Jacinto and we're already splitting into haves and have-nots, along location lines. Now, I reckon your citizens put up with as much shit as the land-based ones, but the others won't see it that way. They're already asking for transfer." Hoffman took his cap off and passed his palm over his shaven scalp. "And I'm saying no."

"I understand your position. And you have complete authority to do whatever you want with these ships."

"Okay, here's a plan. We help each other out on the medical side, and I'll divert more resources to fitting out one of the tankers as accommodation."

Hayman gave the colonel a sharp look. It wasn't in the script. Anya stood by for a diversion in case the dissent was visible.

"I'm very grateful, sir," Fyne said.

"I owe the navy." Hoffman put his cap back on and his eyes met Anya's for a moment. She couldn't imagine this man giving an order for Marcus to be left to die in prison. "Now, have you got any intel on this base? Old stuff, I mean. We've got plans going back to the last major construction here, but that's only seventy years. My men think there's a lot more underground storage here."

"Like the imulsion tanks."

"Merrenat's been a dockyard since the Era of Silence. There must be a warren under the docks."

Fyne seemed fully on-side now. A little stroking worked wonders. "Only people who might know would be some of the retired men."

"The navy *retires?*"

"Only to run the merchant fleet."

"Trawlers and tankers."

"Not always. Counterpiracy patrol. You think all the Stranded are on land? Try Quentin Michaelson."

"Well, I'll be damned." Hoffman lit up. He was in an exceptionally good mood today. Some Gears seemed lost without the routine of combat, but some were changing before Anya's eyes. "Michaelson. I thought he'd be dead by now."

"Old friend?"

"We go back some. Thank you, Commander."

Michaelson was a name that also rang a bell for Anya, even though she couldn't quite place it.

Fyne guided them back to the brow through narrow passages and watertight doors. Hoffman strode away down the quay with a definite spring in his step.

"I like that guy," he said.

Hayman struggled to keep up. She wasn't impressed. "I don't

know what kind of shit you're up to, Colonel, but you're at the age when you'll have prostate trouble, and that's no time to piss off your doctor." She gestured to the waiting 'Dill to collect her. "Make sure Fyne does what he said, or I'll get that tapeworm Prescott to *make* it happen."

She stormed off. She hadn't got what she'd wanted and needed, which was control of the naval medical facilities. Anya allowed herself a brutally pragmatic thought that it was better to end up with 50 percent mortality than 100 percent, and that she was glad that Fyne was an isolationist. Hoffman was now striding ahead of Anya and Marcus, swinging his arms and leaving a trail of vapor as he exhaled. It made him look steam-powered. It was the first thing that had struck Anya as funny since the evacuation.

"Michaelson must be special." The intense cold burned her face. "The old man's not normally like that."

"Former CO, *Pomeroy*." Marcus always did have a prodigious memory. "Amphib. Special forces."

"Ah."

"Yeah."

Anya remembered now. *Pomeroy* was the support vessel for the assault on Aspho Point. She'd been duty control officer in *Kalona* when her mother was killed. It wasn't a happy association for Marcus, either.

"I wouldn't recognize him."

"He was chummy with Hoffman."

"You seem . . . to be on good terms with the colonel now, too."

"He's okay. For an asshole."

Anya wanted to tell him that he didn't have to keep up this front with her, but she suspected it was too much a part of him now to let it go. These days, she could hardly tell when he was in an approachable mood and when he wanted his space; every painful event in his life left him less communicative. She wanted to reach up and touch the puckered scars that ran across his right cheek and through his lip, but thought better of it. That wasn't something she could ever do in public. She just gestured. He seemed to have collected more recent scars.

"So you got a few more in prison, then?"

Marcus closed his eyes, more a long blink than anything. "And I used to be so pretty."

"It's been *six months*. If you're over it, then you'd mention it, at least. It's as if it never happened."

"Maybe that's how I dealt with it."

"I wrote." Screw it, she finally had to get this out of her system, whether he liked it or not. He always seemed disturbed by open affection. It upset her to think that he might not have under-stood—even now, after all these years—that she still lost sleep over him. "I got your message not to visit. But I *wrote*. Twice a week for four years. I'd have written daily if I hadn't thought you'd get pissed off with me."

Marcus's jaw muscles tended to betray how tight a rein he had on himself at any moment. "Dom said he wrote, too. Didn't get more than a couple of letters. The Slab's lousy at guest relations."

Anya had always imagined Marcus reading the letters and throwing them away, embarrassed. Now she could see some prison warder sharing them with his buddies, laughing at this stu-pid girl who was pining for a man who'd die in prison. Life ex-pectancy for an inmate was less than a year once that door slammed shut. She'd actually started grieving. She felt ashamed that she had.

"But you can guess what was in them," she said.

Marcus's jaw muscles twitched a few more times. "Yeah."

"Well . . . that hasn't changed." She could see Hoffman al-ready waiting at the next jetty. For once, he wasn't pacing around in irritated impatience, and he just looked away from her as if he was intruding. "It never has, and it never will."

Marcus made a faint sound in his throat, as if he was going to come out with one of his rumbling all-purpose avoidance com-ments, but he just cut it short and nodded a few times. If any-thing, he looked overwhelmed. It would have been easier if he'd told her to get lost, or had a string of other women; but he didn't. She was competing with ghosts, and whatever padlock his family had put on dealing with emotions.

But it was early days—for everyone. Six months or six years wasn't going to put Marcus right, whatever *right* meant for him. By the time they reached Hoffman, Anya had dragged her worries back to the slightly simpler task of dealing with a community still balanced on the edge of fragmentation.

"Now watch an old man make a total asshole of himself," Hoffman muttered. He kept glancing up to the deck of the trawler, as if he was waiting to be invited on board. He was the head of the COG forces; the vessel was his, under martial law. But he seemed almost excited.

The bridge door swung open, and a gray-bearded man with sun-baked skin stepped out.

"Victor? Victor, you old bastard!"

"You lazy excuse for a maggot," Hoffman growled, grinning like a kid. "Get your sorry ass off that pleasure boat and get used to driving a *real* ship again."

"I thought you'd forgotten me."

"Hell, no. I need a real sailor."

"Spoken like an admiral."

"Don't tell me you were running counterpiracy in this piss-pot."

"Best thing for the job on the coastal run." Michaelson had the most beatific smile. He clearly loved his calling. "You drift along, distract the wrong sort from the freighters, and when they come alongside to relieve you of your catch—bang, and good night. So what can I do for you? Fish? Crabs? Clams? Dead bad guys?"

"Dockyard plans. My Gears want to explore. After the fuel find, they're convinced there's more storage down there that we don't have blueprints for. We need to check out every possibility." Hoffman gestured over his shoulder. "You remember these two? Lieutenant Stroud and Sergeant Fenix."

Michaelson looked past Hoffman. "I don't think I've met Miss Stroud before, which is my loss, but I do remember Sergeant Fenix."

Marcus just nodded once. "Dominic Santiago's here, too. He'll want to say hello."

"Ah, yes, the commando with all the kids and the lovely wife."

"I'm afraid not," Marcus said. "Not now."

Michaelson looked away for a moment, then beckoned them aboard. "That was a bastard of a war."

It was. But they were now using the past tense. Anya could only see that as a cause for hope.

MERRENAT, DRY DOCK C.

Cole thought dockyards were just holes in the coastline with a few fancy buildings, but Merrenat was an education.

No, it was a *maze*. There were tunnels and interconnecting shafts, even stone stairways that vanished under water. A lot of the metal that could be ripped out easily had gone, but the place was still usable. It even looked like people were having *fun* here.

If Cole turned his back on the broken skyline of Port Farrall and just stared out to sea, the world looked like nothing had ever gone wrong. He couldn't even see snow. A flock of seabirds followed the trawlers like a noisy white cloud, and the wind slapped sails against masts. If he'd known what normal looked like, he'd have said it looked *normal*. The only normal he'd ever seen had been old paintings in the House of Sovereigns.

"Okay, this is good." Baird knelt down on what looked like a solid bridge at the edge of a dry dock, and peered over the side. "Look at all these sluices in the caisson. *That's* engineering."

"Man, you need to get out more."

"If we can get the pumps working, we can maintain hulls."

"They ain't gonna let you play with that submarine. How about a nice dinghy?"

With anyone else, Cole could have made a crack about the toys they must have wanted as kids and never got, but there was too much shit in Baird's family history. When Baird mentioned his folks, and that wasn't often, it was like he was quoting a history lesson; they did this, they did that, and he did something else. The word *feel* never came into it. Cole, who coped by imagining his folks being on some long overseas trip and still wrote his mother letters to get it out of his system, thought there was nothing worse than having no happy memories to keep you going in the shitty times.

Actually, that wasn't completely true. Baird *did* have some happy memories. They all revolved around the cool things he'd built as a kid, which he seemed to miss more than his folks. No denying it—Baird was fixated when it came to machinery.

"You keep the yacht, Cole," he said. "Me, I want torpedoes. Shit, where *is* everyone? I'm freezing."

"Marcus is gettin' some chart or something from a crazy old sea captain."

"Man, the romance of the sea."

Cole kept watch on the road, waiting for the rest of the squad. It was hard to think there was any stash of supplies that the Stranded hadn't sniffed out, but there was a whole wrecked world, and maybe only one in a thousand folks had survived, so there had to be plenty of shit they hadn't found yet.

"About time," Baird said.

Cole turned around and saw Marcus, Dom, and Bernie approaching from the opposite direction. *Road* was an optimistic word for it; the concrete was broken up and saplings were growing through the cracks.

Just one little bit of road. How long before we get around to fixing that? Baby, it's going to take forever to repair Sera.

"Dom looks like shit," Baird said.

"He ain't sleepin'."

"Man always sounds normal to me. That's what's *abnormal*."

"You want him to go crazy once a day, just so we're sure he's still hurtin'?"

"You know what I mean."

"He's hangin' on best he can."

Cole was sure he'd have wanted Baird to cap him if the Locust had messed him up that bad. Maybe it was better to tell folks that in advance. It saved them a lot of worrying afterward. But Dom's lady probably never thought she'd end up that way.

You still gotta pull the trigger, though. Don't feel any better, even if you got permission in writing . . .

Marcus walked up to Baird and Cole with a sheet of paper stuffed under his arm and some black cylindrical things dangling from straps in one hand.

"Okay, it took fifteen years." Marcus held up five flashlights. "Maybe we can find a way of attaching these so we're hands-free."

Baird grabbed one and played with the buttons. "This is so what I wanted. A few frigging *years* ago."

Marcus handed another flashlight to Cole. "Courtesy of NCOG."

"We goin' somewhere dark?"

"Tunnels."

"Treasure hunt, baby!" Nobody said that they'd had enough of going underground. Cole knew everyone felt the same way, but this was probably one of the last times they'd ever have to do that shit. And there was a chance there'd be something worth finding down there other than grubs and trouble. "You got the map? Has it got a little picture of one of them brass-bound chests with loot spilling out of it?"

Marcus didn't smile, but at least the line of his mouth relaxed a bit. "Michaelson says there was always talk of an old armory and magazine somewhere between here and the airstrip. He remembers a drain cover in line with the barracks entrance."

"Navy life must have been *really* boring," Baird said.

"He got busted as a cadet for getting drunk and going down there."

Bernie scanned the derelict skyline. "There's got to be another access. They'd have to be able to get supplies down there."

"Find the drain," Dom said, "then work our way out. Let's hope it hasn't flooded."

It took a damn long time. The barracks entrance was intact, but the grounds in between were overgrown, and it was hard to even find concrete in the rubble, trees, and undergrowth. Cole walked along an imaginary path from the front doors—just the stone frame, because the wood had already been ripped out—and kept his eyes down.

The squad ended up doing a line search like a bunch of cops at a crime scene. Eventually Dom squatted down and started scraping away debris with his fingers.

"Here we go." He jammed his knife under the edge of the cover plate. "Give me a hand. Mind your fingers."

"Who's going down first?" Baird asked, peering into the hole. "Thinnest?"

Bernie gave him her shark look. "How about biggest tosser?"

"Let's try the rock test first." Marcus looked around for a chunk of stone, then lobbed it into the shaft. There was a small thud almost right away. "Sounds dry and shallow. Let's get a safety line down there. Hey, Control? Mathieson, we're investigating a possible underground store on the jetty side of the barracks. If we're late reporting in, panic."

The opening was wide enough to take a Gear in armor, and when Cole shone his flashlight inside, he could see brickwork and flagstones. There were footholds in the sides of the shaft, but the metal ladder had rusted through, leaving stumps where the rails had hung. Baird secured a line to the nearest tree.

"Ah, shit . . ." Marcus sat on the edge of the shaft, legs dangling, palms flat on either side. "I've done worse."

He dropped. Cole heard a grunt as he winded himself landing.

"Baird? Stay up top, just in case. Everyone else, down here."

Cole took the rope route. He hit the flagstones just after Bernie, and the place lit up with pools of white light as they shone flashlights around. The first thing that struck him wasn't that it was musty and dark, but that it was warm—warmer than the surface, anyway. They were in a small lobby with a couple of vaulted passages leading off it.

"It's all arches," Dom said. He moved his beam along the walls. "I can see doors in them. Well, it's storage, all right. Let's start here."

Marcus seemed wary, checking the low ceilings, but Bernie didn't look bothered. She went exploring further up the passage. "I'll find the main access," she said. "Don't walk off and leave me down here, okay?"

Her boots echoed on the stone and faded. Cole and Marcus squared up to the first set of doors and forced them open.

"Should have brought Jack," Marcus said.

"Yeah, the bot would have cracked the doors right away." Dom walked in and checked inside. "I hope this isn't eighty-year-old beans."

Cole followed the narrow white beam that was bouncing over wood-lined walls—no, stacks of crates on racks, loads of them. Dom heaved one of the boxes onto the floor and took out his knife.

"Place your bets," he said.

The three of them trained their flashlights on the box as Dom levered the lid free. The wood splintered; there was a layer of wadding underneath. When Dom peeled it back, Cole could see small metal containers.

"We couldn't be that lucky," Dom said.

Cole grabbed a container and pulled off the lid. It was neatly packed with rounds. They looked in good condition.

"Oh man . . ." Lancer rifles hadn't changed much in fifty years, except for the chainsaw. They used the same caliber now as they did during the Pendulum Wars. Cole tossed another container to Marcus. "Now, long as this ain't the only full crate . . . and it's all in this condition . . ."

"Hey, leave me up here freezing my ass off, why don't you." Baird's voice echoed down the shaft. "What's happening?"

"Damon baby, it's Cole Train's birthday. This is just what I always wanted."

"Ammo," Marcus called back. He sounded relieved rather than pleased. "Who says the navy's just for decoration? Check out the rest before we celebrate too soon."

They picked doors at random, forcing them open and cracking wooden boxes for about twenty minutes, and found they were all full. Some tins were rusted through, but it was pretty dry down here.

"There's enough ammo for a siege," Cole said.

"That was what they were expecting." Marcus took off a glove and felt one of the walls. "Yeah, dry. There must be waterproofing behind this."

"Nice and warm," Cole said. "Compared to topside. Maybe we all oughta move down here for the winter. There's cabling and everything."

Marcus had a certain look that went beyond a frown, a kind of deliberate lack of expression that told Cole he really didn't want anyone to see he was rattled. He was doing it now.

"We're not going to be driven underground like grubs," he said quietly. His lips barely moved. "This place smells like a fucking prison."

Yeah, Cole got it. The sooner Marcus was out of here, the better.

Dom had disappeared further down the passage. Cole could hear splintering wood and the clatter of tins.

"You can't eat ammo," Baird called.

"Yeah, but maybe you can eat *this*." Dom came jogging back down the passage with some more metal containers in his hand, small rectangular cans. He held one up and rattled it. "Dry rations."

"Man, you gonna shit yourself for a year if you try eatin' that garbage now." Cole held out his hand for one of the cans. "Looks like some kind of cracker. Don't navy crackers have weevils in 'em or something?"

"Canapés," Baird jeered from the shaft. He must have had his head stuck down there. "How elegant."

"We clear this place out first. Then we worry about the eat-by date." Marcus studied another box with a frown, pressing his earpiece. "Bernie? Found the front door yet?"

Bernie didn't respond. The radios were always a problem underground. But she'd been gone long enough to walk nearly a kilometer, and that meant she could be anywhere. Marcus shook his head and ambled away down the passage, repeating the call.

"That you barking, Cole?" Baird called.

There was a lot more wild noise around Port Farrall than Cole expected, everything from surprisingly loud birdsong to something that sounded like a guy coughing up rustlung, which Bernie said was a stag telling other bucks to stay off his turf. Without humans and their machines around, you could hear stuff from five, ten klicks away. But that was definitely dogs he could hear now.

"I can't tell where it's coming from. Sounds distant. Bernie *said* there was dog packs around."

"Yeah, she'd be thinking about dessert—"

A shot rang out.

"Baird?"

"Shit, what was that? Nothing up here."

It was *inside*, not out. Cole dropped the box he was rummaging through and ran in the direction that Marcus and Bernie had gone.

Dom chased after him. "Marcus? Hey, you okay?"

The comms channel was just stuttering static again. Marcus's voice echoed back in bursts, as if he was running. "I heard it. Shit, it's a maze down here. *Bernie!* Where the hell are you?"

The flashlights weren't much help for navigating tunnels with passages branching off them. Cole found himself right on top of junctions before he saw them, and had to pause to listen or look for boot prints before he could work out where Marcus had gone—and then remember the route he and Dom had taken. The acoustics threw Cole completely. Working out directions from sound bouncing around a warren was next to impossible.

There was another shot, and then his earpiece crackled again—but no voice. It might have been Bernie transmitting.

Shit, how far have we run?

"Bernie, what the hell are you doing? . . . No . . . Where?" Marcus must have been closer to her now, or maybe closer to ground level, because he sounded like he was having a conversation. And Cole was close enough to hear him. "Where are they?"

"Cole here, baby, who we talkin' about?"

Bernie's voice exploded in Cole's earpiece. "Dogs. Bloody wild *dogs.*"

Cole could see shadows without the flashlight now. There was natural light coming from somewhere, and the echo effect was fading. When he rounded the next corner, he found himself on a cobbled slope. Light cut through in shafts from gaps in the planked roof overhead. The air was colder; this was the end of one of the tunnels, back near the surface.

Then he heard the snarling, and a long burst of automatic fire.

"Shit," Dom said. "Just how big *are* those mutts?"

Cole switched his Lancer to automatic out of habit, not expecting anything more than a few hungry strays, but he was wrong. When he got to the top of the shallow slope, he stepped sideways toward the light and saw Marcus—Lancer aimed, taking one slow step at a time as if he was tracking something.

"Where did they go?" Marcus turned. "*Shit.*"

"Oh, fuck—"

That was Bernie.

She wheeled around at the same time Marcus did, and Cole could see blood on her chin. That was when it ceased to be just weird and became a fight.

A pack of at least twenty dogs, big ones, mongrels and hounds of all sorts, came racing down another passage from behind Cole and Dom, like they'd wheeled around the back to ambush them. Cole opened fire. Shit, he'd chainsawed his way through more grubs than he could even begin to count, and now he was under attack from frigging *puppies*?

But they weren't cute pets. They were wild predators, too fast to target, and way too close to shoot without spraying Dom or Marcus, and two got past. Cole spun around to see them leap and bring down Bernie by sheer momentum. Nobody had a clear shot. The big tan dog with a back like a damn pony had its jaw clamped on her left biceps, and the other one—black and tan, smooth-haired—would have had her face off if she hadn't hooked her fingers in the corner of its mouth and ripped hard. Marcus moved in and brought his Lancer down like a mallet. It took Dom two point-blank shots to stop the other one.

Bernie lay there for a moment and then struggled to her feet. Cole caught her arm to steady her. It was the first time he'd seen her really scared—wide-eyed, chalk white, and breathing hard.

"What, you forgot you've got chainsaws or something?" she snapped.

"We might have taken your arm off." Marcus started checking her over, all quiet and calm again. "Dom, are there any more out there?"

"Looks all clear."

All they could hear now was the wind and Baird's shouts. Cole had no idea where the tunnel had come up, but Baird seemed to have found them. Bernie limped out into the open air.

"Whoa, firefight?" Baird said. "What the hell's down there?"

"All done." Marcus held up his hand. "Feral dogs."

"You're shitting me. We can take on the grub army, but we crap our pants when we run into a pooch or two?"

"Man, you didn't see 'em." Cole had never seen a dog set on killing, let alone a pack of them. They didn't run off whimpering. They weren't scared of humans or rifles. They just kept on coming. "Those things are *fast*."

Bernie didn't like losing face in front of Baird. Cole watched her brace her shoulders like she was going to cuss him out. "The idea is to pick them off at a distance," she said, but her voice was still shaky. "Not get cornered and knocked down in a confined space where you can't use your weapon."

"Haven't they got rabbits to chase?"

"It's cold, there's less for them to hunt in this weather, and we've attracted them." She tried to unfasten her elbow plate to roll back her sleeve, but she was trembling too much. Cole grabbed her arm and took off the layers for her. "A human settlement's an easy meal for dogs."

"Skin's not broken," Cole said. "You're still going to see the doc. Your chin's cut or scratched or somethin'."

Baird studied the dead dogs and prodded them with his boot. "So, are we eating these or not?"

"I think I'll pass," Bernie said.

She looked plain wrung out. It just wasn't right for a lady of that age to have to live like this. Okay, she was tough and she could take care of herself, but it still upset Cole that she even had to. They headed back toward Port Farrall, Baird ambling along in front and shaking his head as if he couldn't believe Delta Squad had come to this.

"So, we stop fighting grubs and we start fighting Stranded, the local dog pound, and each other." He flung his arms out in disgust. "Welcome to the new world peace."

"Better get those stores moved out," Marcus said, ignoring him. "At least we know where to bring the vehicles now."

Dom kept turning around to scan the area. "Man, I never knew dogs would try to kill *people* like that. You sure they're not diseased or something?"

"They're just being dogs," Bernie said. "When people disappear and there's no more commands or fences, animals go back to being what they always were. Animals."

Marcus nodded to himself. Cole knew that look.

"Like humans," Marcus said.

PORT FARRALL, CHECKPOINT 8, TWO DAYS LATER.

A steady trickle of junkers and battered trucks was still running between the dockyard and Port Farrall, ferrying the windfall of supplies from the tunnels.

Dom huddled in the shelter of a wall. A dark red down-filled jacket, definitely not uniform issue, had been left without explanation on his mattress a couple of days ago, and that meant someone else had given it up for him.

He needed to know who was prepared to make that sacrifice for him in this weather. When he finished this duty watch, he'd hand it on to the next guy, Jace. For all the agony and privation of the last few weeks, he found the unquestioning comradeship of being a Gear the most comforting thing in his life.

And I haven't blown my own brains out yet. So I can't be grieving that much, can I? What kind of bastard am I?

Dom even found himself distracted, wondering what he'd find to eat in the barracks. He didn't deserve a damn jacket that could have been making someone else comfortable.

Footsteps crunched behind him from the direction of the food distribution center. The snow had mostly vanished despite the lack of a thaw—it had *sublimed*, Baird said—but the ground was still frozen. Cole had given up trying to arrange thrashball games to keep the kids' spirits up because he was worried they'd break bones on a sports field as solid as concrete.

"So what did you find?" Anya slipped close to Dom and tucked her arm through his for warmth. That was the kind of thing you learned to do fast with buddies in this climate. It didn't mean anything else. "Prescott's actually *excited* about it. I don't think I've ever seen him excited about anything."

"What, he's jumping up and down clapping his hands?"

"No, he keeps smiling."

"It's indigestion."

"So, Lancer rounds, high-energy crackers, antiseptic liquid . . ."

"Field dressings, sterile scalpels, painkillers. Loads of drugs, but so damn *old.*"

"Hayman's pleased. She says expiry dates are pretty flexible for a lot of meds."

"So we've got fuel, ammo, and medical supplies, but no damn food."

"Well, the chickens are enjoying the crackers."

"Shit, someone really did bring chickens with them? No pigs?"

"Oh, we have some refugee pigs, too." Anya fumbled in her pocket and pulled out a tiny plastic container. "And I traded a pair of gloves for this tonight. Eye makeup. Half full. We won't be making this kind of thing again for *years.*"

"You don't need it." Dom was simply being matter-of-fact. Anya could stop traffic, makeup or not. People stared at her even in this shithole of a camp. "Do you know who left this jacket for me?"

Anya shook her head. "No. But it's kind of them."

"Everyone knows I shot Maria, don't they?" It was a shrinking community, and gossip was one of the few interesting things left to do. "Are they saying what a bastard I am?"

Anya's arm tightened on his. It was the first time he'd said it out loud to her. "If they're talking about you at all," she said gently, "they're saying that you really have to love someone to be willing to end their misery and take it on yourself for the rest of your life."

Dom didn't want to be let off the hook. He didn't want to be poor tragic Dom, hero and martyr; he wanted someone to punch him out for failing his wife. He thought he understood the weird shit going on in his head that made him react that way, but it didn't actually stop him from feeling it.

"Do you ever *not* do things, really obvious things, and then hate yourself afterward?" he asked.

"Every day." Anna nodded. "Yes. *Every* day."

"You know we came face-to-face with the Locust queen? I was thinking about it last night, and . . . I could have *asked* her. I could have asked why the hell the grubs hate us so much, what they want, why they did that to Maria. And I didn't."

"You really think she'd have given you an answer? Seriously?"

Anya was right, but Dom was still in that place where he could know one thing and yet believe another entirely. "No. Probably not. Hey, you're going to freeze out here. Go back to the mess."

"If you ever want to talk, Dom, you know I'm here."

"Thanks, Anya."

"See you later, then."

Dom went on staring into the darkness, concentrating on the wobbling lights of vehicles as they pottered around. He really wasn't sure if he wanted to spill his guts or not. Maybe he was looking for forgiveness, but there was nobody left to give it to him. So he tried to be the Dom who got on with soldiering.

Okay . . . how much more are they going to haul out of those tunnels?

The underground passages were more extensive than anyone had realized, Marcus told him; they extended under the city, and parts were hundreds of years old, built when the dockyard was first constructed. A lot of the things stored down there were useless, but it was still worth checking every nook and cranny for anything that could be reused. People were starting over with almost nothing they'd been used to having even in the worst days of Jacinto, and no way to manufacture it for maybe years to come.

How the hell did the Locust queen know Adam Fenix?

Dom cradled his Lancer one-handed and stuck his other hand under his arm for warmth. The cold ate through his gloves like acid.

She just said that to fuck with Marcus's head. The bitch was probably the one who killed his dad anyway.

Well, she was gone now, with pretty well all her stinking kind. Dom was disappointed that he hadn't come across more grub stragglers. He hadn't had any closure at all, not even seeing the tunnels flooding, and he understood Bernie's rare loss of discipline in wanting to carve up that grub.

God knows what they did to Marcus's dad, then. And I bet Marcus is still chewing that over, but he'll never say a word about it. Funny—me and him, we know every damn thought the other has by now, and yet there's still some shit we never talk about. His mom. His dad. Anya. Prison.

Dom made up his mind there and then. He'd have a serious talk with Marcus when he rostered off. He'd finally tell him to stop dicking around over Anya, and that he ought to have learned his lesson when he thought she'd been killed. One minute he was distraught when he couldn't contact her, and the next it was back to we're-just-friends business as usual.

Bullshit. You've got no idea how much life will hurt without her, Marcus.

A broken bottle lay in the gutter opposite the checkpoint. Dom watched it for a while, trying to work out how long it had been there, why nobody had collected it to reuse it like every other precious scrap of material in Port Farrall, and why it was glittering in the faint light from the checkpoint post. Then he realized it was moving. Every so often, it would shiver.

It's the wind.

He kept watching, gradually more engrossed in it. It rattled against the curb.

No.

It looked like it was vibrating.

Shit.

Dom didn't trust his own eyes at the moment. He'd seen some weird and wholly unreal things since the assault on Landown, mostly centered on Maria, and the medic had told him it was concussion and stress. He pressed his radio earpiece, just to make sure he wasn't seeing things again.

"Checkpoint Eight to Control, Santiago here."

Don't say it. It's the wind, you know it is.

He didn't get an immediate response from Mathieson. Things were quiet in Port Farrall compared to the usual comms traffic that CIC was used to, so Dom expected some acknowledgment right away. He switched to the open radio circuit to see if there was something happening elsewhere, and the chatter of civilian drivers, Gear loadmasters, and perimeter sentries filled his ear. Proper radio procedure had gone to ratshit now.

"Five-Seven here. Three-Nine, are you gonna move that heap? I need the ramp."

"Three-Nine to Five-Seven—sorry, man, give me two minutes."

"Control, those goddamn dogs are back in the storage vaults. I can hear them scratching. Any chance of some assertive pest control?"

Dom noticed that the city at his back was suddenly silent. It wasn't just the general quiet of a bitterly cold night. It was like a scared, suddenly held breath.

Oh God, it's not just me . . .

Dom felt it with senses sharpened by fifteen years of practice. It made him look down at the road beneath his boots. It made him check his Lancer and start looking around him, 360 degrees. It put him on full alert.

The broken bottle was now tapping gently but insistently against the concrete curb, *chink-chink-chink-chink-chink . . .*

And then voices erupted in his earpiece, and he knew he wasn't crazy.

"Oh God, oh God, oh God—"

"Shit, they're here."

"Where are you? Where the fuck are you?"

"Fire!"

The screaming and yelling lasted five chaotic seconds before the ground under him shook and he started running. He bolted back into the city, not even thinking, letting his reflexes take him. The pavement ahead collapsed into a long narrow trench like opening a zipper, and he jumped clear, but the subsidence was streaking away from him, sucking down concrete and paving slabs as it made for the center of the Port Farrall camp. He could hear screaming already. The civilians were packed into the southern part of the abandoned port, and they knew as well as any Gear what was happening.

The grubs were back.

And all he wanted to do was get at them the moment they broke through the surface. He couldn't *see* them. There was no more radio traffic from the underground stores, so he guessed that was where they'd entered; they'd come in under the city using tunnels obligingly dug for them by humans years before. It didn't matter that these were just a handful left out of a vast army. They could still kill. They'd effectively been let loose in a cage full of humans, at a time when humans were an endangered species.

I wanted to take a crack at them one last time, didn't I?

Tell me I didn't make it happen somehow.

"Control, Santiago here—I'm following the tunnel collapse. You got any sightings?"

"They're emerging around the communal buildings. Food center, medical stations, latrines. All squads, engage."

"How many? I said, *how many?*"

Dom lost track of the welter of voices. He could pick out Mathieson, and then he heard Marcus calling for fire support. A battle had erupted in the center of town. Dom could see the flashes of light and hear the explosions. He was now running against a tide of civvies heading down the street toward him, women carrying kids bundled in just their nightclothes, some folks clutching the grab bags they'd been so thoroughly drilled to snatch and run with when disaster struck. It was blind flight; Dom was still looking for something to kill. The civvies could have been running into more grubs, but he had no way of knowing or stopping them. He just needed to hook up with his squad.

Where's Anya? Oh shit. Did she make it back to CIC?

Thunder rumbled ahead. He saw what he thought was billowing smoke, but it was dust; he inhaled it as he ran on, dodging lumps of masonry in the road. A building had collapsed. By the time he got out of the cloud of debris, he'd reached the city square where the food center had been set up, and then he found his grubs.

The center was always busy. It took all day to serve meals and allocate rations, so there were plenty of people pinned down there. Bernie and Baird were easy to pick out among the Gears firing from cover because they never wore helmets, but Dom couldn't see Marcus or Cole. He would have tried to raise Anya on the radio, but that wasn't what his body was telling him he had to do, and he ended up flat against the nearest wall, taking shots from the cover of the corner of a derelict bank.

A couple of dozen drones sprayed the food center with gunfire as civvies tried to escape or run back inside. A Berserker lurched around the square in a killing frenzy; the chain from her harness flailed wildy. She'd probably tracked the human scent, because that was all the female grubs were good for—mindless, savage bitches, even by grub standards. Dom waited for her to swing around, blocking him from the main direction of the drones' fire, and then ran for Baird's position.

The Berserker stopped and turned to focus on Dom.

Oh shit . . .

Now he'd find out how many reloads it would take to drop her. He was caught in the open. Suddenly he didn't care.

So what? So what? I'm going to kill them all, and if I take out a female, I stop her from dropping any more litters.

Dom ran at her, firing with some half-assed idea that he could hit her underbelly, and knew he was going to die doing it. At that point, life became perfectly clear, sane, the calm eye of the storm. He knew what he had to do, and there was no need to worry about what he would have to live with afterward when the adrenaline stopped pumping.

There wouldn't be an *afterward*.

The Berserker closed the gap. Dom could smell her. He was

sure he wasn't imagining how bad grubs smelled even when they weren't dead.

And I'll die, and so will you, bitch.

He sidestepped to reload, weirdly relaxed and easy. Someone yelled at him and he caught the word *asshole*, but he took no notice until a Centaur roared past on his right. The next thing he knew, he'd been slammed flat on his back with a weight across him, winded, and a massive explosion showered him with wet debris. The firefight carried on. He tried to get up. Grenade rounds flashed over him.

"Are you fucking *insane?*" It was Marcus. He pinned Dom to the ground. *"Stay down!"*

Huge tires passed so close to Dom's head that he could smell them, as pungent as the stink of the Berserker, a choking stench of rubber that caught the back of his throat. He struggled to turn his head to see what was happening. The tanks had moved in to finish the grubs.

Shit.

"Clear! Suck on that, assholes." That was Cole, a few meters away. "Yeah, we're done, baby. Anyone got a flamethrower? Let's clean the drains . . ."

Marcus got up and looked down at Dom for a moment before giving him a hand up. Dom was lobbed back into reality, his detachment suddenly gone, leaving him with a pounding heart and ragged breath.

Oh shit. I'm crazy.

"Dom, don't do this." Marcus grabbed his shoulder onehanded as if he was going to shake some sense into him. *"You're going to get through it.* There's no point beating these assholes if you throw your life away."

Dom could decode Marcus well enough by now. Guilt crashed in on him again, but this time it wasn't about Maria. He tried to be his old self, as much for his own reassurance as for Marcus.

"Sorry, man. I just get mad."

Marcus let go of his shoulder, then walked from grub to grub as if he was tallying the corpses, nodding. "I know. Just remember that a Centaur round up the ass is going to ruin your day, and mine."

The Centaur gunner leaned out of the tank's top hatch and called down to them. She had a good vantage point way up there.

"There's not many. I make it less than forty." She pushed back her goggles and pressed her earpiece, listening for a moment. "Yeah, small raiding party. We're going to keep getting stragglers, but at least they're down to their womenfolk now."

"Small by the old standards," Marcus said. "But not when they get loose among civvies."

Dom watched casualties being carried away. "They've got to stop sometime. The numbers are dropping."

A woman with bright red curly hair walked up to him carrying a little boy in her arms, maybe four or five years old. Dom thought she was just going to ask him for help until she got closer and he realized that the kid was dead. The boy's head lolled right back; there was a clean entry wound in the upper chest. Dead kids were the hardest thing Dom had to cope with.

"We were supposed to be *safe* here," the woman said, completely dry-eyed but shaking with shock. "*You* were supposed to keep us safe, you bastards. What am I going to tell his father?"

She might as well have backhanded Dom across the face. It felt like she had, and he wanted to tell her he knew exactly what it felt like to lose your kids, but he didn't even know where to start. The woman walked off, straight into the arms of one of the civilian medical team, and Dom teetered on the edge between tearful grief and complete shutdown. Then he blanked the whole thing, because he had to. Marcus steered him back toward the barracks.

They were still passing civilians with bags. They were heading out, or at least it looked like it. Marcus stopped a middle-aged man with two teenage boys as they passed.

"It's over," Marcus said. "You can go home now."

"Home, my ass," the man said. "There's no *home* anymore. We're going to find the nearest Stranded community. They seem to survive okay."

Dom watched them disappear down the road. They weren't alone; he passed a few dozen on the walk back to the old school. Whatever had held people together in Jacinto was starting to come unraveled.

"Vote of no confidence," Marcus muttered. "Over to you, Mr. Chairman . . ."

Dom wasn't sure that even Prescott's spin skills could make people feel good about Port Farrall. Like a car wreck, you were relieved to stagger out alive, but then you realized you were hurt and a long way from home with no way of getting back.

This was the core of what was left of humankind, and there was no rescue service on the way.

"Yeah, shit," said Dom.

CHAPTER 6

Don't keep things from me, Mr. Chairman. Not even opinions. I can't do my job if you don't level with me. There aren't enough of us left to dick around with this need-to-know bullshit any longer.

(VICTOR HOFFMAN TO RICHARD PRESCOTT, DURING A FRANK
DISCUSSION AT PORT FARRALL.)

THE HOFFMANS' APARTMENT, JACINTO,
FOURTEEN YEARS AGO, APPROXIMATELY ONE
WEEK TO HAMMER DEPLOYMENT.

"Are you awake, Victor?"

Sleep was getting hard to come by since Prescott had penciled in the end of the world. Hoffman knew that lying awake with his eyes open invited conversation, and discussing his troubles with his wife was the very last thing he could do now.

His head buzzed from lack of sleep and his mouth tasted of metal. "What time is it?"

"Five o'clock," she said. "You told me to make sure you got up."

"So I did. Thank you."

Margaret was a meticulous woman, and he respected that. She was also a lawyer. Her capacity for spotting a man evading cross-examination was unrivaled.

"Are you going to tell me what's wrong?" she asked.

Hoffman padded over to the shower, wondering how much longer there'd be running water in the city. "Well, there's the war, it's bad, and we're running out of body bags. That's about it, really."

"Don't patronize me. We've been married nearly twenty years, and it's *all* been war except for six weeks. Something's changed."

Hoffman turned down the water temperature to cool. "We're going under. But you know that."

"You're doing field showering again, Victor."

"What?"

"You do this every time you're about to go on frontline duty."

Margaret knew him far too well. Hoffman cut short his showers and ran the water colder to prepare himself for the basic facilities he'd get in the field—and he'd been lucky to get a shower at all most of the time. But he hadn't realized he was doing it again now. His subconscious had told him he was going to pick up a rifle and do the job for real again.

Shit.

He switched off the water and wiped the condensation off the shower screen to check the clock on the wall: three and a half minutes. *And the fact that I can tell that means I checked the time before I went in.* He was more strung out than he thought.

"It's gone beyond bad, hasn't it?" Margaret said.

At least he didn't have to lie about that. Maybe it was time he started getting her used to what was going to happen, and why. "It's as bad as it gets. They're going to overrun us sooner or later."

She stood there looking at him in her bathrobe, arms folded, head slightly on one side as if she was expecting him to break down and confess in front of a jury. How the hell did he tell her that most of Sera would be a smoking wasteland in a week or two? How did he *not* tell her?

She'd be safe in Jacinto. She'd be fine, so it was okay for him not to tell her. The law said he couldn't, anyway. He carried the burden of being privy to state secrets.

"Damn," she said quietly. "Is this a case of saving the proverbial last round for yourself?"

"With luck, it won't come to that." *Luck, and Adam Fenix.* "But they're a loathsome enemy, and I would *not* care to be taken prisoner, honey."

"They don't take prisoners, you said."

Hoffman ran the razor over his scalp. "That may be their only virtue."

"How long?"

"What?"

"How long have we got, do you think?"

Hoffman knew to within a few days when most of urban Sera would probably cease to exist. Operational security was just an excuse for not telling her that he'd be responsible for it.

She'd hate him for it.

It's Prescott's decision. Why am I assuming responsibility?

And if I wanted to stop the detonation . . . could I?

They'd do it with him or without him, command key or not. But it needed doing. He could see no other option. Maybe it didn't matter who killed you in the end, just how quickly it was over.

"I'm thinking in terms of weeks," he said.

Margaret didn't say anything for a few seconds. "Is there *nothing* we can use against them? Didn't we have all those chemical stockpiles? The satellite lasers?"

She was a smart woman. She asked logical questions.

"They're in our cities," Hoffman said carefully. "It's not like they're behind their own borders."

Hoffman wasn't sure if he was hoping she would guess the truth to spare him the eventual revelation, if he was encouraging her to see that weapons of mass destruction and 90 percent casualties made sense, or if he was just lying by omission.

"I'm going to ask you something that might offend you," she said.

Here we go. No, she couldn't possibly guess the full plan. Not even Margaret's razor mind could extrapolate like that. "Ask away."

"If it comes to it . . . I wasn't joking about the last round. If it happens that way, if everything goes to hell, will you do it for me? Shoot me? Because I saw that news report from Bonbourg, and . . . I refuse to let them do that to me."

It was one thing knowing that war was brutal, and another actually seeing the detail of an enemy that didn't seem to want anything else but to cause suffering.

"Good grief, woman, you mustn't think that way."

"Victor, I have to know."

"Okay. Yes. I promise." *Would I? Would I know when the situation was that bad? Would I regret it later?* "I wouldn't let anything like that happen to you."

She looked relieved. He'd underestimated how much the Locust advance scared her. He thought she was the last person on Sera who'd let herself be intimidated, and that she'd greet those grub bastards at the gates by slapping a subpoena on them. That was why he'd married her: she didn't take shit from anyone.

"Thank you." Damn, how many women were happier for knowing their old man could give them instant oblivion with one round? It wasn't the best of marriages, but he *respected* her. "You never pull your punches with me, Victor. That's what first appealed, you know? No prevarication. No airs and graces. No lies."

It stung, like ironic compliments always did. "As long as it wasn't my flowing mane of hair."

Hoffman chewed over the comment all the way to the House of Sovereigns. That had been his opening to tell her, to prove he was the plain-talking man she always thought he was, but he hadn't. Everything from now on would compound the deceit. And despite a lifetime in the military, where the ability to keep your mouth shut was both demanded and necessary, this was the ultimate deception.

Margaret had family in Corren, in the far south of Tyrus. That was going to become an issue all too soon.

Salaman was already in Prescott's office when the secretary showed Hoffman in, and the number of empty coffee cups on the chart table said he'd been there for a few hours. Prescott was standing at his desk, one hand in his pocket, phone to his ear.

"Sorry, Professor . . . No, what other data do you need? . . . Well, that's the update . . . No, I'm okay with that . . . Yes, we'll still be here."

Prescott laid the phone slowly back on its cradle and wandered over to the chart table.

"Fenix is almost ready to go," he said. "From tomorrow, he says. He's made allowances for programming new targets on the fly if need be."

"So when he gives the word, you're making the announcement, sir." Salaman looked as bad as Hoffman felt. His face was waxy, very pale, and he kept pressing his fist to his chest as if he had bad heartburn. Everyone's digestion was suffering now. "Still three days?"

"Yes. The longer the delay, the higher the chance of the Locust working out what's coming."

Hoffman traced the main cross-border highways into Tyrus on the chart with his fingertip. There were no civilian flights now; it was too risky for airlines, and they were struggling to keep running anyway. That meant vehicles, trains, and pedestrian traffic only. Maybe some would come into Ephyra via the port of Jacinto.

He found himself calculating how far anyone would get in three days.

If they can get a ride. If they can get a ticket. If they find a ship. Oh, shit . . .

"So when do we start pulling back units?" Hoffman asked. "We can't expect them to make a run for it with the refugees."

Salaman didn't look up from the chart. "That's going to need some careful handling. If we're not giving civilians more than three days' notice, to maintain some element of surprise, then sudden troop withdrawals are going to clue in the grubs even more effectively."

A man never knew where he drew the line until it was tested. Hoffman discovered his.

"If you're suggesting that we leave Gears stranded, General, then *serious misgivings* hardly begins to cover it." He wondered if he was looking for an excuse to get out of the general quandary. No, it pissed him off to his very core. "It wouldn't be the first time we've sacrificed units for intelligence purposes, but this is an army that's given more than everything it has." *So Gears are more worthy than civilians? Wrong argument to sway this guy.* "And what's the point of decimating enemy numbers if we reduce our own at the same time? We're already hopelessly outnumbered. Even if we burn every Seran city to the ground, we won't kill all the grubs. We need an army to crush what's left when the smoke clears."

Prescott and Salaman might as well have been having a conversation that didn't include Hoffman. He wondered why they'd included him in this tiny inner circle. He was Director of Special Forces, and that no longer had any meaning in a desperate war where mechanics and cooks had to fight in the frontline too.

"Nobody thought this was an easy decision," Prescott said. "You understand that as well as any man in the COG. Anvil Gate might not have been on the same scale, but the dilemmas were the same, were they not?"

Ah, now I know. Hoffman, the man who's willing to do the dirty work.

The siege of Anvil Gate had transformed his career, but he wasn't sure if it was worth the nightmares and the nagging fear that one day he would fail and everyone would die because he couldn't cut it.

Salaman said nothing. Maybe it was his heartburn. He didn't look too well.

"Chairman," Hoffman said, "after you deploy the Hammer, you'll need every Gear you have, and you'll need them on your side. Think about how you'll command even a Gear's loyalty once they know you'll waste them in their *thousands* like that." Hoffman paused for a breath to let that sink in. "Giving your life in combat is one thing. But this is without precedent."

See, Margaret, I can use fancy words and arguments. I don't just tell them flat out that they're assholes now. I've learned a lot from you.

Prescott didn't even nod. He knew damn well what society would be like after the Hammer strike; it would need an army to make sure humans didn't tear themselves apart. Ephyra would still have refugees pouring in from the rest of Tyrus, if nothing else, and a state that sacrificed its own civilians would have trouble for many years afterward—grubs or no grubs.

"What about the Gears from the rest of the COG states?" Salaman said. "Not that we have any control over them."

Hoffman hated himself now, so one more step into the abyss wasn't going to damn him any worse. "I bet they'd be really happy to start new lives in the state that unilaterally fried their families and neighbors."

"I may live to regret my double standards, Colonel, but I agree with you," Prescott said at last. "We'd just be reducing numbers on *both* sides. Start pulling back all units south of Kinnerlake."

"Navy too?" Hoffman asked.

"At least we don't have many ships to assemble these days. Yes, bring them home."

Salaman sat with his arms folded across his chest, staring at the chart, and shook his head slowly. "And that'll leave the towns down there exposed to grub attack."

"They'll self-evacuate." Prescott turned away and poured himself a coffee. "We're moving Gears all the time, effectively spinning plates. People will just assume they're plugging another hole that's opened up."

"Are we going to issue misinformation to that effect?" Salaman asked.

"No," Prescott said. "Even a politician has limits."

There weren't any right answers in this war, or any other. There were only bad and worse.

"I'll get things moving," Hoffman said. At least Gears had transport and route priority. "Excuse me, gentlemen."

It was a long walk to the ops room through a maze of splendid corridors lined with paintings of the Allfathers and heroic scenes from COG military history. That gave him time to get his head straight. He'd taken a stand—a quiet one, but a stand nonetheless—for his Gears, and somehow that seemed less selfish and partisan than special pleading for individual civilians.

But I'll still have to lie to the men.

Hoffman walked past the rows of comms officers hunched over consoles in the semidarkened room, occasionally putting a firm hand on shoulders to stop people from sitting bolt upright when they realized the top brass was behind them.

"Get me the COs of all COG naval vessels, Four-Two Logistics, all units in Zone Three-Alpha," he said. "And I mean *all*. Down to the last field canteen. Four-Two L first, then I'll take the calls as they come in. They're all recalled to base. I need to touch base with all commanders personally."

One of the comms officers was Anya Stroud, Helena's daughter, a good-looking girl just like her mother had been. Hoffman was glad she was safe here for the time being, because Helena deserved to live on somehow. Anya looked at him with the faintest of frowns.

Yeah, you've got your mom's radar, haven't you? You know something's moving.

She didn't have to worry about her friends in 26 RTI, though. They'd be back in barracks by the time the south of the country was vaporized.

Hoffman struggled to think if there was anything at all that he could tell Margaret so that she wouldn't think he was a coward and a liar, but there was nothing.

For most of Sera, it was approximately four days to the end of the world.

FIFTEEN KILOMETERS SOUTH OF KINNERLAKE,
SOUTHERN TYRUS, SEVEN HOURS AFTER
RECALL ORDERS.

"So the grubs have moved north." Dom stood with his head out of the open hatch of the APC, elbows resting on the roof. The traffic—some military vehicles, some civilian—had ground to a halt just south of the town. "If we don't get a move on, they'll be in my backyard."

"You don't know that," Marcus said. He had his eyes shut, Lancer across his lap, arms folded on top. "Get some sleep."

"Why else would we be heading back to Ephyra at zero notice?"

"We'll find out when we get back."

Marcus must have been curious at the very least, but he always sounded as if everything was routine, all in a day's work. Dom sometimes wondered how much he knew. It was still weird that he seemed as much in the dark about the war as anyone else, given who his father was.

But Adam Fenix didn't tell his own son any more than he'd tell a stranger. Marcus said as much. That was *right*, Dom knew, but it sure as hell wasn't *normal*.

"Dom," said a voice from inside the 'Dill. It was the driver, Padrick Salton. "Just be glad we're getting out, okay?"

Padrick had been a sniper in the last war, but like everyone else, he did whatever he had to do on the day now. In the seat next to him, Tai Kaliso was sound asleep, head resting against the bulkhead, snoring. Dom ducked down into the 'Dill's cabin again.

"First chance we get," Marcus said quietly, eyes still shut, "we'll get a message through to her, okay?"

Yeah, Marcus was a mind reader sometimes. Maria needed the little scraps of hope; just knowing that Dom was heading back would make her feel better. She never wanted him to leave now. Since E-Day, he'd been back home on leave maybe six times, which sounded generous until he added up the actual time spent in his own home—and that was just days. No wonder she was going crazy. She was cooped up in that house on her own with just the empty bedrooms and the TV, which only made things worse. He knew she spent most of the day watching the news channels. If you spent your day digesting all that shit and misery, how could you ever come out of it normal? She expected every dead Gear to be him. And then there was the never-ending stream of dead civvies, dead kids, and she didn't need reminding about all that.

Why doesn't she just watch a movie? Well, at least she goes out for a walk every day.

Dom had to find someone to keep her company while he was away. She didn't want to mix with the other Gears' wives. Most of them had kids. She'd always been one to keep herself to herself, but this wasn't normal.

"What the hell's holding us up now?" Padrick muttered. He looked at his watch. "We could have walked it faster."

He opened the hatch and got out to walk up the line of vehicles. Dom saw him stop, put his fists on his hips, and roll his head to relax his neck muscles. He came straight back and swung into the seat again.

"Diversion," he said. "I can see it. Shit, we're going to have to bypass this somehow."

"What is it?" Marcus asked.

"Looks like a sewer collapsed. Frigging grubs again." Padrick shut the hatch, revved the 'Dill, and backed up with a screech of tires, almost rolling over the delivery truck behind him in the line. He'd never been a sunny personality, but since his spotter had been killed, he'd been noticeably surlier. "Sod this, I'm going off-road."

'Dills could tackle pretty well any terrain. Urban areas were no problem as long as the road was wide enough. With an impatient South Islander driving, though, a 'Dill became a law unto itself.

Padrick hit the dash controls to release the bot from its housing on the back of the APC. "Off you go, Baz. Find me a route."

Aww, shit. That was his spotter's name. He reprogrammed the damn bot's call sign. Poor bastard.

There was a clunk and hiss from the back as Baz the bot eased out of its compartment and hovered away to look for a path out of the jam. The APC bounced off the highway and barreled along the grass verge, snapping branches off overhanging bushes and trees.

Dom opened one of the side hatches to peer out at traffic. It seemed to be mostly civilian cars and small trucks, all packed to bursting with people, suitcases, and plastic bags. As Padrick almost shaved the paint off a battered station wagon's door, Dom saw kids' faces pressed to the glass. They looked like they were in a trance, wide-eyed and staring. The only thing that Dom could do right then was shut out everyone else's troubles and concentrate on his own and those of the people he cared about most. There was too much misery in the world to worry about strangers.

"You thought of calling in?" Marcus said.

Padrick glanced at the rear view for a moment. "Yes, Sarge." He pressed his comms switch. "Kinnerlake Sector Control, this is APC-Two-Eighty, please advise on the current RV point for A Company Two-Six RTI."

The radio crackled. "Two-Eighty, what's your position?"

"Approximately fifteen klicks south of the sector line, grid reference eight-three-five-five-one-zero."

"Two-Eighty, all A Company units are heading north on Designated Route Theta in twenty minutes. You're two hours adrift."

"Roger that, control. We're not going to make the window, then. We'll make our own way back to base."

"Watch your ass, Two-Eighty. Grub activity five klicks west of your position a few hours ago. Control out."

Marcus didn't comment. Padrick pushed the 'Dill on. Dom wondered if civilians resented Gears for being able to ignore traffic regulations, queues, and obstacles and just roll over everything in their path while everyone else had to wait. If they did, he rarely saw any sign of it. They knew that Gears were having an even worse time than they were.

The next lump the 'Dill bounced over was a burned-out, crushed car that had been pushed off the highway. All four wheels seemed to leave the ground—Dom's gut felt it—and it smacked down again with enough force to wake Tai.

"We'll reach our destined place in the world whether you race there or not, Padrick," he said.

Dom still wasn't sure if Tai's odd pronouncements were weird mysticism or sly humor. Padrick always reacted the same either way.

"Bugger destiny," he said. "Believing in that makes you accept all kind of shit as inevitable."

Tai and Padrick were both from the South Islands, but there the similarity ended. Pad—ginger-haired, freckled, typical of the northerners who'd once emigrated down there—had tribal face tattoos like Tai, but he definitely didn't share his outlook on life.

Tai gave him a beaming smile and a little bow of the head. "Embrace what you can't change."

"What a load of utter toss." Padrick thundered on, stopping to hit the horn when a truck tried to pull out into his private route home. "Baz, where are you?"

Dom thought it would have been nice if the 'Dills had been fitted with monitors so they could get an aerial bot's view of the terrain just like Control did. Instead, Padrick had to wait for Baz to come back. The bot appeared as a speck in the sky ahead of them, resolving into a lumpy gray metal egg with extending arms as it got closer, then matched speed with the APC.

"Okay, Baz, lead us out," Padrick said.

Baz veered left, taking the 'Dill across country into open fields. It couldn't explain itself, of course, so nobody knew if this was just a shortcut or an indication that it had spotted some serious shit up ahead unless the visual data was relayed to Control and the message was bounced back.

"I'd like to know . . ." Padrick seemed to have had the same thought. A squad got that way. You lived in each other's pockets twenty-six hours a day, and sooner or later you ended up feeling that you were transmitting brainwaves or something. "Control, Two-Eighty here. Our bot's taking us the long route home. Assuming he's not training to drive taxis, you seen anything in our area?"

Baz was now *he*, not *it*, as far as Padrick was concerned. Dom was busy noting all the ways that people coped with bereavement.

"Two-Eighty, there's just been a grub emergence five klicks north of your previous route." Control sounded harassed. There was a lot of noise in the background. "Your bot's saved your asses."

Marcus cut in. "We got a job to do, Control. Give us a position and we'll engage."

"Two-Eighty, is that Fenix?"

"Yeah," Marcus said.

"Everyone's got the same orders, Sergeant. Get back to Ephyra."

Shit, whatever was about to go down in the capital had to be big. Dom was torn between gut-gripping worry about home turf and the urge to put down some more grubs. He thought of the civvies expecting military protection and not getting it. It didn't help.

"Give us the location to avoid, then," Padrick said.

It was hard to tell if Pad meant it or not. Control didn't sound sure, either.

"Jannermont, ten klicks south east of Kinnerlake."

"Who's there now?" Marcus asked.

"No Gears units."

"Roger that, Control."

Marcus shut off the comms link. Padrick did one of his annoyed grunts.

"You know how I am about orders," Marcus said.

"We should try," Tai said.

There was no argument; Dom waited for Padrick to object—and he had every right to argue with a sergeant who was defying orders—but he just hit the console and veered right again. A *kerchunk* from the rear of the 'Dill told Dom that the bot housing had opened.

"In you get, Baz." Padrick was heading back toward Jannermont. "I take it you're voting with us, Dom."

What the hell. "Yeah."

The 'Dill had to slow to a crawl to cross the blocked highway. Padrick eventually nudged cars out of the way with the APC's nose fender, scraping metal and getting a stream of abuse from the drivers. The APC bounced down the slope of the shoulder and headed on to Jannermont across an industrial area that looked completely abandoned.

But Padrick didn't need Baz to navigate. Dom could see the rising column of smoke that marked the grubs' visit to the town.

"Step on it, Pad."

"Yeah, okay, Marcus. Tai, stick another belt in the gun. I'll lay down covering fire from the turret. Hey, you might not even need to dismount."

Fat chance; as the 'Dill screeched around a corner into the main street, Pad opened the hatch and Dom saw the carnage. There was a general store dead ahead, flames leaping from its roof, the front glass all blown out. Dom could see the grubs ripping through the store. Shoppers ran between the aisles in panic.

Grubs never seemed to want supplies—what did those bastards eat, anyway?—but they knew that humans would be there, waiting in line to buy what they could. It was all that people ventured out for in most cities. The grubs were like predators staking out water holes, waiting for prey that had to drink sooner or later.

They enjoy this. They could fry that store in a few minutes. But they love hunting us. Look.

If Pad thought he was going to hose them with the 'Dill's machine gun, then he had a problem. There were too many civvies in the way.

"Sod it," he said. He brought the 'Dill to a shuddering halt twenty meters from the doors, close enough to avoid being caught in the open for too long. Marcus jumped out after Tai and used the APC for cover; Dom made for the front of the store, stood off to one side, and aimed at any grub he could get a clear shot at to draw their attention.

"Get down! *On the floor!*" Marcus gestured frantically to the people near the shattered windows. "Just *get down!*"

Some shoppers threw themselves flat; most that Dom could see just crouched with their arms shielding their heads. They weren't used to dropping prone to the ground. Marcus sprinted into the store and disappeared into the aisles, Tai behind him.

Dom and Padrick followed up, jumping over cowering civilians and kicking up dust that Dom realized was flour scattered from burst bags. There was no food in most of the aisles, just long stretches of mostly empty metal shelves and a few displays of dusty hardware—power tools, paintbrushes, bolts, and nails.

Now Dom was between most of the shoppers—the live ones, anyway—and the grubs. Automatic fire rattled into the refrigerated cabinets lining the walls.

"Pad, get 'em out." He gestured to Padrick, indicating the store front. The fewer civvies around the place, the easier it would be to just let loose with everything he had. "Herd 'em out. Go on."

Dom dodged from one aisle end to the next, not knowing what was at the next intersection. It was like the worst kind of urban warfare. This was like a city on a small-scale grid, with all the risks at every street corner when he broke cover, hearing fire at very close quarters but not seeing where it was coming from. As he darted past the next break in the aisles, something zipped past at the far end, and he'd already aimed before he identified it as Tai and held fire. The next aisle, though—

He turned, and found himself face-to-face with a grub.

Dom was so close that when he raised his Lancer, the muzzle smacked into the thing's chest. It was too close even to level its own rifle. His reflex burst of fire knocked it backward, spraying blood on the shelves and tiles. He ran past, surprised at the amount of blood and bone debris underfoot, and skidded in a pool of what he thought was blood. It wasn't. He could smell it now—some kind of sauce, rich and savory, with fragments of shattered glass studded through it, hard as bone under his boots. When he scrambled to his feet, the staccato bursts of fire stopped. He took a guess at where the grubs were from the sounds.

"Marcus!" That was Tai. "Down there!"

The sound of running made him swing around. With the lights shattered, the far end of the store was in semidarkness. *Okay, Tai's to my left now.* Dom started to form a mental map of positions, listening carefully to the thud of boots. Grubs didn't run like Gears—he was sure he could tell the difference—and he heard another set of boots moving very slowly to his right. Marcus was stalking something.

How many grubs left?

Where the hell are they?

Dom had almost forgotten about the civilians. Padrick should have moved them out by now. When he looked back down the riverbed of debris between the shelves, he caught a glimpse of Pad silhouetted against the light, hauling a woman along the floor by her coat.

Hammering Lancer fire started up again, then stopped abruptly. "Stoppage!" Marcus yelled. "Shit—"

Dom rounded the corner of the aisle to see Marcus standing his ground with a dead Lancer as a grub cannoned into him. All Marcus had now was his bayonet. He stabbed two, three, four times; Dom thought he'd managed to get the blade through the thing's hide, but on the next thrust the bayonet snapped and the metal tip went flying. The grub grabbed Marcus one-handed by the collar, too close for Dom or Tai to open fire, and for a second Dom saw Marcus's eyes fixed wide as he went for his knife, as if he knew this was it, the moment he'd finally run out of luck. Dom moved in to take a crack at the grub with his knife. Maybe he could get an eye, an ear, something vulnerable to distract it and move in for a clear shot, and then—

Bzzzzzzzzzzzzz.

The instant whine of a power-saw almost deafened him. Tai appeared behind the grub and there was a terrible smell, a scream, and a spatter of wet mist that Dom felt on his face like a sudden squall. It wasn't until the grub arched its back like a bow and fell to its knees in a spreading pool of blood that he saw Tai with a vibrating saw in his hands and a beatific smile on his face.

He'd carved a slice out of the Locust from ass to waist. Only Tai could smile and do that.

"Shit," Marcus said, staring. "Nice work."

"We must improvise." Tai brandished his saw. "The world is full of weapons waiting to be used."

Marcus aimed the Lancer at the far wall as if nothing had happened, and waited for a few moments before recocking it manually and firing a test shot.

"Some shit I need to ream out." He wiped the bayonet clean

on the nearest grub, pretty relaxed considering that his weapon had flaked out on him and its bayonet had let him down too. "These blades are fucking useless. We need something that actually *cuts* these assholes, not just pisses them off. When I see Dad, I'm going to ask him to come up with something that *works*."

Dom started checking down each aisle. "Yeah, everyone tells Procurement the bayonets are crap. They keep promising something better."

"Well, we can't wait for them to pull their fingers out." Padrick must have kicked something, because there was a dull, wet thud. It was probably a grub. "Maybe we can bolt Tai's home improvement kit onto a Lancer. Worked bloody well, I reckon. Anyway, all clear down here. Anything your end?"

The supermarket was now quiet except for the sound of a man crying for help in the empty vegetable section. Dom and Tai carried him out. At the front of the store, there were seven injured civvies lying on the paving.

"Where's the others?"

"They ran for it. Walking wounded. Not much I could do."

"Okay, we get these folks some medical assistance." One of the men looked like he wouldn't be needing any if they hung around much longer. "How many still alive?"

Marcus studied his Lancer as if working something out. "Seven."

"Okay, there's got to be a hospital or something. Let's move it. Pad, call in our position, will you?"

The time it took them to load the injured into the 'Dill and search the city for a first-aid station meant they'd definitely missed the convoy window by hours. The place was wrecked, burning buildings and bodies everywhere. Dom watched the procession of terrified people heading east out of town with suitcases and couldn't manage to feel sorry for himself. Where were they going? Did they think it'd be any safer than here? The grubs had ripped through Jannermont and gone. They might never come back.

Nobody knew where to run. Nowhere was safe, except the

cities built on granite, and even then the grubs might attack via the surface instead of tunneling their way in.

"Okay, Baz, find us a clear route to Ephyra." Padrick steered the 'Dill over a carpet of rubble and back onto the highway north, which was now pretty quiet. Everyone was heading south and east again. "Lead on."

Dom cradled his Lancer more tightly as the dusk fell. They bounced across rutted fields in the darkness, back onto paved roads, and through woods. Tai dozed in the seat behind, and Marcus took top cover, head out of the hatch. It was usually a sign that he was chewing something over and didn't want to be interrupted.

"We've got to start looking after these crates better." Padrick distracted Dom for a moment, tapping the readouts on the dash. "Can't keep thrashing them like this and trusting longer maintenance intervals. Look."

The engine temperature was climbing; Dom noted the red line edging closer to the STOP mark. Everyone drove 'Dills to the limit, and Pad would know when to pull over and let it cool down for a while. That was something you didn't do if you didn't absolutely *have* to. He kept looking at his watch.

"APC Two-Eighty to Control." The 'Dill was back on the highway now. In some ways that was safer—you could be located easily—but it was also exposed. "Note our location, please. Minor mechanical trouble brewing."

"Control to Two-Eighty, roger that."

Marcus dropped down into the cabin again and shut the hatch.

"Can't think of anything," he said.

"What?" Dom was used to having to fill in the gaps with him. Carlos always claimed that it was what Marcus *didn't* say that usually mattered most.

At least you didn't live to see all this shit, Carlos. End of the damn world.

There were a lot of agonies that Carlos had been spared by dying in the last war. He'd been a devoted uncle. But it would have been nice if he'd known Sylvia, however briefly.

"Can't think of a reason to recall us to base now," Marcus said, frowning. "That's all."

The 'Dill lasted another thirty minutes before it started making unhealthy noises and Pad had to pull over before something seized. They waited in the dark, suddenly aware of how few lights they could see in the distance, let alone any on the road, and noted every rustle and click they couldn't identify. Charging a line of grubs was one thing, but sitting helpless in the dark was another.

"Okay," Padrick said. "Let's try again."

He started the engine, but it died on him. After a few more attempts, he opened the engine compartment, but four diagnoses and a lot of tinkering didn't solve anything. Padrick admitted defeat and called in.

"Two-Eighty to Control, our 'Dill's fucked."

"Okay, Two-Eighty, we're out of engineer units at the moment. Could be ten hours. Are you okay to hold your position?"

Padrick looked at Marcus.

"Start walking," Marcus said. "Any convoys within ten klicks?"

"Stick on the main highway," Control said. "We'll get someone to you as soon as we can."

Dom checked his compass and did a few calculations. "If they don't, we'll be walking for the best part of twenty hours."

It was going to be a heavy slog home, with everything they could strip out of the 'Dill and carry. The Locust took every scrap of COG technology they could find. They reused it and even incorporated it into their own equipment. They got more savvy every day.

"They can keep the engine," Tai said. "It will teach them the value of strength from adversity."

"You're fucking nuts," Pad muttered.

Dom estimated the pack he was now tottering under weighed more than fifty-five kilos. The four of them set off up the side of the highway, moving in the relative cover of hedges, while Baz the bot skimmed in front of them at head height. Its blue power indicators gave Dom some reassurance.

Baz, at least, knew where it was going, and wasn't afraid of the real monsters that lurked in the dark.

CABINET MEETING ROOM, HOUSE OF THE
SOVEREIGNS, JACINTO, 2300 HOURS.

"Jillian, you don't have to wait. Why don't you go home?"

"It's all right, sir." She smiled at Prescott, radiating belief and loyalty. "My sister's moved in, and I could do with the peace and quiet, to be honest."

"Ah, the one from Tollen." Prescott felt a single grain of burden lift from his conscience. "I know it's tough having family around, but it's for the best. She's far safer here."

And when she finds out why . . . at least one person won't loathe me.

He stood in front of the full-length mirror, debating whether to wear a business jacket or the full military tunic. Did it matter? He didn't have to carry any argument, create the right impression, or win minds in this meeting.

He had absolute power over the Hammer of Dawn.

And absolute responsibility, whatever Salaman and Hoffman think. They do so want to shoulder the burden too.

The tunic, definitely. Civilian rule and democracy has to be seen to be suspended. We can't start arguing the toss about this. We don't have the luxury of time.

"Very well, Jillian," he said. "Show them in. And I'd like you to sit in on the meeting. It'll be brief."

Prescott wondered if he should have left his ministers to find out about the Hammer at the same time as the rest of the world. But how much harm could it do the night before? They didn't want an unmanaged panic any more than he did. And they wouldn't want to compromise Ephyra. Their own lives depended on it, if nothing else.

"And Professor Fenix, sir?"

"Yes."

It was a small cabinet now, just five members: Justice and Security, Health and Welfare, Infrastructure, Industry, and Resources. Elections had been suspended shortly after E-Day.
Prescott was fascinated by how few people seemed to crave power
since the Locust attacked, but this wasn't the Pendulum Wars.
There was no subconscious belief that life would eventually get
back to normal and advantages accrued in the war years could be
enjoyed.

"Ladies, gentlemen, thank you for attending such a late meeting," he said, gesturing to the chairs around the marquetry
table. Whatever happened, he needed some cooperation from
them in the days to come, and it was easier to impose some degree of collusion on them now than find new ministers afterward. "You'll realize that this relates to the gravest emergency,
and as such, everything that's said in this room is strictly classified."

Yes, they'd worked that out. Their faces said so. Fenix sat
down next to the Justice Secretary, Janeen Mauris, looking . . .
ashamed.

*But you'll probably save humankind, Adam. You were a soldier.
How did you ever cope?*

"No General Salaman?" asked Mauris.

"As Chief of Staff, I'll speak on defense matters."

Prescott sat down and caught Jillian's eye. She sat with her
notebook open, waiting; poor woman, she thought she was taking
notes. He simply wanted her to hear it firsthand, because —

He wasn't sure, but he knew that he'd need to keep a reliable
secretary more than ever now, and taking her into his highest degree of confidence would ensure that.

Damn, he was sure this would have made his throat tighten,
his stomach churn, *something*. But he seemed to have rehearsed
all his anxiety into submission.

No going back now.

Prescott took a slow, discreet breath.

"This isn't a discussion or a vote," he said. "It's going to be
very brief, but you should hear it now rather than at ten hun-

dred hours tomorrow, which is when I'll announce it world-wide. Sera has two months at most before the Locust destroy us completely. I've sought more coordinated efforts from other COG states, but I've failed, and they appear to have given up hope. So I've taken a unilateral decision, which is within my powers, to reinstate the Fortification Act and ask all citizens to relocate to Ephyra within three days. This is the only place on Sera that we can defend and have any hope of preserving human life, so the Hammer of Dawn will be deployed—to destroy everything where there is Locust infestation, to deny assets to the enemy."

The silence was what he expected; he didn't know how long it was going to last. But it went on longer than he anticipated, and he started counting. The maroon lacquered doors behind Fenix's head suddenly seemed much more vivid for concentrating on them.

"Jerome?" he said.

"We can't accommodate the entire Seran population in Ephyra," the Infrastructure Minister said at last. "And there's no way that they could reach us in three days anyway, with the current state of transport."

Prescott nodded. *Thank you, Jerome. Let's lance the boil.* "But if we had room, then we'd still have no time." Nobody seemed troubled by the Fortification Act—not immediately, anyway. It was academic in a war like this. "To say I don't take this decision lightly is an understatement. And I've taken it alone, because it has to be done, and I don't think it's . . . *right* to ask you to vote on it. If I'm called to account later, then it will be my decision to justify, not yours."

Good grief. I actually meant that.

And then the arguments started, all at once, a hubbub of voices, shaking, angry, disbelieving—*terrified.*

"Three days isn't enough to prepare for any refugee influx on that scale—"

"I won't be complicit in the—"

"What if it doesn't work, Richard? What if it *doesn't work?*"

"Now we know why you recalled the army."

"We're not just killing other COG citizens, we'll almost certainly be killing our own countrymen, too."

Prescott let them argue. He was in no hurry now, and it made no difference to the outcome; he was fairly sure that even after a war that had lasted generations, nobody in this room had any way of grasping what was at stake in this one. It was only when Adam Fenix spoke that they seemed to settle, and grasp the full and necessary horror.

"This is our last resort," he said. "The absolute last hope we have."

"It's easy for you." Mauris looked close to tears. "I have family in Ostri."

"My only son's a Gear," Fenix said. "And he should have been back at base by now. He isn't. I know what's easy and what isn't, Minister."

There was nothing more to be said, but the cabinet went on saying it, a wall of repetitive noise that ceased to have meaning. Prescott got up and leaned over Jillian. Nobody else took any notice. Shock among politicians was an odd thing to watch.

"You can go now if you like, Jillian," he whispered.

Her face was absolutely ashen. "You . . . warned me, sir."

"Yes."

"Thank you. *Thank you.*"

He knew that would be one of the very few thanks he'd get in the next few days. Now he wondered how long it would be before one of the people in this room called friends and family—or the media—and the whole thing spilled over into recrimination and panic.

Civil security is standing by.

We have the bulk of the armed forces back in Ephyra, or within three days of it.

I can handle this. We have to make this work.

"Ladies and gentlemen," he said, "I'm happy to leave you here to come to terms with my decision, but it's made, and I'm afraid I'm going to have to leave you now."

"You can't just *walk out*," Mauris snapped. "We're going to condemn millions to death on the off chance that it might stop the Locust."

"That's it," Prescott said. "Please, do be responsible about this information in the next few hours. It is, as I said, classified. Goodnight."

He walked out, went to his private office, and closed the doors behind him.

Ten minutes later, Adam Fenix opened them.

"I suppose you can spare a few minutes for me," he said sourly.

"Well, that went as well as could be expected. Did they give you a hard time? Call you a monster?"

Fenix ignored the question. "There *was* another way," he said. "But I thought it was better not to start them off."

"Oh, now's not the time to get cold feet."

"I said *was*. It's a much longer shot."

Prescott surprised himself by how quickly he grasped at Fenix's straw of hope. "What was it?"

"That we could try to flood the Locust underground, where they live, using Hammer strikes."

Prescott thought of the scale of the infestation. It seemed odd to use *insect* words like that when the Locust were so large and so powerful. "But there must be millions of them, and to flood tunnels or whatever they have down there . . . we would need to breach sea defenses and divert rivers. We would still lose entire cities. And it would take time we don't have."

"Yes. Yes, the loss of life would still be huge." Fenix sounded as if he was trying to convince himself. "And we ran out of time in the end."

"Besides, how would we know where to flood? We still know next to nothing about these creatures, nothing about their weaknesses."

Fenix stood in front of the desk and just looked at him. Prescott wasn't sure why, but he had a feeling the man was holding back.

"If you want to call off the Hammer strike, Professor, I'm going to want better reasons than a long shot that might simply kill half the population of Sera rather than ninety percent and still not finish the Locust."

Fenix shook his head. "It was *always* a long shot. The Hammer . . . we know the Hammer will work. It's too extreme not to. It can't penetrate beneath the surface, but there's nothing else we have that could possibly guarantee complete destruction anyway."

"So we're back where we started this evening."

"Yes."

"Is this about your son? This hesitation, I mean. I can *see* it, Professor."

"I'm worried sick about him. He's all I've got. I need to know he's safe."

Of course you do. It's a very small price for me to pay to keep you on-side.

Prescott leaned forward, intimate and conspiratorial. "We'll get him back here in time, I promise. It's Marcus, isn't it? Awarded the Embry Star. An exemplary Gear."

"Yes. Sergeant Fenix, Twenty-Sixth Royal Tyran Infantry."

"Leave it to me. We'll locate him and fly him back if need be."

"Please—don't tell him I indulged in any special pleading for him. He's . . . he rejects privilege. Prefers to be an enlisted man. Very independent, very proud."

"I'll be diplomatic," Prescott said. "And we'll need Gears like him more than ever in the days to come."

Adam Fenix studied his hands, apparently embarrassed, and then straightened up like the Gear officer he'd once been. "Thank you, Chairman."

Prescott sat alone for a couple of hours after Fenix had left, gazing out the window at the Jacinto night skyline. The lights that made this district of Ephyra visible for miles out to sea were still mostly burning, and reminded him what he had to do. Whatever mistakes had been made in the past, whatever sins he had committed, whatever the Locust were or wanted, the choice was stark now: save Ephyra at a terrible price, or lose the whole world.

It was actually a very easy decision in the end.

I think I'll sleep tonight, at least.

He picked up the phone and dialed the extension for CIC. Someone had to find Marcus Fenix and get him back home for his father's sake, if nothing else.

Prescott wondered what an independent and principled war hero like Sergeant Fenix would have to say to his father when he heard the announcement in the morning.

CHAPTER 7

*To think we got this far—survived the Locust, survived sink-
ing Jacinto—and now we're in danger of falling apart because civilians think they'll be better off with the Stranded.
Why the hell did we bother evacuating them?*

(COG NAVAL OFFICER—ANONYMOUS.)

**PORT FARRALL, PRESENT DAY: SIX WEEKS AFTER
THE EVACUATION OF JACINTO, 14 A.E.**

"What did we used to do with dead civvies?" Cole asked, looking
back at the city skyline.

"Same thing," Baird said. "Only *we* didn't have to do it."

"Do we *have* to do it like this?"

"Disease, man. We're living in a shantytown. Can't risk it."

The engineers had been the funeral detail in Jacinto, but now
they were too busy keeping the living alive. Cole watched Baird
run the line out from the fuel bowser to the edge of the shallow
pit. At least they hadn't had to drop the bodies in it, which was a
blessing. Shit, even using the grindlift rig, that ground was so
damn frozen now that it was like excavating solid rock. One of the
navy guys said it was the coldest winter for a century.

"Grubs ain't been around for days, so we got to make ourselves
useful somehow."

"Hey, don't get me wrong, Cole. Just saying."

Baird seemed pretty pleased with himself. He had a new spray system for *spreading accelerant*, he said, and that would get the whole business over with faster and more efficiently. Cole took that as the man's best shot at a little reverence for the departed. He watched Baird trot back from the pit like he'd laid explosive charges and was putting a safe distance between himself and the moment of reckoning.

"Shit, am I supposed to say something meaningful?" Baird held a remote detonation key in his hand. He stood there for a second, sort of defocused, like he was trying to remember something. "No, that's all been done. *Contact.*"

There was a loud *whoof* like a distant, muffled explosion as flames leaped into the air. Cole thought it was a real shame that folks had survived all that shit back in Jacinto only to die when they were safe—or as safe as life could be now.

I like an enemy I can shoot. Disease, cold, no damn food—how the hell can a man put a round through that?

Baird watched the flames for a while, then looked at his watch. "We'll come back later. Check that there's been complete combustion."

"Still don't feel right. It ain't a proper cremation." Cole didn't like the idea of cremation, period, but Jacinto ran out of space for burials, and nobody wanted to end up underground now anyway. "Kinda undignified."

Baird jerked his thumb over his shoulder at the flaming pit. "Hey, that's *civilized*. We could stack them somewhere in the open, because they'll be fine until the thaw. But that'll upset the relatives. Especially if the local wildlife starts gnawing on them."

"Damon, baby, you're all *sentiment.*"

Baird jumped back into the 'Dill. "We got to think of this shit, man. Or else we'll end up like the Stranded. A bunch of frigging animals."

The dead were mainly old folks and small kids, which was really hard for Cole to take. Then there were some Gears and civvies who'd died of injuries after the hospital was cleared. No wonder Doc Hayman was such a bad-tempered old lady. Shit, it must have ground her down patching up folks year after year, and then seeing them die anyway. Some people got softer with pain, and some got harder. Hayman was about as hard as they came.

When the 'Dill got back onto the road into town, Cole saw a small truck coming toward them, loaded with people and baggage. It looked like a whole family. Baird made his *ffff* noise, sounding seriously unimpressed, and pulled over to let it pass. Cole had other ideas. Maybe these people didn't understand the risk they were taking, leaving COG protection. Panic did weird things to common sense.

Cole jogged Baird's elbow. "Hey, c'mon, flag 'em down."

"Why? Apart from the fact that we should commandeer their goddamn truck. We *need* vehicles, man."

"Let me talk to them."

Baird *ffff*ed again. "Sure. Charm offensive. 'Hey, ungrateful assholes, we love you really. Was it something we said? Don't go.' "

"They're just *scared*."

"They weren't scared enough to run in Jacinto." Baird's mouth was set on automatic fire as usual, bitching and cussing, but he slowed down and steered to the center of the road. The oncoming truck slowed as well. "This is natural selection in action. The ones without the balls to stay aren't the citizens we want anyway."

"What happened to all the Stranded on the Jacinto perimeter? They must have been flooded, too."

"Not my problem," Baird said. "Look, you be nice to them for a few seconds, feel all warm about it, and then we can RTB. Okay?"

"Damon, don't you ever have no *warm* feelings?"

"Only when I piss myself. Come on. Do the PR and let's go."

The truck wasn't going anywhere unless it wanted to skirt around the 'Dill and over piles of rubble. Cole dismounted and ambled up to the vehicle, mindful of the expression of fixed terror on the driver's face as he put his hand on the hood and tapped on the side window with one knuckle. The window lowered.

"How you doin', sir?" Cole said. "You headin' out?"

"Yes."

"Nothin' but unsavory folk and bad times out there."

"Really?" The guy had two or three days' growth of graying stubble and shabby clothing. "Then we'll take our chances. We can't keep running. We're not moving camp again, especially to the islands."

The rumor was doing the rounds of Port Farrall, an idea that Prescott was thinking of upping camp and moving somewhere offshore where it was warmer and well away from straggler grubs. Some liked the idea and some didn't.

"Okay, sir." Cole stepped aside and motioned to Baird to pull over to let the truck pass. "You mind how you go."

He watched the truck rumble away, venting a cloud of vapor from its tailpipe.

Baird revved the 'Dill. "Very persuasive. Come on."

Cole slumped in his seat. "You'd think folks would all cling together, if only to keep warm."

"What's his problem? Coffee too hot?"

"Don't want to leave Port Farrall."

"Hang on, he just *did* that."

"He means evacuating again."

"Are they still talking about doing that? Great. I'm up for an island. White sand, balmy seas. Bring it on."

"Think it through. Either we find an empty island, in which case we're gonna be worse off than when we started here, 'cause we wouldn't even have piped water and buildings—"

"Yeah, but we'd be warmer, right?"

"—or we find one that's got folks livin' there, and we got to work out how we get along with them."

"Sorry, I stopped at *warmer*." Baird accelerated. "Warmer's good for me. Oh, and you wouldn't have to bury so many little old ladies. It's a win-win."

Cole didn't mind either way. He'd do his duty. The COG had played fair by him, and he'd play fair in return. Port Farrall was never the ideal spot for starting over anyway, not with the shitty winters this far north. It was just closest, and safer.

Only it wasn't safe enough.

"How we gonna do it all by ship?" Cole asked.

"The navy's really good at moving stuff. Here's the chance for them to do something useful for a change."

Well, at least Baird was chipper about it. If there was a flaw in the argument, he was the kind of guy to find it, worry at it like some yappy terrier, and drop it all chewed up at the boss's feet. He hadn't.

"You're *happy*," Cole said.

"Why wouldn't I be? I'm doing shit I *like* now. My dad said I had to enlist or I could kiss goodbye to my inheritance—I wanted to go to engineering school."

"But you didn't *get* any inheritance, you said, 'cause the grubs showed up."

"And the moral of the story is . . ."

"You'll do anything for the right amount of bills?"

"No, skills are the new money."

"And there I was thinkin' you was just content in your oily-fingered vocation."

Yeah, Baird was going to be a useful guy in a world that needed rebuilding and repairing. And he knew it. Maybe it was the first time he felt he was worth anything. That was kind of sad, and explained a lot.

Back at the barracks, Baird started his daily maintenance on the 'Dill like it was his own personal transport, and Cole left him to it. He had his own maintenance to do—keeping himself on top of his memories. He'd run out of paper to write his routine letter to Momma, and he didn't want to beg any off Anya or Mathieson. Now he was down to old wrapping paper, smoothed out as best he could. It didn't matter, because nobody was left to read it; what mattered was just *writing* it, getting his head straight in the process of telling his mom what he'd been doing. All he had to do was write nice and small and make the most of it. There was no telling when he'd get some more.

He settled down in one of the lavatory stalls and braced his elbow on one knee, writing carefully. A man could get some privacy in here if he didn't mind the constant traffic.

Dear Momma, I'm seeing the damndest things in this town . . .

The main door swung open, banging against the cracked tiles on the wall. "Man, I've got to pee just to warm it up." It was Dom, still making a real effort to be cheerful when nobody expected him to. There was the metallic *zzzz* of a zipper. "That you, Cole Train?"

"Yeah . . ."

"I just saw Hoffman and Michaelson looking *intense*, going into Prescott's office."

"*Cupboard.* It ain't that big."

"Well, something's going down."

Cole slipped the paper back in his belt pouch and came out. Dom was washing his face, leaning over one of the few basins that was still in one piece, and his COG-tag slipped forward out of his collar. Cole did a double take. No, it was something else; Dom had his tag, all right, but he was wearing an extra chain attached to it, something silver.

Aww, shit. I bet I know whose that is.

It was definitely a lady's necklace, a thin chain with a ring-shaped pendant. Dom hadn't worn it before. Cole would have noticed it by now.

Dom straightened up, rubbing his face. "What?"

"Nothin'."

Dom looked down for a moment and seemed to notice that the chain had slipped out. He pushed it back inside.

"It was Maria's," he said, not that he owed anyone an explanation. Cole could usually work out the right moment to tackle the awkward stuff, but this was a tough call even for him. "It's way too small for my neck. I looped it on my chain instead. We always retrieve tags, right? Whatever it takes."

Everybody had their own way of coping with shit that was just too much to take in, Cole decided. He wrote letters that nobody else would read; Baird tinkered with that damn 'Dill when it didn't need it, Anya was busy trying to be her mom, Bernie tried to feed everyone, and Dom hung on to his wife's necklace like a fallen buddy's tag. Marcus always looked like he carried on as normal, but Cole was damned sure that he kept something in his head that got him through the day.

"Yeah, we do, baby." Cole went back into the stall and sat down to unfold his wrapping paper letter again. "Nobody's ever really dead unless we forget 'em."

CIC, PORT FARRALL; OVERNIGHT TEMPERATURE, FIFTEEN DEGREES BELOW FREEZING.

"Humor me, Chairman," Hoffman said. "We're not short of fuel, and we only need commit one squad to this, two at most."

Michaelson pulled a rolled chart out of the pile.

"We have options," he said.

Anya helped him lay the chart on the table, flattening it out as best she could wearing gloves. The gloves weren't achieving much. Her fingernails still had a distinct blue tinge when she checked them. Outside the window, the overnight snow was a thin dusting that belied the intensity of the cold. Anya could just about see the old school sports field through a porthole of clear glass that she'd rubbed in the icy condensation. Most of the trees that had taken root after the place was abandoned had already been hacked down for emergency firewood and building repairs. Even a small city's worth of humans changed a landscape fast.

We're going to strip this area completely. What's going to be left in the spring?

"Here's my priority." Prescott shoved his hands under his folded arms. "Keeping this city—this community—together. I'm not actively stopping civilians from leaving yet, but we may have to, and I'm going to have to sell this move to people, because simply giving them orders to go isn't enough."

"Really?" Hoffman's only concession to the cold was a scarf just visible under his collar. "Because it always worked fine before."

"The foundation of the COG's always been that the citizen is protected by the state, and in exchange the state expects the citizen to make a few sacrifices for the common good." Prescott seemed to be trying a softer approach, but Anya suspected that there was a good dose of pragmatism behind it. If the exodus was what he considered to be nonessential citizens, then it was a good way of saving their food rations. "So if we can't keep our end of the deal, what motivates them now?"

"Put it this way," said Hoffman. "If the cold doesn't kill us, the last of the grubs will, because they know we're here and they keep coming. And even if we've drowned ninety percent of them, they'll *still* be able to finish us off if we stand here like goddamn targets long enough."

"Every evacuation costs lives, Victor, however efficiently it's done."

"It's damage limitation," Hoffman said. "Do we lose more people by staying put than by moving? It's a calculated gamble."

Life had been one long gamble since E-Day. Anya found herself thinking almost enviously of the Pendulum Wars, when the rules seemed easy to follow: human versus human, motives known, limitations understood. And somewhere, if you traveled far enough, there was always a border that could be crossed to reach places where some aspects of life went on almost normally: restaurants, warm beds, shops, perfume, books, small luxuries, second helpings.

Anya even found herself missing the squalid bars in Jacinto. There was no haven left on Sera now. Port Farrall was as good as it got—a vast refugee camp of derelict buildings. Anya didn't want to imagine that there were Stranded outposts that had made a better job of things than the COG. It mocked every sacrifice of the past fifteen years.

"Chairman, Captain Michaelson has as good a knowledge of COG naval bases as anyone." Anya decided she had a voice in this, too, damn it; she was an *analyst*. She wasn't just there to answer the phones, she was there to *task Gears*, which meant she had as much to contribute now as any other officer. She bristled, pitching in to back up her colonel. "But even if none of those places is habitable, then at least we're *seen* to be pulling out all the stops, not just sitting on our—"

She wanted to say *asses*, but stopped short.

"*Asses*," Michaelson said obligingly. She could have sworn he stifled a smile. "You're worried about civilian morale, Chairman? Then this could give it a real boost."

"So what are our options? If we're going to relocate, then I need to stop the engineers wasting resources on facilities we'll end up abandoning."

"We need somewhere that hasn't been destroyed by Locust—which means islands on the far side of the abyssal trench. The Locust couldn't tunnel that deep. It's kilometers to the seabed." Michaelson leaned across the table and dragged his finger down a strip of scattered islands. "Then, somewhere big enough for a small city population. Unless you want to spread the community along a number of islands—good for disease control, bad for governance and logistics—then you've got a choice of Erevall or Vectes. Vectes should still have infrastructure, because it was a big naval base in the Pendulum Wars, but it's off-limits because of contamination. Erevall's mostly at sea level, so it's prone to storm inundation, but—"

"Let's try Vectes." Prescott stared at the chart, stroking his beard with his forefinger. "It's within Raven range without refueling, yes?"

Anya knew that fixed expression. Hoffman did, too, because she watched his lips compress into an even tighter line. Prescott had knowledge that they didn't.

"It's off-limits," Michaelson repeated. "It was the old chemical and biological weapons site. We mothballed the base."

"I think it'll be safe now."

Hoffman's face was a study in suppressed anger. Anya always thought he'd have a heart attack at times like this. "Chairman, I was under the distinct impression that we'd agreed need-to-know meant that we *all* need to know."

Prescott looked as if he was embarrassed at forgetting something. If he was acting, then he was at his peak performance today.

"Apologies, Colonel." He frowned as if he was irritated with himself. "It's one of a very long list of things that crossed my desk in previous years and seemed irrelevant. Until now. If I recall correctly, the facility was fully decommissioned by the time we started the Hammer of Dawn project. The quarantine was left in place because we had no immediate plans for the base."

Hoffman took a long, shallow breath that struck Anya as counting to ten.

"Vectes it is, then," he said. *Strained* didn't quite cover his tone. "Captain, can you add reserve tanks to a Raven?"

"I'm sure we can bolt on some extras that Major Gettner will approve of."

"Very well, Victor, make it happen," Prescott said. "No doubt you're tasking Delta again."

"Fenix gets the job done every time, Chairman."

"*Almost* every time."

Anya had to make an effort not to put Prescott straight. It was hard. No, it was impossible. "We'd all be dead without Delta, sir."

Prescott looked as if he was about to say something pointed, but thought better of it. "Indeed," he said.

Anya rolled up the charts and made a point of getting Hoffman to open the door to walk out ahead of her. She didn't want to leave him to have a closed-door argument again. Michaelson gave her a knowing flash of the eyebrows. The three of them headed down the corridor to CIC, saying nothing until they were out of earshot.

"Lying asshole," Hoffman muttered. "Excuse my language, Lieutenant."

"You normally use worse, sir. And it's okay."

Hoffman turned to Michaelson. "Damn, Quentin, we're going to have to wring every last bit of information out of him."

"It's a reflex," Michaelson said. "They were all like that, if I recall. If you ask him if he knows the time, he'll just say yes. Assume any politician is only telling you what he wants you to know, until proven otherwise."

"You think Vectes is safe?"

"Well, I wasn't kept in that loop back in the day. But one thing I'm certain of, Victor, is that politicians need a critical mass of humans to exercise power over, so he's hardly likely to be taking risks with his . . . subjects. Sorry, I almost said *electorate*. How old-fashioned of me."

"Okay." Hoffman put his hand on the CIC door as if testing it. "Better get Sharle in on this, because there's no point finding somewhere if he's not ready to evacuate from here. Oh, and I hereby place you back on active service."

"I never really retired, Victor."

"No, but much as I admire that lieutenant commander of yours, I'm breaking the news to him that *Sovereign* is now your ship and you're going to be in command of all maritime assets."

Michaelson gave Hoffman a mock salute. "A Raven's Nest of my very own. How nice to be free of the smell of shrimp."

"Just make sure those choppers can reach Vectes from here."

Michaelson strolled away with a spring in his step.

"If only everyone was as happy with their lot," Anya said. CIC was now noticeably warmer since more personnel had moved into it. The EM manager's staff were a heat source in their own right. "Don't let Prescott get to you, sir. The captain's right—it's just force of habit."

"Anya, I have to deal with it, because I can't afford to hate him. Nothing's going to destroy this community faster than a feud within its leadership." Hoffman braced his shoulders in a way that said he hadn't quite steeled himself to the idea that even now, he would never be told everything. "You were quick enough to put him right about Delta, though."

"Marcus paid for whatever mistakes he made."

"He did. And we all make them."

"Sir, may I go on the recon mission?"

"Why?"

"There are injured male Gears still on combat duty who are physically less able than me. I can do *more*. I've been bringing my fieldcraft and weapons skills up to speed."

"I know. Mataki's been giving you individual tuition."

"We need *everyone* pulling their weight, sir. Don't you think I'm capable?"

Hoffman didn't have much of a veneer. The man she saw was

mostly the inner core, only his natural fear and guilt kept in check, and he never seemed bothered to learn to lie. He smiled ruefully.

"You're your mother's daughter, Anya. She never took any crap, either. You go right ahead." He jerked his thumb in the direction of the comms desk. "Find me another one like Mathieson, preferably two, because *nobody* should be working twelve-hour shifts every day, and I'll seriously consider you for frontline duties. Now let's get this recon planned. Go find Fenix."

Hoffman could have called Marcus on the radio, on duty or not. He knew that. He was just being Hoffman, still trying to atone for what he'd done to Marcus, and so—indirectly—to her. Dom might have been convinced that the two men were now locked in some mutual loathing, but all Anya could see was that they both still wanted to admire each other despite their respective lapses: Hoffman bewildered by Marcus abandoning his post, Marcus still shaken by being left to die in the Slab. Neither were the actions of the men they knew they were.

You're all guilt, aren't you, Colonel? You'd have gone back for Marcus eventually. You know you would. I know you would.

"Will do, sir."

Marcus was off duty. Anya knew roughly where he was at any given time because she kept the duty rosters, and there weren't yet any places in Port Farrall where he could hole up and hide. If he wasn't with Dom, he'd be patrolling the camp's warehouse block or keeping an eye on a food distribution center on his own time. Nobody wanted any downtime to think.

And nobody with any sense was venturing outside today if they didn't have to. Anya hunched her shoulders against the cold and tried raising him on her radio.

"Marcus, where are you? It's Anya. Hoffman's going for the recon. He wants a planning session right away."

Her earpiece crackled. "I'm in Sector Alpha-Three. You still in CIC?"

"No, I'm about half a klick from you. Just passing the medical station in Alpha-Two."

"Wait there. I'll walk back with you."

It was so quiet that she could hear a Raven's engine starting up in the dockyard. The whine rose in a crescendo, then the *chakka-chakka* of the rotors, and she glanced up as she walked to catch a glimpse of it. No, she was wrong: *two* Ravens. They zipped low overhead at top speed, heading inland. It wasn't a routine sortie. Nothing was scheduled; she would have known. That either meant some refugees had been spotted, even this long after the evacuation, or there was trouble somewhere.

Anya pressed her earpiece and tried to pick up the comms traffic. One was a pilot she barely knew, a guy called Rorry, but the other was Gill Gettner, and she was going for broke. Anya could hear the two pilots trading targeting data; they'd spotted Locust on the surface.

"Yes, run, you ugly fucker." That was Gettner. "Corpser, two klicks dead ahead, asking for it . . . I'm on."

"Six Boomers, three o'clock, one klick and closing, I'm engaged."

"Roger that, Three-Three."

"Targets heading away from Farrall, half a klick west of the highway, repeat, *away* from Farrall, still on the surface."

"Control, this could be a decoy. Advise perimeter security."

"I'm in—engaging now." Rorry sounded detached. Black smoke from the rocket strikes boiled into the sky; Anya could see it even from the center of town. "Confirming that kill, stand by."

Anya stood waiting to pick up Gettner again, finger jammed in her ear, and watched the skyline. Another pall of smoke and flame rolled skyward.

"Corpser down," Gettner said. "Anyone want to dance on it?"

"All targets neutralized. KR-Three-Three returning to ship."

"Roger that, KRs." That was Mathieson. "Dispatching a 'Dill to check the area."

Everybody had scores to settle, comrades in need of avenging. Anya wasn't sure what Gettner's individual story might have been, but it was impossible to find anyone now who hadn't lost family and friends to the Locust or the consequences of living in a city wrecked by war. Like Bernie always said, grieving was a little easier when everyone knew what it felt like.

Marcus ambled up to her, Lancer cradled against his chest. He nodded in the direction of the smoke. "They never give up."

"At least we know what they've got left." Anya started walking back to CIC with him. It was—by their standards—quality social time. "Some Corpsers are still tunneling away from the Hollow, presumably. Wiping us out still seems to be their priority."

"Consistent."

"Yes, you have to give them that."

"They could sit and wait until we freeze." Marcus's mind was definitely on something else. He had that slightly defocused look. "Maybe they're running from the last of the Lambent. Maybe it's nothing to do with us at all."

"Say it."

He blinked a couple of times but kept his eyes straight ahead. "Say what?"

"Your father. Finding all those recordings of his voice in the Locust computer . . . don't tell me it didn't upset you. If that had been my mother, I'd be pretty upset, too. And angry. And confused."

"It's like getting wet. Once you're soaked to the skin, you can't get any wetter no matter how much it rains."

"What was he *doing*?"

"Damned if I know. And I never will."

Marcus must have heard the talk about his father being a traitor; like father, like son, some had said. Nobody said that now. But Anya doubted that he'd forget. She waited a few moments in case he was planning to go on, but he wasn't.

"Anyway, Hoffman's sending you and Delta to Vectes to evaluate it," she said. "That's why I came to find you."

"A trip to Toxin Town. We get all the perks."

"Prescott says it's safe now."

"Imagine that."

Marcus didn't say anything else all the way back, and just kept pace with her. But it was the longest conversation they'd had in a while. Anya settled for quantity over quality.

"Fenix," Hoffman said, not looking up from the chart on the table. "Did your father ever tell you anything about Vectes Naval Base?"

"Not really."

"Me neither. We'll work from Michaelson's data." Anya went to sit down and get on with some paperwork, but Hoffman stopped her. "You'll want to sit in on this, Lieutenant."

"Something you want me to do, sir?"

"You wanted some hands-on time. Well, you've got it. You're going to Vectes, too."

CHAPTER 8

Healthy? How healthy do you expect a Gear to be? Years of chronic sleep deprivation. Exposure to more environmental toxins than I've got tests for. Acquired hearing loss. Rustlung. Depressed immune function because they're totally burned out. Brain damage, everything from blast proximity to serious head trauma. And that's without the psychiatric issues. Traumatic stress is a given. In hospital, those boys made more noise asleep than they did awake, because it was one long frigging nightmare. So nearly all our men of fighting age are utterly—and maybe irreparably—damaged.

(DR. MARYON HAYMAN, SUMMARIZING FUTURE HEALTH ISSUES FOR
CHAIRMAN PRESCOTT.)

OUTSKIRTS OF PORT FARRALL, SIX AND A HALF
WEEKS AFTER THE EVACUATION OF JACINTO,
14 A.E.

"Andresen picks his moments." Baird shuffled from foot to foot in the icy morning air, rubbing his gloved palms together. He had a Hammerburst rifle slung across his back today. Locust weren't the only ones who looted from their fallen enemy. "Why the hell do we go running after every grub that shows up?"

Sergeant Andreson had blown a big hole in a grub on perimeter patrol last night, he claimed, but it had run off and he'd lost it. Now Delta and Sigma 4 were doing a line search near the woods. That was where the things seemed to keep emerging.

"Because they're there, Blondie," Bernie said.

"Or we could be smart and wait for them to come to us. Because they do. We're just wasting calories."

Bernie understood the need to go after every contact. It wasn't just pragmatic; humans would never be able to get on with living again until they knew the last Locust was dead. It didn't even matter if they weren't a viable breeding population.

Do they talk about us like that? In animal terms?

She thought of Prescott's speech. *Genocidal monsters.* Humans were conducting the genocide now. She was fine with that.

"Look, as long as we leave any alive, even a couple, then the bastards will start breeding again," she said. "We have to hunt them down."

"Yeah, but they'd be so inbred they'd look like that nurse in J Sector medical station."

"That's cruel. True, but cruel."

"You like hunting shit, right? Go back down there and hunt for Berserkers. Kill the females, and it doesn't matter how many boy grubs are left."

"So Cole finally sat you down and told you where babies come from. With all the rabbit pictures."

Baird took it in his stride. "You know I'm right."

"You volunteering?"

"It's a better plan than playing hide-and-seek with the assholes."

"Maybe. But we're in no shape now for another Landown-style assault. Even if the place wasn't under water and full of imulsion."

The weather might have been pure frozen hell, but at least the thaw had set in between her and Baird. There was, as she'd hoped, a trace of regular human behind that thick shield of self-centered cynicism. Nobody had ever cared much about Baird except Baird, she suspected, not until he enlisted and realized that there were people who'd put their life on the line for him for no other reason than being a Gear.

Now he'd managed to score a black knitted cap for her, the kind she could pull down over her ears—not exactly flattering, but essential kit for a sniper. She didn't want to think who he'd outsmarted to get it. He was trying hard, and that was all that mattered.

"So you get to go on the all-expenses-paid Delta trip to Vectes," he said. "A perk from Hoffman?"

Ouch. "We go back a long way, Blondie. Nearly forty years. Maybe I lent him my pencil in class once, and he never forgot it."

Baird never really grinned. He just had this *smirk*—there was no other word for it—that got to her when she was least expecting it. He was near a raw nerve now, and he knew it.

"Whatever." The smirk got broader as he kicked through the frozen grass. "I *like* to see old folks happy. If you're going to croak with a coronary anyway, you might as well go with a smile on your—"

"Now go say that to Hoffman." *Play it cool. It only encourages him.* "And I'll make sure Doc Hayman's standing by to reattach your balls."

The smirk took a long time to fade. If she hit him again, it would just be etched there permanently.

The turf sloped away gradually into the valley and the Jacinto road. A hundred meters away, Marcus and Dom paced slowly, eyes down, Cole a little way behind.

If Andresen had chased down a drone here, then there should have been traces. Bernie squatted down and searched for blood in the thick layer of frost. There was no point in anyone wandering into the forest at random. They hadn't even located an emergence hole yet.

"If the grubs are watching us, they'll know we're thinking about leaving." Baird took his earpiece out and fiddled with it, then rubbed his ears. "They're not stupid. They'll see stuff being moved to the docks, like the vehicles."

"Then they'd better give us their best shot, hadn't they?" She clipped his ear. "Wear a bloody helmet. Or earmuffs. You'll get frostbite."

But something wasn't right today.

She couldn't hear birds and animals that she'd become used to. The noises were there, but more distant. It sounded like the area had been cleared. Maybe the wounded grub was lying in wait, gathering itself up for a final effort to take one last human with it. She pictured a doting drone dad with a crib full of little newborn grub bastards, a fresh generation of terror, and knew that couldn't be allowed to happen. She knew how the things bred, too. Hoffman had told her. It was one excess too far, too personal. Any species that bred by rape didn't deserve to survive. She'd heard horror stories about COG baby farms way out in the country, but fertile women knew their worth to society, and she'd *seen* some of them since the evacuation, well fed and healthy, not looking like prisoners or victims of abuse. It was different.

We're different.

Shit, how would I know what a victim looks like? Does anyone think that when they look at me?

No, the COG *was* different. COG citizens were almost a second-line army. They were used to doing their duty—whatever that duty might be—for the greater good, and that was why they were citizens. Anyone who couldn't hack that degree of self-discipline gave up and went with the Stranded.

Fuck them. Parasites.

"Yo, blood trail!" The shout went up from further down the line. "Over here."

Everyone converged on the Gear who'd found something. She couldn't recall his name; Collin or something. Squad designations didn't seem to mean a thing now except as call signs on the day so that CIC had some idea of locations.

Lost my whole squad. Men I'd only known for a week. Cole lost his, too—back with Delta again. Tai gone. Shit, what's left of us now?

Marcus looked down at the frozen black patch, evidently

unimpressed. "Mataki? Pretend you want this asshole for lunch. Track him."

Bernie set off into the trees, slow and careful, noting damage to vegetation. Everyone else kept behind her line.

Blood . . . broken tree root, white inner fibers not oxidized yet . . . boot print in one of the remaining pockets of snow . . . She was now a hundred meters into the woods, and the light was filtered by the evergreen canopy. It was getting hard to see.

Shit, where's the blood gone?

"Lost the blood," she called. "Wait one."

"Over here." That was a guy to her left, too far to be a continuation of this trail.

"You sure you're not looking at rabbit shit, sweetheart?"

"I know what shit looks like, Sarge."

Then another Gear called out, fifty meters to her right. "Blood here, guys."

This wasn't funny. She was cold, tired, and she needed to pee. She waited to hear Baird make that little snorting noise of amusement at her expense. But he was right there behind her, dead silent. She looked around. Every Gear looked seriously alert.

"If you're taking the piss," she said sourly, "this is the wrong time for pranks, and I'll—"

Baird nudged her hard in the back. "Granny, how's your hearing these days?"

"About as good as my right hook, dickhead."

"I mean it. Listen." There was a sharp crack as someone stepped on a twig. Baird whipped around. "Hey, I said *listen.* Hear it?"

Bernie thought it was an animal at first, a distant groaning noise, and then it suddenly became the only ambient sound she could hear. Her brain focused on it and nothing else.

"Shit." That was Marcus. "Kantus."

The sound resolved into a steady, continuous droning. It made the back of her throat itch.

Kantus.

And where there were Kantus, there were grubs ready to attack. *That* was the noise, some weird chant or animal call. It rallied grubs, even badly wounded ones. The sound made them fighting mad again.

Definitely shit.

She heard the creaking and ripping behind her at the same time as everyone else, and turned.

"Ambush!" Dom yelled.

Grubs erupted from the ground in a semicircle right behind them—Boomers, mainly, around thirty or forty—and cut them off. Baird opened up with the Hammerburst. Bernie reached for the Lancer slung across her back, cursing herself for walking in here with the Longshot, and heard a rapid *beep-beep-beep* some meters away. A blast nearly blew her off her feet. Splintered wood flew everywhere like flechettes. The smell hit her instantly: scorched metal, raw meat, scented wood resin.

The Gear to her left, the guy who'd spotted the blood, was already down. Bernie caught a glimpse of a headless body. Something had also sheared off some of the surrounding saplings at head height. Once that registered on her, her conscious brain took a backseat and the primal core that knew how to process information and move her around without thinking took over. She took cover and opened fire. For all the chaos, she could still hear that droning sound.

"*Mines!*" Marcus backed up toward a larger tree, gesturing. "Watch your asses—proximity mines. Sigma—fire position, *there*, now. Delta—*there*. Where's that fucking Kantus? *Mataki!* Find the goddamn thing and shut it up."

The Gears were deep in the tangled gloom, minus vehicles, and if any Centaur or Raven support managed to get to them, how the hell could they open fire? Marcus called for support anyway.

Some of the Boomers had huge cleavers, snatched from the Locust kitchens. Others were Maulers with shields and explosive flails. They looked like a random army wielding whatever weapons they could grab, cobbled together from what had survived, but calling them stragglers didn't do them justice. This was an efficient, intelligent killing machine once again. One Mauler struck out at a large tree, bringing it crashing down at an angle, but it stopped short of crushing Gears in its path when it lodged in the branches of another. It just cut off another exit.

Another explosion cut down trees and Gears, and another.

"Freeze!" Dom yelled. "They're driving us into more mines!"

Bernie, crouched in the flimsy cover of a pine tree, shut out the muzzle flash, screams, and rattling fire and tried to focus on that single, sickening noise.

The Kantus had to be stopped. The first problem, though, was to find the thing in this maze.

Time — it could have been a minute, two minutes, or half an hour.

All Dom knew was that he wasn't dead yet. He could hear Marcus, and eventually he heard Cole and Baird yelling over the sound of chainsaws. Then he realized he hadn't heard Bernie in what seemed like a long time. He felt like instant shit for forgetting her.

"Bernie?" He could hear everyone else on the radio net, so she had to be receiving, too. "Hey, Mataki?"

No answer. *Shit.* Maybe the radio was down. No, that was the dumb and desperate lie he'd often told himself when he didn't want to think that someone had finally run out of luck. He bobbed up from cover, hitting one of the butcher Boomers with short bursts of fire. Marcus got in a headshot while it was struggling.

"I hate it when they think," he said.

"So much for stragglers. They've sharpened up again."

"Shut that damn Kantus up, Bernie." Marcus paused to listen; the droning chant was going strong. Dom was close enough to see a bead of sweat run from his hairline down his neck, subzero temperatures or not. "*Shit.* Sounds like two of them now. Someone find those assholes and take them out."

Boomers wouldn't run if a Kantus was chanting. The droning

sounded like plain noise to Dom, weird and irritating, but to the grubs it must have been like a bugle call or something, because they went for broke when they heard it. Stopping the damn thing mattered.

"Delta, Sigma, all squads—this is Control. Bravo Three's heading your way. Hang in there."

"Step on it, Mathieson." Marcus primed a frag grenade and prepared to swing it by its chain. "And I'd really like some ordnance I can *roll* under those bastards' shields . . . aw, *shit*." The grenade caught the top of the Mauler's shield and spun clear. Two seconds later, it exploded, taking out a drone who stepped over it. It didn't kill the thing, but it lay bleeding and shrieking while its buddies carried on around it. "If we can get them to a clearing, can a KR target them?"

"Delta, KR-Eighty here, what clearing?" That sounded like Gettner. "You want me to *make* one?"

"Can you *see* anything below, Gettner?"

"Not enough to be certain I won't take your guys out, too."

Dom could hear the helicopters overhead, but the forest canopy was too dense for him to see more than shadows, even in daylight. And the pilots sure as hell couldn't see enough to confirm targets. Another explosion deafened him for a moment and he felt something stab into his cheek. When he put his hand to his face, his fingers came away wet with blood and sharp, fragrant wood splinters. He was lucky they hadn't blinded him.

"Man, you okay?" Cole thudded down beside him. Dom could hear via his earpiece, but every other sound—except the Kantus chant, which seemed to be seeping into his brain via his teeth— was muffled now, his hearing pummeled by the noise. "Where's Baird? I hear him, but I don't see him."

"To your right." Baird was panting. "And I—*shit!* Shit, shit, shit—man, that's *it*. My frigging goggles. You *bastard*."

There was another stutter of Hammerburst fire, very close— not a grub, but Baird. Dom tried to look around. All he could see was muzzle flash, smoke, and drifting debris picked out in the shafts of light stabbing down from the canopy. The battle was running in bursts. Every time he dropped behind cover and looked up again, the grubs were somewhere else, waiting, then they started up again. They were pushing the Gears deeper into the forest. Every time they fell back a few meters, another mine detonated. Dom could hear Collin screaming. That was the real nightmare: he was pinned down, he couldn't even see where the screaming was coming from, and the guy needed help.

"Anyone near Collin?" Marcus yelled. "Where the hell is he?"

"Got him." Dom didn't even recognize that voice. "Shit, I can't move him. I'll stay with him."

"This is more than a frigging ambush."

"You said it."

Dom still couldn't see Baird. Cole knelt back on his heels, looking as if he was going to jump up and find him. Dom tried to grab his arm. "Don't, man."

"Baird," Cole yelled. "You okay?"

Baird was there, all right. Dom saw the Boomer with the meat cleaver just before he saw Baird. The Boomer swung, Baird ducked to his knees, and the cleaver skimmed his hair to thud deep into a tree trunk. The Boomer tried to pull it free, but in the heartbeat's pause Baird shoved the Hammerburst at an angle into its gut and fired—once, twice, then a third burst. It fell backward, still hanging on to the cleaver's handle. Cole jumped on it and fired his pistol into its head point-blank.

And it *still* had a grip on the cleaver. Baird smashed at its knuckles with the butt of his rifle until the blade dropped along with the dead Boomer's arm.

"Frigging *cook*," he snarled, picking up the cleaver. "Now it's *my* turn."

The grubs advancing on them suddenly turned to look behind. Bravo 3 crashed between the trees, spraying fire everywhere. Dom dropped back behind the shattered stump of a tree and found himself nose to nose with Marcus.

"Okay," Marcus said, finger on his Lancer's power button. Dom readied his, too. "Steady . . ." Any grub left standing was being driven toward them. The things were about to get a gutful of chainsaw. "Go!"

Dom jumped up from a crouch and swung his chainsaw into the first gray moving object he saw. He wasn't even sure where the blades caught it. He just felt the saw bite and travel like it had a life of its own, and the grub slipped down sideways in slow motion—or so it seemed to him. When he pulled the saw clear, he was staring straight at Gears from Bravo 3.

Where are the grubs? All down. Over. All gone.

The Kantus was still droning. It sounded like an echo. There were definitely two.

"Shit, you guys need to check before you—"

Dom saw movement behind the Bravo line. The ground at the edge of the treeline erupted, and another rank of grubs—Boomers and drones—rose from the frozen ground, cutting off every Gear.

It was a double ambush. For the first time he could remember, Dom found himself wishing a round would just hit him between the eyes, *now*, right now, and get the shit over with, let him go home to wherever Maria was.

The thought was gone in a breath. Marcus lobbed a frag grenade between the trees, clear of the Bravo line, and the explosion bought two seconds to find cover. The battle revved up again. The Kantus was louder than ever; the Boomers charged.

"You better not be dead, Mataki." Marcus dropped and sat back against the tree stump while he reloaded. "Kill that noisy bastard. *Now*."

If Bernie couldn't find the Kantus, then Cole decided he had to.

It was just like thrashball. Once he had his mind set on winning and could visualize what he was going to do, the moves came naturally. There were plenty of damn trees, and those things weren't obstacles—they were an *advantage*, and he was trained to take it.

All he had to do was find where that bitch-ass voice was coming from.

Every time he shut his eyes and concentrated, it sounded like it was coming from everywhere at once; every time he looked around, straining to see through the smoke and gloom, he saw vertical columns and horizontal movement, trees and troops, no freaky Locust cheerleader in robes and a helmet. Where could a thing like that hide? It was damn big, like any grub.

He needed to get some elevation.

Cole sprinted from tree to tree, zigzagging, doing a dangerous thrashball run away from the battle and in the direction he thought the voice was coming from, deeper into the forest. He was expecting to hit a mine at any moment. He thought he saw movement matching his own, but when he turned his head it was gone. Then he looked back. What he saw now—he saw stairs, baby, *stairs*. Explosions had torn up the forest and some trees had been ripped clean out, roots hanging in the air, trunks leaning against others at an angle. If he took a run up the trunk, he'd be halfway up a big tree and a few meters higher than everyone else.

Speed, baby. Just get some speed up.

Cole sprinted. He still had the acceleration, even now. His boots hit the bark and he just let his momentum take him far enough up the slope of the tree to fling his arms around the upright trunk supporting it and hang on. There were two big black pits in the ground thirty meters away—emergence holes. He straightened up, one arm still around the trunk, and scanned a full arc around him.

Shit, fir trees didn't have blue lights. Did they?

In the gloom, he could see triple bars of faint blue, armor indicators—but vertical ones, like they were lying on their side on a branch up in the damn trees.

It took him a few moments to work out what he was looking at: Bernie Mataki, propped in the fork of a branch with her Longshot aimed. Had she seen him? If he called her on the radio, he might distract her. But she'd seen him, all right. She didn't even move her head, just her left arm, pointing down into the trees and then indicating one with her forefinger.

The Kantus must have been within meters. She could see it, but Cole couldn't.

Then she moved her arm wider, circling her forefinger—vague direction, yeah, he got it—and then held up two fingers. The second target.

Shit. What did he have to do? If she wanted radio silence, then he couldn't ask.

Thumbs up. *Yes.*

Yes *what?*

A single shot rang out. The droning chorus thinned instantly into one voice. Something went *thud* on the ground close enough for him to hear it.

Now he could hear the other Kantus, and work out roughly where the asshole was. Bernie's voice whispered in his earpiece.

"He's just standing absolutely still, right next to a tree. Flush him out for me. Preferably *that* way."

"All part of the service, baby."

"Follow the finger . . ."

Cole knew he wasn't one of nature's stealthy types. They didn't call him Cole Train for nothing. He decided to sprint for it, and the instant his boots crunched on twigs and gravel, the Kantus stopped droning and bolted. Bernie didn't fire; the grub went the wrong way, out of her line of sight. Cole dodged the trees and tried to head the Kantus off.

But you can't run and chant at the same time, can you, asshole?

Cole darted around the next tree, just catching glimpses of the Kantus, trying to drive it back toward the battle—or so he thought until it whipped around and he saw the muzzle flash as it fired its pistol. The round clipped his collar armor and went wide. By the time the Kantus aimed again—faster than a Boomer, but not fast enough—Cole emptied a Lancer clip into it, up-down, face to groin. There was no point doing half a job with these guys. They needed shutting up for good.

He reloaded and made sure its chanting days were over. "Tough audience, ain't I, baby?"

Cole could already hear the tide of battle changing as he

headed back to Dom's fire position, more Lancer fire rattling through the forest than Boomshots and Hammerbursts. The injured drones weren't bouncing back into the game all fresh and enthusiastic now that their Kantus were gone, and the Boomers were finally getting the idea that the party was over. Two turned and tried to run. But the moment they emerged from the trees and onto open ground, hammering gunfire from a Raven strafed them.

Gettner was a patient lady, for sure, waiting there like some vulture until she got some trade.

Cole ducked and dodged as he ran after the last grubs. He almost fell over Baird, who was kneeling by a pile of grub ammo, pouring rounds into another butcher Boomer. It was hard to work out where anyone was until the firing slowed, the noise died down, and Gears started calling in as they cleared positions.

Cole pressed his earpiece. "Marcus, that's two more Kantus who won't be performin' again."

"Nice job, Cole. What happened to Mataki?"

"She don't like choral music, either. She capped one."

"She's okay, then."

"Yeah." *Shit.* She hadn't caught up with him yet. "I better go find her."

Baird was admiring a haul of cleavers and Hammerburst ammo. "Hey, we going to come back for all this stuff? Can't waste it now."

"Let's collect Bernie first. What happened to your goggles?"

"Don't ask."

Baird would get another pair somehow. But now that the dust was settling and Cole was feeling the winter chill again, he could see just how high a price they'd paid to put down these grubs. There were too many bodies. They'd lost a lot of Gears. It felt like the killing was never going to stop.

"Bernie?" Damn trees all looked the same. "Boomer Lady, where you gone?"

Baird called for her. "Yo, Granny, where are you?" He still had a cleaver in one hand. "I got you a nice new chopper. For all the dead animals you cut up."

Cole found what he thought was the right group of trees and scanned the branches. He thought she'd already climbed down and headed back until he heard her voice.

"Are we done?" she called.

"Bernie baby, it's real messy down there, but we got 'em all. You can come down now." He beckoned. "I'm impressed you even got up there."

"Yeah, but I'm stuck," she said.

"How stuck?"

Baird managed a smile. "Throw some rocks at her. That usually works."

"I've got a cramp in my leg, dickhead." She tried to shuffle back down the branch and winced. "And it's one thing climbing up here . . . but another getting down again."

"Bernie, you shot so many kitties for lunch that the cat god's passin' judgment on you." Cole roared with laughter. "You got *stuck up a tree*. Ain't that poetic justice?"

It was only raw relief. He didn't think life was funny at all right then, not one bit, but he didn't have any control over the laughter that shook his whole body all the way from his gut. There were too many dead buddies back there, too many hurt. It'd hit him later, he knew, but right then all the folks he was closest to were in one piece, and this just started him off laughing.

"You want me to plummet from here, or try climbing halfway and *then* break my neck?" Bernie called.

Cole held out his arms. He couldn't see straight because his eyes had filled up with tears for no particular reason.

"Come on, Boomer Lady. Trust the Cole Train—I'll catch you. I *never* fumbled a catch in a game, ever."

"Good." Bernie's voice was suddenly small and shaky. "Because I don't think I've got enough adrenaline or energy left to hang on."

Baird muttered and shook his head. "Shit, she shouldn't be doing this."

"You tell her." Cole positioned himself right underneath her, then took one pace back. "Bernie? Just let yourself fall, baby. I swear I won't drop you."

It was like one of those dumb-ass training things where guys had to learn to trust their buddies to save them from a little bit of pain. Cole didn't want to say it aloud, but if Bernie broke something, she wouldn't mend as fast as the rest of them.

"Okay." She took a loud breath. "Incoming—three, two . . . go."

Twigs snapped, and he caught her in both arms, staggering back a few steps.

It hurt a lot more than he thought—her elbow caught him in the chin—but it felt pretty good to make the catch. When he set Bernie down on her feet, she limped a few paces.

"Ow . . ."

"Okay, now you're gonna listen to me."

"I only twisted my ankle." Cole tried to support her arm, but she fended him off. "I can walk. Really, I can."

"Now, I always was a good boy," he said. "But sometimes Momma *don't* know best." He picked her up bodily and threw her over his shoulder. "And I'd carry you nicely, but I know you'd give me hell about that for makin' you look girly and *weak*."

Gears took care of each other. Cole was going to lock Bernie in her quarters until they were ready to ship out for Vectes if he had to, and not let her out of his sight.

"Yeah, you really are a good boy," she said, sounding winded by each stride he took. She started laughing, too. "Thanks, Cole."

Baird ambled along behind. "Hey, don't forget the cleaver."

"Thanks, Blondie. Just what I wanted."

There were still Gears jogging in the opposite direction toward the trees, because it wasn't over yet. There were tags to collect, funerals to fix. Cole suddenly realized Baird wasn't with them anymore, and turned to check.

"He's gone back to join the burial detail, I think," Bernie said, not seeming to mind the undignified lift. "I wish I hadn't been such a bitch to him before."

"Baird's okay," Cole said. "He only gives bloodstained cleavers to people he *likes*."

Vectes was sounding like a pretty sweet idea now. Cole could keep the jokes coming as long as people needed him to, but he had the feeling that if they had to go through this many more times, he'd reach the stage where even he might not be able to look on the bright side again.

CHAPTER 9

As all of Sera has learned, peace is fragile. This new, ruthless enemy has rendered most of Sera's leaders either helpless or dead. This enemy believes Sera is finished. Some in the Coalition of Ordered Governments also seem to believe Sera is finished—a sick, feeble animal waiting for slaughter. But today, citizens of Sera, we—Tyrus, the heart of the Coalition—will take back our planet. To ensure your safety and cooperation, we are reinstating the Fortification Act. All of Sera will be under martial law. No one is exempt. Survivors should immediately start evacuating to Ephyra. These unclean creatures, these Locust, are unable to penetrate Jacinto's granite base. Therefore, in Jacinto, we are safe—for now. We won't let this rampage go further or surrender power. The Coalition will employ Sera's entire arsenal of orbital beam weapons to scorch all Locust-infested areas. For those citizens who cannot make it to Jacinto, the Coalition appreciates your sacrifice. Please forgive us. This is the only way.

(CHAIRMAN RICHARD PRESCOTT, 30TH DAY OF BLOOM, 1 A.E.)

VEHICLE CHECKPOINT, EPHYRA-KINNERLAKE
HIGHWAY, 30TH DAY OF BLOOM, 1 A.E., MINUTES
AFTER CHAIRMAN PRESCOTT'S ANNOUNCEMENT.

There was no such thing as a good time or place to hear news like that.

Dom wished that he hadn't been among civvies at the time. The squad had walked all night along the side of the highway, loaded with salvaged kit from the dead 'Dill, and now they'd reached the bridge over the Tyra River. It was paved with traffic at a complete standstill.

Someone had a radio turned up to full volume, the sound spilling from the open door of a car stopped in the traffic. Dom was caught among people who expected Gears to know what was happening.

They looked at him for answers. He had none to give.

"Did we hear right?" a woman whispered. She put her hand on his arm and shook it gently, as if she thought his mind was elsewhere "It's got to be a mistake. Surely? They can't mean it. They'll *kill* people. What happens to our homes?"

Dom had been leaning on the safety rail of the highway bridge, looking down onto the river, when he heard the broadcast news conference. The words *entire arsenal of orbital beam weapons* hit him with their full force a minute or so after he heard them. He found himself staring at the glittering reflections of the sun on the water, and every starburst point of light was now etched into his memory. Things were bad, but he'd had no idea *how* bad.

I have to call Maria. I have to get to a phone.

"Ma'am, I don't know any more than you do." The woman had her hands cupped over her mouth as she looked up at him, shocked and helpless; how the hell *could* anyone take in what Prescott had just said? He couldn't. "It'll be okay. You're not far from Ephyra now. You'll make it."

"But I don't *want* to go to Ephyra," she said. "I live in New Sherrith. What am I going to do about my son? He's in Soteroa."

The South Islands were on the other side of Sera. Unless the guy had a private aircraft—and that was a privilege even the richest on Sera had been forced to hand over to the war effort—then the poor bastard was weeks away by boat.

If he can get passage at all.

Shit, this is it.

"Ma'am, it's going to be fine." Dom knew he was probably lying, but what the hell else could he say? That her son was screwed? "They know what they're doing. If they didn't think people could get to Ephyra, they wouldn't have given them advance warning, would they?"

Dom looked around at the mass of people—scared, confused, unable to move. How the hell was everyone going to get to safety? He didn't even want to think about it. The enormity would paralyze him and take his mind off what he had to do. He had his orders. He also had his mental list—unnumbered, unplanned, but if forced to recite it, he probably could—of people he would protect whatever the cost.

"Dom? *Dom!*" Marcus's voice got his attention. He was on the opposite side of the stationary traffic with Tai and Padrick, talking to a transport sergeant. "Over here. Come on."

The bombshell dropped by the broadcast was now spreading ripples. Not everyone had heard it live; not everyone had a radio with them. The news was being spread by word of mouth, car to car, truck to truck, person to person, and Dom had to wade through a sea of rising panic. At one point he looked across the bridge in the direction of the checkpoint and saw the Gears there under siege from pedestrians who had now abandoned their vehicles and were trying to cross on foot. The traffic jam was now becoming a permanent, fifty-meter-thick barricade of buses, trucks, and cars. Fuel rationing hadn't stopped many from taking to the roads in the almost constant ebb and flow of refugees shifting from city to city after each Locust attack.

And now that Prescott had announced the decision to smash Sera flat to stop the grubs, the refugee exodus to come would make today look like a minor inconvenience.

"Marcus! Marcus, you heard the announcement? Have you *heard the goddamn announcement?*"

Dom had to slide on his ass across the hood of a car stopped so close behind a bus that he couldn't squeeze through. He felt the edge of his holster scrape the paintwork. The driver yelled at him, just a muffled noise with a lot of *F*s in it, but scratched paint was going to be the last of anyone's problems. By the time Dom crossed four lanes of nose-to-tail vehicles, the transport sergeant was fending off pedestrians.

He was right on the edge, poor bastard, and he looked as if he hadn't slept in days. The name tab on his shirt said MENDEZ. He seemed to be trying to talk to Marcus in one breath and carry on a radio conversation with Control in the next. And anyone in uniform was now a magnet for terrified, confused, angry civilians who'd heard the world was ending in three days. He was trying to keep a man at bay with one hand, but the guy had a baby in his arms and he wanted answers right now.

"I *have* to clear this frigging road, sir," Mendez kept saying. "We've already got a traffic jam ten klicks north because the grubs have trashed Andius. Now the bridge is blocked. You'll have to wait. Don't leave your car, okay? *Don't abandon it.* I can't get the traffic moving if you dump cars on the bridge. Do you understand?"

"What's going to happen?" The guy kept asking that over and over, not hearing a damn word Mendez said. "Where am I going to go in Ephyra? My wife doesn't know where I am."

"Everyone on this road's got the same problem, sir." Mendez looked as if he wanted to manhandle him out of the way, but the guy had a baby, and that made everything awkward and emotional. "Look, go sit in your car. When the traffic starts moving again, you can drive straight into Ephyra."

"Sir," Marcus said, "give me your wife's name and a number. I promise we'll get a call through."

He held out his hand, and when Marcus made a suggestion, even civvies took it as an order. It was the gravel voice and the steady blue stare, Dom thought, the weird combination of looking like a hard bastard while sounding like a guy you could always rely on.

The man fumbled for his wallet. Padrick helped him extract a business card and scribble details on it, then escorted him back to his car. Marcus watched, jaw muscle twitching.

"You're good at fobbing them off," Mendez said. "You should do my job. Now, I got to clear this bridge for military traffic, but you—"

"I meant it." Marcus read the card, then slipped it inside his armor. "I'll call her. Now, what do you mean, we have to wait for extraction? We got four pairs of willing hands here. What do you need done?"

"I got my orders, Fenix. Every crossing and VCP's been told to hold you for pickup."

"We haven't been tasked for a mission. We're just heading home. We can shift the abandoned vehicles."

"Too late. I've flashed CIC and there's a KR inbound. You're going home, fast lane, Fenix."

"Whose idea was *that*?"

"Hey, why ask me?"

Marcus rocked his head slightly as if he was weighing up something, then shrugged. "We can do something here. We have to clear this route, whether it's for convoys or refugees. Just tell us what needs doing."

"You could start driving vehicles or marshaling further back down the road, diverting vehicles onto the side roads. But you're not going to have time."

Dom could already hear the Raven approaching. They were getting out. He wondered how the people stranded here would feel when they saw Gears leaving right after the Chairman announced they had three days to get to safe ground before he fried the rest of Sera. He wondered if they'd be seriously pissed off at the Gears' privilege, for once, getting a lift home out of this chaos while they were trapped here.

And Maria's stuck on her own right now. She watches the damn news channels all day. She's heard this shit, and she doesn't know where I am, and she'll be going crazy with worry.

"My father's fixed this," Marcus said. "Why the hell doesn't he leave things alone?"

"Hey, Marcus, it could be Hoffman. He might have a job for us. Wait and see."

The Raven set down on the other side of the checkpoint in a parking area. The crew chief jumped out and called to Mendez. "Where's Fenix?"

Mendez pointed; the crew chief beckoned. Pad and Dom squeezed through the gap, followed by Tai and Marcus, then ran at a crouch to avoid the rotors.

"Whoa, no, we've got *one* space." The crew chief held up both hands. Dom could see the Raven was loaded to the deckhead with Gears. "Move it, Sergeant. Chairman's request."

"Not without my squad."

"Look, I'm running a shuttle here and I've got a shitload of trips to cover with zero downtime in the next three days. Make your mind up."

Marcus was standing right under the crew bay. One of the Gears leaned down and said something Dom didn't catch, but Marcus shook his head. "Thanks, buddy, but I can't let you do that."

Marcus turned to walk away. Dom had a choice, as everyone did at times like this; he could bleed for strangers whose problems he couldn't fix, or he could do something solid and real. He shoved Marcus hard so that he fell back on the deck of the Raven, struggling for a moment.

"Go!" Dom yelled at the crew chief. "Get him out. Now. Or he'll *never* go."

The crew chief went to slap a safety line onto Marcus's belt, but he was already scrambling off the chopper, cursing a blue streak.

"Fuck that," Marcus said. "I don't leave my squad."

Dom tried to block him. "Go."

"*You* go, you've got a wife who needs you."

"Just go. We'll be okay."

Marcus looked around and made for the cars, ignoring him completely. Dom could see he was heading for the guy with the baby. The crew chief was yelling not to piss around and waste time, and Dom went after Marcus, grabbing at his arm. Marcus shook him off and hauled the father from the car.

"Come on, get going." Marcus reached into the passenger side to grab the bassinet, complete with sleeping baby. "Forget the car, citizen. You got a ride."

"Hey, thanks, I—"

Marcus just marched the man up to the Raven and handed the baby to the crew chief. "One space, one passenger. Kids go free. Right?"

"My orders are to get *you* back, Sergeant."

"And I'm pulling rank, *Corporal*. Civilian evac. Send my dad the bill."

The crew chief strapped in the shocked, bewildered father. "Hey, buddy, you know who just saved your ass?" he said. "Fenix, the war hero."

Marcus ducked out of the Raven's downdraft and the helicopter lifted clear. If he'd heard the word *hero*, he didn't react, but Dom knew he hated the label. It didn't seem to matter to him that people meant it.

Padrick just looked at him. "You're a fucking martyr, Sarge."

"No, I'm a Gear." Marcus leaned into the first empty car in the line and felt around for the key. "Our job is saving civvies. Anyway, I didn't notice any of you jumping aboard, either. *Shit*. Dom, can you hotwire this wreck?"

"Sure thing."

Dom didn't feel so bad right then. The test of any man, his dad had told him, wasn't how he behaved when things were going fine, but how he handled himself when the shit was up to his neck and rising. Marcus passed the Eduardo Santiago test every time. Dom tried to. He felt he had today; they all had.

You're right, Dad. And I miss you so much.

Dom fumbled under the dash and touched wires, and the car rumbled back to life. "Now all we have to do is make some space."

"You say that like it's going to be hard," Padrick said, sliding into the driver's seat.

And Sera was going to be razed to the ground. Every time Dom forgot that, tied up in the physical effort of shunting cars and yelling at drivers who just wouldn't follow the marshaling signals, it came back and slapped him, demanding attention.

No, it couldn't be right. There had to be a mistake, a bluff, some shit even Marcus couldn't guess at.

Dom kept telling himself that right up to the time he saw the first of the convoy trucks rumbling down the shoulder that he'd cleared. This time he'd earned that ride home. He climbed over the tailgate and held out his hand to haul Marcus inside.

VICTOR HOFFMAN'S APARTMENT, EPHYRA, LATER THAT NIGHT.

Margaret never yelled.

Hoffman had often wished she would, because then he would have been able to gauge just how far he'd fallen from grace with her. But perhaps her complete silence was his answer. She stood at her desk in the study, phone wedged between ear and shoulder as she rummaged through the drawers. He stood in the doorway and tried to pick his moment.

"Natalie? Are you still there?" She was talking to her sister. "Damn, it's taken me all day to get you . . . No, I don't care, I know you've got casualties . . . Listen, Nattie . . . *Please*, Nattie, I'm serious, I'm coming down to Corren . . . Yes, I mean it. I'm coming to collect you. Stay at the hospital."

Margaret laid the phone down again. She must have known he was behind her. But she just tidied the case folders on her desk, slipped them into the drawers, and locked them away. It took her a full five seconds to turn around and face him.

"I'll get her on a COG transport," he said, wanting to die of shame. "You don't have to do this."

"Oh, I do. Because I can't trust you any longer."

"I'm sorry." He was; he regretted having to do it, so much that it hurt. "I am so, so sorry."

She made an odd little strangled noise, as if she'd started to laugh and then lost the will to carry it through. "*Sorry?* Fuck you, Victor. Fuck you and all your secret little cabals, holed up in your bunkers while the rest of the world dies."

He'd rarely heard her swear in their entire marriage. He understood why the news had devastated her—she wouldn't have been human if she'd taken it in stride—and he knew this fight was coming. He also knew that even if changing his mind could turn back the clock and make her respect him again, or even despise him a little less, that he'd still nod and say to Prescott that this had to be done.

"Don't go down there, Margaret," he said. "Please. The roads are at a standstill. You won't get back in time, either of you."

"And Nattie won't make it out otherwise. And you *knew.*"

Hoffman could have begged forgiveness, or told her that it was Prescott's decision, or that the best estimate now was that the Locust would reach Jacinto Plateau in ten days, probably sooner, in numbers that the whole army couldn't stop. But there was no point.

"Yes, of course I damn well knew," he snapped. "I've known for a week or more. And what would you have done if I'd told you?"

"Oh, if this is going to be the public-spirited lecture on not spreading panic, Victor, why don't you switch on the goddamn TV and watch the panic *now?*"

"You'd have told Natalie. Then she'd have told her colleagues. She'd have tried to move patients early, and the whole thing would have been a hundred times worse, with numbers of refugees worldwide that we just couldn't handle. And the enemy guessing what was coming, or even *knowing*, and concentrating on Ephyra—because once they take Ephyra, the human race is finished. Do you seriously think I would go along with this if I thought we weren't facing *extinction?*"

Margaret held up her hands to shut him up. "I don't want to hear this bullshit," she said. "The longer I listen and try to believe the man I married might still be inside you, the later I'll be to save someone who actually matters a damn to me."

"So what's it about, Margaret?" She couldn't possibly make

him feel like a bigger pile of shit than he already did. "Me not treating us as special cases who need to be saved when every other bastard has to take their chances, or destroying most of Sera? Spit it out, honey. I don't quite know where the moral outrage is coming from."

"I don't have to justify my outrage to *you*."

She snatched up her jacket and walked straight at him; he thought of just grabbing her and pushing her back, but that only turned the tide of a fight in movies. She wouldn't suddenly see how he'd done a necessary thing, weep for her sister, and fall into his arms. She'd just spit in his face.

It had been a long time since she'd fallen into his arms at all. Hoffman stepped aside and followed her down the hall.

I can get her stopped at a checkpoint and turned around. Or detained. And she'll curse and loathe me, but she won't get killed, and then she can get on with life without me if she wants.

He had a plan, then. She wouldn't get far out of Ephyra anyway, even if all the traffic was heading into town. The intersections were blocked. She wouldn't get off the Jacinto ramp, let alone reach Corren.

Kill it to save it. Kill Sera, and humanity gets to survive. Kill our marriage, and she lives.

Hoffman had traded one catastrophe against another all his army life. "If you want me to explain," he said, "it'll all be clichés. This really is the lesser of two evils. For once, the numbers matter. Because one of them is zero."

"No, you're all murderers," she said. "You must have known that millions wouldn't be able to reach Ephyra. Not in days, maybe not even in weeks."

"And I'll have more deaths on my conscience if we *don't* do this. In ten days, more or less, the grubs will be here. *In this house.* I've got nothing left to stop them, and we all know it."

"Victor—shut up. Just shut up. You *can't* argue this with me. You disgust me. This isn't collateral damage. It's mass murder. And *you kept it from me.* How in the name of God did you think I'd react?"

Hoffman gave up at that point. It wasn't the bigger picture that was pissing her off. Whatever the bleeding hearts said about humanity and its suffering, the only pain they really felt, *could* feel, was for the faces they knew and would miss. Margaret had been lied to—he admitted it—and she wanted to save her sister. That was it. That was the level of distress he could understand.

"Shit, woman, you expected me to blow your brains out if the bastards got here," he said. "And you've never once asked me how I feel when the body bags come back from the front line. And now you give me this shit when you don't have a single fucking option to put in its place."

"I'm going, Victor. I'm taking the car."

"Are you waiting for me to physically stop you? Prove what a loving husband I am?"

Margaret stopped at the door. The hallway was long, High Tyran style with a dado rail on each side, and an overmantel mirror above the console table on the right. She reached for the car keys without looking. For a moment, her fingers tapped around on the polished table, groping for the key ring, but she wouldn't take her eyes off him to look down and locate it.

It told him more about the state she was in than anything she'd said. She was completely terrified, disoriented, unable to cope. But she was Margaret, so she looked totally in control of the situation, except for that few seconds' lapse.

"Would you stop the Hammer strike?" she asked. "Can you?"

He couldn't make matters any worse, and the only lie he had ever told her in twenty years was by omission, keeping the destruction of Sera to himself.

"I can't," he said. "And I wouldn't."

"Fuck you, then," she said, and closed the door behind her.

She didn't even slam it.

Hoffman waited for a few minutes in case she came back, anger deflated, but he knew she wouldn't. She meant what she said about getting her sister out of Corren. Natalie was an emergency doctor; she was always busy, and the chances of her voluntarily evacuating now were slim. Margaret would flash her ID card at checkpoints, use his name to bypass the lines, work her contacts. Hoffman had his uses.

"Shit," he said. "*Shit.*"

There was nothing more he could do tonight except sleep so that he could function tomorrow, so he poured himself a drink, settled down in front of the TV—should he watch the news or not?—and picked up the phone to CIC.

"Control, I need a favor. Pass a message to all VCPs. My wife's gone looking for her sister. I want her stopped and turned back— escorted, arrested, whatever it takes. And tell them to ignore her angry lawyer bullshit. Just get her back into Ephyra."

He hoped it didn't sound flippant. But it was better for everyone to think he was a callous bastard than to hear a man with a Hammer command key break down and sob.

Either way, the marriage would be over. But Ephyra would survive, and so would Margaret.

POMEROY BARRACKS, SOUTH EPHYRA,
REGIMENTAL HQ OF THE 26TH ROYAL TYRAN
INFANTRY, 0500 HOURS, FORTY-SEVEN HOURS
TO HAMMER STRIKES.

"The phones must be screwed," Dom said. "They *have* to be. She wouldn't just ignore it, not when I'm deployed."

He kept dialing home, and Maria kept not answering. In the corridor outside it might as well have been midday. The entire regiment was returning a company at a time, filling the accommodation block with smells of breakfast, soap, and vehicle exhaust. The place hadn't felt this crowded in years.

Marcus stood at the basin, shaving for what seemed like the third time in an hour, putting neat edges on the strip of beard down his chin.

"Overloaded exchange," he said. "Everyone's trying to call everyone else."

"Yeah, I think I worked that out, thanks."

"Dom, it's five o'clock in the fucking morning. She probably took her meds and slept."

"But she doesn't know we've been recalled."

"Okay. Enough." Marcus wiped his face carefully. "We're going to go see her. Come on. I'll talk to the adjutant and beg a ten-hour pass. He owes me."

"Now? We're on standby."

"Just do it, Dom. Then you can get some sleep."

"What's the Hammer strike going to be like? What will we see?"

"If you see it, Dom, you can kiss your ass goodbye."

"Your dad never talks about it, does he?"

"If you're asking if I already knew about this shit, I didn't."

"I never thought you did."

"I'd have told you if I had." Marcus tapped his watch. "Back in ten minutes. Stay put."

Dom tried again to take in the scale of the planned Hammer strike and failed. It was too much to imagine. There was something completely unreal about the way it was being . . . managed. That was the only word for it. A day and a time, a tidy schedule for what was going to be pretty well the end of the world. He had to repeat that a few times in his head and then actually say it aloud before it started to make his stomach knot in the same way it did when he feared the worst for his family.

Marcus reappeared in the doorway and held up a couple of small blue cards—absence permits. "I've got a special way with adjutants."

"How are we getting there?"

"You've seen the traffic. Double time—quick march."

Even for a city so used to war, Ephyra felt on the edge of panic. People were stuck in traffic, waiting in line for besieged hotels— impatiently, Dom noticed—and arguing with law enforcement patrols about where they could and couldn't go. He'd never seen anyone getting mouthy with a cop before, except outside the seedier bars. One guy was suddenly pounced on and hauled away to a nearby patrol car. He looked more shocked than angry.

And none of these people looked like threadbare refugees. It was probably going to be worse at the temporary camps.

"Shit, is that what we're going to end up doing?" Dom asked. "Guarding refugee camps?"

"If Ephyra's all that's left in a couple of days, what else is there for us to do?" Marcus began moving at a steady jog. In combat rig, a Gear could go anywhere and civilians would stand aside for them. Gears had a job to do; it was always urgent. "Going to be hell to manage that kind of influx."

Most milling crowds parted for them—locals, or at least Tyrans. Some didn't. Marcus had to stop and ask them to clear the way, and they seemed pissed off that he expected it. Marcus, always rigidly polite with civvies, had an edge in his voice when he had to repeat himself.

"Where the hell are we supposed to go?" The man who stopped Marcus had an accent Dom couldn't place. "How do we find—"

"Ask the patrol officer, sir. Over there."

They had to be from across the border, not even from other regions of Tyrus, Dom thought. It just wasn't the COG way of doing things. COG citizens—no, *Tyrans*, that was who he meant, that was who he *was*—were disciplined and hardy, stoically accepting necessity. They understood that restrictions were there for a reason. It was the former Indie states, the independent alliance the COG had fought for so many decades, who thought orderly government just crimped their style. They were used to protesting in the streets. Tyrans just sucked it up and made the best of a bad job.

"They're going to get a shock here," Dom said. "This isn't Pelles."

Marcus just moved on through the crowd, leaning slowly against the press of bodies when people didn't get out of his way fast enough—and it worked. He was like a goddamn mounted patrol. Dom had seen horses trained to do that. For some reason, he found it unbearably funny.

"What's the joke?" Marcus said. They were now on a relatively empty backstreet and heading for one of the bridges across the river. "I could—shit, look at *that*."

Dom caught up with him. From the approach to the bridge, he had a grandstand view of the southern side of Ephyra. The cityscape was a single mass of stationary lights stretching to the horizon, each road picked out in vehicle headlights.

"I didn't think there were still that many cars on the road," Dom said.

Marcus shook his head, just a slight movement as if he was talking to himself. "You won't see that again."

It took another fifteen minutes to jog to Dom's home. It was nearly six in the morning, close to sunrise, but lights were on in pretty well every house. Dom imagined families huddled around the TV or radio trying to make sense of it all.

His house was still in darkness. He sprinted the rest of the way, almost dropped his keys in his hurry to unlock the door, and dashed upstairs two at a time.

"Maria? Maria, baby, it's me, are you awake?" He didn't want to sneak up on her and scare her. "We're back at base. I've been trying to call you—"

The bedroom was empty. Their bed hadn't been slept in. He checked each room, but she was gone.

Marcus stood in the hall. "Dom, what's wrong?"

"She's gone. Oh shit—*shit*." The kitchen was tidy, as if she'd cleaned the place up before leaving. He ran back upstairs to check the closets. The suitcases were there, but an overnight bag was missing; he couldn't tell if she'd taken any clothes. "Shit, she's packed and gone. Where the hell would she go?"

Marcus went into the dining room and picked up the phone. "Dom, take it easy. She can't have gone far."

"It's not like we've got any family left. She won't be at my folks' place or hers. Will she?" Dom was really starting to panic now. Maria only went out for a walk every day. She didn't have friends to visit, and if she was out tonight, in this chaos, what did she need to pack for? "Shit, I hope she's not trying to get to Mercy and tend her folks' graves."

Marcus stood with the phone to his ear, looking unmoved except for his rapid blinking. That told Dom the worst. Marcus was worried, too. "Why would she go there?" he asked. "She'd have the sense to stay in Ephyra."

"Marcus, she's not *well*. She does weird shit from time to time. Hell, totally *normal* people do things like that under stress, let alone . . . oh God . . ."

Marcus held up his finger for silence as if someone had answered. "Dad? Dad, it's Marcus. Look, I know it's early, but I need a favor. We're back at Dom's, Maria's not here, and I need to . . . Oh God, really?" Marcus shut his eyes for a moment and blew out a slow breath. Dom's heart was close to hammering its way through his rib cage. "Well, Dom nearly shit himself, so a note would have been good . . . Okay, we're coming over . . . Okay . . . Yeah . . . No, I didn't. See you later."

Marcus slammed down the receiver. Dom could hardly bear to hear what he had to say.

"She's at our place. Panic over."

Dom's legs were shaking. He felt like an idiot. "Shit, man . . ."

"Dad was worried about her hearing the news alone. He sent a car for her and she's been there for a couple of days." Marcus had that tight-lipped look that said he was veering between pissed off and embarrassingly relieved. "Everything's okay. But nobody thought to leave a frigging message. You okay?"

"Yeah." Dom just wanted to see Maria and forget everything outside Ephyra's city limits for a while. "We better get going. It's a long way on foot."

"He's sending transport."

"How the hell is anything going to get to us? You've seen the jams."

"He's Professor Adam Fenix. He can make that kind of shit happen."

And he did.

A COG government car rolled up outside the house, light bar flashing. Dom felt like a complete asshole climbing into it when the rest of the world was going to hell in a handbasket. One of the neighbors watched from her doorstep, maybe thinking he had some urgent official business, or he was being arrested, or something. She just nodded at him as the vehicle roared off.

"So you turn down a Raven ride home, but you're okay with your old man diverting a car for me."

"I never said I was consistent."

"I owe you, man."

"Shit. You know you don't."

"And I owe your dad." Dom didn't feel that the few minutes of utter pants-pissing fear for Maria mattered now. Marcus's father cared enough to look after her when he knew she would be worried out of her mind. "He's always been good to us."

Marcus didn't comment. The driver broke every traffic regulation in the book, mounting sidewalks and ignoring one-way signs, to get to East Barricade. He didn't say a word, either. Dom could see the guy thinking that he had some VIP's son on board, wasting his time, and what an easy life someone with a name like Fenix would have.

Not true, buddy.

The car rolled through the big main gates of the Fenix estate and past formal gardens, greenhouses, and trees, scattering gravel along the drive. The house was a mansion. It wasn't a house at all as far as Dom was concerned, more an antique-filled and wood-paneled museum of a place that had scared him as a kid. He'd always been afraid of breaking something priceless when he visited. It was lavish, imposing, and breathed money; it was also cold and empty. To understand Marcus, you had to see that house.

Adam Fenix was already standing in the doorway. He managed a smile for Dom, but worry was written all over his face.

"How did it go?" he asked. "Are you okay?"

"Bayonet broke again," Marcus said casually. "We need something better to get through grub hide. Maybe a powered saw of some kind."

"I'll have a think about that." Professor Fenix turned to Dom and shook his hand vigorously. "I'm sorry I worried you, Dom. I've been a little preoccupied lately."

Preoccupied. Poor guy; the Hammer of Dawn was his project, and now he'd always be known as the man who made it possible to wipe out a world. Inside, the house opened up into an echoing marble hall with a film-set staircase and corridors leading off on all sides. Maria, sitting in the kitchen at a table big enough for a banquet, looked tired. The housekeeper was making breakfast.

"Dom, I'm sorry . . ."

"Hey, doesn't matter, baby." He leaned over her chair from behind and hugged her as hard as he dared. *How would I cope without her? What would my life be worth if she left?* "You okay? I tried to get you. I wanted you to know we were coming home."

"Isn't it *lovely* here? It's like living in an art gallery."

Somehow, as all hell broke out beyond Ephyra, the high walls of the Fenix estate shut out the real world, and they ate breakfast. A goddamn breakfast with all the trimmings, even small talk, while Sera counted down to its own destruction.

And the kindly, rather awkward man pouring more coffee for Maria had to help make it happen.

Dom gave up trying to grasp it all and settled for holding Maria's hand so tightly that she had to ask him to let go so she could use her knife and fork.

"Come on, Marcus." Professor Fenix pushed back his chair and beckoned to Marcus to follow. "Got something to show you."

Carlos had said that the Fenixes never fought like regular families did. It wasn't the way that old money behaved. They just looked tense, or raised their eyebrows, or quietly disapproved with a tilt of the head; sometimes they really lost it and expressed grave disappointment. It was no wonder they couldn't show enough affection. Bottling up all that stuff became a habit, a locked door that nothing could breach, not even the good things that needed saying and doing. Dom sat with his arm around Maria, listening to whispered voices.

"It's such a shame," Maria said, looking slightly past Dom as if she was talking to herself. "Does Marcus realize how much his dad loves him?"

If Marcus did, Dom thought, he would never say. After a while,

Dom wandered out into the hall to look for them—it was a house you could get lost in, a house where you could hide and shut yourself away from the world—and realized they were sitting on the main stairs, talking.

Dom could hear them. He shouldn't have stopped to listen, but he did.

"I didn't take this decision lightly."

"I know, Dad."

"We just ran out of time. I've tried every damn way to find . . . alternatives, but it's all that's left now."

"Dad, I'm out there. I see it. If we don't do it, *nobody's* going to survive."

"Forgive me."

"Nothing to forgive."

"Oh, there's a lot."

Marcus didn't reply for a while.

"Do what you have to do," he said at last. "That's the best any of us can manage."

Dom felt terrible for Marcus, but then he often did. He found himself thinking that if Adam Fenix was Eduardo Santiago, he would have done this or said that, right from the heart with no holds barred, but that would have all been too much for Marcus. Whatever he felt—it was there, all right, but you had to look hard to spot it. This wasn't the kind of family where people used the word *love* every day. It was probably wrenched out of them only on their deathbeds, if at all.

Dom looked at his watch. They'd need to get back to HQ soon. Whatever was coming, there would be an aftershock of some kind to deal with. He crept back to the kitchen and sat down to rest his forehead against Maria's. For a minute or so he thought they were savoring a quiet and intimate moment, but then he moved a little and could see she was somewhere else entirely, eyes focused on something he couldn't see.

"You okay, baby?" he said.

She took a few moments to drift back. "I need to go for a walk."

"Not today. It's a madhouse out there."

"I have to. I can't miss a day."

"I think the exercise can wait awhile."

"No, I have to. I have to go look."

Dom couldn't shrug that off as misunderstanding her. "Look at what?"

"If I don't keep looking, I'll never find them."

He braced himself for an answer he knew he wasn't ready to hear. "Who, baby?"

"Bennie and Sylvie. I know I saw them. Just once, but they're out there, and they'll be so scared—I have to go find them."

Oh God. He couldn't say it. He couldn't. *They're gone, baby. They're dead.*

"It'll be okay." *Shit.* "It can wait a little."

He held her more tightly. Some days she seemed to go to places in her mind where he couldn't follow, however hard he tried. Now he knew exactly where she went, in every sense of the word.

We stick together however hard it gets. That's the marriage vow. We don't quit when it hurts.

He'd been crazy about her since he was eleven years old. He couldn't imagine life without her. She *was* his life. He had to make sure she never forgot that.

"Hey, baby," he said. "I haven't told you I love you today, have I?"

CHAPTER 10

I can't tell you exactly how many citizens we have here, sir, or who they are, because I don't have a complete census of names yet. So I can't even tell you how many Stranded have slipped in between evacuating Jacinto and today. We have a porous border, and a lot of people who look pretty rough to begin with.

(ROYSTON SHARLE, HEAD OF EMERGENCY MANAGEMENT, BRIEFING CHAIRMAN PRESCOTT.)

KR-80, EN ROUTE FOR VECTES NAVAL BASE, SEVEN WEEKS AFTER LEAVING JACINTO.

"I never thought I'd envy men." Bernie dragged herself through the cargo compartment hatch to squeeze between Baird and Marcus. Anya sat on the bench opposite, jammed between Cole and Dom. It was more diplomatic seating in a crowded Raven than cramming her up against Marcus. "This crate's sanitary arrangements leave a lot to be desired for us girls. I expected better with Gettner driving."

Cole guffawed and deafened everyone. He was a lot louder via a radio earpiece. "All I want to know is why ladies spend so damn long in the bathroom."

"Sweetheart, six hours in the air is a long time." She leaned forward and patted his knee. "Never take the traveling convenience of a dick for granted. If we had one, Baird and I certainly wouldn't—would we, Blondie?"

Baird, arms folded tight across his chest, had taken refuge behind a fresh pair of goggles.

"Don't mind Mataki, ma'am," he said to Anya. "She's old. She rambles."

Bernie didn't actually expect any more than a bucket in a Raven, but she sorely needed to see some levity right then. Cole could always be relied upon to join in and steamroller over everyone's doubts. From time to time, she caught him staring at her, frowning a little, and his unspoken question said that he knew she was agitated but wasn't sure why.

He was a perceptive lad. He'd put two and two together sooner or later. She'd *wanted* to tell him. Shit, she hadn't even told Hoffman, and if there was anyone she felt she could confide in, it was him.

Yes, I'd rather deal with grubs than Stranded now. At least what you see is what you get. They never pretend to be human.

Dom jerked his head at Cole to to get his attention. "Not sick yet? You got it corked or something?"

"I'm picking my moment, baby."

Gettner's voice cut in on the circuit. "Not in my frigging bird you don't, Private. Bag it, then dump it, okay?"

"See, your position as Queen Ratbag's already been filled, Granny," Baird muttered.

Gettner boomed again. "And I heard *that*, too, Corporal Baird. You want a nice refreshing dip with the sonar buoy?"

Bernie took it all as general relief and the gradual return of optimism. Mel Sorotki's Raven was following about a hundred meters behind, carrying the underslung 'Dill and enough supplies to keep the recon party going if they decided it was safe for the fleet to start shipping in refugees. It felt like life was moving on for the first time in years.

"You ever been to Vectes, Bernie?" Dom asked.

"No, too far for most Stranded, and big seas. Easier pickings on the smaller islands. Plus the biohaz marker buoys didn't do much for its tourist trade."

"You never thought of yourself as Stranded?"

"Shit, no." Bernie wondered if Dom would ever really understand how much the idea appalled her. Baird seemed to, at least. "I was just taking longer than expected to get back to base."

She sometimes wondered if Dom believed her, but it was hard for anyone on the mainland to understand just how damn big and empty the world was, and how tough it was to get anywhere when there was nobody else around.

"I don't know how you stood being on your own for that long," he said.

"I left Galangi nine years after E-Day. We didn't even know who else had survived the Hammer strikes until then, remember." God, was it really that long? Had Mick been dead nine years? Grief did lose its sharp edges eventually, for her at least. Maybe Dom's never did. "So that's actually five years completely on my own, roughly . . . the rest was just being alone among people I knew."

I could tell them. I could tell them all right now. I could get it over with, explain what happened, what I did, why I did it. Cole wouldn't blame me. Anya and Baird wouldn't. Dom? Not sure. But Marcus . . . no, he's got his rules. He'd think I was an animal.

Marcus—eyes shut, arms folded across his chest—was definitely *not* asleep. The eye movement under his lids was all wrong, and she was jammed so close to him that she could feel the tension in his arms, as if he'd braced himself so that he didn't lean on her. She'd been cooped up in transports often enough to know that dead-weight sensation when the Gear in the next seat finally nodded off and slumped against her.

"Where did you commandeer a boat?" he asked, eyes still shut.

"New Fortitude." No, Marcus never forgot a damn thing anyone told him. "I got fed up waiting for the ferry."

"For someone who's afraid of water, you don't let it hold you back."

From anyone else, that might have been sarcasm, or even

praise. From Marcus, though, it was a question. She just didn't feel up to answering it in front of everyone when they had nowhere to run to avoid it.

"Marcus, you *know* I hated amphibious training," she said. "I persuaded a trawler to drop me off on the mainland. It's not like I sailed around Sera single-handed on a bloody raft. Well, not quite."

Baird seemed to find that funny. "You hijacked a trawler? Classy. That's so you. There'd have to be dead edible things involved."

"Hey, we can't laugh at them nautical types for their dumb-ass uniforms any more." Cole held up a warning forefinger, diverting the others' attention. Yes, he knew something was troubling her. "The navy's drivin'. We got to *depend* on them now. Specially if we end up livin' on an *island*."

"Okay, day-trippers." Gettner cut in on the radio. "Unless there's been some unfortunate seismic activity on a Jacinto scale, we'll be at your destination in thirty minutes. Met records say it's windy most days."

"Nice bracing breeze." Marcus gave Bernie a look that said he'd finally picked up on her apprehension, too. "I'll man the gun. Last disused COG base we visited had resident monsters."

Anya, staring out the Raven's door, looked swamped by her body armor. She was too slight for the standard-issue plates, so she'd opted to try partial armor on the upper body. Plates took some getting used to. Anya wanted to start.

Bernie still wondered if she'd done the right thing by encouraging her wish to be more frontline. A woman needed to be able to look after herself in a world that was now a lot more uncertain for wholly different reasons, but Bernie wondered if she was just feeding Anya's need to live up to the larger-than-life image of Major Helena Stroud. Anya was surrounded by conspicuous valor wherever she turned: her mother, Marcus, Dom, Carlos, and even Hoffman all had received the Embry Star. It was in danger of becoming her benchmark, a sign that she was somehow lacking.

"If there's anyone on Vectes, then they probably haven't seen COG personnel in fifteen years," Anya said. "That's going to be interesting."

"If that biohaz stuff got out of hand, they'll have two heads. Shit, man, you saw those things we found at New Hope, whatever the hell *they* were." Baird eased his elbow out of Bernie's side and checked his Lancer. "Maybe we'll find Indie troops there who don't even know the Pendulum Wars are over."

"I don't care if we've got pirates coming out the storm drains," Dom said. "Smell that air."

Bernie could. It was the kind of scent that they just didn't get on the mainland, the promise of cleaner skies. Vectes loomed on the haze of the horizon.

Marcus squeezed through into the forward section and settled down at the port-side gun. "Okay, Major, ready when you are."

Gettner took the Raven in a cautious loop around the island. It was a seventy-kilometer crater, a long-dead volcano, and the coast was a hoop of granite cliffs that cradled fertile lowland in the bowl. On a chart, that was just data and contour lines. To the eye, it was another thing entirely.

Despite the warning signs and hazard buoys, the solid buildings of the naval base looked almost welcoming, and mostly intact; the old navy certainly built things to last. The metal jetty structures had seen better days, and some of the dock basins housed rusting, half-submerged wrecks as well as solid-looking vessels in dry dock, but there seemed to be so little overgrowth that Bernie wouldn't have been surprised to see lines of naval ratings drilling on the parade ground.

"Good start," Gettner said. "Sorotki, we're heading inland now. But I think we've got our operating base identified."

Vectes now didn't look at all like the frayed oval on the naval charts. The grid said it was around five thousand square kilometers, and at this height, Bernie could no longer see the sea. She could have been anywhere on the mainland continent in the pre-Locust days. There was open country, forest, fields—yes, fields with clear boundaries, obviously maintained—and a river. In the distance, she could see granite highlands off to the west. It all looked solid and permanent, even comfortable, not a windswept rock in the middle of an ocean at all.

"Shit, rivers?" Cole pointed at the broad ribbon of water snaking beneath. "Man, this is going to be *nice*. I might take up fishing."

This place could support Jacinto's remnant just fine, Bernie decided. It was bigger than Galangi, and that was pretty comfortable. They could start planting crops right away in this climate; people would now see some end in sight for minimum rations. The higher-minded civvies might have been bleating about organizing city governance and councilmen, but average humans didn't give a shit about that. They wanted to eat and stay warm, and not get killed by grubs. It wasn't much to ask at the end of a war.

"Well, maybe we won't need to lynch Prescott after all," she said. "Good call, Chairman."

"Up ahead," said Baird.

"What?"

"I said, look up ahead."

Gettner cut in. "Yeah, I see it. House."

"They'd have needed living quarters here," Anya said, sticking to the past tense, when all Bernie could see now was an island where someone was still maintaining things. "Not just for the naval personnel, either—they'd have needed to be self-sufficient for long periods because resupply wouldn't have been easy."

"You mean like that?" Marcus said. He was staring down the sights of the door gun. "Nice tidy furrows."

Gettner banked the Raven. Fields didn't plow themselves, and as they passed over, a man in overalls straightened up from a power tiller, watched the Raven for a few seconds, and then began jogging in the direction of the house.

"Confirmed, still inhabited," Gettner said. "So, you want to say hi, Lieutenant, or do a covert recon, seeing as they now know we're here?"

Anya straightened up in her seat. Gettner was taking her frontline familiarization seriously, too. Bernie waited.

Come on, Anya. You make life-or-death calls every day. It's no different on the ground, except that you're in the line of fire, too.

"Look for some obvious center of population," Anya said, sounding more confident. "If we go covert now, it could look hostile. Try raising them on the radio. They probably don't get too many visitors."

That's our Anya. Good going, kid.

Anya was in her thirties, but she would always be Major Stroud's kid. Bernie didn't see that as a bad thing. Gettner seemed to cut her a hell of a lot more slack than normal, too. She was even talking her through the procedure, and doing an unusually diplomatic job of it for a woman who could etch glass with her insults.

"Better not buzz their quaint homesteads." Gettner took the Raven higher. "Nothing like low-flying gunships to upset the natives."

The occasional single-story home below became ones and twos, still small scattered farmhouses, but then the horizon resolved into something more familiar—a man-made landscape of roofs. It was nothing like Jacinto, no towers or domes or skyscrapers, but it was recognizably a village. The Raven climbed higher.

"Fenix, what are you seeing down there?" Gettner asked.

"No anti-air batteries, but watch out for assholes with rifles."

"Try the more strategic analysis, Sergeant."

"Low technology level, judging by the roads. Low-rise buildings. Sweep the whole area and I'll give you a better estimate."

"Okay, let's see if anyone's home." Gettner started repeating the radio contact litany. "This is COG KR-Eight-Zero, inbound from Port Farrall, calling Vectes ATC. This is COG KR-Eight-Zero, calling Vectes ATC . . ."

Cole peered below. It was fascinating to watch him forget to feel sick when he had something that completely distracted him. "Cows! When did you last see a cow in a field?"

"Steak." Baird nodded to himself, evidently satisfied. "Cream. I'm in."

"*Farmers,*" Bernie said pointedly. She couldn't imagine them being keen to share this with a city-load of strangers. "If I had a place like this, living on what I could grow and raise, and interlopers showed up, I'd need some serious smoothing over."

"We'll be suitably nonthreatening," Anya said.

"Well, at least we can bang out fast if it all goes wrong."

"How many other human enclaves are there going to be in the rest of Sera, do you think? Not just Stranded." Anya seemed to think of the Stranded as being voluntary outcasts, too, then. "People who couldn't relocate."

"There'll always be some."

And they'd all be small, all isolated, all running by their own rules. Bernie was prepared to hope that some would have retained a semblance of civilization, but so far she hadn't seen much to encourage her.

"No radio response," Gettner said. "Maybe they don't have the tech."

Baird shrugged. "Maybe they're pretending they're not in."

This didn't look like any Stranded settlement Bernie had ever passed through. Maybe the navy had never really left. Life in uniform meant accepting that you'd never be told the full story, even in the senior ranks, but Hoffman vented his frustration off duty with more foul language than Bernie had ever heard him use even in his NCO days. All she had to do was nod when he paused for breath. It seemed to do him some good.

Poor Vic. You used to be so much happier.

That was nearly forty years ago. A lot of shit had slid down the sewer since then.

What a nice, tidy little place . . .

The settlement beneath them now looked like a fishing port. Small boats bobbed inside a breakwater, riding a noticeable swell even in the sheltered harbor. The buildings nearest the shore were older and more haphazard, but the ones further back looked more carefully planned, newer, painted with chalk wash, more . . . civilized. People were visible—looking up, hands shielding their eyes against the sun, some running back toward the town, some with kids.

Stranded? Governance by the most violent, for the most violent. Can't tell until you get down there.

"I'm setting down on that cliff," Gettner said. There was a promontory north of the inlet, an inviting expanse of lush green turf. "High ground, good visibility, unimpeded takeoff. Okay, boys and girls, try not to found a cargo cult, will you? But I doubt they'll think you're visiting gods."

"Ma'am," Cole said, "just wait till they see my best moves."

Bernie caught a glimpse of more people moving onto the shoreline. The town was turning out to watch the show. The Raven descended, flattening a circle of short grass with its downdraft, then settled on its wheels.

"I'll go on ahead." Marcus jumped out. "Delta—stay back, wedge contact formation, and *low-key.* Bernie, Anya—on me. Women can defuse situations. You look less threatening. Usually."

They walked slowly down the slight incline, weapons conspicuously slung and hands well clear, but Bernie could imagine what the locals would notice first—not a gray-haired old woman and a slight blond girl, or the familiar and welcome uniform of a protection force, but a big, surly, scarred, heavily armed man who'd just jumped out of a helicopter gunship.

Gears would scare the shit out of anyone, whether their Lancers were aimed or not. They were physically incapable of looking like they'd dropped by to have a nice chat.

Had the locals even seen a chainsaw bayonet before? Not if they'd been cut off since E-Day. Somehow it looked a whole lot more menacing than the old Lancer she'd been used to.

A path of small rocks and pebbles crushed into the soil led down to the shorefront buildings. Ahead, two men with shotguns, backed up by a crowd of about thirty, had formed a roadblock of bodies.

"Easy, Delta," Marcus said. "If we're moving in, might as well show what good neighbors we can be."

That was the way to do it. Even though they'd just stepped out of a long, dehumanizing war, Gears could snap straight back into being civilized, disciplined, law-abiding—everything the COG stood for, everything Bernie had come back to find again. She'd been like that once, and then—

Crack.

The shot was either very badly aimed or *meant* to go over Marcus's head.

VECTES SHOREFRONT.

"Hold your fire—Delta, *stand down!*"

As soon as the first shot cracked and the insect whine of a round passed over their heads, Dom knew that diplomacy here was going to be basic. His automatic reaction to coming under fire was to drop down and return it. It was hard to override something that had been so hard-drilled in him for nearly twenty years that it was now instinct.

"Delta, maybe you should withdraw." Gettner's voice didn't sound agitated, but Dom could understand why a pilot sitting in a Raven with extra fuel tanks was a little nervous around weapons discharged by strangers. "Barber's covering you."

"Stand by, Major," Marcus said. "They just don't know how lovable we are yet."

Baird muttered something under his breath and pulled his goggles over his eyes. Dom took a few cautious steps forward so he could see better. Marcus seemed to put an awful lot of faith in psychology, but all Dom could think was that even a Stranded asshole who couldn't shoot straight was capable of a head shot at that range, and Marcus never wore a helmet. That do-rag wasn't going to save him.

Dom had to strain to hear what the civvies were saying, but everyone else was loud and clear on the radio.

"Hey, I'm not shooting, citizen," Marcus said.

The man out front—forty-five, fifty, sandy hair—still had his shotgun leveled. "Who the hell are you?"

"Sergeant Marcus Fenix, Coalition of Ordered Governments. Why don't we put down the weapons and talk?"

"All kinds of vermin can get hold of COG armor these days. Prove who you are."

He definitely had Marcus there. A COG-tag wouldn't prove a thing. The crowd was getting bigger.

"If I give you my earpiece," Marcus said carefully, "I can probably get Chairman Prescott himself to talk to you."

That usually didn't cut much ice with Stranded. Dom prepared to open fire if anyone's finger so much as moved on the trigger again, and waited for the frozen pause to turn into the usual abuse about fascist assholes. But the guy with the shotgun seemed taken aback.

"Damn, after all these years . . ."

"I'm *Marcus*." Yeah, he had this crowd control thing down pat. No ranks now, just *people*. "And this is Anya Stroud, and Bernadette Mataki. You want to catch up on the news?"

The guy lowered his shotgun, although the other man just angled his down forty-five degrees.

"Gavriel," he said. "Lewis Gavriel. Head of maintenance at the naval base. Been here since before the COG decommissioned it. More than twenty years."

Marcus held out his hand for shaking. It always surprised Dom that he could switch back instantly to the well-mannered heir to a big estate, who knew the right titles to call people and how to read a wine list.

"Nice place you got here," Marcus said. "We used to call it Toxin Town."

"And we knew how to keep the lids sealed." Gavriel motioned to the other guy to lower his weapon. "That's all gone now. Are you planning to bring the rest of your men?"

Marcus turned to wave the squad forward. Baird trotted down the slope, but Marcus held out his arm to halt him.

"Goggles off." He only had to give Baird the two-second ice-cold stare these days to get him to do as he was told. "Easier to communicate when the other guy can see your eyes."

Well, it always worked for Marcus. Baird parked his goggles on his head again without a word.

Gettner's voice filled Dom's earpiece. "We'll sit this out—call if you run into problems. Sorotki and Mitchell are going to prep the 'Dill."

Dom took the eye contact thing seriously. The growing crowd was made up of all kinds of healthy-looking people, including a lot of kids. Many people here — maybe most — hadn't seen a Gear in full rig before, that was clear. One small boy, seven or eight, trotted alongside Dom, staring at his boots. They seem to fascinate the kid more than the Lancer.

"Why d'you need those big boots?" the kid asked.

Dom missed being a dad. He hadn't been a dad often enough, not when he added up all the days he'd actually been home with his kids. "To stomp big grubs."

"I never seen one."

"You keep it that way. You wouldn't like 'em."

A man's voice from behind him made him look over his shoulder.

"Hey, don't I know you?" The guy was talking to Cole, keeping pace and craning his neck to look him in the eye. "Yeah, you're Augustus Cole! Damn it, you're the Cole Train! What are *you* doing in uniform?"

Shit, have they been totally cut off from the war? How much are we going to have to tell them?

Cole chuckled. "Got to spread the pain to a different game, baby."

"I saw you play in the final for the Eagles. The last season before you joined the Cougars. Man, you were *good.*"

"I *know*," Cole said, grinning. "But that was just trainin' for the really *big* game, know what I mean? Hey, you guys play thrashball here? Want a game? I promise I'll be gentle."

By the time the weird procession reached the center of the town, Cole had fallen back a long way, surrounded by people who remembered him when he was a thrashball star, signing autographs. Dom had almost forgotten that world existed. It must have been strange for Cole, too; he looked happy enough — he almost always did — but it had to feel weird to be reminded of the life he once had.

Bernie, standing off to one side, watched the crowd with an expression that wasn't curiosity or wonder but suspicion. She was shadowing Anya, close enough to be a bodyguard. She was also trying to keep an eye on Cole, and she couldn't do both.

Shit, she really didn't trust anyone who wasn't a Gear. But this place could have been a small town in southern Tyrus decades ago, and the people in it didn't seem like Stranded. It felt more like a COG outpost that had been waiting for the government to finally show up and tell them what was going on.

Dom scanned each street and checked each roofline as he passed, more out of habit ground in by urban patrols than fear. That was when he saw it: a frayed and much-repaired banner fluttering from a polished brass pole, the white cog-shaped symbol still clear on a black background that had faded to charcoal gray.

Hell, that was *exactly* what this place was. Not an abandoned site colonized by passing Stranded, but a community that was still part of the Coalition of Ordered Governments.

It was probably going to take a while for Bernie to realize that.

"Where are we, anyway?" Dom asked. "Does this place have a name?"

Baird nodded silently in the direction of a painted sign on a nearby wall. It read PELRUAN TOWN HALL.

Dom was sure that was where they were heading, but Gavriel went into what looked like the local bar instead. He seemed to be pretty friendly, warning shots aside. Whether he'd still be so sociable when he heard what Marcus had to say was another matter. He stopped everyone at the door, including the guy who was reluctant to lower his weapon.

"Come on, Will, you can see who they are." Gavriel sounded placatory. "We don't need protection from our own people."

"Hey, Dom, company man," Baird whispered. "We lucked out. *Finally.*"

"Check out the banner, Baird. It's home."

Home turf or not, it was pretty hard to sit around in a deserted bar looking casual in armor. Dom tried. He shook hands the way his father had always insisted—just hard enough to make an honest impression, not break anything—and watched Marcus and Anya sit down opposite Gavriel at a small table. Dom felt a vague and nagging sense of guilt that he couldn't place. He was one big tangled ball of guilt now, and working out the particular thing that triggered it each time was getting harder.

"*Fenix,*" Gavriel said, still on the small talk. "I don't suppose you're related to Adam Fenix, are you? He came here a few times. Always a big VIP visit when he showed up."

"My father." Marcus's jaw muscles twitched. "And he died a few years ago."

"Oh . . . I'm sorry."

Anya cut in. She could always time it right. "How long since you had news of the mainland, Lewis? You know about the Locust."

Shit, if they don't . . .

"We had long-range comms until the Hammer strike. After that, we lost day-to-day contact, but we know that it's bad out there. We hear things occasionally."

"But you've survived okay since then."

"We've always had to be a self-sufficient community. The town was here for the naval base—mutual dependence. The town might as well *be* the base."

"Couldn't you get to Ephyra? You heard about the recall."

"Yes, but how could you relocate a town in the middle of the ocean in three days, or even three months? And I thought the government would need to reactivate the base sooner or later, so . . . well, my team decided that if the locals stayed, we *all* stayed. Then, as time went on, we'd get short-range radio contact from passing boats, or an island, or the occasional refugee would show up, and we pieced the news together."

"Did the government realize you were still out here?" Marcus asked.

"No idea. Obviously, we didn't get a Hammer strike, but whether anyone realized we hadn't evacuated . . ." Gavriel changed tack. Dom felt pissed off on his behalf. "The Locust are destroying everything, aren't they? Well, they haven't reached *us* yet. Is that why you're here? Is the COG starting up the biochem programs again?"

Anya was good at breaking awkward news. Marcus seemed to have taken an invisible step back, arms folded, to let her tackle it.

"The war's all but over," she said. "We finally wiped them out. Most of them, anyway. We still get stragglers, and that's a problem, but we need to consolidate what we have left before we deal with that once and for all."

Gavriel's lips parted for a moment as if he had a million questions and they were all jamming the exit trying to get out.

"It's . . . pretty damn strange to know there's been something terrible going on for so long, and we've known next to nothing about it. Except from the Stranded." He didn't sound as if he was about to celebrate. Dom supposed that it was all just too weird, sudden, and disorienting for anyone to take in. "So what happens now?"

"Lewis, everything's gone. Even Ephyra."

He blinked a few times. "What do you mean, *gone?*"

"We even had to destroy Jacinto to stop the Locust. We flooded the whole city to drown them in their tunnels." Anya's shoulders rose a little, as if she'd taken a deep breath to blurt it out all in one go. "That was the last place we held, so we had to evacuate the survivors to Port Farrall—and that's been derelict for years. The majority of the human race is now in a single refugee camp. At least ninety-nine percent of the population of Sera died in the years after E-Day."

Gavriel seemed like a calm sort of guy. Dom thought that was probably an essential quality for a man whose job once had been to look after some of the most lethal weapons in the COG. But there was *calm* quiet and there was *paralyzed by shock* quiet, and this was the latter variety.

"Oh . . . my God . . ."

Anya nodded, as if she was reassured that he'd started to understand just how serious the crisis was. "We have to rebuild Sera from scratch. We're starting over with the few we saved."

Shit, the scale of destruction was too much even for most Gears to grasp. How could Dom expect people like this to take in a fifteen-year war, with no TV or radio from Jacinto, just occasional Stranded passing through? Even Bernie said she hadn't ventured this far.

Dom could hear everyone's breath, each tense swallow. That was how quiet things were right then.

"I suppose you want us to come back, then," Gavriel said at last. "I can see why. Some won't want to go, I can tell you that now, but . . . well, this is desperate." He shrugged. "I rather like it here."

Here it comes.

Oh boy, this is going to sting . . .

"Lewis." Anya leaned in a little and put her hand on top of his. Only Anya could have done that right then. She was just the person to tell you the very worst and make it hurt less, because she had that calming CIC voice honed by years of talking Gears through tight situations. "Nobody's asking you to leave. The mainland's going to be no place for *anyone* for a while. We want to bring what's left of Jacinto here before we lose everybody."

Gavriel definitely wasn't taking it in now. Dom could see that he wasn't focusing on Anya, and his lips kept moving as if he was trying to spit out an insect he'd inhaled.

But he pulled himself back on track. "Sorry . . . how can we . . . how can we feed a *city*? I mean . . . this is *thousands* of people we're talking about, isn't it? We're a small community. About three thousand here, and then there's the other settlement, anywhere up to a thousand Stranded. We avoid them for the most part."

There was a definite dividing line, then, just like Baird's: regular humans and Stranded.

"We've got our own supplies," Anya said. *Well, not quite, but some.* But Dom understood why she said that. The locals would be worried that the newcomers were going to leave them starving. "It was a managed evacuation. If we can set down here, we can rebuild our own camp. Look, you know the Vectes base better than anyone. Is it habitable? Can we make use of it?"

"Mothballed," he said. "Hydroelectric power, run-of-river. One of the reasons this site was chosen was sustainability. We had to be able to keep going if the worst happened . . . well, that definitely came to pass, didn't it?"

"That sounds like a plan."

"I'm only the mayor here," Gavriel said. "I have to put it to the vote."

Marcus just gave her a slow, careful look. Dom wasn't sure if she saw it, or if she was even meant to, but she paused for a moment.

"I don't want to overstate the case," she said. "But Vectes can save humankind. *You* can save it. We have nowhere else to go."

Gavriel licked his lips for a moment, staring at the table, then nodded, but Dom knew damn well that he didn't know what he was nodding about. He glanced sideways to catch Bernie staring at her clasped hands.

"I feel very bad not offering you some refreshment," he said. "Would you . . . ?"

"You're very kind." Marcus had taken over again. He had something on his mind. "I'd like to go check out the naval base first. You probably need to do some explaining to your people in the meantime."

"You'll need Will to show you around, then."

"We've got the plans," Marcus said. He seemed in a real rush to get out. "We just need to get the feel of the place. Any operational defenses?"

"They've been dismantled, but they could be restored."

"And how much trouble are the Stranded?"

"Sporadic raids. I'm armed for a reason. People have been killed here. The Stranded know the deal—if they set foot in the town, we shoot on sight now. They haven't been around for a while."

"Understood," Bernie murmured.

Dom kept right behind Marcus all the way back to the Ravens, doing his best to look reassuring, the kind of Gear who had come to make things better. Cole was glad-handing enough for the whole COG. He was turning out to be quite a distraction, and that was a big help right then. Marcus was pissed off about something, and that didn't help him look more friendly. The civvies stared. No, they'd never seen Gears quite like this before.

But then they hadn't seen grubs, either. That would have made everything a lot clearer for them.

The 'Dill was now parked between the two Ravens while the flight crews lounged on the grass, helmets by their sides, chewing ration bars like they were on a picnic.

"Okay, it's Vectes base," Marcus grunted. "Who's driving?"

"Why, yes, I'd be *delighted* to transport you, Sergeant Fenix." Sorotki got to his feet and did a curtsey. He seemed to be enjoying himself. "Your ill-articulated wish is my command."

Marcus didn't react. "Thanks, Lieutenant."

He turned away to stare out to sea while they waited for Will to show up. Dom saw Bernie roll her head slightly as if she'd resigned herself to doing something, then start the slow stroll toward Marcus to talk to him. Dom decided that was his job. He shook his head at Bernie to divert her and moved in.

"Hey, Marcus, what's the problem?"

Marcus didn't turn around. "No problem."

"Bullshit."

"I said no problem."

"And I said—bullshit."

Marcus did his slow head turn. "You want to know."

"Yeah."

"Okay, the COG's going to roll in here and take over this island. We ought to spell that out, because there's sweet fuck-all the guy can do about it anyway. But instead, we start with a lie—by omission, but that's as bad. Poor reward for a loyal COG servant who stayed at his post waiting for orders for *fifteen frigging years*, and because he has, we can ship in refugees a little easier."

"Hey, Marcus, I'd have done the same, okay? Get them used to the idea gradually, make them think it was their own." Dom put the people he knew and loved first, and wasn't ashamed of that. But Marcus worried and sacrificed just as much for the stranger, too, and sometimes you just couldn't do both at once. You had to choose. "Kinder than walking right in and saying, 'Thanks for your service, asshole. Now beat it.' Right?"

It wasn't like the islanders could have caught the next boat back to Ephyra anyway. Dom didn't see staying put as an heroic last stand on a burning deck, up to their asses in grubs. They'd just been marooned in a pretty safe place.

Marcus stared at him for a few long seconds, then nodded. But Dom could see how a guy who wouldn't abandon his post on doomsday would really touch a nerve with Marcus.

"Baird—stay here in case anyone gets too interested in the other Raven." Marcus turned back to the squad as if nothing had happened. "Rest of you—we check every facility there ourselves. If Will can't open a door, we blow it. I don't want to find any more surprises in decommissioned COG facilities."

"Yeah, even Hoffman didn't know about that last place," Cole said. "Man, was he pissed. He ain't good at hiding it, either."

Dom wondered if Marcus's suspicion was actually a dread of finding more of his dad's activities, not fear of turning up more secret shit. They'd found some weird research stuff in the last COG outpost, but the recordings of his father's voice in the Locust stronghold had really rattled Marcus. He hated secrets. That was clear.

Will Berenz arrived clutching an old leather briefcase so stuffed with papers and plans that he couldn't close it properly. "This is going to take some time," he said, holding up the case. "This is everything you need to know about VNB. I don't suppose they even use the call sign anymore, do they?"

"Everything?" Marcus said.

"Yes."

"I want to know all that chemical and biological stuff really is *gone.*"

"Okay. I can understand that."

It was a silent ride to Vectes base. Marcus did his usual avoidance maneuver: eyes closed, arms folded, don't-interrupt-me frown. Even after twenty-odd years, close as real brothers, there were still parts of him that Dom couldn't fathom. Marcus could go through a two-day firefight and not turn a hair. But little things, little *dumb* things, made him fume. It was almost always about not being told everything.

His father had lied to him about a stack of things, like his mother's disappearance, and probably for the kindest reasons, but Marcus didn't seem to think so. Maybe hearing Adam Fenix's voice on those damn grub computers, or that Locust bitch taunting him about his dad *speaking highly* of him—and none of the squad was going to mention *that* to Marcus again—had dredged it all up.

Marcus wasn't like his father in so many ways.

When push came to shove, Adam Fenix was prepared to kill a world to save at least some of it. His son, Dom suspected, might not have been.

VECTES NAVAL BASE, CALL SIGN VNB, LATER THAT DAY.

"We could speed things up if we helped them out, Anya." Mel Sorotki walked along a faded paint line on the parade ground as if he was walking a tightrope, arms extended. He looked bored out of his skull. "I'm up for a search. So is Mitchell."

Marcus, Dom, Bernie, and Cole had already been gone three hours with Will Berenz. Anya charted their progress around the base as Will drove them from building to building in the site vehicle kept for checking the place over each month. The base was the size of a town, with roads that had colorful names like Admiralty Place, Weevil Lane, and Ordnance Row.

"He likes to keep pilots on standby," she said, pressing her earpiece again. "Marcus, how are you doing?"

"Fine," he said. There was a sound of creaking metal hinges in the background. "As in nothing so far."

Mitchell appeared and began pacing around, too. "Anya, tell him they don't mark dangerous secret shit with a skull and crossbones and the word POISON, will you?"

"Tell Mitchell," Marcus's voice growled, "that we've seen enough dangerous secret shit by now to *know*."

Mitchell smiled. "So ground-pounders *don't* go deaf."

Anya hoped Will Berenz understood that Delta came from a very different world, like every other Gear and Jacinto citizen. She wondered how people in this relatively peaceful island existence would cope with men and women who were constantly on edge, ready to swing a punch, and who didn't even regard that as abnormal.

"Anyway, the environment guys in EM will want to check it out when they get here, too," Sorotki said.

Anya cut the outgoing comms link. "Can't be too careful. At Merrenat, we found fuel. New Hope outpost, Delta were attacked by things we hadn't even seen before. Here—who knows what we'll get in the prize draw?"

Sorotki broke out a deck of cards, one of the two universal distractions for Gears, and dealt three hands. From time to time, Anya could hear the vehicle in the distance. Vectes was quieter than any place she'd known—until sirens started wailing, and she almost tripped in her scramble to raise Marcus on the radio while she tried to find her respirator. Sorotki and Mitchell swung into the Raven's cockpit, ready for a rescue.

Anya imagined the worst. She wasn't even sure why she'd grabbed her gas mask. "Marcus? Delta, anyone, what's happening?"

She could hear Cole laughing his head off. "Ma'am, Private Augustus Cole reporting that the base alarm *works!*"

"Just testing," Marcus said. "Carry on."

"They're so fucking hilarious." Mitchell scouted around for his cards. "Anyone remember what hand they had?"

Apart from a lot of squabbling seabirds vying for roosting places, the base was peaceful again in that echoing, solid way of big empty structures. It was another hour before the battered pickup rattled back through the gates and pulled up next to the Raven on the parade ground. Everyone jumped out looking pleased—not just Will Berenz, but even Marcus. He was closer to a smile than she'd seen in a long time.

"We'll take it," Bernie said. "But the wallpaper's got to go."

Anya savored a flood of relief and radioed Port Farrall, exchanging thumbs-up gestures with Dom. Marcus did a slow turn and walked away again. If anyone was going to find it hard to adjust to peace, it was him. Anya sat down on the Raven's bay steps, hand to her ear.

"Sir? Sir, I think we have a solution."

Prescott let out an audible breath. "Is it viable, Lieutenant?"

"I'll get more solid information sent to Emergency Management later, but yes. Delta just checked the base for hazards. We have a habitable area—power, water, some existing accommodation—and a few thousand COG citizens still living on the island. The base maintenance team's been here since E-Day."

Prescott didn't respond for a moment. Anya thought she'd lost the link.

"Absolutely *extraordinary*." He sounded as if he meant it. "*Sovereign* will be with you in around four or five days, and we'll have Raven units with you in a day or so. The relocation starts now."

"I'll get the local maintenance team moving." She paused, wondering if the next point would be too trivial. But there was now an entire generation who'd only known a shattered, burning landscape and a crumbling city. "It's a very *attractive* island, by the way."

"That's important to know. Deploy the bot to transmit some images back to CIC. It'll be a huge morale boost for everyone to see where they're going—that it's going to be a better life." Prescott sounded as if he'd been interrupted. "Anya, Colonel Hoffman wants a word."

Somehow, she was expecting more discussion. She recalled a time when people had spent longer deciding which restaurant to visit. But when you were out of choices and out of time, the really big decisions tended to make themselves—or they'd already been made.

"Anya? You clearly made the Chairman's day. Now give *me* some good news. How do you assess the security situation?"

"Still on that, sir. I think the local population will be scared of being swamped by migrants, so we have to start handling that right away."

"They're definitely our people, then."

"They seem to be. COG naval base team, and the town that serviced it. There's an aggressive Stranded presence we need to assess, but I think the island's big enough to maintain separate zones if we have to."

"That's COG sovereign territory, Lieutenant, not a private resort, and we are the government. We'll be sensitive to local feeling, but we also have the remnant of humanity to look after."

"When you put it like that, sir . . ."

"Well done, Anya. Good job. And now I owe Michaelson the last of my brandy."

"Sir, they have a bar here."

"*Damn* good job."

The genuinely hard work was yet to come. But Hoffman sounded so caught up in the general optimism that she felt that *this* was the turning point, the moment at which life would change forever. Marcus ambled back across the parade ground, right on cue. Either he had uncanny timing or he'd been listening on the open circuit.

He put one boot on the Raven's deck. "Better go fix the tourist brochure."

"You heard, then."

"It's not like they can choose another destination." He called to Sorotki. "Lieutenant—I want to take a look at the Stranded settlement before we lose the light today. Let's move."

Dom seemed almost excited. "Anya, they've got a hospital wing," he said. "Some medical supplies, too. Doc Hayman might even be pleased for once."

If Anya hadn't known Dom so well, she'd have thought things were back to normal. A couple of months' grieving wasn't long enough, though, so she took it as simply getting the outward signs under control or being exhausted into a numb state of marking time. Sometimes he looked quietly lost, but then he'd find something small that focused him—the clean air here, a generator that still worked—and made him come alive for a while. Grieving had to be taken a moment at a time. Eventually, there were more good moments than unbearable ones in a day, and then you knew you'd turned the corner into a new road.

The Raven lifted clear of the parade ground and set off along the western coast.

"I'd call this *blustery*," Sorotki said. The coast here was much more rugged, a narrow strip rising into the highlands that ran down one side of the island. "Those hills make a good windbreak."

"Good natural barrier for a lot of things," Will said. "Keeps the Stranded out of our way most of the time."

Bernie sat with her hands in her lap, clutching something. When Anya took a discreet look, it turned out to be a few downy feathers, black and white, like some of the seabirds nesting at the base. Anya's first thought was that Bernie had been doing what she did best—scoping out the wild food supply and sampling it. When Anya looked up, Bernie's eyebrows were raised slightly as if she was disappointed.

"No, I didn't kill anything," she said. "Just picked these up. I was going to make a fishing lure for Cole. You said you wanted to try fishing, Cole Train."

Cole grinned. "Bernie baby, you *remember* the little stuff, don't you?"

"If I kill something," Bernie said, "I have to have a good reason. It's not a hobby. It's necessity."

She bunched the feathers by their quills, took out a small tin to extract a fishing hook, and began binding the feathers onto the shaft with a fine thread.

Will gave her a wary look. Bernie returned it.

"I'm the battalion survival instructor. Not just a sniper." She said it as if that would make Will feel safer. "So, are the Stranded that much trouble?"

"They're not welcome in town. This is the COG, and either they abide by society's rules or they leave."

"That still doesn't tell me what they do. But I can guess."

"They steal, and they damage things we can't replace." Will patted his shotgun. "And sometimes they kill. Nobody's going to come if we call the police, so . . . we *are* the police."

Bernie just gave him a nod, as if she understood perfectly, and went on making the lure. Nobody said anything else until Sorotki cut into the comms about fifteen minutes later.

"Next stop, Stranded Villas, five minutes. Very picturesque."

"Anywhere to land?" Marcus asked.

"We could just circle menacingly."

"Just want to look them in the eye and say hello."

Dom raised a finger. "I'm the Stranded wrangler. Let me do the introductions."

Marcus watched Will carefully. "You ever come down here?"

"Only when we had to, once."

That said it all. Marcus did a slow blink. "We're pretty serious about protecting citizens. You won't get any more trouble."

"Unless you want to fast-rope down and really impress the hell out of them, I'm going to try for that area at the top of the slipway," Sorotki said. "If it can take that boat, it can probably take this bird's weight."

A clinker-built motor cruiser that had seen better days sat on blocks. The cement slipway was laid in sections, and already breaking up. Dom jumped out of the Raven after Marcus gestured to the others to wait.

In Pelruan, the townspeople had come out to see who was landing. Here, though, Anya could see signs of everyday life — laundry hanging from lines strung between scruffy shacks, a thin wisp of smoke from a metal chimney—but there was nobody outside. Anya wondered what kind of Stranded could reach this isolated place and survive, and decided they weren't the urban Stranded she'd been used to back home. Armed caution seemed to be what everyone thought was appropriate here.

"Will," Bernie said, "what did Lewis mean about any old vermin wearing armor?"

"A boat landed a couple of years ago. One of the men was wearing pretty well the full rig, but it was obvious he wasn't a Gear. Didn't talk right, didn't walk right. And then . . . he didn't *behave* right."

"Got it," Bernie said, but her voice sounded different. "Now, if they were me, they'd have a sniper position in that boat. Coming, Cole Train?"

"I'm all about fishin' boats now, Boomer Lady. Lead on."

They jumped down from the other door and began walking. Anya saw Bernie circle the motor cruiser, then climb the access ladder to the deck.

"Hey, anyone home?" Dom called. He was still close enough to the Raven to run for cover if he needed to. He turned around full circle, back to back with Marcus and a few meters apart, and waited. "We're from the COG. How about a chat, so we understand each other?"

There was a creaking sound from the cruiser. Anya moved to look, and there was Bernie, Lancer held vertically, leaning against the wheelhouse while a young guy in a heavy tunic backed out of the door and began climbing down the ladder. He seemed torn between worrying about her and sizing up Cole.

"Come on, folks," Dom called. "We know you're in—"

Suddenly doors edged open and men—no women in sight—began appearing in the paths between the shacks. They were armed with an assortment of half the weapons that Anya had ever seen: hunting rifles, a couple of Gnasher shotguns that no civilian should have had, snub pistols, and even a Hammerburst. Why the guy needed that—or how he got it—Anya couldn't imagine, but scavenging had been a daily necessity for fifteen years. Extraordinary things were traded from place to place. It didn't mean the man had fought Locust or even seen one.

"I hope you understand our shoot-to-kill policy now, Lieutenant Stroud," Will said quietly. "We were never armed, and so we've got very few personal weapons. We've traded for whatever we can get."

"You've got us now." Bernie wandered past, right behind the man she'd flushed out of the cruiser, who kept glancing at her as if he was expecting to be shot in the back. "Cole, cover me, will you?"

Anya couldn't sit this out. She jumped down, trying to tread the fine line between looking like she meant it and not provoking an incident. She hadn't managed to nail that Gear body language yet. It was an effortless movement where the rifle became an extension of the arms and eyes, and she knew she'd need to achieve that or remain the useful desk jockey that everyone else had to protect in a tight spot.

One of the Stranded must have passed a ribald comment about Anya to his buddy within Bernie's earshot. Bernie paused and gave him the angry sergeant stare.

"You so much as *smile* at the lieutenant," she said, "and you'll be pissing through a straw."

The man with the Hammerburst didn't look as if he was going to shoulder the weapon anytime soon. "Well, fancy seeing the COG here at last. Welcome to Massy's territory. That's me, by the way. You're on my turf."

"The COG's moving back in." Marcus just rolled over the challenge as if he hadn't heard it. "Looks like we never left."

"Shit, you've come to the middle of nowhere to find another place to kick us out of, asshole?"

"We're just asking you to be more considerate neighbors to our citizens."

Massy was probably forty or so, balding, bearded, unusually heavyset for a Stranded. They looked much better-fed here. "I'm seeing three of you—oh, and the dick from the town hall—and about thirty of us. You good at math?"

"Top of my class."

"You want to check your figures again?"

Marcus just looked at him, then back at Bernie and Anya. "Dom, check my working-out, will you?"

Dom shrugged. "Well, there's *five* of us, and Mr. Berenz, and then there's the missile launchers and guns on the Raven, and a bored chopper crew, so I make that outgunned plus eight. But maybe I forgot to carry the one."

Anya heard the rasp of metal bearings, like someone opening a reluctant jar. Sorotki trained his gun in the vague direction of the shacks, making more noise than he needed to.

Oh God.

Anya felt the jolt of adrenaline flooding her thigh muscles. She was scared. But . . .

I hate even thinking it, but I feel alive. Seriously alive.

She'd never expected that. She wasn't new to life-or-death situations, but she'd never been physically involved in them until the last few weeks. And she didn't want to die, but right then she wouldn't have traded places with Mathieson for anything.

"Okay." Massy sounded relaxed, and he shouldn't have been. He lowered the rifle, and every Stranded male did the same. "Here's the deal. You keep away from us, and we'll let you stay awhile."

Something seemed to have caught Bernie's attention. She walked past the shacks along the shoreline, along a row of small boats upturned on the pebbles. She looked them over as if she was thinking of buying one.

Massy seemed to notice her for the first time. "You got a problem, lady?"

Bernie turned around. Anya could see she was chewing the inside of her lip. A couple of the Stranded men had moved round a little so that she'd have to walk past them. Anya's warning bells went off, but Cole was already prepared and made a noisy show of cocking the Lancer manually and blipping the chainsaw for a second.

"The blue dinghy," Bernie said, fixing on Massy. Anya was sure she had the other Stranded in her peripheral vision. "Anyone want to admit to owning that?"

"You want to make an offer?"

"Simple question. Is the man who owns it here?"

"No."

"Shame," she said. "I'll have to keep looking."

"Okay, we're out of here." Marcus motioned everyone back to the Raven, and the tension seemed to drop. "Glad we've reached an understanding."

Then Anya learned how fast a situation could veer from calm to a fight. As Bernie passed between two of the men, one moved to jostle her. Anya didn't see the moment of contact. He might have just shoved Bernie, or maybe he'd touched her backside or something, but he had just enough time to start a leering grin before she spun and smashed the butt of her rifle hard across his mouth. Metal cracked against teeth. He went down like a stone.

Anya's instinct said to pitch in, to back up her squad. But she'd hardly moved before Dom was on the second guy, Lancer shoved hard in his chest, and Cole was blocking Bernie. Everyone froze; every weapon was now raised. There was an awful pause.

"Anyone else want some?" Bernie said, aiming at the man on the floor. She didn't look like steady, good-natured Bernie now. She looked like she wanted an excuse to fire. "No? Good call."

"Yeah, I know who you are now," one of the men called. "Stupid bitch. You're really going to get what's coming to you now. Didn't you learn your lesson?"

"You need to stay out of my frigging way." She began backing away with Dom and Cole as the Raven's rotors started up. "Because you never learned *yours*."

Sorotki's voice came over the comms. "Move it, people. You'll be late for diplomacy class."

Marcus covered their exit and then jumped aboard. The Raven lifted clear. Nobody said a word while Bernie put her head in her hands for a few moments, then sat up straight again.

"Shit, I'm sorry." She looked dreadful, every year of her age and then some, as if something inside had crumbled. She was a veteran Gear, no stranger to violence; Anya had seen her simply shrug off close calls with Locust. Something was wrong. "I could have got you all killed. Baird's right. I'm a liability."

"There's nothing wrong with your reflexes, Bernie," Dom said. He ruffled her hair as if she was one of the men. "It's okay. Nobody got hurt."

Cole joined in the vigorous hair rubbing. "Well, apart from the guy spittin' out teeth, that is. See, that's why I *never* played ladies' thrashball teams. Girls get *rough*."

"It's *not* okay." Bernie submitted to the horseplay. Anya thought that was revealing, seeing as she'd reacted so violently to someone else touching her. "I just lost it. I'm old enough to know better."

Nobody asked what the man had meant by knowing who she was, and that she hadn't learned her lesson. Anya tried not to guess. But she was already starting to fill in gaps despite herself.

"Bernie, we've all done it." Anya reached across between the seats and grabbed her hand. "Even I've hit a guy. Okay, anyone here who *hasn't* lost it with someone?"

Marcus shrugged. "Got kicked out of junior school for fighting. Had a fight on my first day at Olafson Intermediate, too. And I hit Hoffman."

"Well, I just do friendly *taps*," Cole said. "But yeah."

"See, Bernie?" Anya squeezed her hand. "You're in the company of serious scrappers. Everyone's been there."

"I feel better already," Bernie said, clearly not meaning it.

It was part of a ritual, and Anya knew it. Everyone rushed to reassure Bernie in this awful, semi-joking way, listing their own moments when they forgot discipline and procedure and just lashed out. But the real question wasn't asked, and wouldn't be until the civilian was out of range: what had happened before she rejoined the army?

Will Berenz just gazed at Bernie with undisguised admiration. He didn't seem remotely curious. All he seemed to see was a Gear who would put the Stranded in their place, Stranded who'd terrorized him and his neighbors. Anya had seen the Stranded on the fringes of Jacinto as unlucky misfits at best, and lazy cowards at worst, but she was now starting to see another element—the utterly lawless who'd never been in fear of COG justice in places where civilization had completely broken down.

Back at Pelruan, Will opened up the town hall and gave the squad the keys to the emergency storeroom. "Just somewhere to eat and bed down for the night," he said. "Unless you want to be billeted with families."

"We'll be fine here, thanks," Dom said. "We snore."

Marcus nodded. "Appreciate it, Will. We'll mount patrols tonight, just in case. You'll hear the APC. Anya, maybe you can draw up watch rosters for the Ravens."

Now they were on their own, with no outsiders to limit their conversation. Bernie hauled out folding camp beds while Dom investigated the food stores. Gettner and Sorotki's co-pilot, Mitchell, volunteered to cook dinner. To Anya it felt like a settled and normal night in barracks in Jacinto, except there were no grubs to worry about, just a handful of feral humans down the coast who would have been unwise to show their faces here.

No, not *exactly* like Jacinto: there were no sounds of a crowded city, no urban noise—just the wind, roaring surf, and occasional voices outside. The squad and Raven crews played cards. But there was no barroom conversation this time, just bids and declarations. Cole couldn't keep up the silence forever. Anya watched him picking his moment to steer Bernie to one side, taking an occasional deep breath as if he was about to ask something.

"Bernie, you want to do some liquid resource investigation at that handy little bar?" he asked.

"Maybe tomorrow," she said. "But thanks."

Cole laid his hand of cards on the table, frowning at it for a moment. "Baby, you ain't obliged to explain a damn thing to us. But if you *want* to tell us what all that shit was about, you got a sympathetic audience."

Bernie rearranged her hand in silence, shifting cards around as if she was doing some complex calculation, but Anya could tell she wasn't really concentrating on the game.

"Okay, I'll tell you a horror story," Bernie said. "With monsters in it." She laid down her cards faceup, an obvious bust. "And one of them is me."

CHAPTER 11

There's justice, and there's vengeance. Justice is vengeance administered impersonally by a bureaucrat in a standardized and predictable way, so we all know how much punishment to expect and when we'll get it.

(CAPTAIN QUENTIN MICHAELSON, NCOG,
ON MAINTAINING SOCIAL ORDER.)

PELRUAN, VECTES, SEVEN WEEKS AFTER THE
EVACUATION OF JACINTO, 14 A.E.

Gears were family, and families didn't have secrets.

They had disagreements, and favorites, and annoying dumbass habits, but they didn't keep serious shit from each other—especially if there was something that could be done about it. Cole hoped Bernie understood that.

"Ain't prying, Bernie," he said. The card game didn't matter now. It was just to pass the time, anyway. "But we know you're troubled."

"Who isn't?" she said. "The whole army's a psychiatric ward. Our civvies are stressed shitless, too. Can't live in a world like this and stay normal."

"Hey, Gill, let's check out that bar." Mitchell stood up and went for the door. It was getting too grim and personal for him. Gettner took the hint. "This is *squad* business."

There was a clear understanding of who was *squad* at any given time and who wasn't—nothing personal, just the way Gears were. Bernie took a long time to say anything after they'd left.

"No point pissing around with a long tale of woe," she said. "I was raped by Stranded a couple of years ago. So I went after them. I killed two of the guys, but the third got away. That's about it. Anyone want to play another hand?"

It was hard to follow that. *Real* hard. It even took a few moments for the full meaning to sink in for Cole. Anya shut her eyes for a second or two, and Marcus didn't look like he'd even heard what she'd said. That normally meant he was listening to every syllable but didn't want to react. But someone had to *say* something, *do* something, or poor old Bernie would be wishing she hadn't mentioned it.

Dom was sitting right next to her. "Shit, Bernie, I'm sorry. I had no idea." He was the kind of guy who hugged and back-slapped everyone. He put his arm out automatically, but suddenly looked too scared to touch her. "You're not a monster. You were dishing out justice."

Cole remembered something Bernie said not long after she first showed up in Jacinto. It hadn't all been jokes about her shooting cats for food and fur. He knew damn well—after he'd talked to her and watched her for a while—that some bad things happened to her while she was traveling. Stuff happened to most people; they took their chances out there. But it was tougher for a woman.

What was it she'd said? *I've done some bad stuff. It wasn't just cats I skinned.*

Well, if Bernie had some interesting earrings now as well as kitty-fur boots, then that was fine by him.

"Okay," she said. "It needn't have happened. This gang of bastards spent most of its time cruising the islands, killing, robbing, raping—preying on other Stranded. I happened to have my nice big Longshot, so I put a few holes in them. Then they came back. I can probably handle one man, but three—no."

Cole could see Bernie was going to cry at some point. He just wanted to make things right for her. Maybe getting it off her chest would do that, or maybe he'd opened up something nasty she couldn't handle.

"Any of the gentlemen we just made acquaintance with?" Cole asked. "'Cause me and Baird, we run a really good etiquette program on how to treat ladies with respect."

"I told you they were frigging animals." Baird leaned back in his chair and looked over his cards again. He didn't *mean* to be an asshole, but sometimes he just couldn't put things nicely. Cole stood by to shut him up if he couldn't manage some tact. "Dom's right. Why are *you* the monster? Because you shot a few? They're vermin. You should get a medal."

"I didn't exactly *shoot* the two I tracked down."

Baird shrugged. "Good call. Why waste ammo on 'em?"

Bernie didn't have to draw a picture for Cole. He could guess how she'd settled the score. She knew her way around a carcass, and he'd seen her nearly lose it with that grub back at Port Farrall. But she was still Bernie, still fun to be with, still someone he'd trust with his life. She wasn't one of the monsters. She just had to deal with them too often.

"So," Marcus said slowly, "what are you planning to do when you find the third guy?"

Yeah, he always got straight to the point.

"I know what I *want* to do," she said. "And you're going to give me that disapproving Fenix look."

"Is that what's really bothering you? What I think?"

"I don't know, and *that's* what's bothering me."

"If the asshole shows his face, we got a legal system, right?" Cole was starting to wish he hadn't started this. "Martial law. Rules are clear. The boss man's comin' soon, and we'll be runnin' the place just like we did Jacinto. Can't argue with a legal system."

"I'm not the jury, Bernie," Marcus said. "Can't say I blame you. Can't judge you, either."

Bernie just shrugged. "Well, now you know. I'm not traumatized or any of that shit, because I won't let them win. But if I have a choice, I'll be predator, not prey." She looked like she'd had enough, and stood up to leave. "Okay, wake me when it's my watch. I'll be back to normal in the morning and everyone can forget we had this conversation."

Anya hadn't said a word up to then, but now she moved in. There was some sisterly ladies' stuff going on. Anya probably knew best what Bernie needed to hear. "Come on, Bernie. I'll make coffee."

Cole felt he'd failed Bernie somehow. He thought that a bit of comradely support would work wonders; Gears were closer than family, because there was nothing as tight as a team that'd been under fire together. But whatever was really getting to her wasn't going to be fixed by sympathy.

"Shit," Baird said. "What kind of pervert rapes old women? I mean, no offense, but Bernie's Hoffman's age."

Dom shrugged. "Maybe they were, too."

Marcus gathered up the cards from the table and shuffled them. "It's about power and humiliation," he said. "Nothing to do with animal lust."

"Well, if she catches the last asshole, don't expect me to stop her and tell her to be civilized and legal about it." Baird took the deck from Marcus and dealt new hands. "I'll hold her coat."

"Bernie's right," Dom said. "We're all messed up by one thing or another. If I'd . . ." He seemed to be concentrating hard, like he kept forgetting what he had to say. "If I'd come face-to-face with the actual grubs who did that shit to my Maria, I'd have done just what Bernie did . . . whatever that was, but I can guess. That's all I'm saying."

It was the first time Dom had said anything like that. He only talked about Maria's death in vague and general terms. But now he'd spelled it out to everyone: the grubs had done something terrible to her.

Shit, everyone knew that. But sometimes you had to say it out loud just so *you* could hear it, so you accepted that folks were gone and never coming back.

Baird had dealt Cole a lousy hand. He hadn't done Dom any favors, either.

"I'm out," Dom said, pushing his cards back into the center of the table. "And I'm so tired I won't even have nightmares tonight. Wake me up when it's my watch."

"Yeah, count me out, too," said Baird. "Wow, listen to that silence out there. Isn't it *weird*?"

The sea was pretty noisy, and so was the wind. But there was no traffic, no animal sounds, and no distant thump of artillery or mortars. It took some getting used to. Cole and Marcus patrolled the town on foot, as much for the novelty of breathing in clean, mild air as getting into alleys that were too narrow for the 'Dill.

The locals had built a really nice place here.

"Is Dom really doin' better?" Cole asked.

Marcus shrugged. "Up one day, down the next." He let out a long breath. "Thinks he can save the world if he works hard enough."

"That world's *gone*, man. Gotta draw the line. Save the new one."

"How do you teach a man who never quits that he's done all he can?"

Marcus was no good at letting go of stuff, either. "Well, maybe you gotta *show* him."

If there was anything good about the last fifteen years, Cole decided, it was that shared pain saved you from having to explain what the problem was. Everyone—Gears and civvies alike—had been through a lot of the same garbage, more or less, so you never had to feel you were crazy or abnormal, seeing as normal meant you were just like everyone else. And that meant seriously fucked up.

Pelruan looked like its worst problem might have been feeling lonely. It was so small that they could cover it all in thirty minutes at a slow amble. Every time they did a loop around the Ravens up on the cliff, Sorotki and Barber were sitting in KR-239's bay, chatting happily with buddies on long-range comms.

"It's okay here," Cole heard Barber saying. "I can't believe all this shit is finally over."

Marcus stood staring out to sea.

"What's that?" he said.

Cole followed where he was pointing. It looked like a dim, intermittent white light on the water. Then it was gone.

"Reflection?"

Marcus stared a little longer. "Don't think so," he said. "Cole Train, go wake everyone."

PELRUAN, 0300 HOURS.

If there was anything out there on the water tonight, then it had to be human, and Dom hadn't had to deal with a human enemy in a very long time.

He kept to the spongy grass above the pebble shore so that he could hear better instead of drowning out everything with crunching boots. Once he'd adjusted to the sound of the sea, he tried to filter for other noises. At one point he was sure he heard the puttering noise of an old outboard motor.

Damn, my hearing used to be better than this. That's what comes of never wearing a helmet. Eighteen, nineteen years of noise, noise, noise . . .

Dom scanned the shore with his field glasses, picking up what little moonlight there was. A small flock of seabirds huddled against a cliff north of him, heads tucked under wings; gleaming shapes in the water turned out to be seals of some kind, eyes narrowed in weirdly smug human expressions. If it hadn't been for the voice traffic in his earpiece, Dom would have believed he was the last man left on Sera, alone with more wildlife than he'd seen in years. He was out of visual range of everything and everybody.

It would have been a great place to bring up kids.

Baird's voice in his earpiece made him jump. "Dom, see anything?"

"All clear."

"There's something out there, man."

Anya cut in on the radio. "Marcus, I've just left Lewis. He's disappointed that everyone's been told to stay inside and leave us to it. Some of the locals are pretty pissed off."

"When his guys have trained with us and know how to stay out of our fire, we'll deploy together," Marcus said. "Until then, they're safer indoors."

In the middle of nowhere, the list of potential intruders was short. If it wasn't the heavies from the Stranded camp, then there was a whole new problem out there that they hadn't thought of.

Big island. Long coastline. A few thousand people stuck in one town and a few farmers here and there can't possibly keep an eye on who comes and goes.

"Massy would have to be crazy to start anything," Baird said. "Is he seriously going to go up against Gears? Dumb asshole."

Bernie had been unusually quiet. She didn't have a lot to say when she was working, but she'd been checking in with only the occasional grunt, nothing more.

"Hey, Mataki—what d'you think?"

She took a little while to answer. "He might be doing what damage he can before the whole bloody COG shows up and smokes him. He knows there are only ten of us. And he doesn't seem worried by the locals."

"Rules of engagement," Marcus said. "Remember that we have them, Delta."

"Yeah," Baird said, "but do *they*?"

"Just saying. They're not grubs. Self-defense or defense of COG citizens when presented with lethal or injurious force."

Baird didn't argue. That didn't mean he wouldn't find a reason to shoot, though.

Dom wondered how Bernie felt about that.

"Bernie, can I ask you a question?"

"Yeah."

"If you shot some of the bastards to start with, why didn't they kill you?"

Marcus sighed. "Dom, drop it."

"Hey, I didn't mean it like that."

"Fair question." Bernie seemed relaxed about it, but that didn't mean a thing. "You want a blow-by-blow account, all the details?"

"God, no. I'm sorry."

"I think they wanted value for money," she said. "You have to be alive to suffer, remember. That's why I felt a bit . . . *cheated* after I killed them."

"You got that cleaver with you, Bernie?" Baird asked. Dom couldn't remember the last time he'd called her Bernie. He was definitely doing his best to be nice to her. "The one for making omelets."

"I thought it was for chopping nuts."

"We'll swap recipes."

The squad was now spread out along the kilometer of shore, with Anya patrolling the landward boundary in the 'Dill. She was pretty safe in that; Stranded weren't likely to have grub firepower. But Dom was sure she'd just drive right over anyone who got in her way, because she had that same streak as her mom, the ability to shut out everything else and go for a target.

She was still getting to grips with the physical stuff. When she did, she'd be scary.

"Hey, something moving," Baird said. "Hear it?"

It was running fast along the pebbles, something pretty small by the sound of it, a rapid skittering noise at a gallop pace. Dom picked it up in his binoculars: two goddamn dogs. After the feral pack in Merrenat, he wasn't taking any chances. He could hear the *hah-hah-hah* of their panting as they raced in his direction.

But they streaked past him. They didn't even slow down to check him out. He wondered if they were chasing rabbits, or whatever had left its crap over the short turf here, but a few moments later they started barking their heads off. Then two, three, four shots rang out. The barking stopped.

"Game *on*," Baird said.

Raven engines cut through the night air as the birds lifted in complete blackout. If anyone was coming ashore from the sea, they had to do it at Pelruan, between the break in the cliffs that gave the town a sloping shoreline and a harbor. Dom dropped to one knee, Lancer ready. In the town behind him, dogs took up the barking.

"KR units, on task." Gettner said. "Sorotki, keep an eye on the back door."

"On it, boss." KR-239 broke away and headed inland.

"Contact, hundred meters out, on your two o'clock, Fenix—rigid inflatables."

"I see 'em."

"And here," Cole said. "They're spreadin' out. I got a bunch of three inbound, slow-movin'."

"I see you, Cole, and I have a shot—lead boat of group of three." That was Bernie. "Ready when you are."

Dom ran toward the slope of the next cliff to get some elevation. He could see what Gettner had eyeballed now—another group, four small raiding boats, coming in slowly. The swell hid them in the troughs until they were almost ashore. Then they hit the throttles and stormed in.

Shit, they *had* to be crazy. They *had* to hear the choppers and feel the downdraft, even if they couldn't see any lights. Maybe they assumed the COG was too gentlemanly and civilized to unleash its superior firepower on a bunch of randomly armed civvies.

Wrong call, asshole.

The night suddenly lit up as Gettner switched on the Raven's searchlight. A brilliant white shaft raked the shore and shallows, picking out one of the inflatables like a cabaret spot. For a moment, just a moment, the raiding party stared up, hair flattened by the downdraft, spray whipping around them.

"I really *wanted* to see fishing nets," Gettner sighed. Then the bullhorn boomed. "Drop the fucking weapons, vermin, or I *will* open fire."

Dom's eye caught upward movement as an assortment of rifles lifted and aimed. He didn't take in anything else, only the weapons. A pipe-like barrel jerked up almost vertically just a split second before a yellow ball of discharged gas blew out behind it. A grenade round hit the Raven. Fire spat from the air down at the boats, raising a neat line of water.

Been there. Been on the receiving end of that, a long time ago.

Dom fired out of pure reflex. His save-yourself instinct was screaming: *Watch out for the Raven, the bird's been hit, it's going down.* But nothing hit him, and there was no fireball. When he turned, the Raven was hovering, firing short bursts into the shallows. More boats skidded up the shingle and Dom opened fire again, punching through one of the rubber hulls. Three men jumped out of it and ran ashore, and Dom jumped up to sprint after them. Automatic fire—some Lancer, some not—rattled up and down the beach. The bastards were landing at multiple points.

Marcus cut in. "Gettner, you hit?"

"If they'd done more than clip the boarding step, you'd know all about it."

"Give me some light by the slipway, then."

"On it."

"I have a visual on the 'Dill." That was Sorotki. "Heading for . . . yeah, I see them, three big junkers, heading into town. Going in to welcome them to Pelruan . . ."

"Hey, mind my tanks, shithead." Gettner must have been taking more fire from the ground. "Barber, smoke them before they hit the reserve fuel, will you?"

Dom reached the edge of the buildings, panting. The Stranded had vanished into the streets. That was the last thing he needed. He couldn't see the bastards, and the homes were mainly wooden structures that gave no protection to anyone inside, a bad place for a firefight. It was even worse knowing there were civvies huddled in every building who wouldn't have a clue how to stay down and let Gears deal with the cleanup.

"Dom!" Baird sounded out of breath. "I'm heading right toward you. We're going to intersect by the town hall."

"Where the hell *are* you? Can you see me? I can't see you."

"Running parallel with the road where the bar is." He paused. "Amateurs. Homemade firebombs—"

Glass smashed. A tongue of yellow flame leapt above the low roofline, and the *whoomp* of igniting fuel followed by more Lancer fire gave Dom something to run at. He skidded around the next corner, trying to orient himself by the light of the fire, and caught sight of one of the Stranded running full tilt down the road. He stopped and squeezed off a burst. The guy pitched forward and fell on one side. Dom was suddenly aware of screaming—a woman's voice from out in the open, not muffled by walls.

Shit.

Dom had shot someone in the back. For a terrible moment he thought he'd dropped a civilian who'd come out to defend their property or something. He ran for the body, but Baird appeared out of a side alley and gave him a thumbs-up.

"Locals are firefighting," he said. "Shit, I hate urban ops. You can't hose anything."

"I've lost at least two of them."

"It's a small town. How far can they get?"

"How much damage can they do?"

Wooden buildings, narrow streets, fire. Dom could work it out. Voice traffic had been almost zero for a few minutes, but now Dom's earpiece went on overload.

"Shore, clear." Bernie said. "Boats—clear. Eight-Zero, can you see anything else down there?"

"Negative, Mataki. Heading over to the town."

"Anya, Sorotki—Fenix here. What's happening your side?"

"Roadblocking." Anya was shouting over the noise of a Raven. Sorotki sounded like he was almost parked on top of the 'Dill. "Because I can't drive and operate the gun at the same time."

Machine-gun fire started up in short bursts, and then the distinctive sound of the 'Dill's belt-fed gun joined it. Dom could have sworn he heard Anya whoop. That was so unlike her that it shook him. He ran where the two Stranded had gone, following the light of another burning building, and straight into a knot of men from the town—shit, he hoped he could tell the difference—with a scruffy bearded guy pinned bodily to the ground. One of the men put a hunting rifle to the Stranded's head and pulled the trigger.

Oh God oh God oh God . . .

For a few seconds, Dom was back in the Hollow, one simple movement of his trigger finger marking the line between finding what he'd searched for so desperately and destroying it forever.

Oh God, Maria, I'm so sorry . . .

The group of men looked up at Dom as if he'd crashed a party.

"What the hell's wrong with you? The bastard asked for it." There was a Gnasher shotgun lying on the road, COG issue. One of the men grabbed it. "We told you to let us deal with this. What the hell are you going to do now? Let them burn us out?"

Dom snapped back to being Dom the Gear, ready to deal with anything. "You look after the firefighting," he said, poking his finger hard in the man's chest. "Leave the Stranded to us. Okay?"

"You started this. You provoked them."

Baird caught up with him and they left the civilians to it, realizing that Gears weren't coming across as the heroes of the hour in Pelruan. This wasn't Jacinto. The locals didn't see Gears as saviors, the last line of defense. They were just outsiders that they didn't invite and didn't understand.

"I've lost the other asshole."

"Screw him," Baird said. "Hear that?" There was crazed barking, but it was coming from outside now, not the houses. "They've let the dogs loose. Wow, they must train them to take out Stranded. I'm impressed."

Dom stopped dead. "Marcus? Anya? Anyone need backup? We lost our quarry."

The Lancer fire from the shore had stopped. Dom could hear people coming out of the houses, calling to their neighbors to check if they were okay. Baird yelled at them to get back indoors because it wasn't over yet, not by a long shot. If they heard him, they took no notice.

"Ahh, *shit*." That was Marcus with his radio channel open. Dom had no idea where he was. "Get back inside, lady . . . Cole, get them back inside. *Shit*. Dom? We're clear shoreside. Get down to the road and mop up anyone from the junkers."

Baird ran alongside Dom. "Next time we hit a new town, first thing we do is memorize the street plan."

"Yeah."

"We'd have been screwed without the Ravens."

"I never said Stranded were dumb."

There was one road out of Pelruan to the south, now marked by a pall of smoke and flame. The town was so small that if you stood at the right point, or got some elevation, you could see everything from the road to the shore in one axis, and from one headland to the next in the other. Even in darkness—it was 0405 now—the aftermath of the fighting was visible. Dom climbed up on a dry-stone wall and scanned the area. There were five or six fires, some already being damped down, and both Ravens were now out over the open country to the south, searchlights directed, guns occasionally loosing off bursts of fire.

Dom and Baird ran on. By the time they got to the roadblock, Cole was hauling out bodies, and the two Ravens were heading back, their nose lights visible head-on. Two junkers lay on their sides, burning fiercely, and the third was upright with its roof ripped open like a tin can.

"I'd hate to see the Lieutenant when she's in a *pissy* mood," Cole said. "Damn, you seen the collection of toys these jokers got? There's *grubs* with less firepower than this."

The 'Dill had stopped at a point where the road sloped away sharply into the river on one side and soft ground on the other. Perfect choke point: Anya definitely had the right stuff. Dom just didn't want to see her end up like her mom, killed in a magnificent but crazy single-handed charge. It might have been great for the movies, but it was shit for the people left to grieve. The top hatch opened slowly and Anya eased her head and shoulders clear. Dom wouldn't have said she looked pleased with herself, not quite, but in the light from the fires she had a certain shine to her cheeks like she'd just come back from a brisk walk.

"You can't see much from this gun position," she said.

Baird clapped a few times. "Great debut."

"I think Mitchell did most of the work." She ducked back down and came out through the front hatch. When she saw Cole clearing up, her face changed, and Dom wondered if she'd suddenly made the connection at gut level that the targets she'd been firing at so diligently were actually flesh and blood. "How many of them are there?"

"We'll count 'em proper when the Ravens are done playing fighter jocks," Cole said. "Shit, seen that chunk out of Gettner's bird? Whole step ripped off the crew bay. She's lucky she ain't toast."

"We'll hear all about it." Baird collected the weapons, an assortment that was mainly automatic rifles and grenade launchers. He paused to take a naval officer's ceremonial sword off a Stranded's belt. "Whoa, Captain Charisma won't like you playing pirates with *that*, buddy. Show some respect."

Dom slid his hand inside his armor to check that his photographs were still safe. "You okay, Anya?"

"I'm . . . I'm fine, Dom. Just not trained for this."

"Hell, who is? You ever killed anyone before?"

"I think I hit a Locust or two when we first reached Port Farrall," she said. "But never a human."

Baird just looked at her. "You still haven't . . ."

Cole just shook his head. The flames were dying down in one of the junkers, and he ventured in to pull out a body that was half out of the driver's seat. Dom only saw the movement as he tugged on it.

Cole froze and turned away. "Aww . . . shit, this one's . . . aww, hell."

Dom wondered what could disgust Cole. Any man who could chainsaw his way through a squad of grubs and laugh his ass off wasn't the squeamish kind. It took Dom a while to work out what he was looking at, but then the blackened shapes resolved into something recognizable: the body had come apart in two halves when Cole pulled at it.

"Gross," Dom said, and finished the job for him.

Humans . . . it *was* different. People weren't grubs, not even the really shitty ones.

Baird peered over his shoulder, then went on loading the salvaged weapons into the 'Dill, still whistling. Gears generally despised Stranded—as savages, thieves, cowards, parasites—but Dom had always tried to get on with them because he needed their help. He'd lost count of the number of Stranded he'd stopped in the streets and shown Maria's picture. Had they seen her? It was always no, until the last day, and then it had been too late.

Why don't I blame them?

"Why d'you hate 'em so much, Baird?" Cole asked.

Baird counted off on his fingers with a theatrical flourish. "Failure to engage with the implied social compact between citizens and state. And the fact that they stink like shit." He looked at his gloves, frowning. "Oh, yeah, I forgot—they're mean to people we like."

Marcus's voice cut in on the radio circuit. "Delta, we're done here. Everyone back to the slipway to clean up the debris. Baird—find some welding equipment and fix Gettner's bird so that she shuts up."

Baird drove the 'Dill down the narrow roads back to the shore. Pelruan seemed to have two natural centers, two places where people tended to congregate. One was outside the town hall—not exactly a square, more like a village green—and the other was the row of houses closest to the sea, almost a semicircle looking down the shallow slope into the harbor. Baird parked the 'Dill, headlights angled down onto the shore to illuminate it, and everyone dismounted. A growing crowd of locals had come out to look. Some stood with arms folded, looking shocked, but some were obviously mad as hell, and not just with the Stranded. Dom saw one guy yelling at Marcus while Gavriel and Berenz stood between them, making calm-down gestures with their hands.

"Vernon, nobody got hurt," Berenz said. "The damage can be repaired. But *nobody got hurt.*"

Vernon turned on him. "Yeah, and they wouldn't have come here at all if it hadn't been for this bunch throwing their weight around—when did we last get raided? They don't know how we do things here."

"Vern, Stranded could come back and raid us anytime. But do you seriously think they'll be back now?"

"Face it, Will—our way of life here is *over.* In one damn day, everything's changed."

Dom listened, resentful. *Well, now you know how the rest of the world felt on E-Day, asshole. But we're not grubs. We're your own.*

Gavriel steered the guy away. Marcus, being Marcus, just stood there in silence and let it roll off him, looking more interested in the bodies that were being laid out. Bernie examined them. They were looking for something. Dom jogged over with Baird to check.

"No Massy yet." Marcus rubbed his neck as if he'd pulled a muscle. "Twenty-six bodies so far."

"He might be one of the barbecued ones," Baird said helpfully. "We've got a stack out on the road."

"Either way," Marcus said, "we've got a shitload of Stranded with a grievance."

"So? They try it on, and we cap them, too. Not exactly a legal gray area."

"Why the hell would they even try?" Dom asked. "Last-ditch raid? One for the road?"

Marcus shrugged. "Fifty to a hundred of them, with grenade launchers, assault rifles, and vehicles. Ten of us with two helicopters, reluctant to see collateral damage. We'd have taken those odds, too."

"Yeah," Dom said. "But we'd have *won*."

The Ravens were still hovering over the water, searchlights moving slowly, while a couple of small boats searched for more bodies. Any they hadn't recovered could have washed out of the harbor by now. Gavriel came back and joined the subdued line looking at the Stranded dead.

"I think it would be a good idea to call a town meeting in the morning and calm everyone down, Marcus." He indicated the dead bodies with a nod. "People are quick to forget that those individuals *there* would have cut their throats for the clothes on their backs. And what with the . . . returning refugees, we've got a volatile situation."

"Yeah. I'll do that." Marcus nodded, like it was the most natural thing in the world, no more than a dispute over a parking space. "I've had plenty of practice at explaining why things went to ratshit."

He walked away, and Dom watched him sit down on the front steps of one of the houses, head lowered, finger jammed into one ear. Dom knew who he was trying to raise: Hoffman.

Hoffman, Dom thought, would have done exactly the same.

PELRUAN, KR-239 CREW BAY, LATER THAT MORNING.

Anya sat in the Raven's crew bay with Delta, waiting for Hoffman to call back and explain just how disappointed he was with their diplomacy.

"You can't make allowances for Stranded, Marcus," she said. "One squad can't search thousands of square kilometers in a day."

Bernie shook her head. "I should have postponed my feud until the bloody fleet was here."

"I'm the one who wanted to pay them a visit." Marcus joined the squad competition to take the blame. Nobody could ever accuse them of sloping shoulders. "But we need to put a lid on any complications in town, and fast."

Stranded could be anything from a slight nuisance to a full-scale threat. But nobody was used to a blurred line between Stranded and citizens; you were either one or the other. Some of the residents didn't seem to be too sure about that dividing line, and Anya could see them milling around the slipway, staring at the debris from the skirmish. Some looked stunned, others disapproving. Being isolated from the real war had formed a very different culture, COG banners or not.

"When Lewis is ready, I'll go in and talk to the council," Anya said. "We'll calm things down."

Marcus did his slow head shake. "*I'll* do it."

"You want to address a meeting?" Anya felt that was her responsibility. She was the officer, and she was the one who'd told Prescott and Hoffman that things were fine, more or less. But a little pang of guilt made her wonder if she thought Marcus was too abrupt and aggressive to be trusted with the task. "Maybe I should do it."

"A meeting," Marcus said, "is just a mob that hasn't started throwing rocks. I'll be fine."

Baird obviously couldn't see what the fuss was about. "Hey, we've got the whole COG army coming. This is just a small bunch of seriously underarmed civvies. Why are we wasting energy trying to persuade anyone about *anything*?"

"Because we've got to rebuild society now," Anya said. "Priorities are changing."

"But this is the COG. Everyone's got responsibilities. If they wanted all that flaky free-spirit I'm-an-individual crap, they should have moved to Pelles. Oh, wait—Pelles got creamed by the grubs even before Hammer Day. I rest my case."

Sorotki stuck his head through the hatch. "The master's voice. Hoffman on the line for the lucky victim."

Marcus took a breath and pressed his earpiece, staring up at the deckhead. Anya listened in with her mike switched off, mainly to help her resist the temptation to intervene, and wondered if she should have stuck to CIC. She knew damn well that her mother would have handled this better. She wasn't sure how, but Mom had just had a *presence* that said she knew exactly what she was doing and that she couldn't lose.

And even when she finally lost for the first and last time, she won the battle.

Miss you, Mom. I really do.

"Colonel," Marcus said, "we had a minor incident. The situation's been contained."

"How minor, Fenix?"

"Stranded raiding party—up to sixty dead, no civvies injured."

"So what's your security evaluation now?"

"Can't be more than seven or eight hundred of them, and at least half are women, kids, or old men."

"Prescott wants the usual deal—offer them amnesty and ask them to hand over the criminal element. How are the locals taking it?"

Marcus paused. "We need to get a few things straight with them first. Like whose side they're on."

"You said they were COG citizens."

"They're mostly COG citizens who've never had grubs up their asses. So they aren't as focused or grateful as Jacinto folk when we have to break a few things to save them."

"I hear you, Fenix. Prescott wants to address them live via your bot's video link, but I'll stall him."

Marcus did his silent sigh, eyes shut for a moment. "Tell him he's even more charismatic in person. What's your ETA?"

The link faded to static for a moment while Hoffman seemed to be consulting someone. "Michaelson estimates four days, but we can start flying in teams in a few hours."

"We'll keep a lid on it."

"You *will* call for assistance if you run into difficulties, Fenix. This isn't the war. Policing civilians requires more manpower than shooting troublesome bastards."

"I'll make a note so I remember that."

Marcus jumped down from the Raven and walked toward town. Anya followed with Dom.

"You're not going alone," she said.

Marcus didn't turn around. "I'll try not to drag my knuckles."

The main meeting room of the town hall where they'd played cards just hours earlier was now packed with locals, who might have been representatives or just the first ones who managed to cram in to find a space. Anya took it as a positive sign — at least they weren't rioting in the streets. Lewis Gavriel's first reaction had been to call a meeting, and the population's response had been to attend. That wasn't the behavior of a mob.

Gavriel squeezed through the crowd, clapping his hands to get attention over the hubbub of voices. But it was actually Marcus who silenced them. He walked in behind Gavriel, and the noise level dropped as if someone had turned down a volume control. He cleared a path without even trying. A teenage boy — fifteen, perhaps — turned idly to see what was behind him, and the expression on his face when he saw Marcus was pure animal fear, instant and undisguised. Anya was taken aback by it.

Hey, that's my Marcus, he's not like that, he wouldn't hurt you —

Anya had to remind herself that *any* Gear was an intimidating sight for civilians not used to them—all that battle-scarred armor, the Lancer that never seemed wholly clean of blood, the impression of bulk and sheer unstoppability—but Marcus projected something beyond that. It wasn't just dominant body language. It was a kind of angry weariness. It made people shut up and listen.

He reached the front of the meeting room and stepped onto the low dais with a hollow thud of boots. Anya moved off to one side with Dom, looking back at the packed hall and scanning the faces. Most wore similar expressions of confusion and fear.

Gavriel stepped up beside Marcus, all solidarity. "Citizens, I know you're all worried by what happened earlier, but I really need you to listen to Sergeant Fenix. We're going to have to get used to some changes. I want you to hear him out."

Dom was standing so close to Anya that he could whisper in her ear almost without moving. "I'd like to see anyone try to interrupt him."

Anya kept telling herself that Marcus could handle this. But he wasn't even the talkative type, let alone an orator. She braced herself to step in if he hit problems.

"I want you to understand how serious our situation is," he said. "You might think you know what war means, but you don't. Most of humankind is *dead*. All the cities are *gone*, even Jacinto. The only humans left alive, apart from Stranded, are on their way here by ship because they've got *nowhere left to run*. Do you understand the stakes? We're facing extinction. That's why we're moving in. And it's not a request—it's going to happen. The people we pulled out of Jacinto survived hell, and they're COG citizens, too. So here's the deal, like it's always been—you do right by your fellow citizen, and the COG does right by you. There's no other deal on the table."

Anya never knew Marcus had that many words in him. She almost didn't dare look at the crowd in case she broke the spell—which seemed to be horrified shock rather than admiration for Marcus's brutally frank announcement.

It took a few long seconds to sink in, and then the questions

GEARS OF WAR: JACINTO'S REMNANT

erupted. And they weren't just fired at Marcus; the crowd was arguing, taking sides, shouting. Marcus just folded his arms and waited in silence for them to yell themselves to a standstill.

Okay, that's not a bad strategy . . .

"What the hell's going to happen to us?"

"Are you *invading*?"

"How many? Come on, how many? This is just an *island*."

"You selfish bastards—didn't you hear what the guy said? They're all that's left."

"They're going to be slugging it out with Stranded and we'll get caught in the middle."

"We fended for ourselves when the COG abandoned us—where the hell were *you* when we needed you?"

"They're *our own*, man. They've got nowhere else."

"We don't have room. Why the hell do we have to take them?"

"Because we're COG, asshole, you forgotten something? What do you think the flag is? Why do you think we're here at all?"

"I don't care, they can't just walk in—"

Bang.

Anya flinched. She thought for a moment that Marcus had hit the wall behind him with his fist, or maybe Gavriel had, but it was Dom. He'd knocked over a chair.

Dom took three strides into the crowd and grabbed the loudest guy by the collar while he fumbled inside his armor. He pulled out something: his photographs. He'd taken those pictures out so many times over so many years that he could just flick them out like a card trick. He shoved the photographs right in the man's face.

"See this?" he said. Tears ran down his cheeks. "This is my wife. She's dead." He fanned out the photographs one-handed. "And these are my two kids. They're dead, too. And these are my folks, and her folks. They're *all dead.*" He dropped the pictures, the whole pack, and they fluttered across the floor. "You think they all died so you could slam the fucking door in our faces and tell me you don't have room for the few who *didn't*? I'm telling you—*you have room.*"

Anya held her breath. One wrong word, one move, could set off a fight. The guy just stared into Dom's face even after Dom let go of his collar, and then squatted down to gather up the photographs with him. Dom, suddenly his normal self again, patted the pictures into a neat pile and slid them back inside his armor. Marcus stepped down off the dais. Anya expected some parting shot from him, but it was clear now that none was needed. He put his hand under Dom's elbow and gave him a push toward the door.

Anya found herself alone, standing with Gavriel, with nothing to add.

"It's that simple, people," Gavriel said. "This is COG sovereign territory, and we're its citizens. If you don't want to accept that duty anymore, then this is a big island, and you can go your own way as Stranded. But Jacinto's remnant is going to settle here. That's all there is to it."

Some people got up and stormed out. The rest just stood or sat where they were. If any of them were overjoyed at the prospect of ending their isolated existence, they didn't show it.

"Thank you," Anya said. "You have no idea what a lifeline this island is for everyone."

As Marcus had said, Vectes didn't actually have any choice. The remnant was coming, the COG was asserting its authority, and there was nothing anyone could do about it except develop a streak of self-destructive insanity and try to fight its own government.

But it still never did any harm to say thank you.

An old man with a wonderfully lined face smiled at her as she left the meeting room.

"Didn't Ephyra effectively shut the door to refugees when Prescott ordered the Hammer strikes?" he said, still smiling.

"Yes, it did." Anya couldn't call it a low blow, because it was an inevitable parallel to draw. She wondered what he was going to tell her—and she knew that he would, sooner or later—about the relatives he had lost somewhere on the mainland. "But the people in those ships, *they* didn't do anything."

That wasn't completely true, of course. There was Prescott and Hoffman. But Victor Hoffman had paid dearly for his part in the decision. She liked the old bastard too much to see him pay any more.

"Perhaps we'd have seen things differently if we'd been overrun by Locust," said the old man.

"Yes," Anya said. "I think you would."

CHAPTER 12

I am responsible for myself and my actions; I shall conduct myself honorably, and live a clean and frugal life. I have responsibilities to my fellow citizens; I shall be loyal to them, and humble, because we are equal elements of a greater whole, and without them I am nothing. I have responsibilities to our society; I shall understand and respect my place in it, defend it, and work to make it prosperous, so that I may receive society's protection, and that we may hand on safety and prosperity to future generations.

(THE OCTUS CANON, FOUNDING PRINCIPLES OF THE COALITION OF

ORDERED GOVERNMENTS, AS HANDED DOWN BY THE ALLFATHERS,

AND RECITED BY EVERY CITIZEN.)

PELRUAN LANDING AREA, ONE DAY AFTER THE
STRANDED RAID, 14 A.E.

"I decided Prescott could cope without me," Hoffman said. "And if I had to watch Major Reid trying to crawl up his ass one more time, I might have taken a chainsaw to him. Am I being unreasonable, Anya?"

"One reason I take care of you, sir, is that I'd prefer not to work for him," she said. "Come on. Meet the loyal caretakers."

The Raven circled once before heading back to Vectes naval

base with Will Berenz. The advance party of Ravens had landed to get essential services running before the first tranche of evacuees came ashore. Anya had half imagined some kind of single event, a historic and camera-worthy moment where the remnant set foot on safe ground for the first time, even though she knew that the landings and transfers would have to be done in stages.

Cole and Baird were working on the quay, cutting lengths of wooden planking with their Lancers' chainsaws. Okay, chainsaws *were* chainsaws. You could use them for more than just killing grubs. But it still made Anya smile. A couple of small boys watched the two Gears, clearly fascinated.

"Where's Mataki?" Hoffman asked.

"Visiting the Stranded with Sergeant Fenix. They've gone with Sorotki and a local farmer for an aerial recon."

"Are the local vermin rabid or something? Never known them try to take on Gears. I don't agree with amnesties for them, but Prescott insists. I think they'll tell him to kiss their asses. They usually do."

"They've had soft targets for too long. They're not used to facing superior firepower."

"Well, they're going to get damned used to it now. Crazy bastards. Did anything set them off, or are they always that suicidal?"

Anya wondered how much Bernie had told Hoffman. He probably needed to know that she had more issues with Stranded than the average Gear, but this was thin personal ice to step on.

"I think they were just making the point that they owned the place, but then they found out they didn't," Anya said. "We made contact with them earlier in the day, and it was pretty hostile." *God, do I tell him? Maybe he knows the rest.* "Sergeant Mataki slugged one. But she had good reason."

Hoffman slowed his pace to an occasional step. "How good?"

"One jostled her." No, that didn't cover it at all. "Sir, were you aware she was gang-raped by Stranded?"

Hoffman obviously wasn't. He stopped dead. He didn't even

look at Anya, and his usual reaction to any news was to fix the messenger with a stare that could drill holes in sheet steel.

"I was *not*," he said. "Are we talking about the same Stranded?"

Anya lost her nerve. There was only so much strain she could put on Hoffman's heart before he turned pale enough to scare her. "It's complicated."

"I'd need to know." He hadn't even let loose with his usual stream of expletives. He was definitely shaken; the blood had drained from his face. "Mataki and I go *way* back. Do you fully understand? I'd personally take a Lancer to any man who upset her."

"I believe she dealt with two of them, sir." *I should never have started this. I should have left it to Marcus.* "I'm sorry, I realize you're close. I should have handled this more diplomatically."

"Damn glad you told me, Anya," Hoffman said. "Because she wouldn't. Leave it with me."

He walked on, shaking his head, fists balled. Anya thought better of pouring fuel on the fire by mentioning the boat that Bernie had taken an interest in.

When Gavriel met them in the town hall, Hoffman seemed to snap back to his old self, blunt and business-like.

"So some of your residents think we're going to be a pain in the ass," he said, turning a chair around and straddling it. "Well, we're not going to be on your doorsteps for a long time to come. You'll have seventy kilometers of breathing space. But the Chairman will *not* tolerate segregation and no-go areas in COG territory. There has to be some integration."

Gavriel looked ashamed, if anything. "I think they're afraid of overcrowding and violence. Competition for food. Some remember the Pendulum Wars, and from what Lieutenant Stroud tells me, that was civilized by comparison."

"Gavriel—"

"Lewis, please."

"Lewis, we fought genocide. Do we have to draw a picture? Goddamn it, we're not animals. We're not Stranded. My Gears are disciplined soldiers, and the civilian population is under martial law. They're not some plague that's going to spoil your comfortable existence here."

"I know that, Colonel."

"Remind them that their community only exists because the NCOG *paid* it to be here to support the naval base."

Anya winced. She liked Gavriel, and hoped he understood Hoffman's savaging was nothing personal.

"So how do we achieve integration, Colonel?" Gavriel asked calmly.

"Same way any social animal learns to get along with a new pack. *Gradually.* We allow small parties of the remnant to visit Pelruan, and Pelruan sends small parties to see what life is like in Vectes. Eventually, anyone can go anywhere. But this *will* be one island, one nation. Chairman Prescott is most insistent on that. He's asked me to pass on his invitation to your councilmen to visit VNB and meet the civilian community when they arrive."

Reading the riot act to Gavriel was redundant. The man still saw himself as a COG civil servant, fifteen years' isolation or not, and so did many of his neighbors. But some didn't, and Anya could only guess at where that divergence had started.

And who's the new animal and who's the pack? That's the problem.

Perhaps once they saw how little impact the overnight city at the other end of the island made to their daily existence, then they'd settle down.

And I'll make damn sure they have a history lesson. They have to understand. But why should we have to justify ourselves to them, after all we've been through?

Anya realized she'd almost let resentment get a hold on her. That was how easy it was, how simply it began. And now she knew what her objective would be in the immediate future. She might never become the exemplary fighting Gear her mother had been, but she could organize and analyze—and she could make people understand.

"Martial law," Gavriel said at last. "That would apply to all of us, would it?"

"It would," said Hoffman. "The Fortification Act is still in force." He checked his watch. "It shouldn't make any difference to your daily lives, Lewis, except that we'll provide security patrols here—and at the farms. That should reassure your people."

"Some will see it as enforcement, but we can deal with that."

"Maybe it is. Citizenship is a two-way street. So *we'll* deal with it."

Anya winced. Hoffman had never been a diplomat, but his honesty got him a long way. Now he wanted his walking tour of the town.

"They might as well get used to the sight of me," Hoffman said, "because this is all going to land in my lap. I can smell it."

"It's actually quite a nice place, sir."

The whole concept of a nice place was almost a forgotten memory. Anya thought back a few weeks to when she'd believed that Port Farrall was as good as it was going to get, and that there were no more havens across a distant border where small luxuries were still available. Now she was standing in one of those havens. Her definition of luxury had scaled down considerably over the years, but fresh food, a quiet bar, and clean sheets were now real.

And no grubs.

That was the hardest thing to get used to. The monsters were still very much under every refugee's bed.

A few houses showed signs of fire damage from the raid, but workmen were already up ladders, hammering and sawing and repairing. Word of Hoffman's arrival had spread around town, and people wandered out to look. The colonel looked every inch what he was—aggressive, uncompromising, and short on charm—but he seemed to switch into parade inspection mode, and went along inspecting and commenting favorably on the tidy state of the houses. Anya willed him not to go the whole hog and order some unlucky householder to get down and give him twenty for having an untidy front yard.

He couldn't have looked that intimidating today, though. One of the small boys who'd been watching Cole and Baird now trailed them, and finally caught up with Anya. He looked about eight. He shot Hoffman a glance, but seemed to think Anya was the safer bet.

"Miss?"

"Hi. What's your name? Mine's Anya."

"I'm Josef. Does your gun work?"

"Yes."

"What are grubs like?"

"Horrible. But you don't have to worry about them."

"Is that why the Gears look at the ground every time there's a big wave or a noise?"

Anya didn't quite understand. "What do you mean, Josef?"

"Why don't they look up?"

Hoffman grunted. "I think the boy means that every time there's a noise they're not expecting, Gears automatically look down. Grubs." He patted the kid's head. "You'd look up to see what it was, right?"

"Yes." Josef was now mesmerized by Hoffman and forgot Anya. "Is that because the grubs are under the ground?"

"It is, son. They lived in tunnels and dug their way up to the surface. We never knew when they'd burst through and come to get us."

Josef looked stricken. It was a child's nightmare, all right. "Did they kill people?"

"Millions and millions."

"Worse than the Hammer of Dawn?"

Hoffman missed a beat and swallowed hard. "Yeah. Worse than that."

"Wow," said Josef, and darted off back to Cole and Baird.

"Now there's a boy whose sleep's going to be disturbed for a few weeks," Anya said.

Hoffman shook his head. "I think he grasped the situation a hell of a lot quicker than some of the adults. Kids are better at imagining monsters." He braced his shoulders again as if he was shrugging off a bad memory. He almost certainly was, but he had a long list to pick from, and Anya always had to guess which.

"Now, under martial law we can requisition whatever supplies we need, but you're going to tell me that'll alienate our friends here, so what the hell do we barter to make ourselves feel like *nice* people when we need to take something?"

"Fuel," Anya said. "They're using everything from wind turbines to wood stoves to vegetable oils. Repair the landline network. Provide labor to clear land. Give them TV in a few key places. That sort of thing."

"TV?"

"Easy. Just tell Baird that you don't think he can possibly cannibalize some of the monitors from the ships and make a closed circuit system out of them, and then stand back. Keeps the media busy, too."

"Yes, we really *are* wrecking their island idyll, aren't we?"

"Cooperation takes less effort than enforcement."

Anya was uncomfortable with the new face of the COG that some in Pelruan seemed to see: an occupying army, an invasion. It wasn't how she saw herself or her comrades. It certainly wasn't how Jacinto civilians had regarded the Gears who held the line between them and the Locust advance.

A refugee city of people who still aren't convinced they'll live to see tomorrow, traumatized, hungry, bereaved—and a small town that hasn't even seen a Locust. We've got a big gulf to bridge.

Hoffman sat down on the low stone wall that ran along the quay and watched Cole and Baird sawing wood to length for the repairs. The air smelled of resin, sea, and cooking.

"Damn nice, like you say," Hoffman said absently. "We'll make the new city damn nice, too. Prescott keeps talking about *New Jacinto*."

"When are you going back to VNB, sir?"

"When I've seen Mataki," he said. "I can wait. May I borrow your Lancer, Lieutenant?"

He held his hand out for her rifle, then revved up the chainsaw and went to cut wood with his Gears.

If she hadn't known he was upset about Bernie, then she would have sworn he was starting to look at peace.

"You just got to shoot them when they destroy crops or kill live-stock," the farmer said. "They're a damn nuisance. You from farming stock? You sound like an Islander."

Bernie nodded. "Galangi. That's mostly livestock. Grew up on a beef farm."

"Say *ass*."

"Arse."

He burst out laughing. "You got that accent."

His name was Jonty, and he carried an obsolete shotgun bro-ken under one arm. Three black dogs with wild, mistrustful eyes kept close to his heels.

"What about you?" he asked Marcus.

"Strictly urban." Bernie could tell from Marcus's slow head turns that he was keeping watch on the dogs in his peripheral vi-sion, avoiding eye contact. "Big garden. Nothing more."

One of the dogs edged forward and trotted over to Bernie to sniff at the cat-fur lining that was just visible through the straps on her boots. Bernie squatted down and offered a gloved hand for in-spection, fingers carefully closed. The dog wagged its tail, appar-ently satisfied that she had the right canine attitude.

"Probably wants to chase cats with you," Marcus said.

"No, he's got a taste for Stranded." Jonty snapped his fingers and the dog came back to heel. "They killed my other dog, the bastards. That was when I changed to using buckshot. They know the score now. If I catch 'em on my land, I shoot to kill. They got a choice of being civilized like the people up in town, or not, and they chose not, so I treat 'em like any other predator."

Bernie understood the man perfectly, but Marcus didn't look comfortable. It might have been the smell of manure, because that was one thing you rarely got in Jacinto. Either way, he wasn't happy.

"So we could give you security cover," Bernie said carefully.

She wasn't here to do deals, but she'd struck up a rapport with the man, and it seemed a waste of goodwill not to broach the subject. "We'll be reclaiming a lot of the open land for farming in due course, but in the meantime, we'll need to find food supplies to top up the rations."

"I'm finding it hard to work this farm on my own these days," Jonty said. "Now, if you had some spare hands . . ."

"Oh, I'm sure we can find some."

"I think that would work out nicely, then." He looked over Sorotki's Raven with an expression of mild curiosity. "I never been in one of these things, y'know."

"They're noisy buggers." Bernie mimed ear defenders with her hands. "You'll need a headset just to talk."

It took Jonty a few moments to convince the dogs that they should stay put and that he wasn't being taken away. He talked to them like kids, which Bernie found painfully touching. Poor sod: stuck out here on his own, listening for every noise in the night, in case a gang of Stranded decided to cut his throat. Well, that was going to change.

"So you negotiated a food supply," Marcus muttered, out of earshot. "Nice. But it's all COG land anyway."

"I know, but you catch more with honey than you do with vinegar."

"And if they don't accept the honey, then you pour on the vinegar."

"Feel free to do better, Marcus."

"I'm impressed. Really."

"We're going to need one hell of a lot more than a single farm's output, anyway. One and a half to two hectares per person, preferably."

"You worked it all out. Now wait and see what happens when we have to offer the Stranded amnesty."

Marcus had never been sociable, but he was definitely keeping contact with Jonty to a minimum. Bernie knew she was in no position to criticize the farmer for taking potshots at Stranded or talking about them in pest control terms. But Marcus seemed to want to keep his moral high ground. For a man who had no qualms about killing Locust, he was pretty ambivalent about even the worst specimens of humanity.

Easy to be humane if you haven't been on the receiving end of them. But you must have seen your share in prison, Marcus. You know I'm right.

Mitchell stayed in the cockpit with Sorotki as the Raven lifted and circled the farm. Jonty pointed out the boundaries and the routes the Stranded took to get onto his land by following one of the rivers that ran down to their part of the coast. Local intel was precious. Bernie made notes.

"So you're going to bring all your big guns and troops into harbor," Jonty said. "No wonder the vermin are getting restless."

"If they're that dangerous, why haven't they wiped you all out?" Marcus asked.

"Animals generally stop eating when they're full, and predators don't wipe out their food supply, do they? But now you've shown up and upset the food chain."

"Have they ever asked to join you guys?"

"Not as far as I know."

"Would you accept them?"

Jonty snorted derisively. "They think they can make anyone back down, even you, because we've been soft on 'em. We ought to go down there, all of us, every man and woman capable of holding a gun or a knife, and deal with them once and for all."

"So you've had your own war for survival." Marcus's tone didn't change. "You get desperate, you throw everything you've got at it. Done that. Had to destroy the place. *Twice.*"

"I don't think they realize the size of the force you're bringing with you, Sergeant Fenix."

"Time we told them."

"Hey, Fenix, are we just overflying the farms, or what?" Sorotki asked. "The next one's ten klicks east."

"I want to check out the Stranded camp again."

"Why me every time?"

"Because they shot up Gettner's bird."

"They shot up this one, too. Just a recon, or you want another fistfight with them?"

"Let's see."

Jonty leaned forward in his seat and pointed at one of the door guns, its ammo belt loaded and secured. "You can stop them anytime you want. *Permanent.*"

That was the problem with Stranded. Not the pathetic ones, who just eked out an existence from day to day; Bernie couldn't get worked up about them like Baird did. He saw them as traitors who could have fought the grubs but left better men—and occasionally women—to do it. No, it was the violent, criminal ones that were the problem, but even the COG balked at wiping them out.

And yet we fried Sera to stop the Locust. We sank Jacinto. Where do we draw the line? Who's worth sacrificing, and why? Why only good people, or the anonymous innocent ones? Why not those shitbags?

She didn't have an answer.

"See, there's the sheep farm," Jonty said. It was all bucolic peace down there, green and white and leafy, a world away from Jacinto and what was in her mind right then. "Up in town, they do like their meat."

"Shit," Marcus said to himself.

The comment was too quiet for the mike, but Bernie could lip-read that easily enough. The thought of lavish portions of roast meat was almost shocking. Rationing might finally be over before too long. Bernie let herself feel a little excited.

"So what do you take as barter?" she asked.

"Labor. Entertainment. Beer. Food I don't grow or raise."

She could see why people on Vectes had no idea how desperate the rest of humanity had become. *Is that their fault or ours? Could we have shipped out here sooner?* It was all too easy to tie yourself in knots with the if-only and what-if. Everyone did the best they could with the situation they were saddled with on the day.

"Sorotki, can you take us over the Stranded?" Marcus said. "Come in from the highland side if you can."

"Ah, the old gunship-rising-over-the-horizon trick," Sorotki said. "Always a good laxative. And are you sure you want to do it with a civilian passenger embarked?"

Marcus turned to Jonty. "Promise me you won't use that shotgun, whatever happens."

"Not if it's my life on the line."

Marcus shifted the Lancer on his lap. "It won't come to that."

"Leave it to us, Jonty," Bernie said.

"No *us*, Mataki." Marcus checked his watch. "You stay well back this time. I'm giving them Prescott's amnesty offer and telling them where to pick up their dead. After that, they can go to hell. Jonty, if there's any asshole you can ID as a serious criminal, other than just antisocial, you let me know."

Jonty didn't look too pleased with that. "What goddamn amnesty?"

"Standard procedure," Marcus said. "Chairman's orders. We remind them they can join the human race, ask them to hand over their criminals, and the rest is up to them. We're short of humans these days."

"You won't find any down there."

"They never accept anyway."

"And then what? You kick 'em off the island? You don't know, do you?"

"Not my call," Marcus said.

Mitchell manned the gun as Sorotki took the Raven over the cliffs to set down a hundred meters from the Stranded camp. Bernie knew the Stranded here were afraid, all right. It wasn't just the COG showing up in force and ruining their arrangement. It was the first time they'd realized she was a Gear. They knew retribution was coming—and if not from her, then from the COG itself.

"You wait here until I call you," Marcus told Jonty, and jumped out.

"What makes you think they won't kill you?" Jonty called.

"They've seen what one squad can do. So they can work out how a whole army would ruin their day."

"Leave your mike on," Bernie said. "I want to hear."

She couldn't see enough from this distance. Marcus walked slowly to the beachfront shacks and stood there waiting. Eventually a couple of men came out cradling rifles and walked toward him, stopping about five meters away.

"Where's Massy?" Marcus asked.

"Not here. But you'd know that, seeing as you killed him."

"Got a message for you from Chairman Prescott, then. If you haven't committed a capital crime, then he's offering you amnesty. Citizenship. Just front up at the gates of the naval base a week from today, oh-nine-hundred hours."

"Asshole," said the taller man of the two. "Don't try to play fucking civilized with us."

Marcus had a habit of saying what he had to say regardless of the responses he was getting. It made him seem robotic and implacable. The overall effect was unsettling. "And the locals get to look you over and identify the criminal element."

"Followed by a fair trial, yeah?"

"You get the same treatment as a citizen. If any of them commit capital crimes, they're in deep shit, too. Fair's fair."

"And how are you planning to enforce this crap?"

"The navy, a couple of brigades of Gears, and the civilian population of Jacinto are going to be here in a couple of days," Marcus said. He seemed to be working through a list, not really expecting any dialogue, but determined to do it by the book anyway. "Whatever you've got going here is over. How you deal with that is your problem. You can collect your casualties from last night's shit on the southern approach road, about two klicks out. Now, anything you want to say to me?"

"Yeah. Fuck off."

"Fair enough." Marcus took a couple of steps backward. "And the guy who recognized Sergeant Mataki better have a good explanation for why and how next time I see him."

"Oh, there's going to be a next time?"

"Believe it. Where's the blue boat?"

"Why can't you bastards just let us *live*?"

"Living's fine. It's looting and violence we don't like."

"Where the hell are we going to go? There's nowhere left."

"Yeah, we found that out, too." Marcus shrugged and turned to walk back to the Raven. "Try the other islands."

Sorotki turned over the Raven's engine. "That was a waste of fuel. Home, Jonty?"

"Only if you're not going to let me shoot those two."

Marcus repeated the litany. "Can you identify them as murderers, rapists, traitors, arsonists, looters, profiteers, or sex offenders?"

"You missed theft of war materiel," Sorotki said.

Jonty pondered a mental list of crimes, frowning. "I don't think so."

"Then I'm not," Marcus said. He turned to Bernie. "I suppose you've identified a good observation point."

She had. It was habit. She couldn't look at a situation without working out the best place to keep watch and get the drop on someone. "Nice OP on the ridge as we flew in."

"Okay, we wait there and see who we can see. Give Jonty the binoculars, and he can ID some of them. Take us out of hearing range, Sorotki."

Sorotki took the Raven a kilometer inland and left them to walk back on the observation point. By the time they reached the ridge, life in the Stranded settlement had reverted to normal and the residents were wandering around outside. Bernie settled down to scope through the faces.

"Damn." Jonty lowered the binoculars. "There's one I shot. I thought he was dead when they carried him off."

"You need a Longshot," Bernie said. "Reloading's a pain in the arse, but it'll stop a truck."

She thought she recognized some faces. The Stranded were a small community anyway, but in the islands, the toughest individuals were the most mobile, island-hopping in small boats, keeping some sort of loose organization going like landed gentry visiting the peasants' farms. Some folks turned up everywhere, not that there was much of anywhere left—

Yes. They did.

Her scalp tightened as realization dawned. It took her a while to be certain, and in the end it was the tosser's walk that confirmed it. Gait was one of the things you couldn't cover up with a beard or change of hair color—not that this one appeared to feel he even needed to.

It was him. The one that got away. *Until now.*

He was younger than she'd remembered, but she *did* remember. Some things were hard to forget. But however hard she'd tried to put it to one side of her mind so that she could go on living, she knew she didn't want to forget enough to forgo revenge.

"Well, fuck," she said, surprised that she found herself smiling instead of throwing up. "Now I've got the full set."

Marcus put his hand out and pressed down slowly on the barrel of her Longshot.

"Let's talk," he said.

PELRUAN, LATE AFTERNOON.

Dom knew it would happen sooner or later, but it still hurt when it did.

As he walked through the streets toward the bar, he saw Maria.

She was in a group of men and women clustered around a small truck, checking off wooden crates of something that might have been food—butter, cheese, whatever, but something in identical glass pots. For two seconds, she was solid and vivid enough to stop him in his tracks and make his stomach flip over. Every detail froze sharply for a moment, just to hurt him more; he could even see her necklace and her checked skirt.

It isn't real. This kind of shit happens.

Was it really her that I shot? Couldn't it have been someone else?

But he had her necklace, and she'd been wearing the skirt when he found her. The more he stared in that slow-motion moment, the less she was there, and he found himself looking at a dark-haired woman who was actually nothing like her.

Bereaved people saw the dead, and they weren't ghosts. Dr. Hayman had told him it would probably happen to him, too, and then it would stop after a while. For a woman who spat acid, she'd been almost patient when he wanted to ask her questions about Maria. He described what Maria had been like when he found her; Doc Hayman had nodded and said words like *ataxia, dystonia, nystagmus, bradykinesia, ocular toxin deposition,* and by the way, did he realize what those scars on her scalp were? Dom didn't have the technical words, but yes, he knew all too fucking well that Maria was already long dead when she stumbled toward him. Doc Hayman said that she couldn't cure any of those things, and what was left of Maria would have been a long time dying if she'd tried.

I'm not allowed to shoot patients. I'd be a better doctor if I did.

Yeah, Hayman was a tough bitch. But she was honest, and that sometimes did folks more favors than kindness. Dom found himself hearing her voice whenever he started to waver and berate himself.

"What are you staring at?" the not-Maria woman demanded.

"Sorry." Dom didn't actually feel embarrassed at all. "You reminded me of my dead wife."

Yeah, honesty really worked best, most of the time.

He found Marcus and Bernie sitting in the bar with Hoffman, spaced around a circular table like they were waiting to start a seance. Dom could smell the residue of an argument. Of all of them, Hoffman looked the most pissed off.

"Hey, I bartered cleaning the kitchen for some beers on the tab." Dom tried hard to lighten the mood. "Anyone drinking?"

"I'll take a rain check," Hoffman said. "I intend to claim it, Santiago. But it's time I prepared the goddamn carpet of strewn rose petals for the Chairman's arrival." He stood and picked up his cap. "I want to talk to you before I head back, Mataki."

Dom collected beers from the wooden trestle counter and tried to work out what had gone on. Back at the table, Marcus and Bernie looked grim.

She raised her glass. "The Unvanquished."

Dom followed suit. "You think they'll reinstate the old regiments one day?"

"Whether they do or not, I'll always be Two-Six RTI, and that's all there is to it."

Marcus stared at his beer for a while and didn't join in the sentimentality. After a few moments, though, he lifted the glass, focused on it for far longer than it took to line it up, and took a pull.

"We found our third rapist," he said.

Dom assumed the obvious. Hoffman was edgy because Bernie had done something that he now had to smooth over. "Oh. With the scumbags here, yeah?"

"It's a shrinking pond."

Dom waited, but no explanation followed. "Are you going to tell me?"

"We're debating whether me slicing his balls off and feeding them to him would bring about the final collapse of human civilization," Bernie said. "Eh, Marcus?"

Dom didn't get it. "What's the problem?" The guy had committed a crime that carried the death penalty in Jacinto, and Bernie could ID him. Maybe she didn't want a trial. She seemed more embarrassed than traumatized about the whole thing, for whatever reason. "Haul the asshole in. Shit, do we even need a trial?"

Marcus just deepened his frown. "Let's save this for later."

"You still believe in legal systems after what happened to you?" Dom asked. Marcus was still a Fenix, all let's-not-talk-about-it and heavy silences. "Death sentence? Remember that?"

"I was guilty," Marcus said.

Dom would have carried on, but he could see Bernie squirming. He didn't want to make things any worse for her. The past was going to take a long time to shut up and leave them alone, all of them.

"You want to talk about a nice roast leg of lamb?" she asked. "We made friends with a farmer today."

Food was always a good topic for distraction. Nobody could

possibly get upset about it. Dom couldn't recall the last time he ate lamb, and was debating the merits of a proper steak when the door opened and every head in the bar turned.

Dizzy Wallin walked in with his daughters, and—automatically, not really thinking too hard about it—Dom greeted them with a nod. So did Marcus and Bernie.

"Well, ain't this nice," Dizzy said, ushering his daughters to the table. "Can't remember the last time I saw anywhere *peaceful*."

Dizzy wasn't the most fastidious of men—he usually stank of sweat and booze—but he'd done his best to tidy up today, beard combed and nonregulation hat brushed clean. Dom wondered how long he'd keep that up. Being back with his kids seemed to have made a new man of him for the time being, but he still had that distinctive odor of a heavy drinker, a faint methanol smell that soap didn't remove. And no amount of armor would make him look like a military man.

Marcus looked him over and nodded. "So you're the advance party?"

"Flown in special to get them old rigs in the dockyard going," Dizzy said. "I got the magic touch. Betty's gonna be jealous."

Betty was his battered grindlift rig. "She'll understand," Dom said. "A rig in every port, right?"

Bernie moved chairs around so that the two girls—Teresa and Maralin—could sit down. They were twins, maybe sixteen at most, with that numb, scared look that said they'd been bounced from place to place and didn't know what *safe* meant. Dom could imagine the kind of life they led in the Stranded shanties after their dad was conscripted. It brought home to Dom how damned hungry they must have been for Dizzy to enlist just to guarantee food for them. They looked like nice kids—clean and tidy, their long reddish hair pulled back tight in ponytails. At least they could make a new start now.

"I'll get the beer," Dom said. "Juice for the ladies."

Ellen, the woman who ran the bar—and who'd been sweetness and light to Dom earlier—just lowered her chin and looked torn between annoyance and embarrassment.

"Another beer, please," Dom said. "And have you got anything without alcohol?"

"You can't bring them in here, Dom."

He thought she meant Dizzy's daughters. They were too young to buy a beer in Jacinto, that was for sure, but he didn't think folks would be that strict out here. "Hey, I'm sorry, I forgot the age thing."

"It's not that. You know the rules for their kind."

"What kind?" Dom felt his throat tighten. "Gears?"

"You know what I mean. *Stranded*." She lowered her voice. "Look, I know he's in uniform, but . . . we can see what he is. They're going to have to leave, him and the girls, before we get trouble. He's lucky nobody shot him as soon as he got into town."

The bar was one single low-ceilinged space, more like a sprawling living room than a bar, without one glass or chair that matched another. Dom realized he wasn't having a private conversation. The whole bar was watching and listening.

"He's not Stranded," Dom said. "He's a Gear, just like me. And if he's a Gear, then his kids are Gear's kids."

Silence was a strange thing. It wasn't just an absence of noise. It was unnatural and frozen—tensed muscles, held breaths, spit unswallowed. Dom turned to check what was going to come crashing down on him. The room just had that feeling. It wasn't exactly an ugly crowd, not like some of the bars he'd ended up in and wished he hadn't, but it reeked of hatred.

But it's only Dizzy. He's a great guy. He's one of us. What the hell's going on?

Dizzy bowed his head for a moment. "We didn't plan on staying. Come on, sweeties, let's go. Got work to do."

"This man saved my ass." Marcus put his hand on Dizzy's forearm and pinned him where he sat. "If you're attacked by Stranded again, he'll save yours."

Bernie leaned back in her seat. "Yeah, we're all Gears. If he's not welcome, *we're* not welcome."

Dom waited for someone to make a move. Nobody did. In a way, he would have felt better if they'd just thrown a few chairs and swung punches, because that was easy, honest, simple. Instead, they just *looked*, and the looks on their faces said that they didn't like Gears much, either. *Great idea to remind them, Bernie.* This was their island. They hadn't a clue what had gone on over on the mainland, but whatever it was, they didn't want any of that shit messing up their nice tidy lives. It was like they couldn't connect the pieces of the world and understand that they couldn't opt out of it.

A few grubs would have straightened you out, assholes. You really need to understand what it's been like out there.

"Okay, that was a beer and two juices, yeah?" Dom abandoned the goodwill of barter and slapped his remaining bills on the counter. "That's still legal tender. It'll buy you something useful at any COG base."

Ellen didn't say anything more, but she got him his drinks and took the money. Regimental honor had been satisfied. It probably didn't make Dizzy and his daughters feel any better, but Dom *knew.* He met Marcus's eyes, then Bernie's, and it was what Baird called a primal moment. The Gears bond was unbreakable. And that included Dizzy. It was the indefinable tribalism that held an army together under fire when any sane man would have been running for his life, and it was as powerful as any emotion Dom had ever known. His heart had been broken so often by now that he wasn't sure what it felt like to be his old self, but he knew that heady bond, and it gave him hope.

The noise level in the bar slowly ratcheted up into normal hubbub as everyone tried to pretend they hadn't really tried to kick out a Gear for not being human enough. Marcus looked as if he was counting down the minutes until he could walk out with Dizzy without looking like they'd been driven out.

"First thing we do," Bernie said, "is make sure there's a sergeants' mess set up in VNB." Vectes Naval Base had become a familiar acronym overnight, just through repetition in fleet signals to the Ravens. "Even if we have to wait for the beer to arrive. I'd rather drink water in the right company."

Marcus glanced at his watch again. It was hard to have a con versation under the circumstances. Eventually an older man passed their table and leaned over a little toward Marcus.

"You were awarded the Embry Star, weren't you?" he said. "Aspho Fields."

Marcus braced to repel hero worship. Dom watched his jaw set. "Yeah. So was Private Santiago here. And Sergeant Mataki got a Sovereign's Medal."

"I remember," the man said, and moved on.

Dizzy scratched his beard. "Damn, never knew we was drinking with a bunch of heroes."

"You're not," Marcus said. "You're drinking with your buddies."

After thirty minutes, Marcus seemed to decide that the point had been made, and got up to go. Dizzy showed off a huge, ancient truck that he'd driven up from VNB, and they killed some time debating why it mattered to drag Pelruan into the fold if they were going to rebuild Jacinto to the south anyway. Anya was overoptimistic—Dom would never call her crazy—if she thought that it was going to make for a better society in the long run. It was all about numbers; Jacinto's remnant had them, and Pelruan didn't.

Teresa edged closer to Bernie and eventually managed a few words. Dom was beginning to wonder if the two girls were so traumatized that they didn't talk. That bothered him.

"They hate us, Sergeant Mataki," Teresa said. "Is it going to be like this everywhere?"

"Not if we have anything to do with it," Bernie said. "Right, Delta?"

Dizzy seemed to pick up on Bernie's embarrassment. "Some Stranded are halfway to bein' real people, sweeties. *Domesticated.*"

Bernie looked chastened. After Dizzy and his girls drove off back to the base, Marcus stood staring at the dwindling taillights for a few moments.

"Never thought you had any time for Stranded, Bernie."

"Don't recall seeing any Stranded in that bar," she said. "And don't think that Dizzy didn't make me feel guilty, either."

Dizzy had chosen to be a regular human as far as she was concerned. Dom thought it was interesting to watch where people drew their lines. Marcus just nodded.

"Don't forget Hoffman's waiting to talk to you," he said, and walked off in the direction of the Ravens.

CHAPTER 13

It's as if they waited seventy-nine years for us to finish the Pendulum Wars and drain ourselves dry. Then they made their move.

(GENERAL BARDRY SALAMAN, SPECULATING ON THE TIMING OF THE LOCUST HORDE'S EMERGENCE.)

VOSLOV BRIDGE, THIRTY-FIVE KILOMETERS WEST OF EPHYRA, SEVEN HOURS BEFORE HAMMER OF DAWN DEPLOYMENT, FOURTEEN YEARS AGO—1 A.E.

"What's your position, Fenix?"

"Somewhere between totally screwed and up shit creek, Control."

"Cut the crap. Can you see the convoy?"

"What's left of it." Marcus gestured to Dom for the field glasses. "It's blocked the road, right on the bridge. So no point diverting refugee traffic that way."

"The General says that we have to open that route in the next hour."

"Well, Sherston, tell the General to get his ass down here and help push a few 'Dills."

"Five thousand civvies looking for a way home, Fenix."

"No pressure, then."

Dom was happier when Anya was duty controller. She didn't wind up Marcus as much as Sherston did. On a good day, she could almost keep him happy.

Today was not a good day. They were running out of time. At 0001 hours, Ephyra time, orbital laser strikes would destroy everything outside the city that the Locust could take and use against humans. With any luck, it would catch most of the bastards on the surface, too.

It's got to be done, Marcus. Your dad's right.

But that's easy for me to say—I've got nothing left to lose outside Ephyra. What about Tai and Pad?

"Come on, guys," Marcus said. "Let's get creative. Fast."

The grubs were frugal bastards, Dom had to give them that.

From the cover of the bridge control booth, he could see about fifty of them on the far bank, stripping everything they could carry from a line of trucks, APCs, and Packhorse utility vehicles. The ambushed convoy had blocked the road. The route-proving vehicle at its head was still smoking, skewed halfway across the two eastbound lanes of the bridge, and everything else had piled up behind it. It couldn't have happened more than thirty minutes ago.

Shit, if only we'd moved faster, been here sooner . . .

"Can we take 'em?" Dom whispered. He glanced over his shoulder to see if the others were up for it. "How many Longspears have we got left?"

"We'll just blow up more shit and they'll scatter," Padrick said. "A Raven on a strafing run would be handy, but we're fresh out of those at the moment."

Marcus crouched as if he was about to sprint out from cover. "I want that bulldozer down there left in one piece. Save the anti-armor rounds for later."

The bulldozer could have cleared the bridge of wrecks, but it had its own problems. The cab screen was shattered. The whole rig was off the road, facing west, as if the driver had reversed and turned it to face the oncoming Locust ambush.

And there was a big, open expanse of road—a marshaling

area—to cross before they got anywhere near the bridge itself. It was a bascule structure that opened to let ships pass. Nothing much had ventured downriver for the past year, and the control booth had been abandoned.

"Well, at least I've finally visited Shit Creek," Dom said. "Look at those assholes down there. They must have more of our equipment now than we have."

The grubs were taking everything; ammo, weapons, ration packs, even dismantling the vehicles. The COG convoy was being taken apart a component at a time and ferried back by a chain of drones to whatever sewer the grubs called home. Dom sighted up on one of the grubs as it ripped open the door of a truck and hauled out the Gear slumped at the wheel to strip the armor from him.

When it tried to pull off his helmet, Dom could see that the guy was still alive. He started to struggle.

"Shit." Dom snapped a scope on his rifle, racked up the magnification, and saw blood coming from the man's mouth. "I got to do something."

Marcus must have checked through his own scope, because he just grunted. Dom's instinct said to blow the grub's head off. Common sense said to finish the Gear. He didn't know what to do, and both solutions were bad. In the three seconds he tried to decide, the grub solved the problem for him and put a few rounds into the man's head to finish him. Then it went on scavenging his armor and kit.

"Bastard," Dom said.

"It only did what we would have done." Marcus started prying open the door of the control booth from a squatting position. "Motives don't make any difference to the guy on the receiving end."

And if I'd shot him, done the decent thing, we'd be under fire now, too.

It still didn't make him feel any better. He knew what he'd want Marcus to do for him in that same situation.

"You look like a man with a plan, Sarge," Padrick said.

"If there's still power to the bridge, then yes." The door splintered around the lock. Marcus went on rocking it carefully, forcing a gap he could get his fingers into. The grubs wouldn't hear anything over the noise of their own scraping, hammering, and hauling. "Gravity is a wonderful thing."

The door suddenly gave way and Marcus fell back on his ass. The four of them crawled into the booth, keeping beneath the level of the windows, and Marcus knelt at the operator's position.

"Pad, scope through and tell me what's happening out there." He ran his fingers over the bridge controls, frowning. "Where's the power supply?"

Dom crawled around, looking for clues. "Hey, it's in the on position. Are you going to open the bridge?"

"Ever tipped garbage down a chute?"

"What's that going to do, apart from clear the bridge?"

"Shunt a line of traffic back onto the grubs, and keep them busy while Tai lines up a few Longspears to ruin their day."

"You're nuts."

"I'm out of options." Marcus always looked the quiet type until he opened fire or came up with a maximum-risk plan. He was still getting to grips with the bridge controls. "Okay—power, warning signal, safety gates, motors. I need to bypass the warnings."

"What if they're safety-interlocked with the motors?"

"Then the grubs work out what's coming, but they're still going to be caught in a lot of sliding metal."

Tai assembled the Longspear launcher control with a satisfied expression on his face. No, not satisfied; *serene*.

Pad scrambled to another position in the booth to look west. "Nothing's ever going to wipe that smile off your face, is it?"

Dom could see why Pad thought he was slightly unhinged. Tai just took every bit of shit that came his way with a kind of certainty that it was all going to work out, whether he survived it or not. Faith was a wonderful thing.

Dom preferred taking fate into his own hands, preferably with an assault rifle. He traced the cables back from under the control desk, lifting sections of the floor. It was like a kid's toy down there, cabling sheathed in vivid red, blues, and yellow, with oversized transformers in cheerful bright green housings. Even the nuts and bolts on the metal cases looked comically toy-like. There were also isolation switches for servicing. The COG was nothing if not thorough. Everything was stenciled and labeled.

"This is the power to the gates," Dom said. "I can switch that off. Now, the lights and horns —"

"Found it." Marcus interrupted. "Emergency control. Just raises the bridge, maximum speed. In case of *imminent vessel impact.*"

"Tough shit if you're on the bridge," Pad said.

"Tough shit anyway if a ship hits you. Ship's likely to cost more lives."

It was the kind of throwaway comment that could silence everyone in these last few days. Every frigging decision came down to the same thing. One life or five? Ten or a thousand? The rest of Sera or humanity itself? Nothing was ever easy.

Pad rested his rifle on the sill of the booth's front window, adjusting the scope as he observed the Locust scavenging team. "If you're thinking of pressing that button, now would be good. Nice big bunch of them trying to deal with a truck."

"Handle," Marcus said. "It's a handle."

"Well, whatever it is, Sergeant Pedant, do it now if you want maximum buggeration factor for our ugly friends down there."

"Tai, you ready?" Marcus said. "Do as much damage as you can, but avoid the bulldozer."

The door creaked as Tai ducked out of the booth. Dom got ready for the follow-up.

It wasn't going to kill all the grubs, and they'd have to go down there and finish the fight. "This better work."

Marcus grasped the handle and pushed it to the raised position. It worked, all right. There was a loud clunk as gears engaged and motors started up. The vehicles on the bridge started to vibrate. For a few moments the grubs took no notice, and then those on the bridge itself seemed to realize something was wrong. Maybe they didn't make the connection with the control booth, either, but it was too late for that because the span of the bridge had now clearly opened in the middle, rising faster than Dom expected, sending vehicles sliding onto the grubs standing between them. Some started screaming, crushed between fenders; some jumped clear into the water. As the bridge sections tilted more steeply, the vehicles skidded and tumbled rather than rolled, falling onto the vehicles behind. Dom couldn't see much now and darted outside to start dropping as many grubs as he could from this side of the river.

Tai knelt on one knee, apparently oblivious of the crashing and creaking metal ahead of him, with the Longspear launcher resting on his shoulder. The first round arced high in the air. Dom thought the missile was going wide, but a massive explosion threw up a fireball and visible chunks of truck, grubs, and APCs. A sheet of fire swept under the vehicles and engulfed the whole logjam in smoke and flames. Dom could hear the grubs shrieking.

"I would let the flames die down before we deal with survivors," Tai said mildly, standing up and slinging the launcher on his back again. "It will be easier to see."

"Shit," Padrick said. "Nice shot."

"Fuel truck." Tai bobbed his head in a bow. "Thank you."

"Can you see the bulldozer?" Marcus leaned out of the booth. "Is it okay? Otherwise we've wasted our time, because we can't drive the damn vehicles clear now."

"I can see its back end," Pad said. "It's okay. Can you drive one?"

"How hard can it be?"

"Better let me do it."

Dom took up position in the cover of a tree and picked off any grubs he could see. It was hard to tell what was down there with the smoke and charring. One blackened shape stumbled to the riverbank, teetered on the concrete flood defenses, and fell into the torrent below. Dom took a shot anyway, even though it was a waste of ammo. Explosions still threw debris into the air as fuel tanks and tires burst in the intense heat. One chunk of engine smashed straight through the bulldozer's cab.

"Fuck." Marcus was as agitated as Dom had ever seen him, jaw clenching and unclenching as if he was chewing a brick. "That's just terrific."

"Hey, all we have to do is get it to move," Pad said. "Trust a boy who grew up with combine harvesters."

They waited and took potshots at anything that seemed to move in the inferno. After fifteen minutes, the flames began to die down. Acrid black smoke filled the air. Dom could taste the sulfur.

"Of course," Pad said, making his way down the slope to the bridge, "we'll die of some hideous lung disease now. Lower the bridge, Sarge."

Reaching the bulldozer meant edging along the concrete flood defenses that lined the stretch of river; the crush of burning vehicles had completely blocked the road. While Pad got the bulldozer started and Marcus provided cover, Dom prowled the wreckage, shielding his face against the heat with his free hand, hoping there wasn't another fuel tank simmering away and waiting to take his head off. For a moment he thought of the bodies of the Gears in those vehicles. He couldn't retrieve their COG-tags, and he felt bad about that because their families would need to know for sure what had happened to them. But there was nothing he could do about it.

Tai worked his way down to the tail of the convoy. Dom heard him fire a few bursts into the trees, but there were no grubs left around. If they'd survived, they'd gone back into their emergence holes to whatever cesspit they came from.

It's all going to look like this tomorrow.

Shit, how can I keep forgetting that?

Every big city—burned to a cinder like this.

Dom leaned over, free hand braced on his knee, feeling suddenly sick. It was fatigue, he told himself—everyone chucked up when they were this exhausted. Then he realized that the oily black debris he was looking at was moving.

Oh, shit. It was alive. It was a grub.

What if it's not?

Dom realized he couldn't tell a badly burned grub from a badly burned human. He was looking into a face, but he couldn't see the eyes, so this could have been a guy he knew or the Locust boss bastard himself.' He was so shocked that he didn't react until an arm lifted. Then he saw the bulky outline of a rifle that wasn't a Lancer. He emptied a clip into the body.

It took all his nerve to squat down and feel for a COG-tag. There wasn't one.

What if it hadn't been a grub?

Shit, man, I couldn't let a human suffer like that, anyway.

He wasn't even sure if he would feel okay about leaving a grub to die slowly. Maybe he didn't have enough hate in him, or he'd worn it out.

A sudden rumble followed by screeching metal made him look up. The bulldozer was on the move, shoving wreckage out of the way and pushing it into the river. It was the nearest garbage bin. Padrick never did mess about.

Marcus stepped behind the raised safety barriers, keeping clear of Pad's destructive rampage. Dom joined him, feeling lost for the moment, and didn't bother to switch back into the comms circuit. He didn't want to hear the mounting panic in people's voices. Even here, even in Tyrus, there were refugees who just weren't going to make it to the safe zone by midnight.

Fucking impossible decision.

"Control, Fenix here. Control . . . come in, Control." This was how Dom would always picture Marcus: finger jammed in one ear, head down, face like thunder, apparently pissed off at something or somebody. "Control, Fenix here . . . nice of you to join us, Sherston. We'll have the route clear in thirty minutes. Tell them to reroute the convoy."

He had to feel good about that, didn't he? Dom would rather have been saving people he knew, but that wasn't his job.

That's the real test. Sacrificing one person to save a hundred is pretty rough, but it's the obvious thing to do. Isn't it? I mean, nobody would argue with that, would they? But what if that one person is your mother, your wife, your best buddy? What do you do then?

Dom didn't know, and hoped that he never had to find out.

Control must have told Marcus to get back to Ephyra, because all Dom heard him say before he signed off was, "No, we'll make sure the route's clear."

Dom nudged him. "We've got five hours, Marcus."

"Yeah," he said. "If I didn't think there was plenty of time, I'd send you all back now and wait here myself."

Padrick seemed to be enjoying the release of smashing into inanimate objects. He went on clearing wreckage over a bigger area than he needed to, and eventually Marcus had to flag him down to make him stop. They took the 'Dill west along the highway until they saw headlights in the distance, then pulled off the road until the convoy reached them.

The lead Packhorse slowed to a halt and the driver dropped the side window. "You should join the Engineer Corps, Fenix."

"Maybe I will," he said. "Where do you want us, point or tail?"

"Tail."

Pad went off-road and skimmed past what felt like a neverending line of military vehicles, commercial trucks, livestock transports, private cars, and tankers until they reached the end of the line. Dom wanted to talk, but Marcus was feigning sleep, Tai stared at his clasped hands as if he was meditating or praying or something, and Pad had his eyes on the road. Dom felt there was nothing he could say that wouldn't make him sound like a total asshole.

"This is going to be one of the last convoys that makes it home before the deadline," he said at last.

"Thank fuck we're in it, then," Padrick muttered.

Dom had to ask. "Guys . . . have you still got family out there, in the Islands?"

Marcus made a sound that could have been a sigh, a snore, or a hint to shut up. Tai looked up from his clasped hands.

"The Hammer of Dawn would waste its time targeting most of the Islands," he said. "So I can hope."

Dom had no comfort to offer. The 'Dill kept a sensible distance from the last truck in the convoy and rolled past the Ephyra checkpoint with three hours to spare.

"Home," Dom said.

Marcus opened his eyes at last. "Yeah. Whatever that'll mean tomorrow morning."

CHAIRMAN PRESCOTT'S OFFICE, 2401 HOURS, TWO HOURS BEFORE HAMMER OF DAWN DEPLOYMENT.

Even now, Prescott still watched the door.

He realized there was still enough of the helpless human being left in him to wish for a last-minute reprieve. Perhaps—just perhaps—Adam Fenix would walk through the door declaring that he had an answer, a way to stop the Locust Horde without destroying anything or anybody. Perhaps Salaman was heading this way to say that word had reached the Locust commanders of the planned Hammer strike, and that they now wanted to talk terms.

But Richard Prescott had long ago given up believing that problems solved themselves miraculously. It was when he was around twelve years old and worked out that grown-ups didn't have all the answers, and that even his mighty father, Chairman David Prescott, could not come back from the dead no matter how much his son wanted it to happen.

Prescott wondered how his father would have felt about him stepping into dead men's shoes to lead the COG rather than winning an election. But Dalyell's heart attack now looked like a lucky escape from the hell to follow.

You didn't have to succeed him. A deputy chairman can always say no.

Nobody ever had, of course. Anyone who stood for office *wanted* to sit in this chair eventually, but now there were no deputies to lean on, and no elections to replace them.

No miracles. No luck. Just decisions, and the willingness to stand by them.

I just wish I knew—really knew—what was happening to Sera.

Until then, Prescott was guessing about everything—except the fact that the Locust were close to overrunning Tyrus, almost at the Ephyra border as predicted, and that he had one card left to play.

The door opened, and it really was Adam Fenix.

"Do you have any miracles?" Prescott asked.

Fenix looked taken aback. "No, Chairman. Just data."

"That'll have to do, then." Fenix looked drained, and Prescott wondered if he needed a drink. "That boy of yours is hard to keep on a leash. I hear he's just returned from convoy escort duty. We did try to keep him out of harm's way, Professor, but he's determined not to be special."

Fenix didn't seem to know his son had been on operational duty today. His brow creased briefly, just a flash of a frown. "He'll never manage to be anything *but* special."

"Help yourself to a drink," Prescott said, indicating the decanters on the sideboard. He opened the doors onto the balcony and stared up at the night sky to look for the orbiting Hammer platforms.

If he lined up on the Octus Tower, he could distinguish stars from moving satellites. It was getting harder to see objects in the night sky because of the airborne pollution from fires and destruction, but tonight the pinpoints of light showed themselves in a brief window of clarity, warning him: *Look at us, Richard. Be sure you understand what you're about to do.*

"People think you're bluffing," Fenix said.

"Who's there to bluff?" The thought disappointed Prescott. "The other COG leaders? There's nothing for them to concede now. And we have no communication with the Locust whatsoever. How can I possibly give *them* an ultimatum?"

Fenix looked distinctly uncomfortable. Prescott had catalogued the man's vanities and weaknesses within half an hour of first meeting him, but it was seeing Hoffman skirmish with him that filled in the gaps. Hoffman watched Fenix's eyes a lot. It was more than simple human eye contact or even aggression—although Hoffman had an excess of that. Fenix's eyes were his barometer. He went from an unnerving stare to rapid blinking. The rate seemed to indicate his degree of anxiety.

He was close to off the scale now.

"You're right," Fenix said after a long pause. "But people aren't rational. They want to find a reason to believe we won't carry this out."

We. How collegiate. Fenix was both vain—ferociously gifted, a history shaper, and rightly aware of it—and given to martyrdom. He wasn't prepared to wash his hands of his creation even when it was about to be turned on his world.

"I know you're deeply conflicted over this, Professor," Prescott said.

Fenix laughed, the little desperate bark of a man closer to tears than to humor, and cupped both hands over his nose and mouth for a brief moment. He was still staring up at the sky. He hadn't helped himself to that drink after all.

"You have no idea *how* conflicted, Chairman," he said at last.

"Adam . . ." First-name terms after weeks of rigid formality often helped cement an idea in someone's mind. Names had power. "Either you're a monster who built a weapon that will kill millions, or you're the man whose genius will save humankind." Prescott paused to let that sink in, and realized it was one of those moments when he caught himself telling the raw truth even when he didn't plan to. "You've given us our last hope. That kind of power always has its consequences, Adam, believe me. Governance is about choices. All too often, it's about working out which is the least hideous."

"I'm not a politician," Fenix said. "I'm a scientist."

"You build strategic weapons. Join the club."

"I've failed."

"Only if the Hammer strikes don't work."

"No, as a scientist, I *should* have found a nonviolent solution in time."

"So that's why there are so many scientists and engineers working on military projects."

"That's where the research grants are."

"Ah, science ethics at work . . ."

"I'm talking about my conscience. Not theirs."

"You were a serving officer."

"I was. A major in Two-Six RTI."

"You always returned fire, yes?"

"Sometimes you sound just like Hoffman." Fenix seemed to decide he'd had enough of the sky, and now gazed at the floor. "But I killed men rather than let them kill me. This is not the *same.*"

Prescott stopped short of the lecture on collateral damage. Fenix had done the work the COG needed him to do, but if the man was tipped too far, then he might not cooperate further. Prescott checked his watch and the antique clock on the table.

"It's time to save humanity, Adam. Are you sure you won't have that drink?"

Fenix shook his head. Prescott put his hand on the man's elbow and steered him toward the door.

The offices and corridors were almost empty as they made their way to the command center. Ephyra was safe, but nonessential staff had taken Prescott at his word when he said that they might want to be at home with their families tonight. Only the security officer at the main doors was on duty; he was reading a newspaper while a television under the desk illuminated his face with flickering light. Prescott could hear the faint, tinny voice of a reporter. But he knew that if he stopped to look or listen and saw the streams of refugees or the other cities still full of people refusing to leave— or unable to—that it would only make things harder.

The security guard dropped the paper and stood up, startled. "Good evening, sir." He went to switch off the TV, but Fenix held up his hand to stop him.

"Just a quick look," Fenix said, and walked behind the desk to watch the screen. "That's live, isn't it?"

"Yes sir, from Gerrenhalt."

Prescott watched, too. Gerrenhalt wasn't far from Ephyra— four hours on a light traffic day, perhaps. Now everyone on that screen—the people in cars, the pedestrians, the defiant householders determined to sit it out—would be dead in hours. They weren't going to make it to Ephyra.

They were dead already.

And the reporter.

The TV station had a reporter on the spot. What kind of person would volunteer to do that? Was the man so stupid or so arrogant that he thought he was immune? Or was he just so blinded by the need to do his job, so shocked by the scale of the story, that he *had* to be there?

What kind of person would do my *job right now?*

There was only him. And that was why he had to do it.

CIC OPS ROOM, HOUSE OF THE SOVEREIGNS,
2545 HOURS, SIXTEEN MINUTES TO HAMMER
STRIKE.

"Colonel? Are you all right?"

Adam Fenix was standing right behind him, but Hoffman didn't notice until the man handed him a sheaf of papers. He wanted those papers to be checkpoint reports from Corren, handed to him by Anya Stroud or Timothy Sherston, or any of the other CIC controllers who were in touch with the movement of civilian traffic.

But the checkpoint teams had all been pulled back to Ephyra half an hour ago, and none of them had found Margaret Hoffman or her sister, Natalie. All Hoffman knew was that Natalie had left the hospital emergency room in Corren two days ago and hadn't returned.

"Professor." Hoffman refused to lose face in front of Fenix. It was bad for morale. Every Gear needed to believe that the senior commanders were fully in control, not sweating next to a phone, hands almost shaking, for some word of hope. "I won't pretend I'm fine. If I thought things were just dandy now, then I shouldn't be in this job."

"I understand. I really do."

Hoffman suspected that Marcus Fenix would have understood a whole lot better than his father right then. Fenix senior was more talkative but somehow managed to say less. Hoffman was never sure what was going on in Marcus's head, but he could judge by his actions and fill in the gaps, and that told him he was dealing with a modest soldier, a professional, an honorable man who simply didn't broadcast what he felt. Adam Fenix just struck Hoffman as someone who thought he always knew best and paraded his conscience in half-assed moral debates for lesser beings like Hoffman to admire.

"Your son's a credit to the Coalition," Hoffman said. *Take it as a conciliatory gesture or an unflattering comparison, whichever you like, Professor.* "If anyone lives the Octus Canon, it's him."

Fenix looked a little embarrassed. "I often wonder if he ever thinks of ideologies at all. Yes, he's an exceptional young man— thank you. He has Elain's independent streak."

Well, at least he talked about his dead wife. He'd never done that before, not that he'd ever made small talk with Hoffman. It was as good a night as any for the dead to wander back into conversations and remind everyone just how many of them there would be very soon.

Ten minutes.

Margaret was still out there.

I need a miracle.

What was the last thing I said to her? That I couldn't and wouldn't stop the Hammer strike. What was the last thing she said to me? "Fuck you."

Would I feel any better now if we'd lied and said that we loved each other?

"And how's Margaret?" Fenix asked.

"Missing," Hoffman said.

He didn't mean to hit below the belt. But it was true, and there was no other answer he could give.

"Oh God." Fenix looked genuinely shocked. "I'm so sorry—I had no idea. Colonel, everything's in disarray at the moment, I'm sure she's safe somewhere in Ephyra, but you've seen the chaos—"

"She left for Corren after the announcement," Hoffman said quietly, "and as of this moment . . ." He checked the bank of clocks on the other wall, each showing local time in every major city. "As of this moment, with nine minutes to go, she has not returned."

They just looked at each other. On the wall behind them — and Hoffman was sure that Fenix was avoiding looking at it unless he had to, just like Hoffman — hung a backlit chart of Sera's surface, skinned and pinned like an animal hide into a ragged-edged, flattened shape. Every major city was marked with concentric rings showing blast radii. Many of those rings overlapped, and when Hoffman found the stomach to look at it, he had to search hard to find areas that would be beyond the range of the orbital lasers' destruction.

It was going to take three phases of fire to hit every target, realigning the lasers after each strike. The number of satellite platforms needed for a synchronized apocalypse probably exceeded the COG's budget, Hoffman thought, but then nobody sane would ever have planned for the almost total destruction of the planet's surface.

Not almost. *Ephyra's a speck compared to Sera. It might as well be the whole damn world.*

"Colonel, I have no idea what to say to you," Fenix said. "Other than how very sorry I am."

The room was a blur for Hoffman now. He was aware of everything in it, and he was functioning, competent to do his job, but everything was distorted. The normal focus of his vision, background and foreground, had gone. Everything seemed to be in sharp focus regardless of distance, and as for the sounds — he could hear *everything*, too much, every conversation, without the instinctive filter that told his brain what to concentrate on and what to ignore.

Salaman and Prescott were standing at the Hammer control panel. It needed three separate keys to be inserted and turned simultaneously to remove the failsafe lock. In minutes, Hoffman would have to walk over there and place his key in the slot.

I deserve this, but Margaret doesn't.

"Sir?" Anya Stroud edged close to him, as if she wanted Fenix to walk away, but he didn't. "Sir, just so you know—I've tracked down every Gear who's been on checkpoint duties anywhere within Tyrus, and I'm afraid nobody recorded her outbound, let alone inbound. She must have taken a back-road route to Corren. Every highway and minor road to Ephyra is at a standstill now."

Anya was a sweet kid, all heart if you knew how to listen to her. "I wondered why you hadn't rostered off for so long."

"I'm sorry I couldn't do more, sir."

"You've done more than you'll ever know, my dear." It was far too familiar a way to address a junior officer, but he didn't give a shit right then. Anya was being Anya, so he would just be Victor for a few moments. "Thank you for trying. I won't forget it."

And now he had to carry on. Fenix hadn't moved.

Five minutes.

We're going to incinerate Sera, and all I can think about is one woman.

Maybe that's all any of us can manage tonight. To grieve on a manageable scale.

"Victor?" Salaman gestured to him, beckoning almost casually, like he wanted him to join them for a drink, but his face was that awful pasty yellow again. "It's time. Let's do it."

Hoffman had a terrible feeling of walking to his own execution, not crossing the room to be the executioner. Fenix caught his arm.

"If you prefer, Victor—give me the key. I'll do it. Like you said, it's my bomb."

Fenix rarely called him anything but *Colonel.* The damnedest things happened at times like this; you could never really tell with people, not until they were pushed to the limit, and then they could shock you for good or ill.

"Thanks," Hoffman said, and meant it. His lips were moving, and he could hear himself speaking, but somehow it wasn't him. It was the Hoffman who had to front up and earn it, the one who had to be seen to be holding it together because so many depended on him doing just that. "I won't be the only man widowed tonight. I shouldn't dish it out if I can't take it."

Salaman and Prescott waited. Hoffman just got it over with. He placed his key in the slot first, followed by Salaman, then Prescott.

"Three . . . two . . . *turn,*" said Salaman.

The command keys had now started the arming process.

It's as good as over. Where the hell are you, Margaret? Don't be afraid. Please, don't be afraid.

It was the duty tactical officer's job to physically deploy the Hammer. But there were just two switches on the console to press, nothing requiring expertise because the computer system ironed out the timing, and Prescott had decided it was his responsibility alone.

The officer moved aside without being asked. Prescott held his finger above the illuminated plastic buttons, and took one last glance at his watch before looking up at Fenix. The professor nodded.

"Forgive us," Prescott said, pressing one button, then the other.

Forgive me, Margaret.

And Sera burned.

CHAPTER 14

I refuse to tolerate no-go areas for COG citizens in COG sovereign territory. We are either Citizens or Stranded—there is no middle ground. If we start over with a fragmented society, the divisions will only widen, and I will not allow Pelruan to become an enclave. There will be one community and one law for all.

(CHAIRMAN RICHARD PRESCOTT, RESPONDING TO THE DISCUSSION
ON HOW TO DEAL WITH THE EXISTING POPULATION OF VECTES.)

SMALL VESSELS BASIN, VECTES NAVAL BASE,
NINE WEEKS AFTER THE EVACUATION OF
JACINTO, 14 A.E.

"Damn, that's a pretty sunrise," Cole said.

"Weather's going to be shitty, then. Red sunsets are what you want."

"Baird, freezin' your ass off is shitty. A little bit of rain is good for the fields."

Like every Gear, Cole could sleep anywhere, anytime. Or at least he thought he could. Now he was up at a damn ridiculous hour because he couldn't, and word had gone around that the Pelruan trawlers were coming into Vectes today. Cole wanted to watch. It sounded interesting.

The naval base was now filling up with warships, fuel tankers, and just about anything that would float. Cole walked along the jetty, noting what had shown up since he last looked, and felt sure that some of these tubs hadn't been at Merrenat dockyard. He started counting. It looked like Captain Michaelson had found a couple of extra amphib landing ships from somewhere. Some ships were turning right around and heading back to Port Farrall to pick up the last loads of equipment and personnel. It was getting to be a regular taxi service.

Actually, it looked like a pretty damn impressive navy under the circumstances. The little boats hanging around made it look a bit colorful and unmilitary in places, but the big ships had some serious guns. The Ravens Nest carriers were lined up in the big deepwater berth, deck to deck, so that you could almost walk from ship to ship if you felt like it. They were an island in their own right.

Imagine when we had hundreds of them. And now we're down to maybe a tenth of that.

"They hid those things somewhere," Baird said. "They were supposed to have turned in a shitload of hulls to the breakers to reclaim the steel. Crafty assholes."

"Yeah, those crafty assholes sure came in useful, baby."

Hell, it was only because crazy fish-heads like Michaelson and Fyne hid stuff from the reclaim system that the COG had any navy left at all. Cole wasn't complaining. A man was entitled to tell a few lies in the paperwork if he knew he could save lives one day. The navy hadn't had much attention for a long, long time. It obviously got up to all kinds of shit when Prescott's back was turned.

Cole found himself laughing his head off at the thought.

"What's so funny?" Baird still seemed to have his eye on the submarine. He wandered across the caisson to admire it. "Share."

"The navy's just a bunch of pirates in uniforms. Gotta love that."

"Maybe it's just me, but I don't find all that pirate shit romantic. Stranded are bad enough on land. They're not any prettier when they float."

"Go on, make eyes at that sub. You know you want to."

Anyone who said Baird wasn't capable of loving much besides himself just hadn't seen the way he looked at machines. A sailor was working on the sub's casing, messing around with a hatch, and he looked up at the two of them like he found it funny to see Gears sightseeing at this time of the morning.

"Couldn't you sleep?" he called to them. "Land crabs don't usually get up before thirteen hundred, do they?"

Baird didn't go for the bait. He must have *really* wanted to scramble over that sub. The name plate on the fin said CLEMENT. "Nice boat."

"We *like* Gears smart enough to call her a *boat*." The guy went on working. His sleeve badges said he was a petty officer of some sort, all anchors and chevrons. Cole needed to brush up on the navy's fancy ranks. "In fact, we like you so much we won't even try to sink you."

"Never been in a submarine."

"We can remedy that, for a price . . . You're Corporal Baird, right? You repair things."

"Yeah." Baird looked on the happy side of smug. Word of his skills got around fast. "I do."

"We've got a lot that needs repairing."

"Don't encourage him, baby," Cole said. "He'll never hand the keys back."

"We're heading out to search for a trawler as soon as I'm done here. Seeing as Gears got nothing to do now except overeat and chat up women, come along for the ride and make yourself useful."

Sometimes Cole really *did* feel he didn't have anything worth doing now. It wasn't that he missed grubs; he just liked winning, and there wasn't much he did lately that felt like hard work.

"What's happened to the trawler?" he asked.

"The last radio message was weird. The skipper thought he was on a collision course with another boat, and the others lost contact after that." The chief bolted down the small hatch. "They go around in flotillas for safety, apparently. No wreckage yet, so we offered to help. Might get a few choice fillets out of it . . ."

"Okay," Baird said. "I'll be back in fifteen minutes."

Man, Baird was pleased with himself. Cole had to laugh about the barter system that seemed to be operating here. The navy did tricks for fish, like some goddamn seal. Still, it was decent of them. Families would be worrying themselves sick about the trawler crew.

"You're just dyin' to fire the torpedoes, ain't you?" Cole said.

"If that trawler's been hit by Stranded, you bet. They need to find out who's in charge now."

Baird squinted, staring out to sea at the inbound fishing boats, all bright colors like oversized bathtub toys. As they drew closer, Cole could see that one still had its catch strung up in nets on the deck. One by one the boats tied up alongside, and a crewman jumped onto the quay.

"Nothing so far," he said, as if Cole and Baird knew what was going on, and headed for the submarine.

Cole peered down from the quay as the rest of the crew started sorting their catch. They pulled a cable and the contents of the net spilled onto the deck, some of it still crawling and flapping. There was a regular party going on there.

Cole called down to the crew, just to be sociable. "Boat's still missin', then."

"Yeah. We searched for a few hours. It's pretty calm out there. So something's wrong."

"Sorry to hear that."

"It's damn Stranded. They want the boats, not the catch."

"If it is, baby, they're gonna regret it."

Baird leaned over the rail and looked at the fish being sorted. "Shit, I don't think even Bernie would eat *that*." He tilted his head on one side to get a better look. "That one reminds me of an old girlfriend."

"The one with the big mouth?"

"The one with the tentacles."

"You thought the Locust queen was classy. You need help, baby."

"She didn't look like the other grubs, man." Baird pressed his earpiece. "Control, you awake? . . . Yeah, we want to go check out that missing trawler . . . It's Stranded."

Cole wasn't really listening now. He was much more interested in whatever was going down on one of the boats. The fishermen had started to cluster around something *really* big and weird on top of a pile of other fish scattered on the deck. As far as Cole was concerned, most of the things down there looked weird anyway. He sure as hell hadn't seen them on a plate in any restaurant he'd been in.

But there were all kinds of freaky things in the water down in the Locust tunnels, and flooding the Hollow could have flushed out a lot of them. That thing on the deck did *not* look natural. It was two meters long, like a big length of scaly pipe, with a mouth where its chin should have been. Did fish even *have* chins?

Shit . . .

Cole didn't like the look of it, and he'd seen enough weird shit to know when to worry. The trawler crew didn't seem bothered. But then they'd never seen grubs or the variety of shapes the things came in.

"Man, that looks like it came out of the grubs' tunnels," Cole said. "Don't touch it. Hang on—I'll get Baird to take a look at it, 'cause he knows more about Locust than anyone."

An old guy—who'd probably seen everything in the sea by now—hooked his fingers under the creature's gills and hauled it up. He needed both hands and help from two buddies to lift it. "You never seen anything like this before, then?"

"I'm not jokin', man. You ain't seen the freak show the grubs had." Where the hell could he even start with explaining about things like Reavers and Brumaks? You couldn't make that shit up. Maybe the folks here hadn't even seen the grub menagerie on TV before they lost the link on Hammer day. The COG didn't hand over many ops recordings to the media guys. "Don't touch it. Some of that shit even explodes. They got these other things called Lambent, and they glow, and—"

The fishermen started laughing. They thought it was hilarious. Cole didn't mind a good joke, but he just couldn't get across to them that monsters were *real.* He'd seen them, killed them, seen his buddies killed by them. He'd lived next door to monsters for fifteen years. He'd *ridden* one. He'd even met the monsters' queen face-to-face.

Shit. They don't get it. They never saw it. Any of it. I just can't explain it to them. How they ever gonna understand us?

"Son, this is a shale eel," the old guy said kindly. He seemed pretty pleased with it. "We rarely catch them. Real delicacy. You'd love it. Want a fillet piece when we cut it up?"

A goddamn eel. Was that all? Shit, he'd be crapping himself about every animal he didn't recognize now. He felt stupid, but also worried. The nightmare had been real on the mainland, but folks here couldn't begin to imagine what the grubs had been like, so they'd never understand why Gears reacted badly to the simplest, dumbest things. Everything was dangerous until proven safe. Every rumble and vibration was grubs, nothing harmless. It was going to take years to change that.

"Thanks," Cole said, "but I think I'll pass."

The crew laid the monster eel back down on the deck and debated how to divide it up fairly so that everyone got a decent portion. Cole hoped he hadn't offended them by turning down their offer. Baird came back and watched the operation, frowning.

"Looks like a frigging grub," he muttered.

"Glad it's not just me, baby."

The wheelhouse door swung open and a guy leaned out, a radio headset in one hand. "*Fairhaven's* found debris from the *Harvest.* Fenders, floats, no actual wreckage. So we've got a position."

That killed the interest in the monster eel right away.

"We might not need the submarine, then," said the old guy.

Baird looked seriously disappointed. "Ah, shit."

"If they're out there, we'll find 'em, son." He'd totally misunderstood why Baird was pissed off. "Don't you worry."

"You're gonna need some armed backup if that's Stranded misbehavin' out there," Cole said. "We do that stuff. Want a hand?"

"If you're willing."

Baird paced up the quay, hand to his ear, talking to Control, and seemed satisfied. "Control decided to test the sonar anyway," he said. He'd got his boat ride, then. "Plus a patrol boat."

"Which one makes you more seasick?" Cole asked.

"Depends how deep you dive."

It was turning out to be an interesting day. Man, the Stranded out here were a lot wilder than the land-based variety.

Vectes had its own real-life monsters to worry about.

VNB MAIN PARADE GROUND, 0930 HOURS.

About six hundred Stranded from the coastal settlement showed up at VNB's main gate that morning.

Hoffman looked them over, comforting himself with the thought that most of the Operation Lifeboat men had turned into decent Gears, so maybe there was some hope for this rabble once they were separated from their criminal element. Apart from some nervous glances over their shoulders when the inner gates were locked behind them—Hoffman had no intention of anyone signing up, getting their clothing issue, and then slipping away— they looked pretty docile. They'd all been searched for weapons anyway. The worst they could do was bite.

He opened his radio link. "Lieutenant Stroud, I need a bot. And get Fenix and Mataki down here."

"Sergeant Fenix is still out with the patrol boat looking for the missing trawler, sir. Ready for the ID parade?"

More damn trouble from the Stranded; it made it hard to think of any of them as model citizens. "As ready as we'll ever be. Get the bot images back to Pelruan and see what shakes out."

"Yes, sir. By the way, remember that the councilmen from Pel-ruan are visiting at the moment. You said you'd meet with them."

"Damn, did I?"

"They're wandering around with one of the Jacinto representa-tives. You'll be able to spot them by their dismay when they see the line of Stranded."

"That's not a joke, is it, Lieutenant?"

"No sir, it is not. I've had . . . comments."

The Stranded line was mostly made up of women, children, teenage boys, and elderly men. At least Prescott would be happy to see more women of childbearing age joining the remnant, but Hoffman wasn't convinced they'd take kindly to the do-your-duty-and-get-knocked-up philosophy of the COG. Plenty of women were happy to keep popping out babies, even women he'd have thought would have objected to being treated like broodmares, but some kind of reproductive instinct kicked in that said the species was in trouble. On the other hand, lots of women objected to the baby farms. The Stranded females were probably the independent kind who'd tell Prescott where he could shove his repopulation program.

And not enough adult males here. I need to replace the Gears we lost.

Stranded men were probably the wrong material anyway. Humankind had lost a generation of its best, and that was going to take a long time to put right.

VNB was filling up. Another accommodation block would be ready by the end of the week. People were gradually coming off the ships, which made Michaelson happier, but he was going to have to put up with them in the Raven's Nests for months while extra housing was built.

And that took some organizing. Royston Sharle had his shopping list of urgent tasks, and he expected Hoffman to make them possible. Hoffman delegated it to the civilians playing at councilmen and gave them three companies of Gears to make a start on it.

Okay, we need housing built. We need land cleared for farming. We need sources of raw materials identified and secured. Need, need, need . . .

Michaelson ambled across the parade ground to look over the Stranded. He'd shaved off his beard; the trawler skipper disguise from his piracy interdiction duties had been replaced by his old NCOG officer persona, crisp and . . . Hoffman settled on *raffish.* He seemed to be relishing his new task.

"You'll be lucky if you find a pretty one in *that* line, you old predator," Hoffman said. "Admit you're past it."

"I'm not on the prowl, Victor." Michaelson straightened his collar. "But the navy has *standards*. Just checking out the potential recruits."

"Are we competing for manpower now?"

"Oh, we don't need anyone *that* big and strong in the navy."

"We noticed."

"Seriously, are you recruiting from Stranded again?"

"Not unless I'm desperate."

"The land battle's over, Victor. It's going to be a maritime world now."

Hoffman managed to laugh. It was true, but that didn't make him feel any less redundant. "Pirates. Transport. *Cruises.*"

"Resource investigation—we're going to have to mount missions back to the mainland to find imulsion and other raw materials. Projection of power—because, eventually, we'll need to recolonize the continent. Defense—because this is still a tiny population compared to what might be lurking out there in holes across Sera."

He obviously had his sales pitch ready for Prescott. "And you don't mean grubs," Hoffman said.

"There'll still be a few grubs, but we have no idea how many of our free-range Stranded friends are out there. Nor do they, I suspect. Looks like we've lost a civilian vessel today. It won't be the last."

"So you sail the high seas, and we provide the muscle when you go ashore." *I know you're right, Quentin, but damn it, it still hurts.* "Prescott will have to appoint you admiral."

"We'll always need marines."

"My Gears will be greatly comforted by that. Especially as the navy hasn't *projected power* in recent history."

"We're fast learners." Michaelson turned to look past Hoffman. "Ah, here come your charming enforcers."

Anya and Bernie walked down the ragged four-deep line of Stranded, followed by one of the bots that was going to be used to send mug shots to Pelruan for checking. Halfway down the queue, Bernie must have spotted something that worried her; she walked back a few paces, grabbed a man out of the crowd by his collar, and marched him across to a nearby wall to search him. He was a big guy, so she might have been making the point that she wasn't going to be intimidated by that. Anya watched intently as if she was making mental notes on how to scare and demoralize a man correctly.

Michaelson suppressed a smile. "You always did go for the leonine type, Victor."

"Female Gears need to be able to handle themselves," Hoffman said, avoiding the issue. "Stranded don't make concessions to ladies."

You should have told me what they did to you, Bernie. Why didn't you? Damn it, we've known each other long enough.

Anya handed Hoffman a piece of paper, signed by Milon Audley, Attorney General. For a moment, Hoffman thought the old shark had come back from the dead, but it was just an archive document she'd pulled from the files. Hoffman was still being surprised on a daily basis by what had been saved and not saved when Jacinto was abandoned.

"Prescott's still set on trial or amnesty, applied across the board, sir."

"Trials? We're not going to get convictions if he plays by peacetime legal rules." Hoffman decided it was simply a PR gesture on Prescott's part that nobody was intended to take seriously. "Where's the evidence? Who's going to represent the parties? I'm not letting dangerous scum into this city because we can't convict and deal with them." Yes, he thought of this as a city. Until there was a civilian town out there for the remnant to go to, then VNB *was* New Jacinto. "Martial law's there for a reason—when peacetime rules don't work."

Anya looked awkward for a moment. "You'll have to argue that with him, sir."

"Apologies, Anya. It just cramps my guts something fierce to have to do this."

"I'll make sure the registration team is ready to start," she said, escaping.

Bernie went to follow. Hoffman stopped her with a well-timed bark. "Sergeant, wait up. I'd like you to do some personal check-ing." He didn't plan to spell it out in front of Michaelson, friend or not. Bernie deserved some privacy. "Certain elements of the Stranded are of particular interest to me."

"Understood, sir." She looked uneasy. "But I doubt if anyone would walk in and risk a good kicking."

"Free food makes any wild animal take chances, Mataki. You should know that."

"Indeed I should, sir."

Bernie doubled back and began walking down the line of Stranded again. The crowd waiting to be processed at the security post was three or four deep, and past the metal scrollwork gates where they'd come in. The gates were two meters high, an ornate remnant of the pre-COG era with a wheel-like emblem in each center panel.

"Anything I can do, Victor?" Michaelson asked.

"All under control."

"I've known you a long time, my friend, and it's not—"

Bernie was in the press of bodies now, looking into every face. A movement caught Hoffman's eye. In the section of crowd queu-ing in front of the gates, people were stepping aside and looking over their shoulders, as if a scuffle had broken out. Hoffman saw a head rise above the others, and realized a man was trying to climb the gates. Bernie turned to look at the same time. It was an odd moment to decide that he didn't want the COG's protection.

Oh, shit . . .

The guy could have been any criminal scumbag, but Hoffman guessed that he wasn't.

He knew that he couldn't sprint that distance and get to the man before Bernie did. He started to jog across the parade ground, trying to look casual, but Gears and civvies paused to stare, and he saw the top of Bernie's head as she pushed through the crowd. People in front of the gate suddenly scattered and ducked. In that split-second's clear view, Hoffman saw Bernie swing her Lancer hard into the man's legs like an axe. He fell. Hoffman didn't see anything else for a few seconds—there was yelling, plenty of yelling—until he pushed through the crowd and found Bernie kneeling on the man's back, pushing his arm up between his shoulder blades.

Hoffman wasn't the only one on the spot. Every Gear within fifty meters piled in too.

"There," Bernie said. She reached for her rifle one-handed and slid the chainsaw against the man's face. For a moment Hoffman thought she was going to switch it on. "Take a look around. How do you like the odds now, tosser?"

It has to be him. *Suicidal asshole. Why the hell would he risk coming in here? Maybe he thought she wouldn't recognize him. Maybe he didn't realize she'd be down here.*

Andresen, a couple of men from Bravo 6, and a Raven crew chief crowded around, all ready to dive in, all in a bar brawl mood that had sprung from nowhere. Hoffman was sure they didn't know the details, but they'd certainly picked up on one thing: one of their own had a serious grievance with a Stranded.

Hoffman knew that if they found out exactly what the man had done, then things were going to get out of hand fast, discipline or no discipline. He moved in and shoved Bernie aside, pinning the man's arms. Hoffman decided he was still fit enough to take him. If the bastard gave him an excuse to use his sidearm here and now, he'd take it. He didn't care who was watching.

Jacinto folks will understand. The locals—they've got some learning to do.

"It's okay, Mataki," Hoffman said. "I'll deal with this."

"I don't even know his name." Bernie let go and stepped back. "But that's him."

He was about thirty, pretty damn solid, with curly dark hair and an expression on his face that said he really didn't believe anyone could touch him, not even here. That pissed off Hoffman massively in its own right. This was COG turf, *his* turf. And he answered only to Prescott.

"I don't give a damn what this animal's called," Hoffman snarled, nose to nose with the man. "But it's committed a capital crime, and it's going to pay for it. What's your name? I can't just call you *asshole*, because then all the other assholes like you would think I was addressing them."

"You got some fucking funny double standards, man."

Hoffman drew his sidearm. "Name."

"Jonn," he said. "Massy."

The parade ground was a perfect amphitheater. Hoffman was aware that he had a much bigger audience now. There were civvies—*real* civvies, Jacinto citizens, even visiting Pelruan people—who'd come out from an accommodation block to get a better look. The Hoffman they'd known was formal, businesslike. Now they were seeing the man he'd been when he had to get results fast. He hadn't needed to be that Hoffman for a long time.

"I assume you're a relative of the shitbag who raided Pelruan, then."

"Brother. He's dead, asshole. You fascists killed him."

"So file a complaint. In the meantime, you're *detained*."

Jonn Massy—if that was his name at all—also realized he had an audience, although Hoffman didn't know why the hell he thought anyone other than his own kind would give a shit what happened to him now.

"That bitch killed my buddies," he yelled. "She cut them up, man. She took her time doing it. So where's your fucking amnesty now? Where's your justice? Why isn't she in jail? Because it sure as shit wasn't self-defense, not coming back to slit them up weeks later."

Hoffman wanted this over and done with. He didn't want to broadcast the details. Bernie had taken enough humiliation already.

"Maybe they asked for it," Hoffman said, and hauled him off toward the guard room. "And you did, too."

Andresen came after him. "What did the bastard do, sir? Tell me."

Massy was yelling now. "I want a trial—I want a fucking *trial*!"

Hoffman kept walking. "The bitch is a *murderer*!"

"Sir?" Andresen didn't give up. "Come on, sir, it's Mataki—"

And they're imagining the worst anyway.

"You'll find out when you need to, Sergeant," Hoffman said, and slammed the door.

NCOG PATROL BOAT *CHANCELLOR*, FIFTY KILOMETERS OFF THE COAST.

Dom had forgotten just how terrifyingly big the ocean was.

The haze on the water still hadn't lifted, and he couldn't even see the trawlers. They were somewhere out there on an expanding square search pattern, working from where the *Harvest*'s floats had been found.

He hadn't been in a small boat like this for a long, long time. The steady vibration from the engines and the sound of the churning water brought back faces and voices he'd almost forgotten, bittersweet, right on the limit of the painful memories he could handle these days. Overhead, a Raven tracked east to west.

And even with a bird up there, it's still a damn big ocean to cover.

"I can't see the submarine," Marcus said.

"That's the whole point, baby." Cole was way too close to the rail of the patrol boat for Dom's liking. "Y'know, I think I prefer flyin'. It's over faster."

"Don't lean on the guard rail if you've got to chuck up," Dom warned. "I've seen experienced guys fall in. Kneel down, all fours."

"Shit, this thing ain't got much deck space for a growin' boy."

"Okay, go lean on the gun." The machine gun was mounted forward on a sturdy housing. If Cole puked on the deck, a quick hose-down was a lot easier than recovering a man overboard. "We've got to be close. The debris couldn't have drifted that far."

Marcus stood in the open wheelhouse door, scanning the horizon. "Dom, remember that leviathan thing? The one that hauled the grub boats in the underground lake?"

"Do I have to?"

"If there were others, flooding the tunnels wouldn't have drowned them. It might have let them escape into open water."

"Shit. You think something like that attacked the boat?"

"I *told* 'em, man." Cole perked up, vindicated. "The fishermen trawled up this big ugly eel, and I swore it was from the grub menagerie."

Muller, the NCOG coxswain, peered from the open bridge up top. "You want to share that intel with *Clement*, Sergeant? If there's anything on the loose, the CO needs to know."

"It was at least the length of a grub gunboat and it had scales," Marcus said. "We didn't ask if it was an only child. We just killed it."

"Yeah, very helpful. Next time *Clement* makes contact, I'll tell them there might be some seriously big trouble out there."

"Can't you radio him?"

"He's got to come up to periscope depth to get a comms link in seawater," Muller said. "His trailing wire's screwed at the moment. We don't have a single vessel that's one hundred percent functional, remember."

Dom reminded himself that this was just planning for the worst, nothing definite. Until they found identifiable parts of the boat, then the trawler could just have been drifting without radio comms after losing some floats. But everyone was unusually quiet until the voice of *Clement*'s CO came over the radio.

"*Clement* to *Chancellor*, negative so far. The deep trench starts around here. If anything's gone to the bottom, we're out of luck."

"Roger that, *Clement*," Muller said. "And if you get any *big* sonar pings, it might be a grub monster fish that's bigger than you. *Very* late intel report from our sergeant here."

"Might be a whale, of course. Okay, if we don't recognize the acoustics, *then* we'll worry."

Dom wondered what sailors considered a reasonable period to search for survivors before giving up. That was a strange question from a man who'd spent ten years looking for his own wife. He realized he'd already written the crew off as dead. It was easy to do that with strangers, and impossible to do it with your own.

"KR-Six-Seven to *Chancellor*." Dom listened to the radio traffic between the Raven and the patrol boat. "I'm seeing a white object five klicks west of your current search boundary. Might be an upturned hull—or could be a decomposing whale. I've seen foam from something breaching the surface about twenty klicks from here. I'm going in for a closer look."

"Shit," said Cole. "That don't sound encouraging."

"KR-Six-Seven to *Chancellor*, confirmed, it's an upturned hull. Looks damaged. Want to follow me up and get a line on it?"

"Roger that, Six-Seven." Muller opened up *Chancellor*'s throttle and headed west. "On our way."

"KR-Six-Seven, *how* damaged?" Marcus asked.

"Splintered and holed, from what I can see. Collision with something big, or else it's been shot up."

"Not much it can collide with out here."

Muller called down from the bridge. "Not with one of ours, definitely. Other fishing boats—unlikely. Crazed killer grub fish—who knows?"

Even with the Raven overhead directing them, it took a while to get a visual on the hull. Muller brought the patrol boat alongside. It bobbed at an angle in the water, as if it was weighted at one end. The smooth composite was punched with small, splintered holes, and that meant only one thing.

"So I'm guessing it's Stranded," Muller said. "Unless your leviathan was packing a cannon."

Shit, whoever opened fire kept firing when the boat overturned. Bastards.

"Okay, Muller, let the fishermen know," Marcus said. The other boats were still converging on the position, but their top speed was a fraction of a patrol boat's. "Better check in case someone's trapped in an air pocket. I'll dive under there if—"

"No." Muller came down from the bridge and surveyed the hull from the port side. "We don't need extra casualties. Wait one."

He grabbed the boathook and squatted down to prod the hull. Dom wondered if he was tapping to get a response—damn, someone was going to have to get on that hull to actually listen for signs of life, whatever Muller said—but then the hull flipped over.

"Shit." Muller almost lost his footing. "Wasn't expecting that."

It was just a small splintered section of the boat's outer skin, smeared with black streaks that could have been charring. Dom would have suspected a fuel fire if it hadn't been for the peppering of holes. He couldn't tell if the black smears on the debris were oil or burns.

"Well, the rest of it isn't going to be floating anywhere," Muller said. "Unless those poor bastards were exceptionally lucky and went over the side with life jackets before they got hit, then they're gone."

"Okay, if they *did* get out, what are our chances of finding them?"

"Close to zero," Muller said.

The Raven carried on the search for a while, and *Chancellor* hung around more out of courtesy than in any hope of being useful. *Clement* eventually surfaced a few hundred meters away. Muller went into the wheelhouse for a few minutes, then stuck his head out the door.

"*Clement*'s CO says there's a lot of debris on the slope of the ocean shelf, Sergeant," he said. "But finding recognizable bits of boat down there . . . not a hope in hell."

"Any big fish?"

"Whales. You can hear them right across the other side of the ocean if you get in the right density layer. And some distant engine noise. But no rampant leviathans."

"Okay." Marcus took a breath. Dom could see him wrestling with the decision, and knew what he was imagining: some guys bobbing in the water, impossible to spot in a vast ocean, waiting for help that would never come. "We can't do much down here. KR-Six-Seven, want to call it off?"

"We're okay," said the Raven pilot. "We'll carry on for a while with the other boats. We've narrowed the search area, anyway. Go home, guys."

Chancellor headed back to VNB at maximum throttle. Cole

seemed to find that less puke-inducing, and he definitely perked up as the fortress-like walls of VNB got closer.

"Dom, why the hell would Stranded bother to sink a little boat?" he said. "They steal shit. They *need* boats. Hell, they probably want the catch too. Why trash it?"

"Maybe the fishermen fought back," Marcus said. "I want to know what brought Stranded in so close to Vectes. Not an easy journey."

"Easy pickings, maybe."

"What, they failed to spot the whole damn COG navy steaming in?"

Dom thought of the raid on Pelruan. Some collective craziness had seized the Stranded, and they didn't seem to care how big or dangerous their prey was now. Desperation? Maybe. Ignorance? They didn't seem to know the size of the COG forces they'd be taking on. Perhaps they were so used to being the top of the food chain out here that they'd overdosed on arrogance. The COG was tiny, a medium-sized city and a worn-down army rather than an empire now, but compared to a few pirate vessels it was still the world superpower.

He thought it was, anyway. Dom had a moment of doubt.

Maybe it's more than a few pirates. Maybe we're the ones who haven't got the math right.

"Friggin' *sad*, man," Cole said. "Survive the end of the world, and the first thing us humans do is start fightin' among ourselves again."

Marcus grunted. "We can quit anytime. If we *want* to."

Dom wondered if anyone ever did. The COG couldn't quit now, that was certain. It now had a new enemy to tackle. The almost-peace had lasted nine weeks.

CHAPTER 15

Understand what a world had to do to survive.
(CHAIRMAN RICHARD PRESCOTT, MEMOIRS, OPENING LINE,
UNPUBLISHED DRAFT.)

THE SANTIAGO HOUSE, EPHYRA, FIVE DAYS
AFTER THE HAMMER OF DAWN STRIKE ACROSS
SERA, 1 A.E.

The sky was charcoal gray, a kind of stormy dusk, but it was mid-morning. That was a big improvement; the airborne debris was starting to settle.

"Baby, remember to keep the windows shut," Dom said. "I don't want you inhaling this shit. Okay? Stay indoors. Promise me."

Maria handed him a scarf, the camo pattern one he'd picked up in his commando training days. "At least put this on."

"I said, *promise me.*"

She didn't seem to hear him. "You ought to wear your helmet this time. I know you don't like it, but it'll keep you safe."

"Maria, please. Don't go out today." Dom didn't know if he'd do more harm than good by spelling it out to her. But he knew that going outside to look for something she'd never find was dangerous. "Bennie and Sylvie aren't out there, baby. They're gone. I know folks think they see people they've lost, but it's all imagination. I promise I'll be back as soon as I can."

She didn't meet his eyes. It wasn't avoidance. She seemed to blank him out, then carry on again as if nothing had been said.

"You sure you won't wear your helmet?"

Dom gave up for the time being. He wasn't going to hear what he needed to. "No, the air filters just clog up. Why do you think they're not flying Raven sorties? That stuff gets into the air intakes and engines." He wrapped the scarf around his neck and pulled the folds up over his nose. "Look, I don't know how long we're going to be out there, but don't get worried. Everything's going to take longer than usual. Just *stay inside.* I'll try to call you when I can."

He went to kiss her goodbye and had to pull the scarf down again. With any luck, she'd take her meds, sleep through most of the day, and not watch the news, which was pretty well nonexistent at the moment because nobody was leaving the city. The TV helicopters couldn't fly anyway, and the broadcast system had been taken over by endless emergency announcements about staying at home, covering air vents, and filtering water.

In the street outside, a thick layer of dark gray dust covered everything like a negative image of a snow scene. Cars were parked nose to tail along both sides of the road, and it was only when he walked past one of them that he saw movement through a small patch scraped clear on its filthy windshield; there were people sleeping inside. Shit, he had refugees living rough in cars on his own street. They still hadn't been able to move into reception centers.

He wondered whether to stop and help, but what could he do? He couldn't offer them shelter—there was no way he could leave strangers in his house with Maria. And he had to report for duty. After arguing with himself for a few seconds, he walked on, eyes already stinging from the polluted air, and then broke into a jog all the way to the main road. It was hard going. The sidewalks were coated in the same greasy gray crap as the cars and roofs, almost slippery underfoot even though it felt dry.

Whatever the soot and debris was mixing with, it was going to be hell to clean up.

Dom wasn't sure what bothered him most as he made his way to HQ—the unbreathable air, or the sense that the place was packed solid with people even though nobody was visible on the streets. It felt like everything—people, fear, anger—had been crammed into the houses and the doors slammed shut, and one push would force the chaos to spill out. The situation beyond Ephyra that had caused it just was too much for him to take in. He didn't even try to imagine it.

He'd see for himself soon enough. He was on the first recon today. He'd volunteered.

The 'Dills were still in the vehicle hangar, clean and serviced. The transport engineers had had nothing to do for two days except fix them and bolt makeshift filters over the intakes to keep out the worst of the fine particles caused by the vaporization of . . . how many cities? Dom didn't actually know. He wondered if Marcus's dad had told him that level of detail, or if Marcus even wanted to know.

Padrick and Tai were waiting for the briefing with the three other recon squads, sitting on the Dill's front scoop. Poor old Tai; he had no idea what was happening to his folks in the South Islands, and Dom didn't know whether to talk about it. Comms had been patchy since E-Day. Now the Hammer strikes had destroyed relays across Sera, and if there were survivors in the remote and rural areas, it was going to be weeks or even longer before anyone found out.

But there was no more Sera out there, not as any of them had known it. Now Dom had to drive out there and see how bad things really were.

And the whole idea is to check how little we left for the grubs to salvage.

It was an upside-down war in every way Dom could imagine.

"Seen Marcus?" Dom asked.

"Not yet," Pad said. "You got to pity the guy. He must feel terrible now."

Dom bristled. "Why?"

"His dad. You seriously think that someone isn't going to give him shit over the Fenix connection sooner or later? Watch him try even harder to save the world now to make up for it."

"Pad, shut the fuck up, okay?"

"I'm not saying we shouldn't have done it. I'm just saying that down the line, people will forget why we had to."

"It's not Marcus's problem. Just knock it off."

Dom knew the comment stung because it was true. Marcus always behaved as if he was personally responsible for every damn Gear, which was more than some of the officers managed. Now he was the same with civvies. Over the last nine days, Dom had lost count of the times he'd gone so far out of his way to rescue them that it was verging on a death wish.

It also stung because he knew Pad was right about the Fenix name. Nobody knew yet if Adam Fenix had saved humankind or just hurried along its extinction, so the jury was still out—in Ephyra, anyway. Anyone who'd been the target of the Hammer strikes would have made their mind up pretty fast.

Marcus turned up two minutes before the briefing was due to start and just gave everyone a silent nod. He didn't even say anything to Dom. What was there to say, after all? *Good morning* really didn't cut it today, and there was no point commenting on the weather. Eventually, boots echoed down the corridor, and the Gears snapped to attention beside their vehicles.

Dom wasn't expecting to see Colonel Hoffman this morning. But then this wasn't any old mission, and he got the feeling that the man wanted to confront what had happened and see stuff for himself. Some Gears said Hoffman just couldn't delegate, and interfered with every damn thing, but Dom knew him too well. They'd fought side by side—literally—and nearly died together; the Hoffman that Dom knew was simply a soldier who believed his job was on the front line, not shuffling committee papers or kissing politicians' asses. The irony was that the more Gears who got killed, the more hands-on soldiering the senior commanders had to do, and their casualty rate meant that Hoffman was being forced higher in the command simply by staying alive.

No, he definitely wasn't happy that way. The old bastard still looked naked and lost without a Lancer.

"Stand easy, Gears." Hoffman seemed exhausted and angry. Maybe things hadn't gone to plan. "Sorry if you're pining for Lieutenant Faraday already, but I'm briefing you. We've got no intel whatsoever yet, so anything you can glean on this patrol is valuable. The air's going to be filthy for weeks, so you *will* observe personal safety precautions, and those of you too macho to wear goddamn helmets *will* wear breathing masks, or I'll stick you on a charge for hazarding COG property. Is that clear?"

It was a crisp chorus. "Sir, yes *sir*."

"Good. Now, all I expect you to do is to keep to the main highways as far as you're able, take air samples, assess the degree of damage to property, report any signs of grub activity, and any— well, shit, there won't *be* survivors. Just stick to compass points today. You can't cover much ground."

"What if there *are* survivors, sir?" Dom asked.

Hoffman's voice was hoarse. Maybe he'd been out in the streets. "You ever seen a firestorm, Santiago?"

"Probably not on this scale, sir."

"Nobody ever has." Hoffman took off his cap and wiped his shaven scalp with his palm. "If you find any live casualties, chances are that you won't be able to do a damn thing for them. Okay, get going, Gears."

Nobody ever has.

That summed up the day.

Padrick drove the 'Dill south out of the vehicle compound. Roads in Ephyra itself were still passable because Gears had been out making sure they were clear, bulldozing routes where they had to as far as the ring of barricades and vehicle checkpoints. But the world was already an alien landscape draped in dark gray velvet. Yes, that was what it looked like: not snow, but somber velvet.

It's a fucking funeral.

And they were still a long way from the nearest city that had taken a direct Hammer strike. There was no destruction yet, no firestorm damage, just the debris from it that been swept for kilometers on air currents.

"Control," Padrick said, "I'm going to have to find a cross-country route. I can see the highway ahead, but it's nothing but solid cars."

Dom thought of the refugees sleeping in their vehicles in the city itself. He didn't want to believe anyone might be sheltering like that out here. But there was absolutely nothing he could do about it even if they were. If they hadn't made their way on foot to the city, then nothing could help them here. Nobody could even get ambulances down this far.

"Okay," Pad said. The 'Dill bounced down an embankment and onto the rail tracks, a bit too close to overturning for Dom's tastes. He grabbed the nearest seat. "This is the only way ahead. Hang onto your nuts. It's going to be a *very* bumpy ride."

Tai had his eyes shut, hands clasped. Marcus was glued to one of the secondary periscopes for a while, but swore and gave up after a few lurches that left him rubbing his bruised forehead. Even the 'Dill's huge all-terrain tires couldn't smooth out the ride along the rails.

"Pad, I'm going to grab recon pictures every half klick," Marcus said. "Stop and pull back the front hatch when you can. Don't deploy Baz. The crud in the air's going to clog his parts, too."

Even Marcus had fallen into calling the bot "he." It might have been out of courtesy to Padrick, though.

The roads ran close enough to the rail network in places for them to get a good view of the endless frozen river of cars. Eventually, the dead traffic jams thinned out, and the charcoal velvet roads got emptier. People had given up running at that point; maybe they'd tried to sit it out somewhere. It was like looking at tree rings to see what had happened in history. Dom realized he could read the stages and times of panic and desperation from where vehicles had been abandoned.

Pad halted the 'Dill again, and this time Dom got up to assess the terrain with Marcus. Without the navigation aids in the 'Dill, Dom wouldn't have had a clue where he was now.

It was so fucking quiet. No birds, no traffic, *nothing*. The world was dead.

"Shit." If Marcus said it once, he said it twenty, thirty times. It seemed to be all he could manage. "*Shit.*"

"You've seen enough road," Pad said quietly. "Let's just keep on to Gerrenhalt. It's on this line."

It was hour after hour of utter misery, hammering along the rails and being shaken shitless. There was nothing to see, nothing to discuss, nothing to imagine that wasn't death and fear. There wasn't even the constant background of radio chatter to listen to, because there were only four units deployed, and they were probably looking at the same shit as Dom.

All he could do was sit clinging to his seat, rattled like a can of beans despite the safety belts, and try not to let Tai see how shocked he was. Tai's expression was one of complete calm. But he had to be going crazy inside. As for Pad—Pad never talked about family, so maybe he'd lost touch with home anyway. Dom hoped so, for his sake.

We're not even there yet.

We're not even near the worst shit.

Oh God. What's going to be left now?

How the hell could Sera ever rebuild? It was going to take years to clean the place, let alone anything else. He couldn't even begin to think about the grubs. They didn't seem to matter right then.

Marcus sat with the back of his head resting against the bulkhead behind him, staring up at some fixed point Dom couldn't see, and every jolt and shudder bounced his skull off the metal. It had to be hurting him. But he didn't make any effort to sit forward. He looked as if he was punishing himself for something, but—of course—he'd done nothing, and maybe that was his problem. He needed to *do* things. Everyone knew that Sergeant Fenix could do the impossible, pull any situation out of the fire, beat any odds. But now he could do nothing except take pictures and stare at a man-made disaster on a scale that even he didn't seem able to take in.

And this was what his dad did for a job. It was all around him now.

"Chemical factories," Marcus said at last.

"What?"

"Think what happens when you destroy industrial areas. The toxins that get released. All that shit in the air, in the soil, in the water."

"That's the idea, man. Destroy everything the grubs can use." Dom found himself veering between it's-all-going-to-work-out and blind panic. Maria was waiting for him at home, and life carried on in Ephyra. Out here, though—he didn't even have words for what he saw. He tried hard to sound rational and in control. "With any luck, some of the shit will run into their holes and poison the ugly fucks, too."

Marcus shut his eyes at that point. Dom, like any Gear, grabbed sleep when he could, but he couldn't sleep now. It wasn't just the constant shaking of the 'Dill; he was too scared to close his eyes. He'd fall asleep, wake up, and then have to accept all over again that the nightmare out there was real. He hated those few seconds of forgetfulness every time he woke up before the crisis of the day reminded him it was still waiting for him. The best way to deal with it was to gorge on it, overload himself with the pain until it ceased to have any meaning, and not try to avoid it.

"Hey, we've got an obstruction ahead." Pad slowed the 'Dill. "We're about a kilometer outside Gerrenhalt. I'm going to back up to a point where we can get off this track."

"You're going to roll this damn thing," Marcus muttered. He sounded like normal Marcus again. "Can you get back on the road?"

"Hang on . . ." The engine revved. Pad kept shunting back and forth, trying to turn and hit the bank at the right angle. "Whoa . . ."

"Shit, Pad, take a run at it," Dom said.

"That's what I'm doing."

The 'Dill's engine screamed and for a moment it felt like it was floating. Then Dom's teeth nearly punched through his lip as all four tires hit the ground again. Metal crunched and groaned.

"I think I hit a car," Pad said. "Like that's hard to do here. We need a bloody Centaur for this. Control? This is PA-Five-One. You getting all this? It's useless deploying 'Dills. You better send out tanks next time and just get them to roll over the debris."

He continued along some gap—possibly the soft shoulder that would bog down cars—scraping metal on one side in a near-continuous screech. Dom had had enough of imagining what was going on and moved to open the top hatch.

It took him awhile to work it out, but the velvet-coated land-scape was now different. The shapes of the cars were distorted, and the more he looked, the more he could see they had no tires and their glass was gone.

"Shit," he said. "Guys, I think the fires came this far. Look."

The bitter, sooty smell that filled the air in Ephyra was now overwhelmingly smoky. Palls still rose from buildings in the distance, black plumes on a gray sky. There was no color at all in the landscape. The only color Dom could see was inside the 'Dill—blue lights, yellow warning signs, red emergency controls—and it just added to his sense of unreality, like watching a black-and-white movie. Real life was *colored*. Everything in Dom's brain told him not to believe what he was seeing.

"Pad? Pad, *stop*. Marcus—you got to see this."

Pad stopped the 'Dill and opened all the hatches. With the hatch covers fully retracted, they could all stand up in the crew bay and stare around them. Dom watched their faces to make sure he wasn't going mad, and he knew then that he wasn't.

"Oh, fuck . . ." Marcus did that very slow head shake that he re-served for his worst moments, like he couldn't find even a few basic words to express what he was feeling. His shoulders sagged. Eventually he managed something. "It's just *incinerated*."

Dom had to dismount and look. He knew he wasn't going to like what he found, but he had to do it. He tried to walk between the cars, but many of them looked as if they'd rammed into each other in some pileup, and then he realized that their fuel tanks would have exploded in the intense heat, and he was simply seeing how they'd been thrown against the vehicles around them. A truck was silhouetted against a lighter patch of sky, the bones of a metal frame all that was left of its trailer. So far, Dom hadn't seen any recognizable bodies in the seats.

Marcus called him on his radio. "Dom, get your ass back here."

Yeah, Dom had done what he had to do. There would be kilometer after kilometer just like this, and they hadn't even reached the first city that had taken a direct hit. He made his way back to the 'Dill.

Pad cleaned the periscope glass again. "I'm going to take a pee break. Then we head back. That okay with you, Marcus? Either we use Centaurs or wait for the air to clear and send in Ravens. This is crazy."

Marcus grunted. Pad walked down to the shoulder of the road to unzip.

"You okay, Tai?" Marcus asked. They got back in the 'Dill and waited. "It can't all be like this. The Hammer can't cover every square centimeter of planet." He looked down at his gloves. "Very few of the islands were targets. Grubs can't get to them."

So Marcus knew some detail, then. Dom imagined him trying to extract some information from his dad on behalf of his squad, neither of them able to manage more than a couple of words at a time.

"I can change nothing in the past," Tai said, "so I must move on."

Dom envied his ability to do that. Maybe, though, he was just saying it to persuade himself that he could. Then the sound of crunching boots interrupted the quiet.

"Shit. *Shit.*" Pad jumped back into the Dill like he'd come under fire. "Shit."

"Hey, what's wrong?" Dom's first thought was that he'd seen a fire front approaching. "What is it?"

"It's all *bodies.*" Pad was shaking. "I was having a piss by the wall, and when I looked down on the ground I thought it was just burned wood or plastic or something, but it was all *bodies.* It was *people.*"

He slid into the driver's seat, but he started fumbling with the controls as if he didn't recognize them. Marcus reached out and caught his arm.

"Come on, Pad. I'll drive."

"I'm okay. I'll be all right in a minute."

"I know. Come on."

Padrick wasn't a guy who gave in to anything, but he let Marcus take the controls and sat with his head in his hands. Even on the punishing ride back, he kept that position. The 'Dill was the last APC back to base that night. When they rolled in, the engineers were trying to clean the filth off the other 'Dills.

"Yeah, we get it," one of the guys said to Marcus as he dismounted. "It's bad out there."

Pad only got as far as the Dill's front scoop. He sat down again. Marcus waited, so Dom and Tai did as well.

"You want a beer?" Dom said. "Come on, Pad. Let's get totally shit-faced for once."

Padrick shut one eye, head slightly cocked to the side, and stared into the distance like he was sighting up. "It's so easy."

"What is?"

"Death. Done right."

"What the fuck are you talking about, man?"

"I've seen it maybe three, four hundred times. Because I *see* it, right? I'm the only one who does, not even the guy I hit. Close up. *Magnified.* That's what my job's about. I pull the trigger, and the guy's gone. One minute he's having a smoke or thinking about home, and the next he doesn't even know he's dead. His brain's liquefied like *that.*" Pad snapped his fingers. "In a fraction of a second, he's got nothing left to feel pain or fear with. Good way to go, Dom. Few of us get that privilege."

Marcus just stared at him. Dom was getting worried. Nothing that Pad had said was shocking or new, but his tone was scary: not depressed but wistful, as if he thought that instant nonexistence was something wonderful. Eventually he got up and ambled out of the hangar.

"Tai," Marcus said, "you want to keep an eye on him? We can take shifts."

"To prevent what?"

"Tai, he's losing it. Guys do dumb things when they're like that."

"Once something is seen, it cannot be unseen," Tai said. "Who are we to force him to live with what's in his head when it's not in ours?"

Tai almost smiled—he never seemed to let anything get to him—and then followed Padrick. He wasn't being callous at all, just Tai, but Dom couldn't imagine standing by and letting Marcus put a gun to his own head simply because he had a right to. There was nothing to say that Pad was planning to do that, of course. He just seemed to be making the point that he thought some ways to die were better than others, and being barbecued by the side of the road wasn't one of them. Dom would have said that made sense, too. But the look on Pad's face, that weird hopefulness, scared the shit out of him.

"Go home, Dom," Marcus said.

"You staying here?"

Marcus didn't quite shake his head. It was more a shrug. "I'd better go see Dad."

Dom was relieved—again—that he wasn't invited to supper at the Fenix estate.

KING RAVEN KR-42, FOUR HUNDRED KILOMETERS WEST OF EPHYRA ACROSS THE TYRAN BORDER, ONE WEEK LATER.

It was the most spectacular sunrise that Richard Prescott had ever seen.

He was so mesmerized by its intensity as the Raven banked that he forgot for a moment why the sky looked so breathtakingly beautiful, a wonderful streaked palette of coral, scarlet, and magenta. It was because millions of tons of fine debris had been kicked up into the atmosphere by the Hammer strikes.

For a few seconds, the open bay of the Raven framed only a brilliant sky unspoiled by anything else. Then it tilted down, and the landscape below was just stumps of buildings scattered across charred wasteland, unrecognizable as the industrial city it had once been.

So what did you expect, Professor?

Prescott watched Adam Fenix. He had a fixed safety line on his belt, but he stood confidently on the sill of the bay, hanging on to one of the overhead grab rails like the Gear he'd once been. Prescott expected to see shock on his face at the very least. No man could look at that scene below and not be unsettled in some way. But Fenix just closed his eyes for a moment.

"It's certainly been effective," he said. "In terms of asset denial, anyway. There's little for the Locust to take now. But that's a two-edged sword—we're going to have to rely wholly on our protected reserves of fuel, food, and water for months. You've seen how much contamination's blown across Ephyra."

Prescott gave him points for not degenerating into emotion and regret. "Adam, we knew from the start of the Hammer program that the consequences of using it would be serious."

"Yes, but even I can't tell you what the full repercussions will be. Noticed how much cooler it is? That's simply sunlight being blocked by the dust in the atmosphere. The climate effects are already here. The pollution—we'll be living with the consequences of that for decades, perhaps centuries."

"Modern life's always a trade-off between the easy life we want and the poisons it creates." Prescott tried to work out if his own numbness was normal human shock at the scale of the horror he'd been forced to unleash, or fear that he might have made the wrong decision. No; terrible as it was, there was nothing else anyone could have done. "Better that we live to find a solution than letting the enemy slaughter us."

We've been through all this. God, how many times did we argue about this over the last three years?

But that was before anyone had thought of deploying the entire orbital network at once.

Yes, that was me. That was my decision.

It was simply a chain of intense fires raging across the planet. Who needed chemical weapons when you could just set fire to Sera and release the toxins already in factories, refineries, and homes? Prescott sometimes let himself be shocked by the complexity of the world he tried to manage, and how little control he found he had over it. But then he shook it off and did what he could. Nobody could ever have all the answers.

"Why do we keep having this conversation?" Fenix asked.

"Perhaps we're rehearsing our excuses for posterity," said Prescott. "How's your son?"

"I'm not really sure." Fenix stepped back from the sill and sat down, buckling himself into his seat again. "He said it was like walking through dark gray snow. The first patrol, I mean. His squad did the first patrol after the strikes."

The Raven looped around and headed back to Ephyra. Beneath it, the landscape developed more detail as the blast radius expanded, showing how the destructive force had diminished with distance. Rain had washed a lot of the airborne pollution into the rivers. The dark snow was now more like slicks of oil, wet and shiny where the water had pooled, and Prescott began to believe that he had only to wait a few more weeks for nature to begin its own cleanup, and things would look more encouraging.

No, that was wishful thinking. He'd just be able to see more of the consequences of his decision.

The closer they got to Ephyra, the more black dots Prescott could see in the sky—other Ravens mapping the blocked roads and directing engineer detachments to where they were needed. The most they could do would be to clear a route to hell. He wondered what the rest of Sera looked like, but much of it was beyond the range of a Raven, and he would simply have to guess that whatever he'd seen in the last few hundred kilometers was a sample of the rest of the planet.

"Still no Locust," he said.

Fenix shook his head. Something below had caught his eye, and when Prescott leaned to look, it was an APC picking its way along the remains of a road that had buckled in the heat. "But we can't possibly have wiped them out. They're underground. Even if we killed all those on the surface, there'll be more of them deep in the tunnels."

"The pollution runoff should kill a good few of them, too, then?"

"Perhaps." Fenix watched the APC with intense interest until the Raven left it behind. "It'll poison the water table in places, and they must be making use of that, too."

"You always sound bewildered rather than hostile when you talk about the Locust, Professor."

Fenix paused for a moment. "I am," he said. "I don't know how to deal with them now, other than destruction. But I'm not someone who has the energy to hate anything, I'm afraid. Call it sorrow."

Prescott imagined Fenix having been one of those boys who kept scorpions and venomous spiders as pets, and found them appealing. It was the scientist in him. What would he do now? He was a weapons man. If the Locust were crushed, he'd have to find something else to occupy him.

Well, there was Sera. It would need the best minds left alive to heal the planet again. Fenix could make a start on that.

Back at the House of Sovereigns, Prescott passed cleaning crews hosing down the headstones next to the Tomb of the Unknowns. The neat, austere gardens looked almost back to normal, on the surface at least. Ephyra was an orderly city where citizens knew their place and purpose, and now they were doing what they did best: getting on with life and doing their civic duty.

Jillian, his secretary, greeted him with a folder of reports and a cup of coffee when he reached his office. Yes, life did go on.

"Sir, the catering manager is worrying that we might run short of coffee," she said. "I mean, they're not going to be harvesting this year, are they? Shall I start putting some aside?"

"I can live with herb tea," Prescott said. He loathed it, but it didn't hurt to be seen to make small sacrifices. "If I have to."

He sat down at his desk and let the chair tip backward as far as it would go on its tilt mechanism. As he leaned back, he looked at the two phones on his desk: one for routine calls, the other a dedicated line that was used only by ministers and other COG heads of state. Normally that line would be moderately busy, but it hadn't rung in nearly two weeks.

Prescott tried to remember the last conversation conducted on it, and he thought it might have been Deschenko calling him from Pelles—overrun by Locust, close to collapse—to tell him what an evil, murdering, genocidal bastard he was, and how he would surely rot in hell before too long.

Hell was a little too far in the future for Prescott at the moment. He had only to look outside the window to get his priorities in order, and hell had to wait its turn.

He stared at the phone a little longer, but it still didn't ring. He knew it would never ring again.

CORREN-KINNERLAKE HIGHWAY, SIX DAYS LATER.

Private Padrick Salton now sported a ripe black eye, and seemed reluctant to share the story of how he acquired it.

He walked beside Hoffman on a stretch of what had once been road. The bulldozers had driven through for the first time the day before, shoving aside debris so that Ephyra now had a clear route to the sea. Why the hell it needed one at the moment, Hoffman had no idea. There was no sea freight in or out because there was nowhere left to ship it from any longer. The NCOG—what little was left of it after E-Day—was crammed into ports along the Ephyran coast and at Merrenat to the northeast. The route clearance was a monumental waste of frigging time and fuel.

But he was here, walking that road, because he needed to. For some reason, Salton needed to do it as well. The paving and substrate was crazed with deep, narrow fissures down to half a meter where the temperatures had fired it like ceramics.

Shit, Margaret was probably nowhere near here. I just don't know. That's what I hate. Imagining.

"No word from the Islands yet," he said.

"I know, sir." Salton's buddies called him Pad, and sometimes Hoffman did, too. He'd been one of the most successful snipers in the Pendulum Wars. "But there were islands we never heard from after E-Day, too, and they turned out to be okay. Just no comms."

Hope was evil. It seduced you, then dumped you on your ass so hard and so fast that you were worse off than when you started. Hoffman ignored it. "Kaliso hasn't mentioned his."

"Well, he's got this mystic fate and eternity shit going on, but me, I think that when you're dead, you're dead, and that's the way it should be, so you finally get some peace."

"You ever going to tell me how you got that black eye? I'm not going to stick you on a charge."

Hoffman tried to walk the fine line between cutting his Gears some slack and letting discipline collapse. In the lunatic asylum that was post-strike Ephyra, knowing how to hang on to civilized conduct was what mattered. People were shocked and grieving. The curfew didn't stop anyone having arguments over a drink at other times of the day.

"I got totally rat-arsed in a bar last night, sir, and one thing led to another," Pad said at last. "Someone mouthed off about Sergeant Fenix's father. So I got *regimental* on him. I'm still Two-Six RTI."

Hoffman nodded, searching for the right response. "Okay, Private, we've all done it. Just don't let it become a habit."

Loyalty was an astonishing thing. Hoffman accepted it like faith. It didn't have to make sense, and it almost certainly didn't, but the things it could inspire men to do were extraordinary. Coupled with the stress and nightmares, though, it made for flash points.

And I'm a fool. Why am I here now?

He walked down one road out of thousands in the blast radius in the hope of closure. If he had his wish and Margaret's death had been instant, then there'd be nothing left of her or the car. If he found anything—and where the hell did anyone start looking?—then he'd agonize over how long it took her to die.

"I'm sorry about your wife, sir."

"Thanks, Pad. I'm not unique, though." *God, Anya probably told Dom Santiago, and now every bastard knows what went on.* "It's a shitty broken world."

"Do you know where she was? Sorry to ask, but that's why you came out on patrol, isn't it?"

"You don't know, then."

"All Dom said was that she didn't make it back to Ephyra."

Hoffman felt a pang of guilt for even thinking Anya had done anything more than warn people off asking him painful questions. The kid was incredibly loyal. There it was again: loyalty. Hoffman would take loyalty over genius anytime, not that Anya Stroud wasn't a smart girl.

"Pad, I know I'm not going to find her alive. She's gone." Hoffman surprised himself every time he said that. He hadn't even cried yet. Part of him was an old hand at grief and could stand back and watch the other Hoffman going through the same stages without trying to hurry it along. "I think I just needed to see *where*. Why the hell are you here, anyway? You're rostered off today."

"I lost it walking down a road some days ago. I need to be able to patrol again without seeing bodies under my feet." Pad stopped dead. "Got a last reported location? I'm up for it if you are, sir."

"It'll be a waste of resources." All Hoffman needed to do was put out the word to patrols that if they found anything in the months to come, anything at all, to let him know. "Pad, I'm grateful for your support. But there's not enough intel or reason to do this. I think I needed to walk this road to convince myself of that."

They walked on another two or three hundred meters to a mound of rubble the height of a two-story house. The highway was straight at this point; if Hoffman stood dead center, the debris pushed aside almost looked like monuments, a conquering army's triumphal route into an ancient city.

Am I letting you down by not searching, Margaret? Shit, it's too late to bust my ass for you now. I despise people who show more love at funerals than they ever did in someone's lifetime. Including me.

Pad moved around the mound cautiously, checking. It was still a dangerous job. Fires had raged underground, too, burning through ruptured pipelines and sewers, and subsidence was always a threat. There were probably forests and open land where the fires were still burning deep in the soil and would smolder for years.

And they couldn't burn those bastard grubs underground?

Hoffman was about to call Pad back—there was no reason to do this, no urgency—when he lost sight of him. His earpiece crackled.

"Contact, sir," Pad said. "Movement, over there. Left of . . . shit, left of what?"

"I hear you, Pad." It was time to alert CIC. "Control, this is Hoffman, possible grub contact, approximately one klick inland from Corren coast, just off Kinnerlake highway. Stand by."

There weren't enough landmark features to get bearings. Hoffman checked his rifle and went after Pad. The rubble was about knee high, so it shouldn't have been hard to spot anything, but Hoffman couldn't see what had grabbed Pad's attention until something moved and he turned in time to catch a glimpse of something gray.

"It's an e-hole," Pad whispered. He indicated a line at shoulder height. "Grub breaking cover."

Hoffman didn't see enough to make the call on what it was— drone, Boomer, whatever. Did it matter? *Bastard.* He moved in with Pad. They were about ten meters away before they could even see the hole in the ground, a sharp-edged pit that might have been a swimming pool or even a basement before the fires scoured the place.

Neither of them knew if they were chasing a single grub or if they were about to engage a whole platoon of the things. It was a dumb position to get in when there were just two of them with the nearest backup being a Raven that was at least ten minutes away.

They edged up to the pit and looked down, Lancers aimed. It was a big rectangular hollow with arches at chest height that looked like tunnels or very deep recesses. There was so much scattered debris that it was hard to work it out.

"It's a cellar," said Pad. "And that's either a tunnel or a sewer down there. But that doesn't mean it's not an e-hole, too."

"Shouldn't we be more worried about this?"

"Only if a few dozen of them rush us."

Pad jumped down, boots crunching the black wood to dust, and squatted to peer into the sewer. He sighted up.

"Whoa!" He jerked the Lancer's muzzle to one side. "Human. It's *human*. Shit, someone's *alive*. How the hell did they live through this?"

A stupid, desperate thought went through Hoffman's mind. No, it couldn't possibly be Margaret. He was furious with himself for even thinking it.

"Hey, come out," Pad called. "Are you hurt? COG forces here—we're on your side. Come on out."

Hoffman could hear sounds of rubble moving. Eventually someone crawled out on all fours like an animal. It was probably a woman. He decided that from the long mud-caked hair, but it wasn't until she knelt back on her heels that he could tell. She was completely covered in gray ash, wearing a rucksack back-to-front on her chest.

"Are you hurt?" Hoffman said. "How did you get here? How did you survive the fires, let alone the strike?"

She rubbed her sleeve across her mouth. "I hid." Her accent was heavy, not Tyran at all. She'd come across the borders. "I hid in the drains."

"Shit, you better come with us." Pad held out his hand to help her to her feet. "We'll get you cleaned up. You're not local, are you? What's your name, sweetheart?"

It was a perfectly ordinary question. It was simply what you said to scared civvies to break the ice and get them to do what you asked. Hoffman found himself trying to imagine how this woman had survived, and only then did he begin to realize how she might see them.

Enemy. Hostile. The ones who did all this.

Pad pulled her upright. She paused for a moment, unsteady, then launched into him, screaming in a foreign language, fists pummeling. He held her off one-handed, rifle still gripped tight in the other, but she managed to get in a few hard blows before Hoffman jumped down and pinned her arms. Maybe she didn't speak enough Tyran to understand Pad was trying to help her.

"Whoa, whoa, steady, steady . . ." Pad avoided a kick, but Hoffman caught it in the shin. She was completely nuts. She stank of smoke and sweat. "Lady, calm down. It's okay. We're not going to hurt you. We're COG. We'll get you to a hospital in Ephyra, get you some help. Look, you want some water? I bet you need water." He reached for the bottle on his belt. "Come on, it's okay now."

"You help me? You help me *now*?" She spat in Pad's face. Somehow that was always more shocking than a fist. She struggled to find the words in Tyran. "You let us die! You killed everyone! I come here to find Ephyra, find safe place, but we have no time, and you bomb us!"

What the hell could any man say to that? Pad just stared back at her. She'd exhausted herself, and Hoffman now needed to hold her upright rather than restrain her. Her rage was focused squarely on Pad. Maybe she only had enough energy left to hate one Tyran bastard at a time.

What am I going to do, tell her it's all about asset denial? How it's a sensible strategy? Bullshit.

"I'm sorry," Pad said. "I'm really sorry." His face was bleeding; she must have caught him with her nails and clawed him. "But you're safe now."

"My family is gone. Why should I care about *safe*?"

Hoffman let go of her and tried to turn her around to face him. He could hear a Raven approaching. "Ma'am, please, let us help you. I'm sorry, but we had to stop the grubs somehow."

"Grubs don't kill my family," she said. "*You* kill them. You left us stranded. I stay with people I *trust.*"

She backed away and ducked into the opening again. Pad crouched down and tried to coax her out, but she was gone. Hoffman heard her scuttling along the echoing concrete tunnel like an animal. If they went after her without some plan or support, there was no telling what they'd find. They'd have to come back later and do a proper sweep of the area, and maybe send in civilian aid workers.

"Shit," Pad said. "There must be more of them down there. What if they're everywhere?"

Hoffman radioed in to CIC. A Raven circled overhead. "Control, this is Hoffman. There are *survivors.* I repeat—we've found survivors. They've been stranded outside the boundary. So far, one female, age and nationality undetermined, but she's refused aid or evacuation. I expect there'll be more, so advise patrols accordingly. Hoffman out."

Pad was still staring into the tunnel like a cat watching a mousehole.

"Come on, Pad," Hoffman said. *Why did I ever think that poor bitch would see us as the good guys now?* "Nothing we can do here."

Pad bent down and placed his water bottle just inside the tunnel. He waited as if he was expecting the woman to come out, then shook his head and took a ration bar from his belt pouch. He laid it next to the bottle and walked away. Hoffman wasn't sure if it was practical compassion or some kind of peace offering.

I'm going to have to make a lot of those now.

"Control," Hoffman said, "scrub the KR unit. We're done here."

They set off back to the Packhorse. It was always the small detail, the broken fragments of tragedy on the ground, that either made you wonder why you were fighting or reminded you why you had to. And most of the time, it boiled down to the most basic level: staying alive, and watching your buddies' backs. The big ideological stuff was strictly bullshit for politicians and career officers who'd forgotten what they signed up for.

Not me. I remember. I'm still a Gear, colonel or not.

Padrick Salton was probably going back to base more distressed than he'd left it. And there was nothing Hoffman could do for him, any more than he could help the stranded woman who'd spat in his face.

"Damn, Private, what kind of world are we living in now?" Hoffman asked.

"I don't know, sir."

"Collateral damage. Collateral fucking *damage.*"

Padrick just shook his head.

Hoffman had been the enemy before, but never on his own turf.

CHAPTER 16

The COG isn't a superpower any longer, and we're not a national government. We're just city hall with an army, a navy, and the power of life and death. Prescott's a mayor with weapons of mass destruction. That simplifies things a great deal, but it also means small issues have big consequences.

(CAPTAIN QUENTIN MICHAELSON, DISCUSSING POLITICAL REALITY
IN A SHRINKING WORLD WITH COLONEL VICTOR HOFFMAN.)

"Victor, he can't expect leniency for rape. A trial would send out a very clear message."

Bernie could hear Prescott's polished, expensively educated voice in the corridor. She'd never heard a wrangle between Hoffman and the Chairman firsthand before. It was like overhearing the grown-ups fighting, both terrifying and fascinating, and somehow all her fault.

"Make your mind up, Chairman." Hoffman's voice strained at its seams. "Either we have a tribunal for Stranded criminals, your precious one law for all, or we do what martial law entitles us to do. You can't run both systems at once."

"Our women need reassurance that we'll protect them in an uncertain world." Prescott sounded more distant, as if he was walking away, a man with something more important to do. "I'm not politically squeamish, but I want to avoid descending into governance by vague terror. Much better that everyone knows *why* people suddenly disappear."

Good old Prescott. Squeamish? Press that Hammer of Dawn button and stand back . . .

But Bernie saw his point. She was on the verge of going out there and saying that it was fine, okay, whatever they wanted; she'd go through with a trial. She wasn't ashamed. And didn't everyone—normal, *average* everyone—think that rapists and perverts in general deserved a hole in the head? She'd get a medal, just as Baird had told her.

But how's the average citizen going to feel about Gears when they hear how I did it?

The fact that she'd been a civilian when she killed the other two rapists was irrelevant. She was a Gear again now. And nothing could take the regiment out of her blood.

Hoffman sounded as if he was walking after Prescott. "I won't have one of my Gears forced to tell the world exactly what those animals did to her. And we don't want civilians to hear how she dealt with it. Do we? Undermines respect. They wouldn't understand."

Vic's ashamed of me. Oh God. He's actually ashamed of me.

Prescott went quiet. Bernie thought he'd walked off.

"Good point," he said at last. "Deal with it, Victor."

"Chairman, give me a clear instruction for once, goddamn it."

"Do whatever you feel will do least damage to morale. I'll back you completely."

I bet you will . . .

Bernie found it sobering that even a man with an army at his disposal couldn't piss people off too much in this microcosm of a world. Everything existed on a knife-edge. Hoffman stormed back into the office and stood with fists clenched, shaking his head slowly.

"I'm sorry, Vic," she said.

"Don't you dare apologize." He grabbed her shoulders, harder than he probably meant to. "Damn it, woman, why didn't you tell me right away? I'd . . . I'd have handled you *better*."

"Vic, I'm *okay*. I don't bake a cake to celebrate the anniversary, but it doesn't stop me living, either. Every good time I have is a big fuck-you to that bastard in there."

"I'm not having all that paraded at a trial."

"I'm in two minds about it."

"You don't seriously want to give that filth his day in court."

"Chairman's right—he has to be seen to be punished. I don't care who knows what happened. But what *I* did—what will that do to the reputation of every other Gear? We're the good guys, remember? Mr. Average Civvie out there won't see me as a civilian victim."

"So no trial. Good." Hoffman nodded, looking at the door on the other side of the office. Jonn Massy was locked in an adjoining room, waiting. How long he had to live and how he died would be decided in the next few minutes. That was sobering, too.

"Are you ashamed of me, Vic?" she asked. "Because it's okay if you are."

"No, no. Never."

"Not even slightly worried about what's in me?"

"It's in all of us, Bernie."

"I didn't believe I could do it. And once I started, it was all too easy."

Hoffman snorted. "You think Massy and his kind agonize like this? They just rob, kill, and rape. Then they get up the next morning and do it all over again."

"Is that the decency line, then? They do it and don't lose sleep, but we do it and wrestle with our conscience? Or we only feel guilty when it's another human and not a grub? Because I still carved those bastards, either way, and they felt pain as much as any grub. And I don't feel bad about causing pain—I feel bad about finding it was easier than I thought."

"We should have had this talk months ago." Hoffman locked the door. The room was sparsely furnished, not yet filled with the paper and general mess of a long-used office. "All I care about now is what happens to you, and what happens to all my other Gears. Prescott can take care of the rest of civilization."

"You know something? I *fled* back to the army. That's civilization to me. I didn't want to become like the vermin I saw. That scared me a lot more than combat ever did. I don't think it's even morality talking. Just dread."

Hoffman stared her straight in the eye for what felt like forever, but with no judgment, just a sad kind of regret. He'd had to do some serious shit in his time, too. She knew that. But he'd acted in the moment, not gone back to settle scores in cold blood. And she still didn't know if that made the difference or not.

"Come on, let's get this over with." He checked his pistol again and gripped the door handle. "What do *you* want to do? Just say the word."

Bernie never doubted Massy was the right man. She didn't doubt that a death sentence for all his gang's crimes—not just for her, for all the innocent Stranded killed and terrorized—was the right one. There were just parts of her that were more troubled by other things these days. She felt her anger was getting threadbare. She wasn't even sure now if it *was* anger.

What the hell do *I want?*

"Let me talk to him," she said.

Jonn Massy was handcuffed. Part of her said to take the cuffs off rather than kick the shit out of a bound man, which suddenly struck her as bizarre: she was a lean woman—not frail, *never*, not yet—pushing sixty, and he was half her age, built like a brick shit-house. The regiment embedded a sense of manly, square-jawed fair play even in its women.

What a joke.

Hoffman stood to one side, looking ready to put himself between her and Massy. For a moment, Bernie thought of Marcus, that sad disapproval or whatever it was on his face when she showed signs of going feral, and realized just how much his opinion bothered her.

I know he's right. Once I kick off the revenge killings, it becomes the way we do things. And then we fall apart as a society.

But Massy needed to pay for everything he'd ever done. That was what held society together: facing the consequences of your actions.

Even now, he had that same arrogant leer on his face. She could smell him, too. It wasn't body odor. It was just *him*, and it had been a long time before she'd been able to get that smell out of her nostrils.

"So why come here?" she asked. "Your buddies must have told you I was back. You didn't think I'd recognize you?"

Massy still looked confident, if not relaxed. "And I just walked in here. Didn't I? How many others have you let in that you didn't recognize, who didn't leave witnesses? We're inside your walls, bitch. You'll all pay for my brother." He winked slowly. "Maybe I came in to finish you off. Just so the COG knows it's not untouchable."

"So why did you crap yourself and make a run for it?"

"Live to fight another day . . ."

"Okay, I'll shoot every last damn one of you, then, just to be certain," Hoffman said. "Because I can do that."

"But you *won't*, you dumb old bastard, because you *haven't*. The COG's gone soft. That's why the grubs forced you out. We'll be here long after you've gone—we're fit to survive. You're not."

Hoffman drew his sidearm and handed it to Bernie, all matter-of-fact. She had her own pistol, but there was a hell of a lot said silently when he did that.

"You going to gloat, bitch?" Massy asked. "I'm not afraid of you. I taught you that you're nothing and that we can do whatever we like with you. You're never going to forget that."

Bernie had a sudden urge to pull the trigger. It passed as soon as it came; she actually wanted to laugh, and wasn't sure why. Stress made you do all kinds of weird things at the wrong times, but—this was a sense of revelation.

It's a contest. He keeps setting the rules for me. Okay, that stops now.

She handed the pistol back to Hoffman. He put it to Massy's temple without a second's hesitation.

"I'll finish the job," he said. "You want to wait outside or not, Bernie? You don't have to be involved."

Massy smirked. "See, no guts—"

Hoffman grabbed Massy's hair in his free hand and jerked his head back. The old bugger was more frightening when he was ice-cold, and he certainly was now.

Massy still wasn't pleading for his life, though. Did she want that? Yes, she *did*. He had to be brought down and then obliterated, so that others could see that men like him could be broken.

He managed to look Hoffman in the eye. "You'll have nightmares about me after you pull that trigger, old man. I'll still own you."

"You're too young to remember Anvil Gate," Hoffman said quietly. "You think this is the first time I've done a dirty job?"

You don't tell me everything, Vic. Do you?

Bernie closed her fingers over the pistol's bulky barrel and pressed Hoffman's hand down slowly. It was a dangerous thing to do to a man with a chambered round and the safety off. She might have been a millisecond from getting her hand blown apart, or worse. But *she* had control now. She knew it.

"No, he doesn't get to jerk anyone's else's chain," she said. "Here's what I'm going to do. He's *mine*. I'll do what I want with him. I'll think of something."

Hoffman just looked at her, questioning, Massy's hair still gripped tight in his fist.

"Yes, I'm *sure*," she said.

But Massy wasn't.

She saw it for just the moment she needed to, that look in his eyes that said he didn't know what was happening now, what would happen next, or how bad things might get, because this wasn't in his rule book at all. *That* was fear. That was what he did to others. And that was what she wanted to inflict on him. The rest was academic.

Hoffman let go of Massy and shoved him aside. Massy found his voice after a few seconds. "You think you can threaten me, bitch? You think you can scare me?"

"I already have," Bernie said. "Let's see what happens next. You know how unpredictable women are."

Hoffman opened the door to let her out, then locked the room behind them.

"Whatever you want, Bernie," he said. "I'll go along with it. But I really wish you'd let me cap the bastard and put it all behind you."

"You were willing," she said. "And that's enough for me."

Hoffman had had enough nightmares. She wasn't going to add one more. If there was any dirty work to be done, she would do her own.

VNB MARRIED QUARTERS, FAMILIARIZATION TOUR, THREE DAYS LATER.

"So remind me, Boomer Lady, how many words ain't we allowed to say now?"

Cole and Bernie stood at attention in the second rank of the Gears guard, watching the small crowd gather in the square—a tree-lined square, like the ones Jacinto used to have—to hear the Chairman say something meaningful to the visiting civilians from Pelruan. Cole wondered if he would ever get used to any duty that just involved standing around looking good.

"*Refugees*," Bernie said. "If you say the R-word, I have to wash your mouth out with carbolic soap. We can call ourselves *Jacinto's remnant*. Or *survivors*. But he really wants us to get used to being *citizens of New Jacinto*."

"Man, I hate that coy shit. We're refugees. We *ran*, baby. We found *refuge*. So what?"

"He thinks it makes the worthy citizens of Pelruan see us as charity cases rather than the masters who've come back to see how well they've looked after the place for us."

"If I ever talk 'bout runnin' for office, Bernie," Cole said, "shoot me. Because I can't be doin' with all that *semantics* shit."

"Come on, look earnest and wholesome, Cole Train." Bernie

shifted her weight slightly. She had all kinds of aches and pains these days, but she didn't seem to be planning on taking things any easier. "The civvies are watching. Our beloved Chairman is about to address us."

The best rooms in town—in VNB, anyway—were the married quarters on the western side of the base. Prescott was so keen to make the Pelruan folk feel united with the Jacinto folk that he'd invited more of them down to see the work being done. The buildings were the same style as the grand old apartment blocks in Jacinto, but if Prescott thought he was going to build a nice replica of the old place here on Vectes, he had a lot of sweat ahead.

Cole found it weird to watch the guy shift from stirring battle speeches to Gears about exterminating grubs to being Mr. Nice and practically kissing babies. It wasn't like the man needed votes. Nobody had voted for years. Folks were only just starting to talk about that election stuff again, so maybe he was getting his campaign started early.

"I'm sure you never imagined this day would come," Prescott said, hands clasped behind his back. "But Vectes—New Jacinto—is now the capital of the Coalition of Ordered Governments. From here, humanity will rebuild. From here, we will recover our strength and numbers, reclaim the mainland, and restore civilization. Your contribution—keeping this outpost going for so many years, and your willingness to welcome the survivors of Jacinto—has made the difference between extinction and a future for humankind."

"*Willingness,*" Bernie muttered. "But not in their backyard . . ."

Gavriel and Berenz were in the crowd. They gave Cole a discreet wave. Well, they'd been willing; they'd kept the flag flying. Cole hoped they got whatever reward made people like that happy. They were probably just grateful to be told they could finally hand back the keys.

"So when we goin' to stop callin' Stranded *Stranded*?" Cole whispered. "They're all different. I feel I oughta reflect that in my *semantics.*"

"Are you taking the piss?"

"I'm serious, baby. I need to know if we're talking about gang-sters, or bums, or homeless, or unlucky, or messed up in the head, or too afraid to go home, or what." Cole liked Bernie too much to let her go on being bent out of shape every time that damn stupid S-word came up. "Or missin' for ten years. Or just takin' a long time returnin' to base . . ."

Bernie didn't look at him. She couldn't. Eyes front, that was the drill. "Low blow," she said.

"Shit, wasn't *meant* to be, Boomer Lady."

"I know, sweetheart. And I know you're right, too."

Baird was going to be a tougher nut to crack. He hadn't been around the buoy a few times like Bernie. Cole decided he'd just have to learn the way she did, by hitting his head hard against the real world for a lot more years.

Cole tuned back in to the speech again. Damn, was the Chair-man still boring the asses off those Pelruan people? He was. The man had stamina. Cole had to admire that.

"We still have a great deal of work to do bringing our people ashore," Prescott went on. "We may ask a lot of you in the days to come. But your lives will improve, too. The first improvement you'll see is to the security situation. You'll no longer be subjected to attacks by Stranded. The criminal elements will be eliminated, and the rest have been offered a choice—to accept the rule of COG law or to leave."

Man, he'd been doing so well up to then. Cole saw the fidget-ing begin, and some folks looked down at their boots, because some of the audience really didn't want to hear that Stranded could have a place at the table if they learned which fork to use. Cole also wondered just what Prescott meant by *eliminated*.

He had to admit he was starting to squirm a little more every time the lawlessness thing got dragged out into conversation. Fighting grubs was something you didn't have to debate about— they wanted every human dead, they didn't have much else ex-cept that on their minds, and it was clearly a Gear's job to stop them. *No gray areas there, baby.* But Prescott needed a police force now, not an army.

The Chairman finished his pep talk and the small crowd broke up. Cole and Bernie hung around, under orders to look reassuring and helpful with the other Gears until the civvies moved on. Prescott still didn't want them having free run of the place, so maybe he hadn't gone totally soft yet after all.

"Bernie, you've fought humans, right?" Cole said.

She laughed. "Yeah. Hate 'em. I want them off my planet."

"I mean the Pendulum Wars. I never fought another human before. I kill grubs. You think I can cap a human if I ever need to?"

"Course you can, sweetheart." She patted his back like he was a kid. "Once some bastard fires at you, experience takes over. You won't care what the enemy looks like, and your forebrain won't be making the decisions." She looked at her Lancer. "I'm not sure how I'm going to cope with using a chainsaw on a human, but we used to use the old blade bayonets, and they're pretty nasty in a different sort of way."

Cole tried to imagine having this conversation with a local civilian. It would have been like trying to explain why he freaked out at the sight of that weird eel. People around him acted like two species now, those who got it when it came to the war with the grubs, and those who didn't.

"Thanks, Boomer Lady."

"Cole Train, you've never doubted yourself, ever. No reason to start doubting now."

He almost asked her why she was worried about using the chainsaw on a human when she'd obviously done some pretty creative knife work on some guys, but he accepted that folks had limits that didn't always make sense.

Three kids from the Pelruan party came over to stare at them. Cole had seen them around for a few days now. Bernie seemed to be her old self again since she'd caught her rapist, like she'd put all that shit to rest even without cutting his nuts off, and she squatted down to talk to the children like she hadn't a care in the world. Damn, she was a pushover when it came to little kids.

"Hi, are you having fun?" she said. "I'm Bernie. This is Cole Train. He plays thrashball. What's your name?"

Two of the kids just backed away and ran off. The little boy stood his ground. "Samuel," he said, looking up at Cole. "Are you going to shoot us?"

"We only shoot monsters," Cole said. That kid's impression of Gears just didn't seem healthy. "But only if they're real ugly ones."

Bernie frowned but kept it all quiet and soothing. "What makes you think we'll shoot you, sweetheart? We're here to look after everyone."

"My mom says you will."

"Really? I think she's got that a bit wrong."

"She says you're all jumpy and you beat people up."

Cole tried to imagine what the boy's mom had actually said. Kids got the wrong end of the stick about detail, but they usually got the sentiment right, and that worried him. He squatted down next to Bernie—he often forgot how big he must have looked from a kid's height—and tried to reassure the boy that Gears didn't bite. Then a woman rushed up and grabbed Samuel like she was snatching him out of the path of a car.

"Let's go, honey," she said. "Don't pester the Gears."

"He's no trouble at all." Bernie stood up with her let's-you-and-me-have-a-talk face on. "He thinks we shoot civilians, though. I was explaining that we don't do that."

"Okay, Sergeant." The woman was backing away a step at a time "I don't know what hellhole you people come from, but I don't want any of you near my kids. You're looking for a fight all the time. You're angry at everything and everybody. You're dangerous."

"Ma'am, we—"

She stabbed a finger at Bernie. "I *saw* you assault a civilian. You hit an unarmed man with your rifle. Just stay away from us, okay?"

Bernie didn't even try to explain, and just watched them go. The shock was written across her face.

"Shit," she said after a long pause. "I terrify small children, and mothers think I'm a danger to society. Is that what I've become, Cole?"

"Bernie, she's just a flake, okay? Forget it."

"Yeah, I gave Massy a smack with the Lancer to get him down off the gate. If I think that's normal, have I lost it?"

"Baby, listen to Doc Hayman. She said the whole damn city's stressed as hell, not just us." He thought of the eel that almost made him crap himself—just a damn ugly fish. "But these folks been livin' in a nice little cocoon, so they're naturally gonna think we're all psychos."

Bernie rubbed the back of her hand across her mouth. Shit, that had really upset her. She was scared of turning into an asshole like Massy and his thugs. Cole was almost starting to look back on Jacinto as a happy memory, a place where everyone understood that Gears had the kind of job that pushed them over the edge sometimes. It wasn't like anyone was out of control—just messed up by a long war, nothing more than that.

"The day I was discharged from Two-Six RTI was like losing my family," Bernie said at last. "Twenty-two years. My old man said he didn't know who I was when I got home."

"Shit, baby, I never knew you *had* an old man."

"Farmer." That was all she said. It explained some things but unexplained a lot of others. She glanced back over her shoulder at the civvies. "Stupid cow. She'll come crying to us when she's got Stranded swarming all over her."

"Talking of which, what you gonna do with your pet asshole?"

"They don't do well in captivity, do they?"

"You can't hang on to him forever. Whatever the Chairman thinks, we ain't got the spare food and manpower to keep folks locked up doing nothing for years."

"Yeah, I realize that."

"Not saying folks shouldn't have justice, but it gets kinda complicated the longer you take over it."

"If he was a grub, what would we do with him?"

"Slice and dice, baby. You wouldn't have blinked."

"The shitbag was right, then. We *do* have double standards, and we *are* soft."

"See why I asked you about shootin' human enemies?"

Bernie shrugged. "Then Massy's business associates will want to avenge him. And so it escalates."

"Yeah, grudges never rust."

At least that made her laugh. Anyone who could laugh was still in one piece.

"Come on, we've got stevedore duty," she said. "Plenty of ships still to be unloaded. Honest sweaty work."

Cole looked back over his shoulder a couple of times as they walked away, and caught sight of two of the Pelruan women watching with mistrust all over their faces. So some of the locals thought Gears weren't properly civilized like decent folk, and the Gears in turn thought the Stranded were a step outside the human race.

Man, there was a league table of society set up already. Nobody could ever accuse humans of being slow to find someone new to look down on.

SMALL SHIPS' JETTY, VNB, NEXT MORNING.

"I don't give a damn if it's unsporting," Michaelson said. "First sign of trouble—open fire."

The small inflatable boat puttered slowly toward the jetty, trailing a square of grubby white sheet on a long radio aerial. Dom could see one man at the tiller: twenty, twenty-five, rifle slung across his back.

Marcus aimed down at the small RIB. The jetty was well above the water line, patrol boat level. "Yes, Captain . . ."

"I detect doubt in your voice, Sergeant Fenix. When we have a quiet moment, allow me to stand you a drink and tell you some unsettling stories about my experience of piracy tactics."

Marcus grunted. "You got it."

Dom wouldn't have put anything past the Stranded now, rubber boat or not. He made a show of sighting up on them, too. The man cut the outboard motor and let the boat drift onto the jetty wall, grabbing the bottom rung of the metal ladder to hold his position.

Michaelson looked down at him from the top. "So you want to talk," he said. "I'm Captain Quentin Michaelson. You look familiar. Haven't I sunk you somewhere before?"

The Stranded guy didn't look amused. "Call me Ed. You're holding a member of our *management*, and we'd like to talk terms."

"What makes you think we'd want to?"

"We hear he's not dead, and you haven't shot me up yet."

"Assuming we're interested, what terms could you possibly offer us?"

"If you hand him over, we'll stay clear of Vectes." Ed cocked his head and seemed to be keeping an eye on Marcus. "And you stay clear of our territories."

Dom expected Michaelson to give Ed the full COG speech on whose territories all the islands were, but he just ignored the comment. "Why should I negotiate with criminals who attack un- armed fishing vessels?"

"We haven't touched your boats, man. Not for a while, any- way."

"Very public-spirited. Perhaps another subsidiary of your Stranded enterprise sank the *Harvest*, then."

"I tell you, we haven't been near your fishermen." Ed sounded wary. He was probably expecting Marcus to open fire. Dom was fascinated at his willingness to come right into the naval base, trusting the COG not to ambush him. "You lost one?"

"You know damn well we did."

"I ain't wasting my breath trying to convince you."

"If I were to hand this gentleman back to you, instead of stand- ing him in front of a firing squad as he deserves," Michaelson said, "then I would want that done by your *management team* in person."

"I'll ask. I'm just the messenger boy."

"And to show goodwill, I'd like the handover to be at your main location."

"We're not that stupid. Or trusting."

"Then they can meet us here. Discuss how things are going to be from now on."

"I think," Ed said, "that they'll want a neutral location. At a time of their choosing. You know how it is."

Michaelson just folded his arms. "You'd better be able to put something substantial on the table and enforce it. Come back to me if and when you've got something to offer."

Ed pushed off from the ladder and started the outboard. He left a lot faster than he'd come in, leaving a wide wake. Dom waited for Michaelson to tell everyone what he was really planning.

"Sounds like a nice simple deal." Marcus lowered his rifle. "What's the *real* one?"

"I imagine Ed is trying to work that out, too," Michaelson said. "But this isn't international diplomacy, Sergeant. We don't have treaties with organized crime. And they are *very* organized. Let me show you something."

He gestured to them to follow him and strode back toward the deepwater berths. It was a constant route march to move around VNB. Dom felt he spent most of his day walking around the place, and wondered if it would have been so hard to free up some vehicles and fuel to save time.

But I can walk anywhere without expecting the pavement to rip open and grubs to spew out of the hole. That's got to be worth some boot leather.

He caught up with Marcus. "I always wondered what the navy did all those years when it wasn't ferrying supplies. I'm starting to find out."

"And Hoffman knows he's doing this?"

"As long as *Prescott* knows."

"Yeah," Marcus said. "He always tells us everything. Never pulls need-to-know shit on us."

"I think Michaelson's making for *Clement*."

"Shit. Armor off . . ."

Clement was a tight fit. A fully armored Gear wouldn't even get down the hatch. They left their plates, weapons, and boots on the jetty—Marcus insisted on a guard for it all, even here—and squeezed into a whole new world that smelled of fuel and stale coffee. It wasn't designed for really big men. Marcus kept scraping his shoulders on bulkhead instruments along the narrow passages, clusters of dials and tiny handwheels packed so tightly together that they looked almost comical. Dom tried to imagine locating the right control in a pitch-black boat after a lighting failure. That alone scared him enough to kill any thoughts of serving at sea. He'd take grubs any day, thanks.

"Welcome to the control center," Michaelson said. The passage opened out onto a slightly less confusing space that spanned the beam of the boat. "Commander Garcia here is one of our last Pendulum War submariners, and this is our only boat, so we take very good care of both. Even so, we haven't been able to maintain all the boat's systems."

Garcia was a lot younger than the grizzled old sea dog Dom expected to see, maybe forty or so, hunched over a small chart table. *Not much older than me. Shit. How much combat experience has he got, then? Can't be much.* When Garcia unhunched, he didn't manage to expand much in the space available.

"We like Corporal Baird," Garcia said. "Very able engineer. Can we keep him? Trade you a few packs of coffee."

"Tempting," Marcus said. "But I have to decline."

Michaelson tapped one of the gauges on the bulkhead, frowning. "Okay, here's the plan I've put to Hoffman. We could afford to ignore a lot of piracy when the COG had a mainland presence. It wasn't our problem so long as it didn't affect us. Now we can't—Vectes shipping's going to be the single richest target they'll have, and we'll depend on safe seas until we can reclaim the continent. So now's the time to give them a serious smacking and not just dick around picking off the occasional boat when we run into it."

"What did you have in mind?" Marcus asked.

"Find their bases. Cream their vessels and eliminate their members. Sends out a message to the noncriminal Stranded, too."

"And pirates are harder to pin down than you think," Garcia said. "We don't have the reach or the kit these days. But at least we can listen better now, thanks to Baird."

Garcia fiddled with a control panel that Dom couldn't even begin to recognize, and a very broken-up radio signal filled the small space. Dom had to concentrate hard to make out anything. But then the sounds started to fall into place, and he realized he was eavesdropping on intercepted radio chatter between pirate vessels. It was patchy, but it was better than nothing.

"We know roughly *where* some of them are, and *who* they are," Garcia said. "Some of these guys have been around for years, like the gang Massy's linked to. So now we know that they want him back, he's finally going to be some use to decent society for once in his life. As bait."

"I'm still not getting this," Marcus said. "You lure a few gang bosses to a handover. You blow them up. And?"

"You knock out a chunk of their command," Dom said. "It puts them off balance for a while."

"And there'll always be another asshole to take the job."

"But there won't be replacement vessels," Michaelson said. "And knowing there's an operational submarine around that can take them out will make them think twice about even going fishing."

Marcus looked dubious. It was pretty clear that Michaelson had penciled in Delta to do some of the work. Dom wondered if Marcus was having a moral moment about all this, because even if he wouldn't admit it, there was a lot of his father in him, especially the urge to do things right. *Right* could be very hard to define; *lawful* didn't cover it. Dom recalled Hoffman's barbed comments about Adam Fenix getting edgy over what to do with the civilian scientists in the raid on Aspho Point.

"I'm not used to fighting that kind of war," Marcus said. "And it sounds like overkill. Torpedoes can sink a destroyer."

"We don't have many of those, so we won't be wasting them until we can replace them," Michaelson said. "But don't underestimate the deterrent value of a submarine."

"Don't you have to leave someone alive to tell the tale for a deterrent to work?"

"That, or surface in the right places occasionally."

"I accept it's a step beyond entrapment," Garcia said. "But the pirates got used to that. They won't be expecting this."

Marcus nodded. Dom couldn't tell if it was grudging approval. "Sneaky."

"*Submarine.* Are you missing something here about the word *submerged*?"

"I meant double-crossing them over a deal."

"If they were gray, scaly, and lived underground, would you do it?"

Marcus shrugged. "Sure as shit, sir."

"Well, there you go," Garcia said. "We've asked Hoffman for your squad for the surface element of the mission. So if you want to feel up front and honest when you kill them, you can."

Marcus just looked at the chart on the table, nodded a few times, and then gazed around the control room as if he was memorizing the detail. Maybe he was wondering how anyone coped here if the lights failed. It was the kind of thing anyone trained to strip a weapon blindfolded would consider.

"If Hoffman tasks us," Marcus said, "then we do our jobs."

Back on the quay, Dom and Marcus put their armor on and stared at each other in silence for a moment.

"Okay, I'll say it." Dom sometimes got frustrated with him for not leaving that kind of high-level moral wrangling to his commanders. "The day you start worrying if we're being fair to fucking *pirates* is the day I haul you off to Doc Hayman for a brain scan."

"Fair?" Marcus started walking back to the barracks. Getting him to stand still and talk had always been hard. He always seemed to be on the run from conversations. "They're assholes. They prey on people who've got nothing. I just feel . . . *uneasy*. That's all."

"Would you feel better if we declared formal war on them first?"

"Probably."

"Talk to Bernie. Get yourself mad. Then declare your own war. I have. I'm fine with it."

Marcus never talked about his time in prison. The Slab was a cesspit for the worst of the worst, and Dom had no doubt what those who were let loose when the Locust overran the area ended up doing. They didn't all go into the army, or even stay in uniform. Maybe Marcus was trying not to let what he'd seen shape what he did as a Gear, a man with rules and standards. It was hard to tell. He didn't say another word until they were almost at the barracks gate.

"I don't give a shit about them as human beings," Marcus said. "I just wonder what kind of society we'll rebuild every time we bend our own rules."

Dom decided to drop the subject. It was all what-ifs and exceptions, theoretical shit that might have been a great debate over a beer but didn't help him deal with the here and now—his job, his task.

And that was to protect the people he cared about, and the civilians who couldn't protect themselves. That was the deal. He served the COG and defended the way of life he knew.

The pirate gangs had declared war on all that the moment they hit their first target. He was happy to play by their rules now.

CHAPTER 17

We're willing to meet you. Neutral water, time and coordinates to follow. No more than two vessels each. Nothing bigger than a patrol boat. No tricks. And we want to see that our colleague is alive and unharmed before we do or say anything.

(RADIO MESSAGE FROM CORMICK ALLAM, CHAIRMAN
OF THE LESSER ISLANDS FREE TRADE AREA,
TO CAPTAIN MICHAELSON, NCOG.)

CNV *FALCONER* APPROACHING HANDOVER
LOCATION, EARLY MORNING, SOUTHWEST OF
VECTES, NEARLY TEN WEEKS AFTER THE ESCAPE
FROM JACINTO, 14 A.E.

Anya now understood the insistence on the time and place, and also why few Stranded ever made it to Vectes.

Just to reach this mid-ocean point was a long, rough journey by sea even at patrol boat speeds. Tackling the distance by sail alone would have put anyone off. And now she saw another hazard for herself.

"Fog," she said.

"Mist," Franck Muller corrected. He stood with one hand on the helm and the other on the radar console, pressing buttons.

"It's not fog until the visibility is half this, ma'am. This time of year, it's almost guaranteed around here. It's two currents meeting."

Anya stood in the open wheelhouse door, scanning the mist bank through binoculars. There were three vessels in there, bouncing back small profiles on radar, but that didn't seem to tell Muller everything he wanted to know. The intermittent radio chatter they'd picked up had stopped eight hours ago.

"So much for two vessels," Muller said. "I'm glad they're not going soft on us."

Anya shrugged. "Well, we didn't tell them one of ours was a submarine, so we're even."

Marcus was leaning on *Falconer*'s starboard machine gun as if he couldn't find a comfortable firing position. The shoulder braces hadn't been designed for someone in heavy armor. Michaelson stood to one side of him, watching.

"I didn't expect them to stick to the rules," Michaelson said, checking his watch. "I hope you'll feel better about us blowing them to kingdom come now, Sergeant Fenix."

It was hard to get a sense of scale with nothing on the water to use for comparison. Anya found that if she lowered the glasses and changed her focus slowly, the cloud layers transformed themselves into distant mountains, and the sea below became a lake, an empty plain, a desert—or even more cloud. It could look like anything you wanted it to be.

And I could make a hell of a lot of mistakes out here if I don't learn fast.

"Lesser Islands Free Trade Area," Anya said. "Have you come across them before, sir?"

"Not by name. But gangs often pool resources and intelligence, so they'll probably have links to my old customers, friendly or otherwise. Some of them operate entirely from ships."

"A few torpedoes would shut them down for good," Anya said.

"As if anyone would do such a thing." Michaelson winked at her. "I just wish I knew where they got their fuel. They certainly get around."

Marcus peered down the sights of the machine gun, apparently ignoring the conversation beside him. Anya didn't need telepathy to work out that he thought this wasn't a safe place for her. It was just as well that Michaelson was rather malleable when it came to women asking favors of him.

I've been stuck behind a desk for nearly eighteen years. I'm retraining, Marcus. Give me a break.

The empty vastness was unnerving, but somehow it also made Anya feel safer. There was nothing lurking within derelict buildings, nothing hiding in the dark, nothing that would erupt from the ground. Beneath *Falconer,* the sea was probably just as dangerous in its own way as the Locust-infested mainland had been, but she didn't feel that constant uneasiness in the same way she had in Jacinto. She was simply aware of safety precautions to be followed.

And who would try to take on *Falconer?* The boat wasn't a *Raven's Nest,* but she looked twice the size of *Chancellor* and better armed—several deck-mounted guns and a grenade launcher, just on Anya's quick inspection—so with *Clement* skulking around somewhere, Anya felt as safe here as anywhere.

Sergeant Andresen walked around from the foredeck and stood watching Marcus, brow corrugated with intense concentration, taking everything in.

"Enjoying yourself, Rory?" Anya asked.

"Learning plenty, ma'am." He took out a small notebook and scribbled from time to time. "I'm okay with the guns. We need training to carry out boardings, though."

"It's like building clearance with nowhere to run," Marcus said, gaze still fixed on the water. "For us *or* them."

Andresen took no notice. "Ma'am, we're going to have to do things we never did on land. It's a whole new game for us now."

"Yes, we'll need to cross-train Gears," Michaelson said. His binoculars hung from a leather strap around his neck. He seemed in his element now, as if this was his war. "It's going to be about maritime operations now."

Marcus grunted. "Somebody better tell Cole. He might want a transfer."

Keeping a constant ear on the radio net, Anya bit back a reflex to plunge in and start directing the operation. Either *Clement* must have been close to the surface or Baird had repaired her towed antenna, because she heard Garcia report in.

"*Clement* to *Falconer*, I'm not picking up any engine noise at the moment, just sporadic sounds I can't identify. If they've got working radar, they must have detected yours by now."

"I thought submarines could hear pretty well everything over huge distances," Anya said.

Michaelson looked amused. "They can hear plenty, but sometimes they can't pinpoint something until they hit it. Omniscience isn't in their armory. But don't tell anyone."

Anya was a little disappointed, but if she believed a submarine could do anything, then pirates probably believed it, too. That was all that mattered in the deterrence game.

Whatever the pirate vessels were doing, it didn't make sense yet. Anya put it down to missing a few reality checks over the years, in much the same way as the Stranded out here didn't seem to grasp the size of the COG forces they were provoking. Perhaps Massy's comrades were too used to targets with the bare minimum of technology, if any, or maybe they thought that NCOG was in an even worse state of repair than it was.

Everyone has a blind spot. Everyone on top of their food chain gets lazy until something goes wrong.

The urge to check everyone's position was hard to resist; old ops room habits died hard. She needed to keep that three-dimensional plot in her head, visualizing every asset and man, every position and movement. It wasn't that she didn't trust *Falconer*'s radar. She simply felt lost without information streaming into her ear. Her perception of the war had almost always been a stream of sound converted in her mind's eye to an image of the battlefield, rarely the real thing encountered this closely.

Vessels one, two, and three there, Falconer *here . . . and where's the submarine?*

Clement had broken contact now, so she could only imagine the submarine drifting below in a watery twilight. But it was in her head, plotted and visualized, even if her location turned out

to be wildly wrong. She was beginning to realize that the navy
wasn't just limping along with obsolete and failing equipment—
its crews were below the safety minimum, and they hadn't had
much serious practice for fifteen years, if ever. The most competent COG asset was still the average Gear.

*But the armaments work. And the ships float. That's all that
matters. Right?*

She pulled her concentration back to the boat when Andresen
and Michaelson moved along the deck. Marcus looked over his
shoulder at her, a fraction away from actually smiling.

"You look happier," he said. "Suits you."

These were the conversations that hurt. They were just the
throwaway things that other lovers said without thinking, but they
were so rare between her and Marcus that she had to treat them
like fragile peace negotiations. One wrong word, and the shutters
would come down again.

*Seventeen years. And we're still at the stage where I never know
if the relationship's on or not. And when it is, I'm wondering when
he'll stay the whole night. I must be insane.*

She tried to look casual. "As our gallant captain would say,
nothing like the prospect of firing a broadside to put roses in a
girl's cheeks."

Marcus never reached the smile. What little he'd managed
faded slowly. "Yeah. He'd say that."

Anya balanced on the knife-edge of a response but found she
wasn't ready to risk it. She'd settle for the broadside. Firefights
seemed less fraught with danger. She was almost relieved when
Muller's voice diverted her.

"Range three kilometers. We should have a visual on them
soon."

"And they're well within firing range, once I see them," Marcus muttered.

"Corporal Baird," Michaelson said. "Bring Massy to the wheelhouse, please."

Dom and Cole edged along the waist of the boat toward her.
"Are we actually going through the motions of transferring

Massy?" Dom asked. He was wearing minimum armor, clutching a life jacket in one hand. "I'll take the Marlin. I can do that."

"Plan is to just to parade him on the foredeck while we confirm we have targets that Michaelson wants, and then . . ."

Then what? It was the unanswered question. It was also still unasked. Exactly what would happen to him? This was too far into the murky territory of COG Intelligence, as she remembered it, and she wasn't sure if she was cut out to be part of that. Either way, Massy didn't know the plan. Baird was still guarding him in one of the stores compartments. Bernie was on deck, wandering around as if she didn't trust the sea if she couldn't keep an eye on it.

"Confirmed, modified gunboats," Muller said. "I can see the lead vessel now—twenty-five meters, thirty tops, machine gun mounted. Nobody visible. The other two are twenty meters or thereabouts, and I can't see any armament. Shall I call them up, sir?"

Michaelson came out. "Anya, you might want to get in the wheelhouse now."

She took it as an order to keep her head down. The wheelhouse felt rather un-nautical, more like the cab of a grindlift rig, with instruments arranged like an oversized dashboard. Baird had brought Massy up to the wheelhouse, and now the man was sitting on the bench seat behind the helm position with Baird, trying to look out at the boats. Then he saw Anya and stared at her. She stared back. Muller's voice—repeating *Falconer's* call sign and waiting for a response from the pirate vessels—faded into the background.

Anya had never been this close to a rapist and a murderer, as far as she knew. She found herself searching his face for something that would show her how very different he was from the people she knew and trusted, but there was nothing. He was just another man—aggressive, arrogant, and repellent, but that described a lot of men who didn't do the kinds of things that he did.

"No response, sir," Muller said. Anya could see the hulls now, just sitting in the water less than two hundred meters away. *Falconer* slowed.

"Lookout, is anything moving?"

"Can't see any life, sir."

For a moment, Anya's gut tightened and she wondered if the ambush was about to be turned back on the navy. Michaelson looked around, unfazed.

"Mr. Massy," he said, "any idea what your colleagues might be playing at? Busy taking tea below, perhaps?"

"No idea, asshole." Massy didn't seem worried. "But you're safe as long as I'm aboard."

"How comforting." Michaelson flicked switches on the comms panel and picked up a mike. "This is warship *Falconer*, warship *Falconer* to Lesser Islands FTA vessels, are you receiving?"

There was no response. The crewman on lookout gestured over the side, and his voice crackled on the radio. "Sir, there's drifting debris. Wood . . . fuel slick . . . paper, metal drums. Not sure if it's a vessel that's broken up, or just old garbage doing the world tour."

Michaelson definitely wasn't acting now. "Collision?"

"Possibly."

Massy went to stand up but Baird shoved him back in his seat.

"You assholes expect me to believe all this shit?" he snarled. "Let me look. Let me see what's out there."

"Good idea," Michaelson said. "Muller, take us in closer. Corporal Baird, walk Massy out on the foredeck. Perhaps they'll feel better if they eyeball him."

Anya watched the foredeck as Baird frog-marched Massy onto the deck. Bernie stood off to the port side with Dom, checking her ammo clips and giving Massy an occasional glance. But there was no sign of life on the boats, no movement—nothing at all.

Massy seemed to be getting rattled, though. He stood on the deck with his back to the wheelhouse, head turning right and left as if he was searching for something. However pirates did business, this didn't appear to be going the way he expected.

"Hey, Cormick!" he yelled, as if he could be heard at that distance. "Cormick? Man, what the hell are you playing at? It's me! Get me off this frigging ship, will you?"

"Baird, ask him if he recognizes the vessels," Michaelson asked.

There was a pause while Massy checked. After some discussion, Baird came back on the radio. "He got technical on me. He says he knows the two smaller boats but not the bigger one."

"Maybe it's a new acquisition." Massy couldn't hear Michaelson anyway, but the captain dropped his voice when responding on the radio. "Okay, let's assume the worst here. *Falconer* to *Clement*, where are you?"

The submarine commander came back on the comms net, and Anya started to understand why the submarine was so unnerving, whatever its limitations. She had no idea where it was at any given moment. It was like having grubs tunneling beneath her. It was another monster lurking under the bed.

"*Clement* to *Falconer*—we just pinged something, and we thought it was a cetacean, but the acoustics weren't right." Garcia paused. "Is Sergeant Fenix there? Ask him about the Locust leviathans."

Marcus cut in. "No idea what they sound like underwater, Commander."

Anya took another look at the vessels through her binoculars. The machine guns on the main boat were still secured. "If they're planning to open fire, they're going to have to step outside to do that."

Michaelson nodded. "And we didn't intend to board, so we've lost the advantage of stealth. Massy's our insurance—if they want him alive, that is."

"You think they don't?"

"Perhaps he's expendable and they've got other plans," he said. "They wouldn't abandon vessels like these for no good reason. Too valuable. And we need to know what that reason is, for our own security if nothing else."

Anya kept an eye on the largest boat's wheelhouse. As the distance between the vessels gradually closed, the lookout's voice came over the radio again.

"Small arms damage to the main boat, sir—inboard. Just above the wheelhouse door."

Michaelson raised his binoculars to check. "Might not be recent, but given the debris, let's assume it is."

Anya tried to focus on the damage, but something else caught her eye as she adjusted her binoculars. There was suddenly movement on the lead boat. She saw a man come to the wheel, waving slowly and deliberately.

"I see him," Michaelson said. "Stand by, all guns."

The radio crackled again. "*Falconer*, nice of you to join us. You've got something we've been looking for."

"This is Captain Michaelson. Am I speaking to Cormick Allam?"

"No . . . Mr. Allam can't come to the bridge. This is Darrel Jacques, and let's just say we've carried out a company takeover. We'd really like to have Massy, please."

Anya interpreted that as a mutiny. Michaelson gestured to Muller, then picked up his radio mike again.

"Baird, see if the name Darrel Jacques rings a bell with Massy, will you?"

Anya watched Baird dip his head slightly as he spoke to Massy, and suddenly it was clear that Massy knew the name, and not in a good way. Baird still had hold of his arm, but Massy pulled back as if to make a run for it—just reflex, because there was nowhere to run. Anya heard a few words of the argument as Baird jerked him back. Bernie watched, no expression visible at all.

"You can't do that, man, he's gonna frigging kill me." Massy didn't look as if he was putting on an act. "No! Fuck you, you can't *do* that to me!"

Baird got on the radio. "In case you missed that," he said, "Jacques is from a rival gang. He's got plans for Massy for stiffing his guys over something. It sounds painful."

Michaelson scratched the side of his nose. "How convoluted. Well, I came here to remove the threat of piracy, so I don't care which camp they're in. And we can only use Massy for this sting once, so let's hand him over and see what else we can get out of this."

So that was why Massy didn't recognize the main boat: it wasn't one of his. It was a hijack. That explained the damage to the wheelhouse. The whole mission was starting to veer off course, but Michaelson didn't turn a hair. Anya had him pegged as a gambler.

"Either they tailed Massy's people, sir, or they intercepted the messages about coordinates," Anya said.

"Good point." Michaelson flicked the mike's switch again. "Mr. Jacques, you'll excuse my directness, but what's in it for us?"

"Maybe we can do a deal."

"Explain."

"We'll deal with the likes of Massy's people in exchange for being allowed to carry on our normal business—taking care of the islands. We're not pirates. The worst you can call us is vigilantes, and I'm not sure that's such a bad thing anyway."

"Will I notice the difference?"

"We see our job as getting supplies where they're needed, making a fair living from it, and looking after our communities. We're in the same profession, right?"

Michaelson paused for a moment and seemed to be thinking it over. Anya had no idea what he was going to do next. Perhaps he didn't, either.

"Let's both show some goodwill and step out onto our respective decks," he said. "You'll understand why I'm reluctant to send my crew across to you on trust."

"Same here," said Jacques. "Let's do that."

Michaelson broke the link with Jacques and switched to the crew frequency.

"All hands, I think we can modify Plan A," he said. "As soon as Massy is handed over and the boats are clear, let them go, unless things start to come unraveled. *Clement*—this is our chance to track them back to their home port. I think your deterrent value is best kept for when we have an audience to appreciate it."

"*Clement* to *Falconer*, understood." Garcia sounded disappointed. "And we're still picking up odd acoustics. Is Fenix sure about that leviathan?"

"No, I'm not," Marcus said. "But if I see it, I'll be sure to let you know."

"Don't waste a torpedo chasing phantoms, Garcia," Michaelson said, and stepped out onto the deck.

Massy wouldn't shut up. He was still spitting abuse and demanding his rights when Baird slammed him down on the deck to stop him struggling.

"You can't do this to me, asshole. You'll regret it. I got rights. And *friends*."

"Do you come with an off switch?" Baird said. "Tell me where it is, or I'll have to make one the hard way."

Dom looked down at him. "If he wants to swim for it, let him."

"Maybe Jacques is his best buddy and this is some dumb-ass act." Baird had his knee on Massy's back. "Hey, how close are we going to get to that boat? You think Michaelson knows what he's doing?"

Dom didn't think Massy was acting at all. He was crapping himself. He didn't seem too scared of the COG, but he obviously knew what his own kind did to settle disputes. If that was worse than anything Bernie had in mind, then Dom wasn't sure he wanted to know the details.

"He's run counterpiracy operations before," Dom said. "And we've got three guns trained on them. We're as safe as they are."

Michaelson strode out onto the deck. The pirate gunboat started up its motor and chugged slowly forward, edging clear of the mist that was now starting to lift as the sun rose higher. A short, thick-set guy with close-cropped white hair came out of the wheelhouse and took up position at the bow. So far, so good; nobody had opened fire. Dom grabbed a pair of field glasses from the nearest crewman and checked out the gunboat for himself.

There were at least three men in the wheelhouse, and half a dozen more came out to stand and look conspicuous. Dom checked out the two smaller boats as best he could, but they were still dead in the water, with nobody visible. There was now less than a hundred meters separating the lead gunboat from *Falconer*. It slowed and stopped twenty meters away.

"So you're based on Vectes, yeah?" Jacques called.

"News travels," Michaelson said.

"We pick up stuff here and there. Now, we owe Jonnie Boy some justice that's long overdue, so how about you bring him over?"

"How about telling me how you plan to keep his colleagues in line?"

"Well, here's a token of our intent." Jacques turned around and gestured to one of his men. "Bring him out."

Dom glanced at Bernie to see how she was taking all this. She had her Lancer resting on its sling, cradled in both arms, with an expression on her face that gave no clue to the personal stake she had in this. He wondered how long it had taken her to come to terms with it. Maybe she hadn't and was just good at acting normal. Her occasional lapses told him it was the latter.

Life goes on. It has to.

Two of Jacques's men hauled a battered figure up to the gunboat's bows. He slumped between them. Dom could see they'd made a mess of him. It was hard to tell if he'd been shot as well. He was still alive, though.

"Captain," Jacques said, "let me introduce Cormick Allam."

Massy squirmed. Baird hauled him to his feet.

"Take a look," Baird said. "Is that your boss?"

Massy blinked a few times, then his face contorted. "Shit, Cormick! *Cormick!* What did they do to you, man?"

Allam raised his head a little, probably as far as he could.

Jacques did a big theatrical shrug. "Like I said, Captain, we'll deal with these shits." Then he pulled a handgun from his belt, turned to Allam, and put a round through his head. The crack sounded extra-loud in the quiet, damp air. "Job done."

The two men threw the body overboard.

Dom flinched. But for the first time in weeks, it didn't bring back memories that he couldn't fend off. He simply noted that it wasn't a straight link to Maria. It was just a bad bastard shooting another one of his kind. It was always shocking to see execution in cold blood, but it wasn't the first time, and Dom was pretty sure it wouldn't be the last.

Massy didn't even manage to swear. He just took in a long ragged breath as if he was going to scream, but nothing emerged. He'd be lucky to get the same quick end that Allam had.

"Fifteen down," Jacques said. "A few hundred to go. Leave it to us."

Michaelson looked unmoved. "And what else would we be leaving to you? Or would we just be allowing one gang to oust another?"

"Like I said, we're not scum." Jacques put his handgun back in his belt. "We take a cut to survive, and we make sure nobody profiteers or hogs supplies. We don't want to touch COG vessels."

"How about the fishing fleet? We lost a trawler."

"Definitely not us. But don't underestimate the number of criminals with boats."

Dom didn't see how Michaelson could strike any deal with Stranded without Prescott's say-so, but *Falconer* was a long way from Vectes, and he needed to get something going right now.

"How about an interim agreement?" Michaelson said. "I give you Massy, you prove you're not going to give me problems, and I'll stay away from you unless I hear you get into bad ways."

Jacques considered it, head cocked on one side. Dom didn't believe for one moment that either man meant it, but he'd seen stranger alliances in the war.

"Done," Jacques said. "Although I'd be interested to know how you plan to monitor that."

"Oh, I'll hear," Michaelson said. He turned to Dom. "You wanted to do the cross-decking, you said."

"Yes, sir." Dom wasn't sure if any of the sailors was up to doing a risky job like that. He was still waiting for something to go badly wrong. "And what are we going to do about the two smaller boats? I could bring one back with us."

"Good question. I was hoping to liberate at least one." He turned back to Jacques. "As a gesture of goodwill, we'd like to keep one of the boats."

Jacques thought it over for a few moments and nodded. "They've got a lot of holes now. But feel free."

Baird shoved Massy ahead of him toward *Falconer*'s stern and Bernie went to follow. Dom put his hand out to stop her.

"We can do this, Bernie. You make sure Cole doesn't puke so hard he falls overboard."

She gave him that look, as if he hadn't done his homework and she expected better of him.

"Okay," she said. "They probably wouldn't let me stay and watch them beat the shit out of him anyway."

"It's their justice," Dom said. "He gets what's coming to him, and you get to keep a clean conscience. I think that's a good result all round."

"I wouldn't have lost any sleep over that." Bernie took a few steps back. "But Marcus has a point about hanging on to the few rules we still have."

Andresen was manning Marcus's gun when Dom squeezed past him. He jerked his thumb aft to indicate Marcus was already heading for the Marlin to lower it over the stern.

"He doesn't delegate well," Andresen said. "He still expects an ambush."

"So do I," said Dom. "Life's like that."

Baird had a hell of a job getting Massy over the side and into the inflatable. Dom had a moment's hesitation: should the COG have been doing this? But if it didn't, what else was it going to do with Massy—execute him under COG law, or let him go? Someone had to do something.

"You know what they're going to do with me?" Massy demanded. He landed on the Marlin's seat with a thud, rocking the whole boat. "You know what those assholes do? You know how long they take to kill you? What they do to you?"

"Shut up," Baird said. "Mataki would have taken longer."

"You can't do this. You're supposed to be the decent guys. Civilization. Remember?"

Marcus stood aside to let Dom take the helm. He kept looking down at the water as if he was expecting something to emerge. All that talk of the leviathan had made Dom edgy, too, and he kept trying to tell himself that the thing they'd seen had to be a fresh-water creature, and this was saline, so it couldn't have come this far . . . could it?

But there were unpleasant and dangerous things much closer to home to worry about.

"Can't help noticing you never denied you did it, Massy," Marcus said at last.

Massy didn't say anything else. Dom took the Marlin wide of the garbage drifting on the slow current. The scattered books, cans, and clothing made it look like a houseboat had been blown up. As they closed on the lead vessel, the flotsam became a thin mat of assorted debris. Dom assumed he was now in someone's sights. Someone was usually in his, after all. When he glanced over the side at the debris, his stomach lurched. A body was floating facedown in the water, life jacket in place, but minus most of its head.

"Anyone you know, Massy?"

Massy swiveled on the seat. It took him a few seconds to react. "No. *Shit*."

"Who is it?"

Massy just shook his head. "How can I tell? He hasn't got a frigging *head*."

Dom brought the Marlin up against the stern and tied a quick-release line. The name on the transom was TRADER V; the boat looked like it might have been a sport boat in a previous life before it was cannoned up. Marcus waited, one hand on the stern ladder, the other on his rifle.

"Up you go," Baird said to Massy, shoving him ahead. "Just in case this isn't as cozy as it looks."

Massy caught the rungs while Marcus held the boat alongside. Three faces appeared over the stern; Dom was ready for a double-cross, and knew only too well how vulnerable a Marlin was to gunfire. But pirates or not, they just hauled Massy aboard and made no attempt to do anything else.

Dom didn't even have to set foot on *Trader*. The last thing he saw of Massy was him struggling as he went over the stern rail. "You'll regret this, you assholes," he yelled.

Dom wasn't sure which assholes Massy was referring to, but there wasn't much he could do about revenge now.

"You think Michaelson knows what he's doing?" Dom asked.

Marcus shrugged. "Garcia can't have had much warfare experience. Long time since the navy deployed a submarine in anger. But Michaelson's been doing this for years."

"Hey, do I get to drive the boat?" Baird said. "Captain Charisma wants that one, right?"

Dom listened in on the radio as Michaelson talked with Garcia.

"Just shadow them," Michaelson was saying. "I want to know where they operate from. No point wasting a lead. I want the nerve center, not the odd vessel."

Baird was listening in. "Is Michaelson too much of a gentleman to actually blow the shit out of them when he's done a deal?"

Dom wondered if Jacques had a point about being vigilantes. It wasn't as if the COG could do anything to reclaim or even protect the islands scattered across Sera, and the COG's enforcement could be pretty brutal too. It all came down to legalities.

When Garcia responded, he seemed a lot less concerned about the definition of pirates than the underwater sound that he still couldn't identify.

"There's something down here, sir," Garcia said. "I'm not going to use active sonar and advertise our position until I work out what it is."

It bothered Dom, too. But he forgot about it when he came alongside one of the drifting boats and helped Baird board it. It was badly shot up, and there'd obviously been a firefight before Massy's chums had been overwhelmed. There were still bodies on board.

"Shit," Baird said. "Doesn't any asshole clean up after himself these days?"

He manhandled the bodies overboard. As they hit the water, Dom wondered for a moment if the guys had families who'd now never know what happened to them, but that was their occupational hazard, and there wasn't much he could do about it.

Marcus didn't say a word. He just kept looking over the side until Baird got the boat started, and both vessels headed back toward *Falconer*.

CNV FALCONER.

Jacques hadn't been joking about Massy. He really was making him pay for something.

Sound carried. And Bernie felt she had to stay and listen. She'd chosen to remain on deck, because if she went below to get away from the sounds of Massy screaming his head off, then she had to ask herself if she'd been wrong to take her vengeance on his two buddies.

If I'd caught him when I did the others, I'd be doing the same as Jacques. Can't turn squeamish now.

She didn't know what they were actually doing to Massy, or what he'd done to get their attention, but she could only imagine his fate within the limits of her own ingenuity. Michaelson was waiting for *Trader* to finish putting a tow line on the other salvaged boat and head back to base. Bernie wasn't sure what he was trying to achieve, other than making sure Jacques left the area and *Clement* followed her home.

It was only postponing the problem. You couldn't do deals with these people. But Michaelson probably hadn't. He didn't seem to see any agreement with Stranded as binding.

Cole wandered up to her and leaned on the rail. His skin tone looked distinctly gray. She didn't think the boat was moving around that much, just gently rolling on the swell as the wind picked up. The mist was gone. It had the makings of a nice day.

"I'm all puked out, Boomer Lady," he said. "I ain't gonna be much use in this new seagoin' world that Michaelson keeps talkin' about."

"I don't think we're going to run out of things to do ashore, somehow." Bernie patted his back and took a firm grip on his belt. She hadn't a hope in hell of stopping a man of his size from falling if he tipped over the rail, but she did it anyway. "We used to have drugs for seasickness. Maybe we can find some."

"You got a cast-iron gut."

She tilted her head in the direction of *Trader*. "Massy, you mean."

"That as well."

"I'm not gloating. I'm just making sure I've still got the courage of my convictions."

"And then you leave it all behind you, right? Promise me."

"Yeah. I think I purged my anger a long time ago. But some things get to be habit."

Cole frowned and shook his head every time Massy shrieked. The sounds were muffled; the man was begging now. So his gang didn't own the sea around here after all. She wondered if they were doing this in *Falconer*'s earshot to make the point that Jacques now ran the show and wasn't afraid to go to extremes to enforce it.

"You gonna come inside, Bernie?"

She wanted to, but she couldn't. "In a while. You go and get some fluids down you. You'll be dehydrated."

She went back to leaning on the rail, and Massy fell silent for a while. A couple of men from *Trader* boarded the second patrol boat they'd captured from Allam's gang. After a few minutes, *Trader* got under way and headed west at a leisurely pace, trailing a wide wake of churning white foam. The patrol boat followed a hundred meters behind. And somewhere below, *Clement* was tracking them.

If Massy was still screaming for mercy, she wouldn't hear him now. It was over. The sense of finality surprised her. Beneath her boots, the deck shivered as *Falconer*'s engines picked up speed and the patrol boat turned back to Vectes. The other gunboat bobbed in the wash as *Falconer* swung around.

Bernie walked down to the stern to watch *Trader* vanish and found Baird eyeing the salvaged gunboat with a frown, binoculars hanging from his neck.

"They wouldn't let me drive it home," he said.

"Let 'em do their sailor thing, Blondie."

He pressed his earpiece. "Garcia's not happy about something."

"Really?" Bernie listened in to the voice traffic. "You reckon there's a leviathan loose? Whatever that is."

"Dunno." He pointed. "Look. *Clement*'s got her radio mast up. Just breaking the surface."

Bernie strained to look, but the entire ocean was spotted with foam and reflections. It was impossible to see whatever Baird was looking at. On the radio, Garcia was debating whether to ping the area with sonar and risk being detected.

"Can't he tell what he's hearing?" she asked Baird.

"The sea's a noisy place. Picking out the sounds takes a skilled operator or really fancy computer analysis, and I don't think he's got either."

"Fat lot of good he is, then."

"It's not like he's up against a fleet of subs. But if we had a Raven here, some have sonar buoys."

"*Clement*'s got sonar."

"Yeah, but it's about stealth. If he pings, he's given away his presence and exact position. The Raven's just dunking a buoy."

They both stopped to listen to Michaelson's voice.

"*Clement*, whatever the object is, is it going to compromise us?"

"If it's a biologic, leviathan or not, it's a collision risk, but—oh *shit*."

"Say again, *Clement*."

"Torpedo—*brace brace brace*."

Bernie froze. She didn't look at Baird. A few seconds later, an explosion launched a plume of water into the air nearly a kilometer away. Was that *Clement*? She had no idea where the submarine was.

"Shit, she's been hit." Baird fumbled for the binoculars. "What the fuck did that? If it's a leviathan packing torpedoes, then we're in deep shit."

Bernie's gut knotted. "Grubs don't have that stuff. What can you see? Come on, is there debris?"

"Wait—no, *Trader*'s gone. That was *Trader*."

Michaelson's voice cut in. "*Clement,* what the hell have you done? I said *follow* her, not *sink* her."

"That was *not* us. I say again, we did *not* fire, that was not *Clement.*" No, Garcia was still there; that was his voice on the radio, remarkably calm under the circumstances. "We heard the torpedo launch. *Not ours.* Time to worry."

"Have you got a fix on it?"

"Nothing's pinged us. We have an approximate bearing from the torpedo."

By now, sailors and Gears had rushed out onto the deck to look. Bernie and Baird hung onto their front-row seats. If Garcia hadn't accidentally fired a torpedo—and how the hell could someone do that, anyway?—then Bernie couldn't imagine what else was out there, unless some Stranded had a submarine, and that was impossible. She'd have heard. It was just too big a deal for them to hide. They'd have used it before. Wouldn't they?

Even Cole and Anya came out to watch. Marcus seemed to be checking where the life rafts were, which worried Bernie more than anything. She shut her eyes to concentrate on the radio, and the next thing she heard was the crew on the small gunboat. They were in one piece.

"You *bastards.* You gave your word."

"We have *not* fired on you," Michaelson said. "We have no idea what's happened, but it wasn't us. We keep our word, I assure you."

Almost. Weren't you going to follow them home to fry them later?

"Deal's null and void, Coalition," said the voice. "We can't do business with you. Gloves off now."

The small boat shot off at high speed. Bernie waited for it to vanish in an eruption of water too, but whatever had sunk *Trader* didn't follow up. Maybe it had his hands full now evading *Clement.*

"We're picking up faint propulsion sounds," Garcia said. "It's not biologic."

"Locust bolt all kinds of devices onto living creatures."

There was a pause. "Including ballast tanks?"

"What?" said Michaelson.

"Hydrophones just picked up something blowing its tanks. It's another sub. Stand by."

"You're clear to engage."

"We need to know what we're firing at first, Captain."

Bernie didn't have a clue what submarines were capable of doing, or even if they could tell where a sound was coming from. Baird muttered something about needing hull sonar for *Falconer*. It was the first time Bernie had felt that this patrol boat, which seemed as solid as a fort to her, could be blown out of the water at any moment, and the only warning she'd get would be a streak of bubbles in the water seconds before a bloody torpedo ripped the hull apart. The guns mounted on deck were no use against that.

She added it to the list of reasons why she didn't like the sea.

Michaelson, shouldn't you be heading away from here at maximum speed or something?

It felt like a long time before anyone spoke again, but it was less than a minute.

"Something's surfacing," Garcia said. "We've got a fix on it. About thirty degrees off your port quarter, range eight hundred meters. Standing by to fire torpedoes."

Baird was glued to his binoculars. "I see it. Look for the foam."

Dom squeezed into the gap next to Bernie. "If it fires on us," he said, "we're really going to regret standing around watching."

"At least we don't get trapped below," she said. "Have we got enough life rafts and RIBs for the whole crew?"

And then a completely unknown voice broke into the comms net. It had a slight accent.

"*Clement,* this is *Zephyr,*" said the voice. "We're surfacing. We're not hostile. Stand down."

Bernie saw a sudden pool of foam, and followed it until a dull black sail rose out of the sea. It sprouted masts almost immediately, and when the submarine settled on the surface, she didn't look like *Clement*. Her bows were smooth. She looked smaller, like a stubby cigar.

"Holy shit," Dom said. "They're breeding."

As they watched, another sail broke the surface in a cascade of foam, then a distinctive black sonar dome appeared. It was *Clement*. By the time the submarine was fully surfaced, Bernie could see crew already at the top of the fin, scanning the scene just like *Falconer's* crew.

"*Zephyr*," Michaelson said, "who are you, and why did you sink that damned ship?"

"Commander Miran Trescu, Republic of Gorasnaya, Union of Independent Republics," said the unknown voice. "It's been a long time. May we talk, *Falconer*?"

Michaelson usually had a smart line for every occasion, but even he took awhile to respond to that bombshell.

The UIR hadn't existed since before E-Day. The COG had been at war with it for nearly eighty years before those short, *short* weeks of peace. *Gorasnaya*. Shit, they were one of the tiny lunatic republics that refused to accept the cease-fire. Nobody took account of them. They had very little left to fight with.

Unbelievable didn't quite cover it, though. They still had a submarine, and they still thought they existed.

"No hard feelings," Michaelson said at last. "But I suggest you explain what you're doing before this becomes a very short conversation."

"You might want to let pirates go free," Trescu said, "but we take a harder line, and we've been tracking Jacques for days."

"We?"

"We may be a small presence compared to you, but we're still worth plundering. As I said, may we talk? I have as many questions for you and your Chairman as you have for me."

Marcus finally reacted. "It's a frigging *Indie*. Fifteen years after the armistice, and he shows up *now*?"

Bernie saw a crewman come out to the starboard bridge wing to take a photograph. Dom stared. "This is a joke, right?"

"Baby, I'm gonna take my seasick pills and lie down somewhere dark till this morning goes *away*," Cole said.

Falconer's deck had fallen silent—mostly. The only sound

Bernie could hear now was Baird, and he was chuckling to himself.

"I'm glad you find it so fucking funny," Marcus said. "Because we just made a new bunch of enemies."

"Shit, we were going to finish off Jacques and his gang anyway." Baird handed the binoculars to Marcus. "At least we got another submarine and a gunboat out of the trip."

"You think Trescu is going to hand it over?"

"Why else would he surface and not just run?"

Bernie had once found Baird an irritating know-it-all, but now she understood that he really did have a good brain in that head, capable of shrewd assessment. Trescu wanted something beyond settling scores with pirates.

And Bernie was keen to find out where the rump of the UIR had been hiding.

Falconer headed back to Vectes, trailed by the small gunboat, and *Clement* kept a close tail on *Zephyr*. It was a strange flotilla by anyone's standards. Bernie spent an hour or two hunched over the chart table, trying to work out where Trescu might have come from, and then a thought struck her—a surprising one simply because it had taken so long to dawn on her.

Jonn Massy had been given his quick release. And she felt neither guilty nor cheated. Now she could move on.

CHAPTER 18

Until we can get radar ground stations in place, we'll rely on ships. Reassure the people in Pelruan that we can maintain a radar picket that should give us almost complete coverage of the coastline to a range of sixty kilometers. Tell them not to worry—the navy's here.

(CAPTAIN QUENTIN MICHAELSON TO LEWIS GAVRIEL.)

"Where do you want me to start?" Hoffman asked. "It's a long goddamn list today."

From the window of Prescott's office, he could see the Indie submarine, real and black and troubling. The appearance of a boat from history was something of a sensation. A growing crowd of seamen and Gears had shown up to stare at it.

"Let's start with Michaelson's private war," Prescott said. "We give him free rein to maintain maritime security. I don't mind how many pirates he sinks. But I'd like more intelligence on who's out there—the island communities we don't know about. We didn't destroy Jacinto to resume another war. We did it to save what little was left of humankind. We need people—*numbers*."

"He says that was the idea. *Clement* didn't attack Darrel Jacques."

"Perception is everything. In due course, we might have some damage limitation to do."

For a man who'd taken the decision to incinerate most of Sera, Prescott could have weirdly prissy moments. Hoffman gritted his teeth. The Chairman seemed to have forgotten that the last city-sized remnant of humanity was clinging to life here, however idyllic the country seemed. Most of it was still living on board ships or in crowded dockyard accommodations. Hoffman decided he couldn't get too worked up about a few gangs until the more pressing problems had been solved.

It wasn't a grub leviathan. That was all that mattered. A few time-forgotten Indies—he could handle them just fine.

"So is the Indie submarine a surprise to us all, or just me?" Hoffman didn't expect to get an answer, but he asked again anyway, battening down his natural urge to bang Prescott's head on that damn desk. "If there's any more classified material around, it would be a good idea to declassify it now, because we don't know what's relevant and what isn't."

Prescott did a slow head shake, apparently racking his memory. "I can't think of anything."

Hoffman decided he no longer had an obligation to be straight with Prescott. It wasn't sulky retaliation, just the last exhausted stage of trying to maintain a one-sided relationship. There was no point asking about the freakish life-forms—the sires—and other bizarre discoveries that Delta had made back on the mainland. He bet that he wasn't alone in his frustration, either, because Marcus Fenix was almost certainly feeling the same way about his father's connection with the Locust. That was in the past now.

If I sat down with Marcus over a beer, would he discuss it with me?

Hoffman realized he was thinking of him as *Marcus* again, not *Fenix*. It was a barometer of the state of their relationship.

"So we're moving from a land forces doctrine to a maritime one," Prescott said. "How do you feel about that?"

I know you're going to enjoy playing me off against Michaelson, and you won't even realize you're doing it, you bastard. So give him my job, if you like. He's a good man. And I'm frigging tired.

"Feelings don't matter, Chairman." Hoffman was still watching *Zephyr,* moored alongside *Clement,* and marveled at the endurance of damned pointless ideas. What kind of fool would bust a gut maintaining a submarine for all those years, wasting precious resources and sweat on something that was useless without a fleet to work with it? *Maybe a fool who just hoped that one day he'd find that fleet.* "We're recolonizing our own land. We'll need to secure fuel and mineral supplies back on the mainland, and then we'll need to reclaim it, grubs or no grubs. It's a maritime operation."

"You don't feel threatened by it, then."

"No, just conscious that Gears will have to adjust to being seagoing soldiers."

"Perhaps *threatened* wasn't an appropriate word," Prescott said. "I meant that change is unsettling for us all."

"I'm all for a change that lets my Gears sleep and get their sanity back."

"You're more diplomatic than Dr. Hayman." Prescott looked Hoffman up and down as if he was checking for leaks. "She says traumatic stress is endemic, and we're such a small population that it's already become a *culture of abnormal psychology.* Sometimes she says we're all *frigging lunatics* instead, of course. Now that we'll have to mix with relatively . . . *normal* people, we have to take account of that."

We're all fucked up. You don't need a medical degree to work that out.

"I know Pelruan folk think we're all dangerous psychos," said Hoffman, "but I *like* us that way. It's what we are. And it's not exactly abnormal to be strung out when you've had grubs chewing your collective ass for fifteen years. It'd be abnormal to be *relaxed.*"

"Yes, but it concerns me to hear evacuees and Gears looking down on the local population as having had it easy here."

"Well, they *have.*"

"Even so, we have to build bridges. We need them, Victor. As support, as *people.* We need *cohesion.*"

"One happy family."

"We can't afford to rebuild Sera from a divided society. Schisms only get bigger. We'll learn from history."

Of course we will. The new political will. My ass.

And now the Indies were back, in small bite-sized pieces, so Prescott could test his will right away. Gorasnaya was only a tiny fractious corner of the old alliance, a bunch of guerillas rather than a major player like Pelles, but it had the potential to be trouble. In a world that had shrunk to a small city, people like that punched above their weight. Hoffman wanted to see their credit rating before he'd accept them on the lifeboat.

Prescott checked his watch again. "Commander Trescu's late."

"He's a whole *war* late, Chairman."

Hoffman resisted attempts to fill the small-talk gap. There was nothing to do but wait for Michaelson and Trescu. Prescott had set up his offices in a former sail loft in the oldest part of the base, a relic from a navy that predated the COG by centuries. The room was light and airy, at odds with the utilitarian furniture, chart boards, and filing cabinets that had been taken out of storage. If Hoffman wanted to leave anything in the past he'd get little chance today. Not even the UIR would let him forget it.

Prescott got up and shunted papers and maps around a meeting table that looked like a canteen trestle. It probably was. "And Sergeant Mataki's issue is resolved, I take it."

"I haven't had a chance to speak to her yet, but I believe so."

"Don't you think it's time she retired? I'm very uncomfortable about a woman of that age doing such a physically grueling job."

"Islanders are hardy people, Chairman, and I can't afford to lose specialist skills like hers." *No, this is my turf, Prescott. You stay away from my Gears, and most of all you stay away from her.* "And it's not a job. It's a way of life, a tribe. Nobody wants to rob her of that comfort after all she's been through."

"Just trying to be a gentleman," Prescott said.

For God's sake, hurry up, Quentin.

It took ten long, silent minutes for Michaelson to arrive. Trescu was about forty, with a close-trimmed beard and buzz-cut hair.

Michaelson took Hoffman to one side while Prescott showed Trescu the naval base panorama from the loft.

"Don't mention the war," Michaelson whispered, winking. "He's got some rather useful assets."

"So you've gone through his pockets and stolen his wallet already."

"Wait and see."

If Trescu recalled Hoffman's name, then he showed no sign of it. Most Gears over thirty-five were Pendulum Wars veterans anyway, so there was nothing remarkable about any COG officer that Trescu might meet. They'd all been enemies, and neither side had much to boast about.

But Hoffman had to remind himself that it was Anvil Gate that Trescu might link to his name, not the fact that he was one of the commanders responsible for the Hammer of Dawn assault. Nobody outside the COG military knew or cared about Hoffman and Salaman, anyway. It had always been Prescott's baby in public. Trescu seemed to be managing not to punch Prescott in the face, so perhaps it was an issue that time and a lot more deaths had closed for the time being.

If Trescu did finally swing for the Chairman, at least Prescott had a great comeback. He'd incinerated a large area of Tyrus, too.

"So you finally used the Hammer of Dawn against Jacinto," Trescu said, glancing into the cup that Prescott offered him. Now there was a man used to a contaminated water supply. "We got word from the Stranded network that the Locust have been very few and far between lately."

Well, at least the Hammer raised its head early in the conversation. Boil lanced, then.

"So where has *Zephyr* been all these years?" Hoffman asked. "Not that we could keep track of all our own damn ships, of course."

"We've moved her from place to place, Colonel. Gorasnaya's ports were overrun several times, but the grubs couldn't sweep the whole continent every day."

"Are you going to tell us where you're based now?"

"Not on the mainland," Trescu said. "But that's all I'm saying until we work something out."

"What do you want from us?" Prescott asked. "We're always relieved to find more human beings alive, of course, but you made it clear you had an offer for us. And why now?"

Trescu reached for the large-scale map on the table. He ran one fingertip down a meridian and intercepted with his other forefinger along a latitude line. The point was in the sea, around seventy kilometers north of the Lesser Islands chain.

"We still have an offshore imulsion rig near a Gorasnayan protectorate," Trescu said. The UIR had never admitted to having *colonies* or invading poorer countries that had something they wanted. They always *protected* the lesser nations they walked into. All the old arguments came flooding back to Hoffman. "It's still producing. More than our small community can make use of."

No wonder Michaelson had pounced on Trescu like a mugger. He couldn't run a working fleet without a lot of fuel, and even the windfall from Merrenat would run out. Yet again, Hoffman felt the future change on a single throwaway line in a meeting.

"How small?" Prescott asked.

"Four thousand people, maximum." Trescu smiled. "You see my point already."

"Your fuel in exchange for sanctuary here."

"I really do think of it as the strength of pooled assets, Chairman Prescott. You get fuel without having to drill for it on the mainland, plus our modest fleet, troops, and population. We get the protection of being part of a larger community. I'm sorry for ruining your operation with Jacques, but what he sees as vigilantism is what we see as hijacking our fuel supplies and food."

Prescott persisted. "You still haven't answered my question. Why now? You've had years to contact us."

"We wouldn't have been much better off in Jacinto, but out here, things can be very different. When you put to sea . . . a submarine can hear a lot, Chairman Prescott. Especially when targets don't even try to be stealthy. How do you think we knew where you were? Your fleet made a lot of noise shuttling back and forth to the mainland. And we keep good tabs on piracy."

Hoffman avoided meeting Michaelson's eye. He seemed desperate to make this deal work, but Hoffman wanted to be sure it was what it seemed to be. If Trescu wanted in, then he was going to have to answer a lot more questions.

"You have people and assets that you can't move, in places you can't reach easily and defend, is that it?" Prescott said.

"Yes. There's a limit to how long a small group can survive on its own." Trescu took out a pencil and held it over the map. "I'll show you where when I know your intentions."

Prescott sat staring at the map, stroking his upper lip with the knuckle of his forefinger. Hoffman could guess what was coming next. *No enclaves.* It was the bedrock of his policy.

"If you come here," Prescott said, "then you join the Coalition. And then you get full protection and benefits. I have to insist on unity."

Trescu chewed his lip for a moment, eyebrows raised, which looked more like amusement than indecision. His pencil hovered over Gorasnaya on the map. Hoffman wondered how the good folks of Pelruan would take another influx of strangers.

"Ah, my father's no longer alive to call me a traitor," Trescu said. "He wouldn't have understood Sera as it is now, anyway."

Prescott extended his hand for shaking. Trescu took it. One war had ended, at least.

ARMADILLO PA-207, EN ROUTE FOR PELRUAN, TWO DAYS LATER.

"I thought they had two squads permanently billeted at Pelruan already," Cole said. "Sending us in too is a bit overkill for a little town of nice fisherfolk an' that. Not that I don't like the place."

The 'Dill rumbled along with its hatches open, another sign that Cole's world had changed a lot. Back on the mainland, open hatches would have earned a faceful of Hammerburst fire, not a fresh breeze that smelled of trees and green stuff. Baird even seemed to be driving more carefully, not tearing the ass out of the 'Dill's clutch for a change, so maybe the relaxing feel of the place was settling him down, too.

"Prescott's worried about the natives getting restless over the Indies," Marcus said. "They know us. If anyone's a safe bet on the ground today, it's us."

"You mean we're the friendly face of the COG?" Dom laughed. Cole hadn't heard him laugh in weeks, so maybe the guy was on the mend. "Shit, things are worse than we thought."

Cole felt sorry for Lewis Gavriel. The poor guy had done his bit for the COG—done his bit for Pelruan, too—and now he was getting shit from the locals because he was the COG official in town and they didn't like what was happening. That was just *unfair*. Pelruan had to suck it up like everyone else, not that there was anything to suck up other than knowing that a load of strangers had moved in at the far end of the damn island. It wasn't like having the water supply cut or rations being halved. It was just that dumb scared panic that human beings were good at, and that turned to something nasty if it wasn't smacked down and dealt with.

"It would be funny," Dom said, "if the Indies turned into the loyal COG citizens and Pelruan went rogue."

Marcus grunted, scanning the fields around them like he was expecting trouble from the cows. "No, it'd be a pain in the ass."

"I *told* you there'd be some Indies around who still didn't know the war was over," Baird said.

"They know it's over, baby." Cole could see the sea now, which meant they'd be in Pelruan in ten minutes. "They just didn't want the fun to stop."

"Imagine keeping one submarine going."

"They got a tanker, a frigate, and some patrol boats, too, Muller says."

"So when are their people arriving?" Dom asked. "In other words, how long have we got before some civvies start spitting on us for being the bastards who launched the Hammer strike on them?"

"Aren't they all technically Stranded?" Baird asked.

Dom shrugged. "I suppose so."

"You saw active service in the Pendulum Wars. I didn't. Does that make you feel weird about having Indies around?"

"Not half as weird as knowing what the former Indie states looked like after we fried them."

"We fried COG states too," Baird said. "Hey, Marcus, did Gorasnaya take a direct Hammer strike?"

Marcus turned his head and gave Baird the real acid blue stare this time, even though Baird's line of sight was blocked by the 'Dill's periscope. "You think I was given the complete fucking list?"

Sometimes Cole could work out what was really on Marcus's mind. The guy didn't get mad often, but occasionally he got *snappy*, and it was always over stuff that went deep and personal. This was all about his dad. Baird was just asking, Cole knew, but the Hammer was old man Fenix's baby, and that twanged a raw nerve in Marcus. Cole tried to imagine how he'd feel now if he'd found all kinds of shit recorded by his dead dad in the Locust computers, but with no damn explanation. *And in front of his squad.* Shit, Marcus knew everyone was asking the same questions as him, too scared to talk about it because they knew he didn't know either. That had to be driving him crazy.

"Baird, you just want to play with another submarine." Cole went for a diversion. "Admit it. Too many old movies. You're all *up scope* and *crash dive*."

"Just saying that if human beings run out of enemies, they have to invent new ones. Or get the old ones out of the attic."

"Hey, if our Indie sailor boy brings a load of fuel with him, I think folks will settle down real fast."

"Hilarious irony. We all got along when the grubs were around. If we've really wiped out those assholes, we'll need to breed some more so we don't have to kill each other."

"Welcome to Dr. Baird's school of social psychology," Dom said. "But he's right. And I *hate* it when that happens."

Pelruan looked pretty normal when they rolled in. Folks were going about their business, and there was no mumbling discontent going on that Cole could detect. Gears had a sixth sense for trouble brewing. Rossi's squad was rostered to do the day patrol, and there was Rossi himself, standing around talking with a bunch of locals outside the town hall, helmet under one arm. Baird stopped the 'Dill a few meters away. Civvies around here tended to get nervous when APCs rolled right up behind them in narrow streets.

Rossi broke off from the chat and walked over to the 'Dill. "Oh, look—they've sent Hoffman's big boys to check up on us."

"We're just here to make the place look prettier, baby," Cole said.

"Well, we might not be pretty, but at least none of the houses burned down on *our* watch."

Marcus looked around. "Nobody rioting, I see."

"Only because they're confused," Rossi said. "They don't know what to riot about first—the fact that we've moved in, or that we've invited complete strangers to join us for cocktails in our new resort."

"Prescott should have told them in person," Dom said.

"Yeah, that would have made all the difference. What are you here for, anyway?"

"Reassurance," said Marcus.

"Ours or theirs?"

Marcus dismounted. "Baird—park up on the shore where they can see you. Everyone else—it's walkabout time."

Cole was okay with that. He had a choice of being the Cole Train or a Gear for these folks, and if he played up his thrashball star side for them—shit, he was still a *name* in Pelruan—then maybe he'd get through to them a little better than just being a big guy with a rifle. The squad split up and ambled through the streets, working on being nice. When Cole passed the town's main store, a couple of guys in trawlermen's overalls came out, and Cole recognized the older one from the boat that had put in at Vectes when the *Harvest* was lost.

"So is it true?" the man asked. "The Indies are back?"

"Only a few. They sink pirates, though. That's got to be worth something."

"Are we going to be safe to fish now? We've been stuck in harbor for days."

They had a point. "Maybe we need to talk to Captain Michaelson about getting you some protection, and then you can fish again."

"That would help a lot."

Cole decided to tread on the thin ice. "You mind answerin' a question for me?"

"Go ahead, Mr. Cole."

"Do folks think we're bringing nothing but trouble here?"

The older guy looked embarrassed. "Well, some people are saying that you're provoking the pirates. But there's nothing to say they wouldn't have come here anyway, sooner or later. Tell us the truth—should we be afraid?"

"The folks from Gorasnaya won't be a problem, if that's worryin' you." Cole meant it. The COG needed extra help, and a few more boats and extra fuel made a lot of difference. "Hell, they might even look after your trawlers. But they *need* somewhere, sir. They really do. My family had to leave their own country—it ain't fun, I'm tellin' you. And we tend to be real grateful for the chance to earn our keep when we get to somewhere that lets us stay."

Cole could have reminded them that they didn't have a say in this at all, but he still believed most human beings had a decent streak that he could find if he pressed the right button. These fishermen offered to share that butt-ugly eel thing with him; they were basically nice people, just scared shitless. And he couldn't blame them. There was so much happening to them after years of relative quiet. Stranded pirates were a known quantity, but Indie submarines were right out of nowhere, and they hadn't even got used to the idea of having Jacinto folk move in next door.

"Your family still alive, Mr. Cole?"

"No, they got killed. All of 'em." *Forgive me, Momma—I ain't using you to persuade 'em to be nice to refugees. Just happens to be true. But you'd want 'em to welcome folks in need, wouldn't you?*

"Makes you see the world *different.*" Cole began walking away. "I'm gonna ask the Captain about some protection for your boats. I promise."

Fishery protection. *That* was what they called it. Cole remembered the phrase just as he got to the waterfront and saw the 'Dill. Baird and Gavriel were standing alongside it. Baird had his finger pressed to his ear, talking on the radio, while Gavriel stood with arms folded, occasionally turning to look out to sea. Baird waved Cole over.

"There's a pall of smoke." Baird seemed to be talking to CIC or Marcus. "You don't say . . . You think they burned their toast? I said *pall* . . . No, I'm not looking at it, one of the farmers called it in. I thought there was a Raven patrol checking that shit daily."

Cole listened in on his earpiece.

"Control to Delta, KR-Eight-Zero is going to check it out. Stand by to hear from Gettner."

"Roger that, Control."

"Baird, it's Marcus. I'm on my way to you. Vigilante action?"

"I'll check. Wait one." Baird turned to Gavriel. "You're *sure* nobody decided to settle a few scores now most of the Stranded have moved in with the COG?"

"It's not our doing," Gavriel said. "We let the dogs run loose in case the Stranded tried to disappear inland, but Dilland Jonty is the only one might torch their camp, and he's the farmer who called this in."

Now that Cole had seen Stranded waging their own civil war at sea, his first thought was that it was gang-on-gang violence. It would be damned hard to keep an eye on everyone who came and went on Vectes. The coastline here had to be at least 250 kilometers, and that was an impossible border for anyone to patrol.

Serves me right for telling 'em they had nothing to worry about. Temptin' fate.

Dom showed up, walking fast but definitely not running. That always made civvies nervous. Townspeople still paused to look, though.

"Gettner will be pissed off she didn't get to set the place on fire herself," Dom said. They all clustered around the 'Dill, listening for comms traffic. "She took that damage to her bird *personally*."

Marcus caught up with them and all they could do now was wait for Gettner to take a look at the place.

"Have we got any Stranded still pending on amnesty while the locals check them out?" Baird asked. "If any fail the vetting, we'll have nowhere left to dump them."

"No. But if we did, we'd find somewhere." Marcus spread out a map on the 'Dill's front scoop and squatted down to look at it. "Michaelson's talking about a radar picket to pick up inbound vessels, but that's not going to be airtight."

Cole leaned over Marcus's shoulder. Yeah, if some gang had slipped through for some retribution, then that really was a lot of coastline to patrol.

Gettner was back on the radio in less than ten minutes. "Control, Delta—this is KR-Eight-Zero. I'm over the site and I'm just seeing burning huts and a few junkers on fire. There's nothing else down there. Going in for a closer look."

"Gettner, we'll follow up and do a search," Marcus said.

"Roger that, Delta. Okay . . . confirmed, no boats, no bodies, no live ones, nothing. Nearest I've seen to clean. Cleared out, unless they're all piled up in the huts for some reason. I'll take a look and see if they've just moved inland. That many people leave some kind of visible track, usually."

"Wouldn't they take the junkers?" Dom asked.

Marcus climbed into the 'Dill. "Not if they left by sea. Let's make sure they're gone. I don't know how these people share information, but if they know what happened to their buddies, then they've got one more grudge with us."

Baird took the 'Dill down the narrow track that led from the inland cliff and stopped a few hundred meters away from the settlement. Cole thought that was extra-cautious, but they'd been caught out once too often in the last week. Gettner was right. It looked tidy. That was a damn odd thing to say about a burning shantytown, but it was true. The flames had already died down and the place simply smoked and smoldered, stinking of burned plastic and unburned fuel. The houses here had just been flimsy huts and shacks, quick to catch fire and crumble into ash.

Cole realized why it looked so clean when he passed the first charred wooden frame of a house. Fires didn't always burn every last scrap, and all kinds of lightweight stuff got scattered around in the drafts, sad little bits and pieces that said something about the folks who'd lived there. But there was nothing like that here. The shacks looked like they'd been picked clean of everything the Stranded could carry.

Marcus ducked his head down to look inside one of the buildings that still had a roof.

"Don't go in, man," Baird called. "The roof might collapse on you."

"Just looking." Marcus walked across to another house where there was no sign of walls, just a big sheet of corrugated metal on the ground—probably the roof, all that was left. He lifted the edge of the sheet and peered underneath. "Nothing. No bodies."

It was sometimes hard to tell charred bodies from other stuff, but Gears had learned to do that pretty well over the years.

"Looks like they did it themselves," Cole said, scuffing through a pile of ash. The sky was still clouded with smoke. It was so much like the places he'd had to pick his way through back on the mainland that his gut still said grubs, but he knew it wasn't. That still didn't stop the reaction. "Looks too orderly. Not enough burned stuff here."

Marcus nodded. "These guys just wanted to destroy everything they couldn't take with them."

Marcus had said it, so it was true, and Cole felt it was safe to breathe again. "Trouble is, I can never see anything for what it is anymore," he said. "I see a damn ugly fish and I think it's grubs. I see a pall of smoke and I think it's grubs." He tapped his skull. "The war ain't over up here."

Baird snapped his goggles into place. "Peace hasn't broken out, in case you hadn't noticed."

There was something else that bothered Cole now. Most of the Stranded from this camp had taken amnesty. Most of those who hadn't—the ones who seemed to have made a run for it—were the menfolk. That meant an awful lot of families had broken up, or else there were plenty of women and kids who were expecting to see their old man back again sometime. Either way, that didn't sound like a happy foundation to become a loyal citizen of the COG.

Nothing got sorted out cleanly anymore. Baird was right. Peace hadn't started yet. They were all in limbo. Nobody could come up with an instant cure for all the problems the war had left behind.

"Wasting all that fuel just to stop us using their shitty wood and plastic," Baird said, pausing to examine a melted lump in the ash. "Asset denial. Like we're goddamn grubs or something."

Marcus squatted to touch the remains of a length of water pipe like he expected it to still be hot. Some of the metal in the ruins was. He picked it up and hefted it in his hand.

"Imagine that," he said.

VNB, 1800 HOURS, FOUR WEEKS LATER.

It was always the dumb-ass little things that started Dom off.

Today, it was walking through the locker rooms and catching someone singing his head off in the shower—nothing out of the ordinary, but it was a song that Maria loved. Even off-key and mangled by a Gear, the lyrics hurt like hell. He found himself heading blindly out of the barracks just to get away from that song, looking for a quiet spot where he could think in peace, but privacy was getting harder to find every day; the base was full. Every spare building had been turned over to accommodation, and it was going to stay that way until new housing was built.

He walked to the dockyard walls, up narrow brick steps to the old sentry points where men had once stood guard with muskets. It was a hell of a view of the sea. Nobody would look twice if an off-duty Gear went up there and stayed for a while. People who'd spent way too much time underground needed to see open, infinite space.

Dom folded his arms on the granite blocks, rested his forehead on them and just let the sound of the waves below erase everything.

How long was it now? Nearly fifteen weeks since he'd found and lost Maria forever in a matter of minutes. He bounced between wanting to go on living because something good had to be around the next corner, and a sense of loss so bottomless that he thought he'd never be able to breathe again. His up days were getting better and more frequent. His down days still left him worse then empty.

She wasn't around for ten years. *What sort of Maria did I recreate in my imagination in that time?*

He took out his pack of photographs. On some days, he hadn't been able to look at Maria's eyes. That was how he gauged his progress. It wasn't even pulling the trigger that haunted him now; it was everything he didn't know. *Ten years.* He knew now that she'd been one of the Stranded. He couldn't kid himself that she'd been killed soon after she went missing, or taken by the grubs right away—because nobody could have survived that long in grub hands. He knew how Stranded lived, the miserable lives they had, the scum in their own communities who preyed on them. Now he couldn't stop himself filling in the blanks, hoping Maria had been with people like Dizzy but terrified of even thinking that she might have stumbled into the likes of Massy. It was a terrible thing to add to imagining what the grubs had done to her to make her into that shell he found. He hadn't even realized it until the last few weeks, when his mind was squarely on Stranded.

My wife *was a Stranded.*

She survived ten years because someone looked out for her. She wasn't like Bernie. She wasn't trained to survive. She couldn't have done it alone.

Somebody else must have cared about her.

It was obvious now, but he just hadn't thought it through before. Somehow, even though it was yet another unanswered question, it lifted him like nothing else had. One of the underclass he tolerated—didn't love, didn't respect, just *tolerated*—must have helped Maria. Maybe a whole group of them did. Now every Stranded he met who wasn't an obvious bastard would look very different to him.

It was turning out to be a pretty sunset again. Dom watched a patrol boat heading out, a black speck on choppy amber water. It might have been a radar picket ship, or it might have been joining the trawler fleet as fishery protection. But whatever it was, this felt routine and normal. Life went on if you wanted it to.

I do. I know I do.

Boots scuffed the steps beneath him. It had to be Marcus, or at least Cole or Bernie. He knew they still kept an eye on him, which was comforting, but his moments of wanting to die had melted down to not caring if he lived, and then to accepting he was staying around and so he had to make things work. He turned around, ready to tell Marcus—or Cole, or Bernie—that he was fine.

But it was Hoffman.

The colonel looked a lot smaller out of armor. He was still the squat wall of muscle he'd always been, but in fatigues he looked built to a more human scale. He took off his cap and leaned on the wall.

"I like it with more purple bits, myself," he said, squinting into the setting sun. "Few more clouds for contrast."

"It's nice and peaceful."

"Well, make the most of it." Hoffman checked his watch. "They're testing the sirens again in a few minutes."

Dom waited to find out what had really brought Hoffman up here. The guy was his old CO, still with a mental list of Gears who were *his*, chief of staff or not.

"It's working out, isn't it, sir?"

"I do believe it is. How about you?"

"Yeah. This place feels solid. Port Farrall never did."

"I meant how are *you* working out."

"Doing better. Thanks."

Hoffman was building up to something. Dom could see his jaw clenching. "You know how I lost my wife, don't you?"

"She couldn't get back to Ephyra before the Hammer strike."

Dom had heard other things, that the checkpoints had been told to turn her back to the city because she'd stormed off, but he didn't want to unpick the private misery behind that. "You know what it's like to pull the trigger. Is that what you were going to say, sir?"

"No. I was going to say that Prescott managed to tip off his secretary to get her sister back to Ephyra, but I played by the rules and never warned my own *wife*. And I lost her. I did it wrong at every stage, and she's dead because of me." Hoffman gave Dom that I-can-see-your-soul look. "I don't know what her final moments were like and I wasn't there to make them easier. But you were there for Maria. Nobody can ask any more of a man, Dom."

Hoffman glanced at his watch again. Dom was still trying to think of some response when the air shook and he thought someone had rammed nails into his eardrums. The emergency sirens wailed all around the base, a rising and falling scream of a noise that instantly churned human guts on a primal level. Even if you'd never heard that sound in your life, it made you want to run for cover. And the sentry post was positioned right over one of the sirens.

Hoffman just put his hands over his ears and waited, still looking out to sea. Dom tried to block out the noise, but his sinuses *vibrated*, he was sure of it.

The silence that fell was sudden. Dom's ears still throbbed.

"I think we can hear that okay, sir," he said.

"Combine that with the radar picket, and everyone feels reassured. Time I was going. The sergeants' mess is officially open tonight, and I'm *expected*." Hoffman turned to make his way down the steps again. "Thanks for listening, Santiago. It never got to me in Jacinto. Now it's like someone took off a tourniquet and the feeling's come back. Every time I look at a line of 'Dills here, I can see those burned-out cars."

Dom stayed at the sentry post for a while after Hoffman left, knowing damn well who had actually done the listening, even if Dom hadn't been the one talking. Hoffman was okay. Everyone— *everyone*—had done crazy, out-of-character things in this war, and the war before that, but it didn't mean they weren't fundamentally decent.

It was definitely time for that drink. An invite to the sergeants' mess was something tribal and special, not about getting shit-faced at all. It was hospitality. It was also a symbol of normal life making a comeback. Andresen and Rossi had gone to a lot of trouble to fit out the place, and not showing up when invited was bad form. He'd have to go.

The mess was a cramped space even before a lot of bodies tried to squeeze into it. Dom worked out from the plumbing and drains in the stone floor that it had been an ice store in the days before refrigeration, although how they got the ice there was any-one's guess. A stack of ammo crates served as the bar; a couple of grub cleavers hung on the wall behind it. There was beer, or what passed for it, and something piss-yellow and evil-smelling, dis-pensed from a steel drum by Dizzy. One of the engineer corpo-rals stared into its depths before tipping back his tin mug.

"Shit, that's *nasty*." He drained it on the second gulp, eyes screwed tight shut, and held it out for a refill. "We can rig some better distillation kit for you, Diz. Let's discuss *design*."

"That's my finest vintage," Dizzy said. "You just gotta let it rest some and get some bottle age, that's all."

"Mataki did the catering, guys," Rossi yelled above the noise. "Those things on cocktail sticks are *not* meatballs, okay?"

Everyone was laughing their asses off. People needed to find something to celebrate, and being alive in a clean, dry, warm room—a stiflingly warm room now—with a drink and all your buddies around you was as good a reason as any. Dom couldn't see Marcus, but Hoffman and Anya were there, and Bernie held Baird in a playful headlock while Cole guffawed and made no at-tempt to rescue him. "Who's a clever boy?" Bernie pinched his cheeks one-handed. Dom had never seen Baird tolerate her like that before. "Who made the guns work? Did you get the big guns working? *Did* you? *Clever* boy! Granny's *proud* of her clever boy!"

"What gun?" Dom asked.

Cole wiped his cheeks with the back of his hand. "The cannon, baby. The naval base defensive guns." He shook his head and started laughing again. "He's been helping the artillery guys. Shit, there's *nothing* Baird can't fix."

Humiliated or not, Baird looked pleased with himself. Dom felt guilty for ever thinking of him as a cocky, selfish bastard who didn't belong in Delta Squad. It was that kind of evening. He decided to stick to one beer in case sentimentality got the better of him again.

Eventually, the door edged opened, and Marcus stood on the threshold of the mess like he was preparing to charge a grub position. Dom was sure he would have closed the door and walked away if someone hadn't seen him and hauled him in by his sleeve.

"I'm still on duty, Dom," Marcus said, holding up his hand to fend off a mug of beer. "Just being polite."

"It's your mess, *Sergeant* Fenix."

"So it is." He had his earpiece in place. Dom couldn't remember seeing him without it lately, on duty or not. It was too easy to keep the comms net open the whole time just in case, and Dom couldn't work out if Marcus did it for distraction or because he still felt personally responsible for fixing the world's problems. "You know that shit makes you go blind."

"All quiet out there?"

"Couple of drunk Stranded had a fight. That's all."

"They're not Stranded now."

"Okay, then two drunk assholes had a fight."

Marcus was doing a discreet scan of the mess, and Dom knew damned well that he was checking where Anya was. *Yeah, she's over there with Hoffman, buddy. Do something about it.* Then Marcus's gaze settled across the room, target acquired for a moment, before he looked Dom in the eye again. It tipped the balance.

"I swear I'll never stick my nose into your private life again," Dom said. "But shit or get off the pot, okay? I saw your face when you thought she was dead. And I know what too late feels like."

Marcus didn't even shrug. He looked paralyzed for a moment, then put his finger slowly to his ear. Dom thought he was just avoiding the issue again until the chatter and raucous laughter around them was drowned in a noise that began like some huge animal gulping air. The gulp turned into a bellow that rose to a scream and fell again. The base alarms had gone off. They waited, but the siren showed no signs of stopping.

"Is nobody going to kill that goddamn siren?" Hoffman yelled. Dom could just about hear him. "How many times do they have to test it?"

But Marcus still had his finger pressed to his earpiece. His attention was somewhere else.

"Hey, not a drill, people," he shouted. "Listen up—we got an incident. A raid on Jonty's farm."

The mess fell silent for a moment. "What kind of raid?" Dom asked.

"The farmhouse and barns are on fire. One of the Ravens called it in. First six duty roster squads—get moving."

The mess emptied and they pounded down the passage to collect weapons and armor. As Dom jogged toward the 'Dill, he could hear the whine of Raven engines as pilots did their preflight checks. Cole listened in to the voice traffic.

"I'm not convinced that siren is a good idea." Marcus pushed past Baird and climbed into the 'Dill's driving seat. "Scares the civvies too much."

"You thinking what I'm thinking?" Dom said.

"Stranded settling scores?"

"Yeah."

"Does that mean more landed?"

"Maybe they never left."

Marcus headed off through the base and waited in the holding area near the main gate for the rest of the vehicles. There was a storehouse near the gates that had been converted to temporary accommodation, and when Marcus opened the 'Dill's hatches, Dom could hear a bullhorn echoing. He got out to look. Someone was driving around the civilian quarters, repeating a message that there was no danger, and that there would be further instructions if the situation changed. Yeah, the siren system needed a rethink.

Dom could guess immediately which civilians were from Jacinto and which were locals who'd relocated. Jacinto people opened their windows to listen to the announcement, then closed them and got on with whatever they were doing. The locals were coming out into the roads, stopping any Gears they could see and asking what the hell was going on. They were terrified; Dom could hear their panicky questions. They were convinced they were going to die.

His guess was confirmed when a window flew open and a woman leaned out.

"Get a grip, for goodness' sake," she called out. The Pelruan civilians looked up to the window. "Whatever it is, it's got to get past every Gear in the COG. What's *wrong* with you people?"

The locals stared up at the window long after the woman had slammed it shut. Dom decided not to get involved, and climbed back into the 'Dill.

"Our civvies believe in us," he said. "It's kind of cute."

Cole grinned. "That's 'cause we're so damn *good*, baby."

Marcus switched the comms over to the 'Dill's radio and listened to Control while they waited. Anya was back in CIC. Three 'Dills and a very old fire truck rolled up behind them. It was just like old times. The gates opened, and Marcus drove out in the direction of the farm.

"You know this guy?" Cole asked.

"Yeah. Met him the other day. Poor bastard lives alone."

There was no traffic to speak of on Vectes, and it was a fast run out to Jonty's farm. Dom could see the reddish glow in the distance long before they reached the place. Where were the nearest neighbors? There was no fire service and no ambulance. It was now down to Gears and any locals who managed to get there to tackle the blaze and sweep the area — if the locals knew about it, of course. When the 'Dill turned the corner into the long tire-rutted lane up to the house, the buildings were well alight. The barn was a ball of flame, and the roof of the farmhouse was gone. Given the distance between the two, it had to be arson.

Marcus jumped out to direct the squads.

"Dom, Cole, Baird—with me," he said. "Everyone else—find the assholes who did this."

The fire crew ran hoses and pumps from the farmyard supply and concentrated on the house. There was no sign of the farmer. If he'd been in the house when it went up, then they weren't going to find any remains until the blaze died down and the debris cooled.

"He's got dogs," Marcus said. "Three big black dogs. Where are they?"

The blaze lit up a large area around the farmhouse, but it was still hard to pick out shapes in the hard contrast between shadow and the fierce yellow light. The ground was a mix of short grass and poured concrete. Dom was poking around the hedges at the back of the farmhouse when he heard Cole call out.

"Got 'em," he yelled. "Shit, I'm losin' my faith in human beings, I swear I am."

Dom went running in the direction of his voice, toward the north side of the yard. Marcus and Baird were already there, staring down at something in the beam of Cole's flashlight. Dom could guess what it was before he got there.

"Assholes," Baird muttered. "But at least we get to shoot to kill now."

Dillond Jonty was dead, laid out flat on his back in a pool of black blood that looked like lube oil in the light from the fire. His three dogs were laid out beside him. Dom could see that someone had intended them to be found and the message to be clear.

Marcus squatted down. "Shot, and throat cut. The dogs too. Shit."

"I'd take a guess that our displaced Stranded just moved inland," Dom said. "But if more have come ashore, then we've got a different problem."

"Any bets as to how they're going to take this in Pelruan?" Baird asked.

"We'll worry about that later," Marcus said. "Looks like we're going to have to guard every isolated farm now."

It wasn't just about protecting citizens. It was about the threat to the food supply. Thoughts started racing through Dom's mind about who was going to sort out the farm and if there were animals to take care of. If the Stranded were looking to cause disruption, they'd found some soft but effective targets.

"At least we're not dealing with grubs," Baird said. "The fight's going to be a lot more equal."

Cole looked at the bodies and shook his head. "Great start to New Jacinto," he said. "Excuse me, gentlemen. I'm goin' asshole hunting."

Dom paused for a moment to watch the arcs of water playing on the burning farmhouse. He wondered if grubs ever did anything like this to their own kind. It didn't matter now; humans did, and this was the new war, one that few Gears had fought before.

Somehow, it was the dogs that troubled Dom most.

ABOUT THE AUTHOR

KAREN TRAVISS is the author of four *Star Wars:* Republic Commando novels, *Hard Contact, Triple Zero, True Colors,* and *Order 66;* three *Star Wars:* Legacy of the Force novels, *Bloodlines, Revelation,* and *Sacrifice;* two *Star Wars:* The Clone Wars novels, *The Clone Wars* and *No Prisoners; Gears of War: Aspho Fields;* and her award-nominated Wess'har Wars series, *City of Pearl, Crossing the Line, The World Before, Matriarch, Ally,* and *Judge.* A former defense correspondent and TV and newspaper journalist, Traviss lives in Devizes, England.